BROKEN FALCON

RACHEL GRANT

Books By Rachel Grant

Evidence: Under Fire

Into the Storm

Trust Me

Don't Look Back

Zero Hour

Evidence

Concrete Evidence

Body of Evidence

Withholding Evidence

Night Owl

Incriminating Evidence

Covert Evidence

Cold Evidence

Poison Evidence

Silent Evidence

Winter Hawk

Tainted Evidence

Broken Falcon

False Evidence

Fiona Carver

Dangerous Ground

Crash Site

Flashpoint

Tinderbox

Catalyst

Firestorm

Inferno

Romantic Mystery

Grave Danger

Paranormal Romance

Midnight Sun

Writing as R.S. Grant

The Buried Hours

This book addresses sexual abuse suffered by the hero. As a survivor of sexual abuse myself, I am aware that descriptions of abuse can be painful for readers, and I never want my work to be harmful. To that end, most of the description of the abuse he suffered is not detailed. However, there is a section in Chapter 27 in which more detail was required. Please be gentle with yourselves and know that I did my best to be gentle as well in the telling of Chase's story.

Chapter One

Washington DC
September

The five-inch blade glinted in the light as the girl—who was only fifteen and looked even younger—brandished it in front of Chase's face. "Who are you?" she demanded.

He was glad to see she was prepared for danger, but a knife wouldn't do her much good with the guys she was supposed to meet tonight.

"I'm here to help you." He paused, then added, "Jessica."

The girl was tiny—five-three at most and skinny as a rail. Her pale face had deep hollows under her eyes, which widened at his use of her real name. The hand holding the knife shook. "Who are you?" she asked again. This time, her voice was softer, suspicious, but less angry.

"Someone who knows the guys you're here to meet are bad news. The job they're offering you isn't online."

"How…how do you know about that? Are you one of them?"

He shook his head. "I'm not, but I know who you are because I'm watching them. When I see a young woman is taking their bait, I intervene before it's too late."

"You—you watched my audition?"

Chase shook his head. There were many things he wouldn't do for this sideline of his, and watching child pornography pretty much topped the list.

"No. I read your reply to the ad and saw the selfie you sent. I have access to missing kids databases and ran your image. You ran away six weeks ago, so you were pretty easy to identify."

She still looked suspicious, and he didn't blame her. He could hardly tell her he worked for a large private security company that employed a hacker who could find his way into anything once he knew where to look.

And Chase had made it his life's mission to figure out where to look. He was haunted by a face he couldn't even be certain was real. He'd given up on finding her, but he would find the people who'd hurt her.

Who'd hurt him.

And in the meantime, he'd use his dark hobby to find girls like Jessica and intercept them before they were taken in by CamDames, a legal online camgirl operation that had branched off into sex trafficking underage girls on the side.

Jessica was their favorite kind of target. Young, homeless, and on the run. No money and out of options. This gig was her last shot, but she couldn't walk in the front door to apply because she was underage.

On the legitimate side of the organization, CamDames offered a room to perform eight-hour shifts in front of the camera and maintained a dormitory-type living situation until each new recruit had earned enough tips to afford their own place. The backdoor portal made the same promises to underage girls. But none of the underage girls who answered the ad went to the official dormitory with the legal hires.

No. Girls like Jessica found themselves imprisoned and forced into prostitution with offline clientele. The girls never received payment for the sex acts they were forced to perform. It was sexual enslavement, but Chase's only evidence of this wouldn't stand up in a court of law.

CamDames had a squeaky-clean, legitimate setup on the outside, but someone in the organization was making a lot of money by trapping girls who applied for the job using a back door that had been set up just for the purpose of luring runaways like Jessica.

Because Jessica couldn't be seen entering the premises, they arranged for a street-side pickup, and this was their favorite location. Out in the open, so it was supposed to feel safe for the girl. But it was a side street with less traffic and there were no cameras to capture a young girl waiting on the sidewalk in between two buildings with a dark, narrow alley at her back.

Just up the street was a coffee shop that had security cameras, but Chase knew from experience the cameras were for show. They hadn't worked for months.

If Jessica balked at getting in the car, there would be no witnesses. And she was already a runaway, so no one to report her missing.

He nodded to the coffee shop on the corner. "They're going to be here soon. Go inside Vivace Coffee. Now. Before they see you. There's a blue-haired Black woman with a redheaded white woman sitting at the corner table. They'll help you."

The girl's eyes flitted to the shop, then returned to his face. "Why should I trust *you*?"

"These men aren't safe, Jessica. They're going to sell your

body, and you'll have no say. Talk to the women in the shop. They'll show you their IDs and take you to a safe place."

"I—I can't go back to my parents. My stepdad—"

Chase nodded. "I know. We found your social media posts. They won't send you home. They'll help get a guardian ad litem appointed so you'll have an advocate to get you into a safe living situation until you're eighteen."

Chase and Tricia had done a lot of digging the moment they identified the girl this morning.

Jessica's eyes narrowed. "I don't believe you." She lifted the blade higher, as her hold had drooped as they talked in the darkened section of sidewalk.

"I'm glad you're prepared to defend yourself, but I'm not the enemy. Please, go to the coffee shop."

Tricia's voice came through his earpiece. "A dark cargo van is heading for the intersection."

Shit. He turned to the girl. "Go inside. Hear them out. Tricia and Isabel will help you. It's a public place. You can walk right out the door if you don't trust them."

She looked at him warily, then her gaze landed on the lit coffee shop. There were people inside. Witnesses who would remember her.

"They chose this spot because there are no cameras nearby and less traffic on this side street. You need to hurry. Go where people will see you and ask for help, so the guys in the van can't risk taking you." Chase pulled a ski mask over his face. "Tuck the knife away and get inside."

Her eyes went wide with alarm at the sight of the mask. "What are you going to do?"

"Make sure they don't go after you." Chase slipped into the alley as the girl turned and ran.

The van rounded the corner as Jessica neared the crosswalk on the opposite side of the street.

The light changed just in time, and she darted across the intersection.

The driver stopped the van and called out the window, "Hey! Jasmine! Come back!"

Chase knew these guys always gave their marks names of animated princesses to use as an alias. They seemed to think it made the girls feel safe. And maybe it did, because girls like Jessica kept showing up. But then, Jessica was homeless and hungry and running out of options. Maybe the name Jasmine was the comfort of an old friend. And a promise of a happy ending.

Chase stepped out of the shadows when the passenger, a thickly-muscled white man, opened his door and jumped out, prepared to run after the escaping girl.

"Forget it. You can't have her."

The guy whirled around. "Who the fuck are you?"

"Her fairy godfather."

The guy whipped out a knife lightning fast and lunged forward. Chase had been expecting it, and this was his absolute specialty.

Part of him wondered if he'd cut the meet time so close —changing the message the girl received so he could meet her a mere five minutes before these assholes showed up— because he'd been spoiling for a fight tonight. He wanted to see the face of this monster, to add him and the driver to his memory bank. To see if any fresh memories were triggered. But most importantly, because he wanted to beat the crap out of someone, and child traffickers were the ideal target for his rage.

Plus, if he could send one of these guys to a hospital, maybe he'd get a name from a police report.

Chase blocked the guy's knife strike and followed with a jab to the sternum. The blade swooped down again. Chase met his wrist with a roundhouse kick that sent the weapon flying.

The guy wasn't ready to give up, though, and came at Chase with fists.

In seconds, it was over. The guy lay on the sidewalk cradling his arm with a snapped radius and ulna.

He met the gaze of the chickenshit driver who'd stayed in the car while his buddy was getting his ass kicked. "I suggest you get him to a hospital. The arm will need setting."

"Shoot the motherfucker, Terry," the wounded man said.

"No gunshots. They've got the girl. It's too late."

"Shoot him!"

"Get in the fucking car," Terry said.

At least Terry was smart enough to know the score. A gunshot would draw too many witnesses. If the goons were identified, the girls who'd been taken already might be found and rescued. Plus Jessica could testify and connect the dots. Jessica would be believed because her statement would be backed up by her two current companions—a former DC police officer and a US senator's wife.

Of course, these guys didn't know who was in the coffee shop, but they knew to cut their losses and get out if things went south. Coming after Chase with a knife could be the trigger that took down the whole operation.

Which was sort of Chase's plan.

He definitely wanted to take down the operation, but it would be a long, slow process if he was going to uncover the top dog.

In the meantime, Chase got a chance to take out his burning aggression in a knife fight. Well, the other guy had a blade. Chase believed in fighting fair, so he'd been unarmed.

The injured guy cursed and groaned as he got to his feet and lurched into the open passenger door. He wasn't fully inside before the van tore away from the curb.

Chase snapped a photo of the license plate as the van raced down the street and slipped into traffic. The license plate would go nowhere, he knew, but still, he had to try.

Once the van was long gone, he pulled off the ski mask and tucked it in his pocket, then headed the opposite direction from the coffee shop. Some would see his role here as that of a vigilante, so he didn't associate with Tricia and Isabel in front of witnesses.

He reached his SUV and climbed inside, then pulled out the one-way earpiece—Tricia hadn't been privy to his conversation with the goons, plausible deniability and all that—and donned his Raptor headset to check in. "All clear on my end. How is Jessica?"

"Scared, but she's willing to come with us to the shelter once she looked up who Isabel is on her phone."

"Glad to hear it."

Last fall, after a chip had been removed from just behind Chase's ear and his memories started coming back, he'd confided to Isabel some of what he knew…and some of what he feared. She'd been tortured with similar methods years ago, and they'd long shared a bond because of it.

He'd known she would understand. Wouldn't judge. Would listen.

She was the friend he'd needed and never really knew he had.

And he'd desperately needed friends after the chip was removed. He had a lot of damage to work through, and it wasn't like he could see a therapist. It was a bitch of a therapist who'd abused and tortured him in the first place.

Over the course of their conversations, Isabel had formed a plan to fund a shelter for runaways, especially ones like Jessica, who faced abuse if they returned home.

Within weeks, Isabel had quit her job at Talon & Drake so she could devote herself to the endeavor full-time. Her husband, Chase's former boss, Senator Alec Ravissant, set up an endowment to fund the home, and it was off and running by mid-March. Isabel's work was kept from the press because the shelter was confidentially located—not even Chase knew where it was—and her involvement could bring unwanted attention. She was a high-profile senator's wife who'd been the target of scrutiny twice already, the last being nearly a year ago when Rav had received threats that might have been intended for her, followed by an explosion at their Maryland estate.

At the shelter, Jessica would get the help she needed, including an advocate who would help her legally separate from her parents. It wasn't a permanent home, but they'd do everything they could to get her placed in a safe foster home with ongoing support and supervision from the advocates at the shelter.

There were no guarantees given that she was a minor, but she also hadn't just handed herself over to sex traffickers to escape her sexually abusive stepfather, so it was a win for now and hopefully forever.

He cracked his neck and took a deep breath. He was wound up from the fight, and adrenaline coursed through him. He put his SUV in gear and set out for home sweet home, Raptor's Virginia compound. Maybe the company gym would help him work off this energy, but then, it never had before.

The last time he'd felt this way had been in Portland, six weeks ago, when a group of white supremacists abducted Raptor operative Josh Warner's girlfriend, Maddie, and his teenaged niece, Ava. Chase had a rousing fight with the prick who'd threatened to cut Ava. He'd needed a few dozen stitches after Chase turned the guy's own knife against him.

It had been scary how good that fight had felt. The exhilaration of releasing his rage on a nasty target. He'd been craving it like a drug ever since.

Even better, this time he didn't have to sit down for hours of debriefing with federal, state, and local cops and prosecutors in the aftermath.

He needed to figure out how to better channel this energy. How to deal with this flood of emotions. Because it was all new since the chip was taken away. For two years, the chip had spoken to him with silent words, controlling his actions, his memories, his emotions.

Eleven months after the chip was removed, the range of emotions he was able to feel once again remained both terrifying and exhilarating.

He hadn't known there'd been a mute on his feelings until it was stripped away, and the first thing he felt was horror over what had been done to him, followed by earth-shaking rage.

Two years' worth of banked rage meant he had a mountain of it inside him.

Rage he'd let loose tonight when he snapped a guy's arm like it was a popsicle stick.

He wanted to do it again.

He breathed through the ferocious urge as he navigated the busy city streets. He tried to exhale the fury, as if that was a thing. This wasn't who Chase was.

The violent vigilante was who they'd made him into.

He didn't want to be a man who craved violence. A weapon they'd wielded like he was some sort of monster.

Wake the sleeping monster with the ring of a silent bell.

He'd seen the note. Knew what it meant.

When he tapped into the rage, was he waking the monster? Or was he merely releasing the demons that haunted him?

He reached the compound and parked in the fleet garage.

He nodded to the guard at the front desk as he passed and made his way to his quarters. Thankfully, he didn't have a scratch on him from the fight, or he'd find himself facing questions he didn't want to answer. The only compound residents who knew about this extracurricular sideline were Tricia Rooks and the tech wizard who insisted everyone call him Mothman. Isabel hadn't even told her husband about the vigilante aspect, and he owned the company.

The hacking they were doing was illegal, but then, the business they were going after wasn't legal, and they weren't looking to gather evidence for arrests and convictions. They were trying to save kids from being trafficked.

Chase could be fired for using company computers this way, so he only used a personal computer, as did Mothman and Tricia. They used the company network, but there was no way around that. Mothman had set up firewalls and VPNs to prevent anyone from following their trail into Raptor's system, and the company had their own internal setup for Mothman's…sometimes questionable security work.

Chase wasn't really worried about getting fired, not after what had been done to him—all because he worked for Raptor—but still, if he were, so be it.

He was doing what needed to be done in a feeble attempt to save his sanity along with the lives of runaway teens. And one thing was certain, without this work—this lifeline Isabel had thrown him last winter—he might well have given in to his demons months ago.

One foot in front of the other. It was how he made it through each day and how he made it to his quarters now. He was on the first floor and had a two-room suite with a window in deference to his status as a member of Falcon team but also because he'd been to hell and back—twice—thanks to Raptor.

He'd play that card if he had to with the company CEO,

Keith Hatcher, but he had a hard time believing it would ever come to that. Not when the owner's wife was working with him and using the man's money to rescue teens at risk of being trafficked. The majority of the runaways they rescued identified as female, but there were a growing number of trans and nonbinary kids who were unsafe at home, and they were especially vulnerable and targeted by predators.

He punched his code into his door and pressed his thumb to the reader. He trusted everyone who lived in the compound—a year ago, *he'd* been the threat within—but he would never leave his quarters unlocked. Aside from not wanting his extracurriculars found out, deep down, he wondered if there could be another like him. Another sleeper.

But eleven months ago, every single Raptor operative had shaved the spot behind their ear in solidarity and to submit to inspection. Plus, Dr. Parks was in prison.

There weren't others like him. There couldn't be.

And yet the fear was there. Deep inside. With nowhere to go.

He locked the door and leaned against it. He radioed to Tricia that he was back, then signed off. He was alone. Safe. He remembered everything.

No blackouts. No glitches. Tricia would have told him if there was a gap in time.

He hadn't had a gap since October, but still, he tracked his movements every time he left the compound. The lock on his door was his time stamp. If he left in the middle of the night, Mothman would alert him and ask why.

He'd built this structure of check-ins and tracking to keep himself sane. After his cabin burned down, he'd tried to rent a few for away time, but quickly realized he needed others available to track him one way or another. The five weeks he'd spent in Oregon had been fine because he'd been with Josh, Ava, and Maddie. Josh knew his concerns.

Now he was back and pumped with adrenaline, and there was only one thing that appealed, and it wasn't the gym.

No. The thing he wanted most right now was what he'd promised himself he wouldn't do again when he returned to Virginia.

He'd also promised himself he'd never go there when pumped on adrenaline like this. Was it dangerous to mix the two? Would the adrenaline heighten his reaction?

Would it become another drug? Would violence and Desiree become the hit he needed to keep going?

He hadn't logged in to that account in six weeks. Since before Portland. He was done. He didn't need her.

Well, he did. But he didn't want to. He wanted to be *normal.* He wanted to be attracted to women who weren't pixels on a screen. He wanted to walk into a bar and see an attractive woman and feel *something,* even if it was nothing but a mild attraction to a pretty face.

But out in the world, he was numb. It was only here, in this private room, and only Desiree who made him feel.

He was so utterly *broken.* He hated that the only time he felt strong emotions was when the violence was triggered.

Sure, he laughed. He cared. He had spent many hours enjoying being in Portland with Josh and his family.

But right now, he was in his skin, *feeling* in a way he couldn't process. And he wanted to see Desiree when he was feeling like this.

He needed to see her.

He sat down in front of his laptop and logged in, hoping she was online tonight and looking to earn a little money.

Chapter Two

Eden O'Keeffe's feet ached and her hand throbbed where she'd burned it earlier in the day. One would think after six months as a barista that wouldn't happen anymore, but there were some lessons that had to be learned over and over.

She cricked her neck as she scanned the counter to make sure everything was restocked or put away for the night. This wasn't her usual store; she'd filled in tonight when an employee was hit with a stomach bug and the closing protocol was different.

A loud bang sounded, and she jolted, her gaze going to the locked coffee shop door. Two men stood on the other side of the tinted glass. She couldn't see their faces in the dim light, but their skin was white and both appeared to be squat and beefy, like bouncers at a nightclub. One wore a sling on his right arm.

They looked like trouble, and judging by the way they pounded on the door, that was what they were here for.

With the front lights dimmed, she stood in the shadows. Curtains had been pulled down over the large front windows.

Only the door wasn't covered, because she hadn't been able to get the blind to release. Given that she was on the interior side of tinted glass, there was a chance they couldn't see her. Maybe she could just ignore them?

She inched toward the back where her coworker for the night, Tony, was balancing the cash drawer.

"We see you in there!" one of the men shouted.

Whelp.

"Open up!"

"We're closed," she yelled as she continued to inch along the rear counter, staying as far from the light as possible. Had it been a mistake to answer them? Maybe they'd lied about seeing her. She cursed her probable blunder.

The man's meaty fist hit the glass again, causing the door to rattle. "Where did they take Jasmine?"

She had no clue what that meant and decided it was unwise to engage again. She ducked down below the counter and crouch walked through the doorway to the back of the store. "Tony, there are two creeps pounding on the front door, asking for someone named Jasmine."

Tony frowned. "Wonder if this has to do with the girl who came tearing in here earlier like she was being chased?"

Eden knew exactly who he was talking about, and the girl's terrified face flashed in her mind. Her eyes had been wild as she'd searched the tables. She'd calmed when she spotted the two women in the corner. "If it does, we could probably track them down. The redhead is Senator Ravissant's wife."

Tony's brow furrowed, then he laughed. "Shit. Yeah. Isabel Ravissant. I didn't recognize her. Good catch."

She wanted to correct Tony that Isabel Dawson hadn't taken her husband's name, but that hardly mattered right now. "Well, red hair with curls like hers is distinctive." The woman had been in the news last year after there had been some threats made against her and then a building on the Ravissant estate blew up.

Eden had recognized her the moment she entered the shop and had been surprised when the frantic girl joined the two women who'd been quietly chatting for over an hour at that point.

"The other woman," Tony said, "the one with the blue hair, left her card. She said if anyone asked questions about the girl to call her."

That explained how Tony was quick to guess this was about the girl. "Do you have the card?"

"I put it in the register." He waved to the desk in front of him. He'd emptied the drawer of all cash, then returned it to the front. "It's still in there."

Eden frowned as she faced the front of the shop. The pounding was muted back here by the desk, but as she moved closer to the front, it got louder and more menacing.

"We should just call the police," Eden said.

"It'll take them forever to respond. I'll get the card."

"The door blind is open. I couldn't get it to close," she reminded him. She'd asked him to close it earlier and he'd agreed, telling her it was sticky if the cords weren't pulled just right.

He nodded and crouched down as she'd done and disappeared into the front. A moment later, he was back, smiling as he studied the card. "Raptor. Of course. Makes sense given she was with the owner's wife."

Tony dialed the number on the card, which was answered immediately.

Eden could only hear his side of the conversation, but she gathered that an operative would be sent ASAP to check out the front and back entrances and to escort them to their vehicles, but if they felt there was immediate danger to call 911 because police would be able to use sirens. Raptor had to obey traffic laws, and the drive would take at least forty-five minutes.

She glanced at her watch. She had hoped to put in a few hours tonight on her other job, but given the long Metro ride home, this would make her later than late. She shrugged it off. When she'd agreed to the shift at Vivace, she'd known it might mean missing a night at her work-from-home job.

There was back-and-forth conversation between Tony and the person at Raptor, then he put the shop's landline phone in the charging cradle on the desk. "Do you want to call the police?"

She wrinkled her nose. She doubted it would speed up the process of getting out of here and could delay things quite a bit. She listened for more pounding, but the front of the shop was quiet. "We can wait. It feels weird to call the police just to walk me to the Metro. But the Raptor folks seem to have expected something like this, so they can do it."

Tonight would be a good night to use the rideshare app, but she found those scary. She cursed her car, which had given up the ghost a few months ago. She was saving up to buy a decent used car because she'd sunk all her money into buying the townhouse and setting up her home business.

She'd had to make the difficult decision to take a semester off from grad school because she couldn't afford tuition and a vehicle, and she'd need a car for practicums in the spring. Until she had extra cash for a car, she was taking the Metro.

They waited in the back of the store. Tony paced. "I'm kind of feeling like a pussy for not just escorting you out the back."

She frowned at that. She understood why he would feel that way, but still, it triggered her internal psychotherapist in training who wanted him to understand the meaning of his words as well as the emotions behind them. "First of all, don't insult vaginas by using them pejoratively."

"Sorry, I shouldn't have used the P-word."

"I have no issues with the word 'pussy.' I'm pussy positive. My issue is using it as an insult. But also, there's no shame in not stepping into a back alley when there's potential danger. Just because you have a penis doesn't mean you can protect yourself or me from being blindsided by a baseball bat. We don't know if they're out there, but we do know those men were hostile and came after they knew the store would be closed and no one was around. The strength of a man—or woman—isn't defined by willingness to face danger, it's in how smart they are in protecting themselves and others once a threat has been identified."

"I suppose, but it's not very…manly."

He was young—barely twenty-one—and she didn't expect him to jump on board with her take, but it was always worth repeating. Maybe someday it would sink in for him.

"It's always okay to seek help." She pointed toward the front of the shop with her chin. "Those men out front scared me with their pounding and shouting. I don't feel safe. I'm glad we've got someone coming who's trained to deal with this, and who'll be able to ensure the alley is clear before we exit."

As a woman, she was taught to respect her response to fear early—before she entered her teens, but she wouldn't point that out. Tony might just take that as further emasculation, that he needed to embrace the fear that is ever present in the female existence.

Of course, Eden had a healthy respect for fear given that she'd been a runaway teen once upon a time. She trusted the instinct of fear probably more than any other.

And these days, her healthy fear was heightened because of her other job, which made her cautious about everything, including rideshare apps. If she were recognized, she would be extra vulnerable, which was one reason she'd gone solo and started her own business six months ago—so she could block all IP addresses that were in the Maryland, Virginia, and DC area. It wasn't foolproof, but it increased the odds that no client would stumble upon her in real life.

About forty minutes later, the landline phone rang. If it was Raptor, they probably had broken a few speed limits. Tony answered and put it on speaker.

"This is Tariq Mirza, from Raptor. I've got you on the line along with operative Chase Johnston. We wanted to give you the heads-up that I'll be at the front door and Johnston at the back in one minute. If all is clear, we will knock and say the password you provided on your initial call. If you hear the correct password, it's safe to open the door."

"Understood," Tony said, then hung up.

"What's the password?" Eden asked.

"Pancakes and horseradish."

"What kind of password is that?"

"They asked for a breakfast food and my least favorite condiment."

"That's pretty random." But she figured the random part was the point. "You want front or back?" she asked.

"I'll take the front," he said, and she guessed he was attempting to show bravery, since the door blind remained open.

She'd let him have the macho assignment. She was content with the windowless back exit that opened into a dark alley. At least no one would see her through breakable glass.

She moved to stand beside the portal, feeling a surge of adrenaline at the idea that there was someone in the alley now, clearing it if there was a threat there.

Had the men gone into the alley? And would they still be here after forty minutes?

A moment later, she jolted at the pounding on the heavy

metal door. She'd been expecting it, but still, the sound startled her in her jumpy state.

The pounding stopped, and a man said, "Pancakes and horseradish."

She let out a huff of relief and threw back the dead bolt, but left the alarm engaged, just in case, and pulled open the door.

A tall white man stood in the center of the light mounted above the alleyway exit.

He looked young—her age or possibly younger, which surprised her given that she was only twenty-six. For some reason, she thought all Raptor operatives were hardened postmilitary men in their thirties or forties. That was the case with the ones who'd made the news, anyway.

He held up an ID card. "Please confirm my ID, then key off the alarm."

She read his Virginia driver's license that listed him as Chase Johnston, which, she believed, was the name the other guy had mentioned. Used to carding people because the coffee shop also sold beer and wine, she flicked her gaze to the birth year and was surprised to see the guy was twenty-seven. Older than her by three months.

She stepped back to let him enter and keyed off the alarm.

He closed the door and bolted it, then tapped the headset at his ear. "Front clear, Mirza?"

There were two rooms between the back exit and front of the shop, so it didn't surprise her that she heard nothing from the front as the man appeared to be responding through the headset. Not wanting to stand in the small corridor in the night security light, Eden stepped back and flipped the switch for the bright overhead light.

The young operative—or rather, same-age-as-her operative—appeared about to say something when his mouth snapped shut.

"Sorry! Was I not supposed to turn on the light?" She flipped it off.

He cleared his throat and stepped forward. His arm reached behind her, and she felt his body heat as he invaded her personal space. With another click, the room was bright again.

"N-no. Just s-s-surprised me is all."

He stepped back, and his gaze scanned her from head to toe.

The look in his hazel eyes… Wow. The intensity of his gaze sent a frisson up her spine.

She just couldn't tell if that was a good or bad reaction to his nearness. Her instinct—and the heat that fluttered through her—said good, but caution was always the rule.

He was safe, right?

It occurred to her then that neither she nor Tony had told anyone that they were calling Raptor. They hadn't specifically decided not to call the police. That might have been a dumb move.

Hell, the phone number had come from a business card left by a patron earlier in the day. It could have been fake.

She took a deep, calming breath. The card had been left by the woman who'd been having tea with Isabel Dawson. Dawson was married to the senator who owned Raptor. It was well known they lived in the DC area.

The card was legit.

But what if not everyone at Raptor was safe?

That had certainly been the case once upon a time. If she remembered correctly, the previous owner was still in prison.

"You okay?" Johnston asked, his dark brows furrowing with concern.

She gave a sharp nod. Just because the guy had an intense gaze was no reason to freak out.

The flutter—or chills, whatever—were probably because he was handsome, and it had been ages since she'd been able to go out on a real date. Her side job was too emotionally draining and she couldn't imagine dating someone who would be supportive. She had bills to pay, and financial security was her first priority, so dating was out.

But it didn't mean she didn't enjoy a pretty face, especially when the guy was tall with dark hair, a smattering of freckles, a warm smile, and cheekbones that reminded her of Cillian Murphy. Come to think of it, the shape of his eyes did too. He was a younger Cillian Murphy, and now she wanted to binge-watch *Peaky Blinders* again.

"I'm just jumpy and feeling a bit foolish. I mean, it looks like we didn't need to call you at all. We could have left a while ago."

"Actually, th-that's n-not true."

It took her a moment to realize he had a stammer. Given his line of work, it must make things difficult given how others tended to perceive stuttering and an operative's need to project authority. And she couldn't help but wonder if his was a case of Child-Onset Fluency Disorder or neurogenic as a result of a brain injury at some point. He would make an interesting subject for her studies if it was the latter.

The other operative, Mirza, entered the room with Tony. Mirza was shorter than Johnston—she estimated he was five-eight or so, given her own height of five-four. He too was handsome, with brown skin and black hair and thick brows. She guessed from his name and coloring he was of Middle Eastern descent.

Like Johnston, he had a wiry build and walked with the confident, commanding gait of a soldier. As long as these guys were legit, they were in good hands.

Johnston gave Mirza a sharp nod, and Mirza addressed her and Tony. "It's good that you called us. When we drove up, we did see two men jump into a vehicle and drive off. Johnston pursued while I circled the premises to determine if others remained. When the pursuit was unsuccessful, Johnston returned." He nodded to the taller man with to-die-for cheekbones to pick up the report.

Johnston pulled out a cell phone. "In the alley, I f-f—" He paused and took a deep breath, concentrating before he spoke again. "Found. I found this." He held up the phone with a photo on the screen. It was the back door of the shop. Spray-painted on the door were the words: JASMINE IS OURS.

"They said something about Jasmine when they pounded on the door," Eden said.

Johnston spoke with his voice pitched lower, making her wonder if it was a method of controlling the stutter. "We've reached out to the operative who was here today with a friend. She believes she knows what the message means and apologizes profusely for unintentionally triggering this harassment tonight."

"We'd like to ask you both about the men who were here," Mirza said.

"Should we call the police?" Eden asked.

"We've already handled that. We have a working relationship with the Metropolitan Police Department, and they're content to let us help you fill out a report that includes photos. If there's a need to follow up, they'll come by the shop tomorrow, when they aren't as busy as they are tonight."

"If it gets us out of here faster," Tony said, "that's fine with me. But I didn't really see anything. I was in the back. Only heard the banging when Eden pointed it out."

"You saw the men?" Johnston asked Eden.

"I did." She wanted to go home, and she was with Tony

on expediting the process. They could go through the inter-view now and let these two men submit it, rather than waiting for an hour or two for an officer to show up. "Let's sit down and get this over with," she suggested.

Tony led them to the dining area, and she was glad to see he had closed the door blind when he let the operative into the shop.

Mirza sat across from Tony at a two-top table. Johnston chose a booth, and Eden slid into the seat across from him. His compelling eyes were fixed on her face in a not entirely unpleasing way, but the intensity of his gaze continued to make her belly flutter. She was certain now it was in a good way.

It was those cheekbones. The guy was just that good-look-ing. And there was something puzzling in the depths of his eyes that the future psychotherapist in her noted, but the woman in her wanted to explore.

She needed to earn enough money for a car and tuition so she could leave behind her second career and date again. Get laid again. For real.

She glanced at her watch. Maybe she should pull a late shift tonight after all. The way Johnston looked at her made her hot, and she could use that energy.

He pulled out his phone. "Th-this." He paused and closed his eyes, and her heart twisted as he flushed red. He cleared his throat and lowered his voice to the whispery tone he'd used earlier. "This shouldn't take long. I've got the forms all here."

"Thank you for doing this. I mean, it's not like we're Raptor clients."

"It's our responsibility to follow up in situations like this. We're deeply sorry for the fear and inconvenience this has caused you." He glanced at his phone. "Now, to get started, I need your name, date of birth, and address."

"Eden O'Keeffe." She spelled out her last name for him. The double Es and Fs could be tricky.

After typing it in, he set the phone down and offered his hand. "It's a little late for this, but it's nice to meet you, Eden. I'm Chase."

She smiled and took his hand, surprised that he went for the formal greeting, but liking the sweetness of it. Her gaze landed on his left hand on the tabletop.

No ring.

Not that that meant anything, but it was a positive sign at least.

But surely someone as handsome as he was, in his super-sexy line of work, had a girlfriend. Or boyfriend. She knew better than to make assumptions.

She again reminded herself she couldn't date right now. "It's nice to meet you too."

He released her hand with a soft squeeze. "I'm just sorry it was necessary." His words made her wonder if he had anything to do with Jasmine and the men at the door.

He returned his attention to the phone. "I need your contact information. Address, phone." He glanced around the room. "Place of employment."

"Actually, I don't work here—or, I mean, this was my first shift at *this* store. I work at the one in Fairfax. I filled in for an employee who was sick tonight." The woman was a friend—well, acquaintance, really—who'd suggested Eden apply for a job at Vivace Coffee, so Eden hadn't balked at helping her out even though it meant working her midday shift at her regular shop and then catching the Metro to fill in here.

Penny was the only person in Eden's orbit who knew about her other job, because they'd met when they were both working for the same employer, before Eden struck out on her own.

Eden frowned at Chase's phone as she considered how to answer his questions. She was always careful about giving out her address, and nice though he might be, she didn't know him. "Let's use my work address for my contact information." She rattled off the details, including the store phone number, and he entered the information without questioning her reasons.

With the basics filled in, she did her best to describe the men she'd seen outside, but there wasn't much to tell.

"You said one of them wore a sling?"

She nodded. It had been the only detail that stood out in the darkness.

Tony and Mirza had wrapped up at that point—Tony had seen far less than she had—and they listened as Eden gave her account, scant though it was.

She wished she'd seen more, but she'd been too eager to get in the back, away from the glass door, and hadn't been about to pause and take notes.

"I think this about covers it," Chase said in his whispery voice. "We'll escort you to your cars and call it a night."

She cleared her throat. "It's the Metro for me."

His gaze met hers, his brows furrowed. "This late? Alone?"

She shrugged. It wasn't like she had a choice. "If you walk me into the station, I'll be fine."

"Where are you headed?" Tony asked. "Maybe I could give you a ride."

She didn't know Tony any better than she knew Chase, but at least he worked for the same company and could be held accountable if something happened. "Fairfax," she said, avoiding being any more specific than that.

"Damn. I'm Takoma Park. Other direction."

"I can give you a ride," Chase said. "Our compound is just outside Fairfax."

She hesitated. A ride would be nice this time of night. But she didn't know this man.

Was she being paranoid?

Probably.

But still, paranoia won out. "Can I text your driver's license to a friend of mine?"

He smiled. Gah. His *smile*. It was a beautiful thing. "Of course."

He pulled out his license, and she snapped a photo, this time noting the address, which had to be the Raptor compound. Did he live there?

She texted the photo to Kelly, a fellow grad student and close friend, telling her she was getting a ride home from the coffee shop from him.

Kelly's response was immediate.

KELLY

You go, girl! He's hot.

She laughed. If only this were a hookup. But no such luck. Plus she'd never take a hookup to her place. No way.

"Okay then, let's go."

They left the shop through the back alley, with the two operatives scanning the alley first to confirm no one had returned. Tony set the alarm and locked the door, then went with Mirza to his car parked in a lot a block away, while Eden walked beside Chase to a large black SUV parked at the curb by the alley.

"Do all private security folks drive black cars?" she asked.

"Pretty much. It's boring, but it makes clients feel secure."

He unlocked her door with a remote. She noticed no lights flashed or sound went off, and when he opened the passenger door for her, the dome light didn't turn on. Stealthy.

She'd never thought much about private security, but living in the DC area, she was aware it was a big business, with all the politicians who didn't necessarily qualify for Secret Service protection but who might be targeted for various reasons. Especially as doxing became more common and conspiracy nuts were ready to believe lizard people were trafficking children in the basements of pizza shops that didn't have basements.

Add to that all the VIPs who came to town to testify before congress. They always had a big entourage, probably to convince the world they really were a big deal.

She climbed up into the high seat. Her five-four frame made it more difficult than she'd like. She was on the shorter side, but this SUV made her feel downright tiny.

Chase slid into the driver's seat, and they were on their way, silence settling between them.

She wanted to pepper him with questions, but usually that was an invitation for the guy to ask her similar questions, and she didn't want to tell him anything about her life. One could never be too careful in her line of work.

It was a shame, though, because he was so easy on the eyes, and someday, when she could date again without guilt, he might be a fun hookup.

She was willing to bet anything he sported impressive muscles on that lean, wiry body. It had been so long since she'd touched a man. Since she'd been touched. What would it be like to strip him down and run her hands over his smooth skin?

She jolted, realizing how far her brain had gone on that path in just a few minutes.

He was a virtual stranger.

And she hadn't had a sexual fantasy like this since she started her sideline. She was too busy spinning fantasies for others to concentrate on her own.

Now here she was, in a car with a beautiful stranger, and she was turned on. Intensely so.

A wild, rash part of her wanted to proposition him. Ask if he wanted to go to a hotel and get naked with her. Would he be shocked? Angry?

Would he say yes?

Was he regularly propositioned by damsels in distress?

Given his looks, she'd guess he probably was. But he also might have a significant other. And he probably didn't like being objectified any more than women did. He might be offended, and rightfully so.

She kept her wild thought to herself. But she smiled. She'd take this energy home and would log in and do a shift after all. It could be fun.

Chapter Three

$\mathcal{C}$hase didn't know how he'd managed to contain his reaction when he recognized Desiree. It had taken a moment—she looked different without the wig, makeup, colored contacts, and fake eyelashes—but he'd never mistake those full, beautiful lips even without the bold lipstick. And he'd always known she had dark hair, because, well, her eyebrows were dark, and she didn't always shave everywhere.

Now he had her in the passenger seat beside him, a companionable silence having settled between them as he drove her home, not quite able to believe this was really happening.

What did it mean that Desiree—or rather, Eden—was working at the coffee shop tonight? Was it a coincidence?

That would be a rather massive coincidence, and yet it was hard to see how it could be anything else.

Eight months ago, she'd worked for CamDames—the legitimate, legal front side—and he'd found her online as he researched the business. But within two months of finding her, she quit and started her own private site, a one-woman camgirl operation. Chase, along with several other regulars, had followed her when she left CamDames.

Subscribing to her new site had forced him to acknowledge that he hadn't continued visiting her online room because he was searching for information on the company she worked for. Truth was, he'd passed that point within the first few weeks and had continued visiting because she made him feel good. More than that…she made him *feel*. Period.

She'd been the first person to stir his physical desire since Parks put the chip in his head and used infrasound frequencies to inhibit and trigger pleasure. To erase his memories. To force him to commit crimes against his friends. His employers.

Parks had used his body as a weapon, and she'd used his body for her personal entertainment.

He hadn't remembered any of it until the chip was removed, and slowly, over the last year, more and more memories surfaced. But with each new recollection, he became more certain key interactions with Parks remained buried. What he did remember was traumatic.

When she used him, he'd ejaculated. But he'd never given his consent. One weekend a month for over two years, he'd been raped by his psychotherapist.

In the months that followed the emerging memories of being sexually exploited, it wasn't surprising that he felt no sexual desire. He'd been certain he'd never feel any such thing again.

Then he'd met Desiree. She was safe. Online. She couldn't touch him. He couldn't touch her. She made him want to explore desire again, and…she'd given him hope that someday he could feel again. Want again.

Because he sure as hell wanted her.

But she was also a woman on a screen. No woman in the

flesh stirred his desire, and he'd made a point of going out to meet women and test his reactions.

Nothing. Not once.

It was like the damn chip was still implanted.

Until tonight. Tonight, he'd seen Desiree in the flesh, and even though she wasn't doing any of the things to turn him on that he'd enjoyed online, he'd felt an instant surge of attraction. Lust.

Desire.

He could have cried right then and there for the shock of the feeling, but crying was also an ability he'd lost with the chip, so maybe not.

Now he was driving her home, and she had no idea who was at the wheel, that he knew her secret.

She was inches away from him. He could smell her. Reach out and touch her—although he wouldn't, as that would certainly, and rightfully, freak her out. But also…for the first time ever, she could see *him*. But she didn't know who she was looking at.

She had blockers on her site that rejected IP addresses within the Maryland/Virginia/DC area, which likely made her feel safe that she wouldn't be recognized, but Chase had always used a virtual private network that pinged from Alaska, and that was what his online alias had always claimed as his location.

She had no reason to suspect him, and he needed to keep it that way.

While he was in Portland, he'd made the decision to give up Desiree. He hadn't visited her site while living with Josh and his family, and it had seemed like the right timing to quit cold turkey. He should return to trying to meet women in person, or maybe even try a dating app and see where it went.

Instead, earlier, when he'd been hyped up with adrenaline

from the fight, he'd broken that promise to himself and logged in to her site.

She hadn't been there. He'd perused the photos and other OnlyFans-type content she posted for her regular subscribers —but it wasn't the same without the personal interaction. With Desiree, it had always been the way she talked. Flirted. And even listened.

Listened.

She knew his voice. Thank God he'd only said a few clipped words to her before he recognized her. Then his stutter had come roaring back when faced with the woman of his fantasies, forcing him to drop his voice to just above a whisper to get the words out.

He'd never in his life been so grateful for the speech impediment he'd battled since early childhood and had mostly conquered.

There was part of him that appreciated the fact that the stutter was his own affliction, for lack of a better word, and not something Parks created. The stutter was part of who he truly was, which was the thing he was most trying to figure out these days.

Who am I now? Are my thoughts even my own?

He didn't think he was the man full of aggression looking for targets to beat up. Not at his core.

He tried to remember who he'd been four and a half years ago, before Ted Godfrey took him under his wing. Godfrey's goal had been to mess with Chase's mind in a trial run of an infrasonic weapon that was likely a precursor to the sonic weapons that were suspected of having been used on diplomats in the American embassy in Cuba a few years ago.

Who had he been then? He'd been twenty-two. Fresh out of the police academy. He took the job with Raptor to gain experience as he waited for an offer from one of several police departments.

He'd gotten an offer that first summer—after Ted had taken control. Chase still didn't remember turning it down, but he'd seen the correspondence. The chief of police for the department said they'd had a video conference interview because Chase had been in remote Alaska and couldn't fly down for the interview.

Chase didn't remember the interview either, but apparently, he'd nailed it. Then Godfrey had wiped it from his mind, because he needed a test subject for their weapon.

Chase needed to go further back if he was to figure out who he really was.

One thing he did know, given his mental history, there was no way he'd ever get a job as a police officer in the future. He was really only fit for Raptor at this point.

He was okay with that—Raptor was a good company, and his coworkers were like family now—but sometimes he wondered if the person he'd been at twenty-two would be fine with that. Did he accept it because he'd been programmed to, or was this his calling?

He had no fucking clue.

He was a man who literally didn't know his own mind.

And the woman in his passenger seat was the only person in the last year who'd offered any kind of respite from the constant questions and doubts.

He had to focus on the road, or he might simply forget how to breathe. Having her so close flooded his brain with reactions he couldn't process—but for once, it was in a good way.

He felt exhilaratingly *alive*.

Why on earth had he decided to give Desiree up?

Was it because he wondered if the old Chase would frown upon him engaging in a transactional relationship with a camgirl?

If that were the case, then judgmental old Chase could just fuck the hell off.

This Chase needed to have some emotional interactions, and this was the only safe way he knew to do it for now.

Eden gave him directions after the exit to her townhouse, and he wove through streets that were still busy even though it was nearing eleven p.m. on a weeknight. A few blocks farther and things would spread out and get quieter, but she lived closer to the central hub—walking distance to a Metro station.

He pulled up in front of her unit. It was a nice one, narrow, but long, with the apartment being a one-story unit above what he assumed was a deep garage.

Why did she have a garage if she didn't have a car?

But then, she'd never said she didn't have a car, and he wouldn't ask. None of his business.

He'd wonder how she afforded such a nice place if she lived alone, but then, that was another assumption—that she lived alone. She could be married for all he knew.

And it wasn't a stretch to think she could afford the place on her own because of her secret job. He'd researched the business enough to know that some camgirls made upwards of twenty grand a week. Desiree wasn't at that level—especially since going solo and she clearly had a day job as a barista—but she could probably easily make rent even without a roommate.

"Thanks for the ride," she said as she pushed open the door.

Damn. He'd wanted to run around and open her door. Get one last chance to stand close and breathe in her scent, even if all he got was the smell of ground coffee. He'd never once considered what Desiree might smell like, and now he couldn't get enough. Eden was so damn beautiful. Everything about her was alluring, from her straight dark hair that was probably soft to the touch, to her petite frame and gently rounded curves.

But it was better this way. Keep it professional. "You're welcome. Can I walk you to the door?"

She cocked her head. The outer stairs to her front door were just a few feet away and well lit. His security duties were over. And now he realized that was the kind of thing a man said when escorting a woman home after a date.

At least, he thought that was the kind of thing men said. He hadn't been on many dates. In the Before Times, his stutter had contributed to a shyness that he finally managed to beat when he was in the police academy, but the impediment meant he'd dated infrequently. And Parks had done her best to muddle the memories he had of the few dates he could remember. They came back in bits and pieces now, disjointed and unconnected to any emotions.

He knew he'd hooked up here and there—he hadn't been a virgin when Parks dug her claws into his head—but he'd never been in a relationship that started with a proper date and a hope for a goodnight kiss. At least, he didn't think so.

"I think I can make it all the way up to the door without help."

He laughed. "Okay. Just know I'm right here if you need me."

Now she chuckled, and the sound was even better in person than the throaty way she did it online.

She closed the door, and he watched the sway of her hips as she walked up the stairs.

He didn't know a lot about women, but he damn well knew that ass sway was for his benefit, because she hadn't walked like that down the alley or through the coffee shop. That was pure Desiree.

Interesting.

Once she was safely inside, he put the SUV in reverse and pulled out of the short driveway. As he headed to the compound, he wondered if Desiree would be online tonight.

Chapter Four

DESIREE

Even though I'm in a hurry, I force myself to take my time as I apply my makeup, thinking about Chase Johnston's wiry body as I blend foundation and choose eye shadow. Tonight, I will pretend everyone in the chat room is him.

I pull on the blonde wig and wonder if Chase would like me as a blonde. It's ridiculous to be thinking about him this much, but it's been a long time since I've felt any kind of zing with a man, let alone the wild sparks I got just from being near the Raptor operative. I'm going to use the energy boost for all I can tonight.

I think my sessions are getting stale. I've lost a few regulars in the last two months. Men who had made the move from CamDames with me, but who don't show up anymore. Have they moved on to younger, sexier women?

These are the kinds of questions that come to mind as I consider the consumer psychology of online sex work. What keeps my clients coming back for more? When do they reach a saturation point?

I'm not seeking an online sugar daddy—that would be dishonest given that this is my sideline until I'm financially stable. I don't have the time or energy to give a sugar daddy what he'd deserve given the financial outlay. So maybe I should focus on the drop-off point. What makes a guy move on, even when everything seems to be going great?

Falcon hasn't been to my site in more than a month. Probably longer, but I'd need to check my tip ledger to be sure. More nights than not, when Falcon showed up, he would pay for a session in my private room. I miss that income, but also, I kind of miss him.

He never once turned on his camera in the private room, but at least there, I could hear his voice. And I liked it. Smooth and deep. Friendly.

Commanding.

Falcon always took control of our private sessions. It was sexy as hell.

He's one of the few clients who legitimately turns me on, so I'm not doing all the work myself. I'm not acting. I'm enjoying.

And I do like this job. I wouldn't do it otherwise, but Falcon always made it more fun, so I've been disappointed by his long absence.

Plus, I miss the income. I need to replace him and the other regulars who've fallen away if I'm ever going to be able to buy a car without going into debt. I have a mortgage that already keeps me up at night. A car loan would send me into a tailspin.

I should consider running ads on some of the bigger porn sites, but you never know who you'll get with those, and the cost is exorbitant. My biggest hurdle is always how to grow the business without throwing money away. I need every penny I can get now that I've gone solo.

I didn't quite realize how good I had it with CamDames,

but still, I have no regrets. I'm the only person who profits off the sale of my body now, and that thought gives me a jolt of spine-straightening pride.

I've worked hard for this body, and I will monetize it for as long as is necessary. And then Desiree will disappear.

Until then, what I really need to do is put in more hours, which is why it's good that I'm going online tonight. I need the money. But I don't usually log in this late, so it's highly likely none of my regulars will be online.

Subscribers—men who have unlimited access to my static content and the group chat room I usually spend at least an hour in, five days a week—have provided an email address or text number so I can ping them that I'm online and looking for company. Maybe I'll offer up a coupon for a private session to get them online this late. Fifty percent off fifteen minutes with me should do the trick.

I focus on my makeup. I need to look hot tonight if I'm going to get someone to redeem a coupon this late. I'm usually logging out in fifteen minutes, not just starting an online shift.

I study my face in the mirror. I don't look like me at all —at least it seems that way because I've never left the house like this. It's not Eden who stares back at me. It's Desiree.

I think Desiree is pretty, but a bit overdone.

Desiree learned makeup from National Treasure Dolly Parton. One of my favorite Dolly quotes will always be, "It costs a lot of money to look this cheap." And now that I have a vast supply of quality makeup, wigs, and costumes, I know exactly what Dolly meant.

When I put on the makeup, I can feel a shift inside myself. Like this sultry woman who lives inside me breaks through to the surface. She says things I would never say. Does things I've never done—not with a partner, anyway.

I'm fascinated by her. By me. But that seems strangely egotistical, and I want to analyze that too.

Desiree is interested in trying all the naughty things I would never consider in real life.

Like tonight, for example. I had a perfectly good opportunity to ask a stranger if he wanted to go to a hotel room and fuck me all night long. Desiree, if she were real, would have asked the question without hesitating.

And maybe she'd have been turned down. Or maybe she'd have had a fantastic night with a hot man.

Sadly, I will never know.

I head for the closet and start digging through my costumes. I'm going all in, starting with a sheer teddy so my nipples will be visible from the start. No need to make them pay to see tits when I'm feeling this hot.

When I first started this job, CamDames wanted me to get a boob job. My C cups weren't big enough, they said. But I don't want fake breasts. I know how to use my assets, and my cup size goes with my body. I work hard to stay slim, because that's what my clients like, but it's a constant struggle.

I spend an hour each day exercising in the homeowner's association gym up the road, and I'm careful about portion size and sweets. My natural weight is too rounded for my clientele, but I'm not rounded enough to get near the plus-sized market, which is a great demographic and would mean I didn't need to exercise constantly if I want to eat carbs.

Sometimes I have dreams of pizza.

I think this, more than anything, is why I'll give up this job when I get my degree.

As much as I'll miss Desiree's bold, vibrant, sexual autonomy, I'll be delighted to welcome french fries back into my life.

And ice cream.

God. How I miss ice cream.

I imagine being in bed with Chase with a pint of Häagen-Dazs. I would lick it off his chest. I have no idea if he's got a nice chest, but in my mind, he's ripped and his body pairs well with pralines and cream.

My tongue slides down from his nipples to his abs, and then I follow the trail to treasure and take his hard cock in my mouth. He cups my head between his hands as I go down on him, and he shouts my real name as he comes in my mouth.

I pause in the middle of my camera room after donning my sheer teddy, shocked at my own vivid fantasies that came from nowhere. I'm so hot and worked up, I need to get on camera *now*.

There is money to be made tonight, and now I have the fantasy that will feed my performance.

I log in to the site and then move to position myself on the bed in a demure pose with my fuck-me makeup and sheer-top green teddy that matches the colored contacts I put in.

I hit the button on a tablet I keep next to me on the bed and take my session live.

There are two men in the room, waiting. They both logged in when my shift was supposed to start but never left. They might be at their computers or not. I clear my throat and smile at the camera. "Sorry I'm late, guys. I had an... interesting time at the day job."

One guy types into the chat window, saying he's glad I'm online and hopes everything is okay at work. He's always sweet, always offering me sympathy, concern, and compliments. I know from our private conversations that he's married and in his sixties. His wife doesn't want to have sex anymore, and he doesn't want to cheat. So this is their compromise. His wife even gives him a budget!

I really like her and the way they've openly navigated an

arrangement that works for them both. I wish I could make them part of a psychological study.

"Thanks, Hank. I'm fine. Just sad to be late to the party tonight because I'm feeling really hot and a lot needy. I'm hoping you guys can help me out."

Hank: What got you so hot?

Before I can answer, another client enters the chat.

My belly flutters when I see the screen name: *Falcon*.

I had been sure he was gone for good. But here he is. Given how eager I am to play tonight, he's *perfect* for a private session. I just need to give Hank and the other client, who uses the alias "Thor," about ten minutes so they get their subscription's worth, then I can move to a private room with Falcon and he can move to voice, not text chat.

If he wants to, that is.

I dearly hope he wants to.

Tonight will be one of those nights when our session goes further than a striptease and dirty talk.

"Falcon! I've missed you! Where have you been?"

Falcon: Extended business trip. I hope you
weren't worried about me.

I give him a throaty chuckle. "I'll admit I was a bit. I was sure you'd found someone younger and prettier to entertain you."

Falcon: No one is prettier or sexier than you.

I bite my lip for the camera then smile just a little wickedly. "You are so sweet."

> Falcon: My thoughts about you are anything
> but sweet. They're raw, and very, very dirty.

I brush a thumb over a nipple as I give the camera a hot look. I'm not even pretending. I'm full of want. "Oh my. We *do* have some catching up to do."

> Hank: You still haven't said what has you so
> hot tonight, Desiree. And you do look
> especially…ready. What happened?

I debate how much to say. I never mention my work—no details of my real life are ever shared. I am Desiree, not Eden, in this room. It's one reason why I use the extra bedroom as my workspace. I don't want clients to see any part of my real life.

But I also know it's fine to mention other men. After all, I'm flirting with two men right now as a third may or may not be silently watching. There's no illusion of fidelity. This is who Desiree is—a woman unabashed by her sexual desires.

"I had a chance encounter with a beautiful man tonight. He was so hot, and his gaze so intense on me, I wanted to ask him to take me to a hotel and fuck me all night long. But I didn't, so now I'm hoping one of you can help me out. I'm wound up and hot with no cock to play with."

My guess is Hank will bow out at this point. He likes to go to the private room to chat and talk about his family. For a guy who's doing this to avoid cheating on his wife, what he really wants from me is the intimacy of friendship. Things are rarely sexual between us, even though I know he likes to look at my body. Even the fantasies he asks me to spin for him revolve around me with other men, not him.

He's not the only one who just wants a friend with a little voyeurism attached. Ninety percent of my private sessions are more like therapy and friendship than they are sexy times and getting off. I find this fascinating.

Falcon straddles that line. He definitely wants to fuck me, but I'm not sure if he ever jacks off during our sessions. Not when we're talking anyway. I presume he does after because I think he likes the heightened desire but prefers to come when he's alone and in control.

I don't judge. I only occasionally orgasm on camera, but I'm really, really good at making it look like I do. But I have come for Falcon, and that's one reason why I want to play with him tonight.

And I want him to come too. I want to hear the sounds he makes as he tips over that edge. I would love it if he turned on his camera and I could see him. But he's never shown any interest in that, and he's the one paying. His body, his choice.

I'm well aware he probably won't live up to my fantasies as far as looks and body, but the thing is, I just love the male body in general. The male form is beautiful in all shapes and sizes. The only thing that turns me off is an ugly soul, and I've spent enough time with Falcon to know he's sweet and kind, but there's an edge of hardness that I think comes from internal pain.

He could be ripped or he could be plump and soft as a marshmallow, and I wouldn't care. And seriously, given how much I resent having to stay in top form for this gig, I wouldn't project this misery on anyone.

I hope Falcon eats all the pizza and ice cream that he might crave. And now I'm fantasizing about licking ice cream from *his* chest. But that's what this is all about. Transferring my fantasy away from the man I met in real life to the online client.

> Falcon: I'm game for a private room if you are. But I don't want to jump the line. Hank was here first.

> Hank: You kids go play. I just wanted to be sure Desiree was okay. It's not like you to miss a session.

I blow a kiss at the camera. "You know I wouldn't miss or be late without a reason! Thanks for watching over me. I need angels like you in this business."

> Hank: I'm always here for you, Desiree. Just say the word.

On his way out of the room he clicks the "$50.00 Tip" button. Clients didn't get much better than that.

Since Thor never chimed in one way or another, I send Falcon the link to a private room and close the main chat for the night.

A moment later, Falcon follows the link into the private room. His camera is off as expected, but his microphone is on.

"What, no charge, Desiree?"

He noticed that I didn't ask him to drop a hundred up front before we went solo. I'm too hot to risk him deciding not to pay.

"Consider it the long-business-trip discount. I've missed you."

"I think you mean you want to get fucked."

"Well yeah, that too."

I hear the chime that means he's tipped me, and I startle when I see he hit the five-hundred-dollar button.

"That's quite generous considering this was going to be a freebie."

"Let's just say I've missed you too. A lot."

"Where were you?"

"I'll tell you if you tell me something personal too."

I debate this offer. It's a dangerous game. In the end I say, "Never mind," even though I really want to know where he went. He's from Alaska, but I don't know his line of work, so I have no idea where work would take him.

I have an idea, though, which I blurt without thinking. "But I will tell you something if you turn on your camera."

He chuckles, and his deep, warm laugh just makes me hotter. "No, Desiree. Not yet."

"Yet?" I'm genuinely hopeful. I want to *see* him.

"Maybe. When you're ready."

He says that with such authority. Like I can't handle how amazing he is, and this is a turn-on because of the two of us, *I'm* the successful sex worker. He's paying me for my time. And yet he has this hot confidence that gets me every time.

I think he's right too. I'm not ready to embrace how hot he is in real life. I need to work my way up. Built up a tolerance.

Then he does the thing that never fails to turn me on in our private sessions. He takes control. And this is one way in which he's so different from my other clients. So many of them want me to entertain them.

Which is fine. They're literally paying me to do that.

But not Falcon. No. He always makes it clear that he's here to service *my* needs. This guy must totally rock in bed. And I *so* want to find out.

"Touch yourself, Desiree. Show me how happy you are that I'm back."

His voice is deep and clear, and it skips along my nerves. He is ice cream. The treat I'm always denied.

I shift on the bed so he can see everything, but my pose is tasteful—for now. I slide my fingers over the satin of the teddy, moving down, down until my index and middle fingers are between my legs.

I press softly and stare at the camera, letting him see the arousal in my eyes.

"Damn, that's hot, but it can't be enough. Not with the fabric between your fingers and clit. Unsnap the teddy. Expose your pussy, and touch yourself."

I do as he says. I want nothing more. It has killed me to wait this long. It's been more than an hour since I climbed out of Chase's vehicle all alone, and I've been waiting for this touch with his imaginary fingers, six times a minute ever since.

Usually when Falcon and I play, he makes me go slow, draws out my pleasure with his commands that push me to the cusp over an achingly long time. But he's been gone for weeks, and I'm ready to combust. It's not a go-slow combination.

"I want a dildo. I want to imagine you inside me." I'm breathless as I say this. I've used vibrators with Falcon before, but never a dildo, and tonight I want to take things to the next level. But he's in charge—after all, he's paying for this fantasy I get to share—so he gets to determine what toys I can use. I add, "Please?" and hope he's not turned off by dildos.

The pause goes on long enough for me to worry he'll say no. Leave me desperate and hanging. But I shouldn't underestimate this most generous of cyber lovers, because finally he says, "You may."

"What color?" I ask. I don't want to grab the wrong one and pull him from the fantasy now. I have a full rainbow of options, including several different skin tones.

"White."

I don't ask size—some men will specify what they want, but without instruction I always go for my favorite. Not too big. I don't really like the extra-large ones, but a lot of guys want to see that. They always require lube, and while I'm a hundred percent pro lube, it's nice when I'm fully aroused and can choose a toy that doesn't require it. No break in the sexy flow, so to speak.

I settle myself on the bed, positioning myself so Falcon will have a good view at an angle where he can mentally place himself between my thighs.

I want him here with me mentally, if not physically. "Are you naked, Falcon? Touching yourself?"

"Naked, yes. Touching myself, no. That won't happen until I'm deep inside you."

The ache in his voice is hot. I slip two fingers inside, then bring them to my mouth. "Do you want to taste me?"

"Desperately."

I wonder if I'd propositioned Chase tonight, would he have gone down on me? I might miss oral sex more than penetration with a penis, because I have dildoes that aren't perfect but a decent stand-in. But I have yet to find a sex toy that's equal to a tongue licking my clit.

I miss giving oral sex too. Hence my earlier fantasy of going down on Chase.

It's the giving and sharing part of sex that's so immersive and wonderful. I could have all the pleasure in the world on my own with my toys, but I miss the feel of a man losing himself as I suck him to orgasm. And I miss the same loss of control when bestowed with the same gift.

I run my fingers over my lips, mouth open for the camera so he can imagine his cock sliding inside. I lick my bottom lip.

"What now?" I ask, moving the sex toy between my thighs, on the cusp of my opening. "What do you say before you slide your cock in me for the first time?"

"I tell you you're incredibly beautiful. That I've ached for you from the first time I saw your face." He chuckles and adds, "And that I'm about to give you the best damn orgasm of your life."

I laugh at that too. It was a joke, and yet...I believe he can deliver on that promise, considering how hot I am when he isn't even in the actual room.

But maybe that's just me giving Falcon too much credit and Chase not enough?

Does it even matter? This is all fantasy. Falcon lives in Alaska, and Chase, well, he and all men who live in the DC area are completely off-limits.

Chapter Five

FALCON

*D*esiree really is beautiful, but now that I've met Eden, I see the even more stunning woman beneath the makeup and wig.

She tries to hide, but I see her. I see the cool woman who was oh so protective of her contact information, but who then reluctantly allowed me to give her a ride home. She's smart to be so cautious, and I'm glad for it.

And now here she is, on my computer screen, telling me she wants to fuck me. And by me, I mean *me*, Chase. The Raptor operative she met two hours ago.

That Chase is the new me, and she likes him. Me.

Whatever.

All I know is he—*I*—am a little darker than the man I once was. Is it the darkness that attracted her?

Because I'm pretty sure old Chase never triggered the kind of reaction she's showing now.

Desiree and I have played in her private room many times before, but I've never touched myself. Never let myself come until after the session is over and I go over it in my mind. I'm all alone and in complete control. No one can share my pleasure or force it on me.

It's important for me to be alone when I orgasm because then it's entirely my choice, how I come. Who I think about. What it means for me. It's a way of reclaiming what Parks stole from me.

Before Desiree, I couldn't even jack off. I thought Parks had stolen my sexuality completely.

Then I found Desiree and discovered I could come after our sessions. The first time it happened had been such a wild relief. And I didn't think about Parks once the entire night.

She always insisted I call her Elizabeth and wanted me to treat her like an adored lover. She would get angry if I didn't, and I think that's when she started playing with different drug cocktails, some of which trapped me in a kind of paralysis. That was one of the first things I remembered after the chip was removed. So now in my mind I only call her Parks. I don't even give her the "doctor" address I always used in her therapist's office.

I focus on the screen, angry with myself for letting Parks have a piece of this moment with Desiree. She's not allowed here.

Desiree's room is my safe space, and tonight, I'm going to do something that I haven't been sure I'd ever be able to do—I'm going to come with her. I'm going to share the moment with her.

She wants me. *Me.* And she's thinking about me as she pretends to fuck Falcon, who is also me.

This has to be the most erotic moment of my life, and we're twelve miles apart, she in her townhouse and me in my suite at the Raptor compound.

Desiree places the dildo between her spread legs and asks me what to do. She likes it when I direct her, and for me, that's the ultimate turn-on. She lets me have total control with an eager woman who wants nothing more or less than my cock.

A pleasure transaction.

I'm leaning against the headboard of my bed, on top of the blankets, totally nude with my laptop open beside me. I'm hard as a rock, my erection pointing to the ceiling and I haven't even touched myself yet. This is what Desiree does to me.

I'm so turned on by her open, unabashed sexuality. And I love that she draws the same open energy from me. Eight months ago, before Desiree, I never could have lain on my bed like this and wrapped my hand around my cock as I'm doing now.

On the screen, she's pressing the tip of the phallus into her vagina, and then she uses her thumb to rub her wetness over the head, preparing it to slide deep.

I run my thumb over the tip of my penis, rubbing the precum over the head, mimicking her movements. Imagining her hands on me.

There are sex toys I could use that attempt to replicate the feel of a vagina. I tried one once and couldn't use it. At least my hand is living flesh, even if it is my own.

"Do you like dildos?" I ask, curious if it's the same for her, but still a necessity for her job.

"Sure," she says. "I mean, it's not as satisfying as the real thing, but still enjoyable. Especially when you're the one telling me what to do with it."

I'm under no illusions that she has singled me out as a favorite client, but still, her words are pleasing.

She places the dildo at her opening again and waits for me to tell her to insert it, but I don't. Instead, I say, "Before I fuck you, I want to go down on you."

She sets the dildo aside and grabs a vibrator shaped like a tongue.

"Put it on the lowest setting. Tease yourself, but lightly. Not enough to satisfy you, because I'm running my tongue over your clit but not sucking. Not stroking hard. I'm playing with you. Getting you wetter and wetter. Driving you mad as you ache for hard licks from my tongue."

She follows my instructions and barely lets the vibrator touch her.

"I slip my tongue inside you and thrust as deep as I can."

She inserts the vibrator and lets out a soft groan. I know she likes the feel of the vibration inside her, even on the lightest setting.

I imagine a future moment in which I'm really in bed with her and we have all her toys at my disposal. I know exactly how to drive her wild.

Of course, that can never happen between us, but still, it's a perfect fantasy made stronger by the fact that today I met Eden.

Later, when I replay this session in my mind, I'm as likely to see Eden in my fantasy as I am to see Desiree.

I'm not sure if that's wrong or not. After all, I didn't seek her out, even though I knew she lived in the area because she'd worked for CamDames' DC headquarters. I could have found her easily. Mothman wouldn't have batted an eye if I'd asked for his help in finding her, given her past association with the website.

But I didn't. Meeting her tonight was pure accident on my end. I don't feel bad about not telling Eden that I know who she is. I'm pretty sure that would have freaked her out and exposed her secret online job to a coworker.

Should I feel bad that I'm here now? In her private room? Would she want to know it's me?

I'm at a loss with this ethical dilemma, and it's not exactly something I can get advice on.

No one knows about Falcon or my regular visits to Desiree's site.

I shove those thoughts aside. I'm not doing anything wrong, and neither is she.

She keeps playing with the tongue-shaped vibrator, and I tell her to stop. She's ready for me, and I'm desperate to be inside her.

If this were real, I'd be sliding on a condom right now.

Someday, maybe I'll get to find out what that's like—the condom ritual when hot and ready and eager. I vaguely remember it from my pre-Raptor days. I remember enjoying when a partner rolled it on for me. How sexy it was to include the condom as part of foreplay. Now I can't bear the thought of letting a woman have that kind of control over my body.

I want to be touched, but how do I keep control? This is yet another reason I can't have sex with a partner. Not yet.

Maybe I should practice with condoms. Retrain my brain.

But not tonight. Tonight, I'm bare and so hard, I could pound nails.

"Falcon?" Desiree says, her voice almost pleading.

I realize I've been silent too long. I'm not telling her how she makes me feel, which is something I know she likes, since she can't see me. "I was just thinking about how hard you make me. Touch me, Desiree. Run your hand down my cock."

On the screen she touches the silicone penis as instructed, and I take myself into my hand, just like she's doing. This is the first time I've done this with her, and I'm so deep in the fantasy, I let out a low groan.

Desiree's eyes pop open and her face is flushed, pupils dilated with arousal. "Are you touching yourself, Falcon?" She runs her hand down the phallus, holding it at just the right angle so I can pretend it's me in front of her and not a camera.

"Yes." I mimic her actions with my hand.

"Am I right in thinking you've never done that before? With me?"

"You are," I say.

"Why is tonight different?"

Because I saw you tonight, and you said you wanted to fuck me.

Of course, I can't say that, much as I want to. "Because I've missed you these last six weeks. And tonight, I can't wait. I need to fuck you now."

In my pre-Raptor sex life, I never spoke like this to a partner. At least, I'm pretty sure I didn't, but it feels right for the new me. It turns me on, and I can tell it turns her on too.

"Slide your fingers inside," I say. "Are you wet for me?"

She does as commanded, and her thumb brushes her clit. Naughty girl. She really can't wait. "So wet." Her voice is breathy.

"Put the tip of the cock inside you, but don't slide it deeper."

She does, and I wrap my palm around the tip of my penis.

She holds it expectantly, and finally, I say, "Take me deep," and thrust into the circle of my palm as she pushes the dildo as deep as it will go.

Watching it slide inside as I do the same with my hand is more intense than I'd imagined it would be. But then, I've been priming myself for this for months, so of course everything is heightened.

"I'm going to fuck you deep and slow at first," I say.

She obeys, moving the toy in a sensual rhythm. I copy her timing. Another groan escapes. I feel an intimacy with her that would be missing if I'd done this months ago.

The intimacy drives me wild because I still feel safe—which was impossible for me before now.

I'm *feeling*, really feeling. And I don't just mean the pleasure sensations coming from squeezing and stroking my dick.

It's the other stuff that has been locked deep for years. I'm happy. Not just happy, joyful. I think I forgot what joy felt like. At least, intimate joy.

I had fun in Oregon, hanging out with Josh and crushing him at Mario Kart. Beating the fuck out of racist trash. Visiting Owen at R&R, and spending our days kayaking on the lake or hiking through lush green forests. But none of that required reaching deep into my broken head.

This…this requires I go to the heart of my pain. So here I am, I've finally broken through layers of protective barriers my mind built and having an intimate moment with a beautiful woman. I'm experiencing intense sexual pleasure without inhibitors.

"Faster," I command.

The dildo slides in and out, and she strokes her clit with her thumb, letting out soft panting sounds as she does it. She's not faking. Not at all.

I've seen her put on an act. When I was a new client and still figuring myself out, we had some very basic sessions. But this isn't that.

This is real. She's fucking me in her mind and enjoying every moment of it. I don't know if she's thinking of Falcon or Chase. Both work for me. "Get the vibrator." I want her to come, and I want it to be powerful. She's earned it.

She grabs a small pink vibrator from the bed next to her and turns the dial on the end.

"All the way up," I say.

"Thank you," she says. She's still sliding the cock in and out as she works the vibrator with the other hand. She stares at the camera, and I expect her to ask if she can place the vibrator on her clit, but instead she says, "I wish you would turn on your camera. Hearing you is driving me wild. I want to see your cock."

"Not this time," I say, even though I want to give her that. Maybe if I keep the camera low…but I'd probably screw it up somehow and she'd see me. Yesterday, that wouldn't have been a problem, but now that she's seen my face, it's impossible.

"If you won't turn on your camera, will you send me a photo? There's an upload button on the bottom right of the screen."

A solicited dick pic? I didn't think such a thing was possible.

I stroke my dick and cup my balls. I have never in my life considered taking a picture of my penis and sending it to someone. But now, as I watch her on the screen, licking her lips, hot for me, I decide to go for it.

I grab a burner phone and snap a photo. She must've heard the digital shutter sound because she asks, "Did you just take a photo?"

"I did."

She grins wickedly. "Send it."

I transfer the photo to my laptop and run it through a widget that strips all data—date, time, location, all the stuff that gets embedded—and upload it to her site.

She lifts her tablet from the bed and clicks on the file. She lets out a soft purring sound, then turns the tablet toward the camera so I can see my dick filling the screen, and she licks the glass.

Damn. It's crazy how hot it is to see her lick my dick like that. But then, everything she does is hot.

"You need to come," I say. Because I'm ready to blow and there is no way I'm getting off first.

She drops back on the bed and resumes sliding the dildo

in and out as her other hand picks up the vibrator and turns it back on.

"Put it on your clit."

She does.

"Pleasure yourself. Make yourself come while I fuck you."

She works both toys, freed from waiting for my commands. I can see the pleasure building in her. Her body gets tighter, her legs squeezing together and her shoulders curling forward. Without a man between her legs, she's closing up around the vibrator and dildo.

I'm stroking my cock fast and hard, on the edge right with her.

She lets out a groan, then goes still except for a slight rocking of her pelvis as I presume wave after wave of pleasure hits her, held at the peak by the powerful vibrator.

Watching her, I come apart. Semen spills from my cock in short bursts. I'm groaning along with her as pleasure seizes me.

I drop back against the pillows, spent. Overwhelmed.

Emotions swirl through me. This was so much more intense than any sexual encounter I can remember.

Usually, after Desiree comes, we chat for a bit before I log off.

Tonight, I stare at the screen on which a beautiful woman is splayed on her bed panting, as if she's had an equally mind-blowing orgasm.

I hit the button that drops two hundred dollars in her bank, then close the laptop without saying goodbye.

Chapter Six

As she did every Friday since the start of the fall semester, Eden went to campus. She'd been hired to work four hours a week as a research assistant for a new study of depression in children with autism spectrum disorder. The study was in the beginning stages, still identifying candidates, and Eden's role for now was to go through candidate files and enter their information in a database. It was tedious work, but it would get more interesting when the study was going in earnest, and it paid well and kept her involved with the department during her semester break, so it was still a win.

She was thankful her advisor had hired her for this study when he had other favorites in the department. She was aware a few students were disgruntled she'd gotten the job when she wasn't taking classes right now.

As with every graduate department, the psychology department was filled with students who wanted to be friends and those who saw the others as competition. Eden didn't care for the games. She wasn't interested in being Dr. Dearborn's or Dr. Howard's favorite, and she didn't particularly care that she wasn't popular among her fellow grad students.

Between two jobs, her course load, and sometimes teaching the intro classes plus the practicum hours that were required, she didn't have time to go out for drinks every Friday night. Or even any Friday night. And she was fine with that.

Being homeless at sixteen had instilled in Eden a deep need for financial security, but the social worker who'd helped her had also inspired Eden's drive to become a psychologist like her. To help people, especially young girls who had nowhere else to turn. To do that, Eden needed school. Years and years of it.

To pay for school, she needed money, lots and lots of it.

She'd found her balance to achieve her goals. She'd make friends later. In the meantime, she had a few people she'd bonded with in the department to keep life from being too lonely, and she stayed in touch with undergrad friends who remained in Colorado.

Working as a barista was a social job, and her night job was...*extremely* social, even if she didn't always get to choose who she spent time with. As an extrovert, she was getting her needs met.

And last night, she'd gotten other needs met. She couldn't stop grinning every time she thought about it. Who knew her job could be quite so...*rewarding?*

The door to the lab opened, and Eden turned to see Kelly, her closest friend in the department and ally against frenemy grad students. She plopped down on the chair next to Eden.

"Okay, spill. Who was the hottie who drove you home last night?"

Eden worked to contain the smile that lingered from thinking about Falcon and turned her mind to the operative she'd probably never see again. "He's a guy from Raptor."

"The private security company owned by the hot senator?"

Eden laughed. "Yep. Mr. Hot Senator's wife was in the coffee shop yesterday, actually."

Kelly let out a dreamy sigh. "Man. She's one lucky woman. The guy is rich, smart, and, well, you didn't live here when he was running for office, but the photos from when he was an Army Ranger were all over the local internet news and TV. He could be in his combat uniform, sweaty, dirty, and rumpled, or all polished up in his dress uniform, and it didn't matter. Formal, casual, whatever, he was hot in every single picture."

"I'm kind of sorry I missed that."

"It was the only time I haven't completely hated political advertising, let me tell you."

Eden chuckled at that. "I can imagine."

"So why did you need a guy from Raptor to drive you home?"

She told the story of the men pounding on the window and the belief it was connected to the girl who'd joined Isabel Dawson and the other woman who was a Raptor operative.

"Why didn't the woman show up at the shop, then?"

Eden shrugged. "No idea. Anyway, since I don't have a car and by the time we finished, it was really late, Chase gave me a ride home."

"You going to see him again?"

Two more students entered the lab. "There you are, Kelly," Evelyn said. "We've been looking all over for you." Her smile stiffened when she spotted Eden. She was one who'd resented Eden getting the research assistant job over her, even though Eden had been in the program a year longer. "Oh. Hi, Eden."

"Hi, Evelyn." She dipped her head to the man with her. "Tobias."

"Hey, Eden," Tobias said. "Great that you're here. You can join us for lunch."

Beside him, Evelyn's face fell. She clearly didn't want Eden to tag along for what appeared to be a group lunch. But it was no secret to Eden that Evelyn wanted Tobias's attention, while Tobias never hid his interest in Eden.

"I wish I could," Eden said, which was a complete lie. "But I've got too much work to do." She waved to the thick stack of files she'd barely made any progress on. "And I have a meeting with Dr. Dearborn in an hour."

Kelly pouted. "You never join us for lunch."

"Tell you what, next week, I'll come an hour early so we can catch up."

"Next week's no good. I've got a thing. Maybe the week after?"

Eden pulled out her phone and unlocked the screen. "Putting it on my calendar now."

Kelly nodded. "You aren't off the hook. You haven't finished the story of the hot Raptor guy. Are you going to see him again?"

Evelyn perked up at that. "Hot Raptor guy?"

Again, Eden was forced to hide a smile. Evelyn wasn't even remotely subtle in wanting Tobias to hear all about a guy Eden might be involved with, and she suspected Kelly had laid this bait on purpose. Kelly always aimed for harmony.

"There's not much to tell, really. I doubt I'll see him again." To appease Evelyn's need to deter Tobias's interest in Eden—and her own desire to have Tobias cease even his subtle advances—she added, "But he really is beautiful. I wouldn't complain if we crossed paths."

"How did you meet him?" Tobias asked.

She gave an abbreviated version of the story, made even shorter without Kelly going on about how handsome Alec Ravissant had been in his Army days.

Story complete, Kelly rose from the chair. "Keep me

posted if you hear from him. And then tell me if he's got a friend."

"Mirza was good-looking too. No clue if he's single. I actually don't know if Chase is either, but a girl can dream."

"You going to be able to join us for happy hour this evening?" Tobias asked.

She shook her head. "I picked up a shift at the coffee shop. Another time, maybe." But that too was a lie. She didn't usually work at the coffee shop after putting in her four hours in the lab, but she always worked in front of the camera on Friday night. It was her most lucrative night of the week.

*A*fter meeting with her advisor to go over the schedule for the autism study, Eden took the Metro to Vivace Coffee for a short shift to fill in for another coworker who had to leave early for a doctor's appointment. Her brain swirled with the shifting gears. There was a reason she tried not to work at the coffee shop on days she was in the lab, but at least this was only a two-hour shift, and she'd be home in time to cam tonight.

Whenever she looked at her bank balance, she wondered if she'd made a mistake in going solo, but then, if she'd been at CamDames' DC office last night, she never would have had the intimacy she'd shared with Falcon, knowing that corporate executives would have access to the footage. Everything was supposed to be dumped within forty-eight hours, but all private sessions remained reviewable for that long in case complaints were filed by either the talent (aka herself) or the client.

It was a necessary safety net for a big corporation, but

Eden was on her own now and could cut off a client at any point without having to provide a reason. She'd exercised that privilege twice, and it had been glorious.

Desiree didn't have a two- or three-strikes rule. All it took was one and she could banish anyone from her presence.

By the same token, she could have a more intimate session like she'd had last night and know it remained private. It was possible Falcon had recorded it, but she didn't think he was the type to do that. Probably foolish faith on her part, but she trusted him just the same. Plus even if he had recorded it, she didn't think he would share it with anyone. He certainly wouldn't upload it to a porn site and attempt to monetize it.

She reached her Metro stop and walked three blocks to the coffee shop where she usually worked. Vivace Coffee was a small chain—only eight shops in the DC area—and in the six months she'd worked there, last night had been her first time picking up a shift at a different store. It had been a perfectly fine change of pace until closing.

And even that wasn't so bad. Meeting Chase Johnston had been a highlight after a long dry spell. On the long Metro ride to school and back, she'd spent her time alternating between mooning over Chase and Falcon. Last night had been more fun than she'd had on her side job in a long time, and she'd made a nice chunk of change to boot.

Once she was behind the counter of the shop, she found herself watching the front door like a hawk, wondering if her inspiration for the hot online encounter might come up with an excuse to visit her at her real workplace. But every time the bell over the door chimed, she would eagerly greet the new customers with a fake smile to hide her disappointment.

It had been a chance encounter last night and would end there. After all, she had no reason to call the guy, and he didn't have her number. The phone in the back rang, and her coworker, Lainey, answered. A minute later, Lainey called out, "Eden, call for you!"

Her heart beat rapidly as she slipped into the alcove at the end of the counter to pick up the extension, glad there was no line or customers who needed attention right that minute. She lifted the receiver and hit the button to connect to the caller on hold. "This is Eden."

"Eeed!" a female voice said, drawing out the hard E of her name. "I just wanted to thank you for taking my shift last night. Food poisoning is the *worst*."

Once again, she felt a pang of disappointment, but really, she shouldn't expect to hear from Chase ever again. She shouldn't have gotten her hopes up. "Hey, Penny. I hope you're feeling better."

"I am. Finally able to keep fluids down. Last night was ugly, though. Glad I wasn't scheduled for today, because I'm still feeling weak."

"I've been there." Eden kept her eye on the door. They were deep in the afternoon lull. She had time to talk. "You missed something interesting. Some guys came by and pounded on the front door, demanding to know where someone named Jasmine was. Turns out they spray-painted 'Jasmine is ours' on the back door while Tony and I waited for help."

"Wow. You called the police?"

"No." She explained the girl who came running into the shop and the Raptor operative who'd left her card. "So Raptor sent two operatives to check out the shop and escort us to our cars." No need to tell Penny she'd gotten a ride home from the guy. Penny might want to know more. She was the only person who knew about Eden's double life.

Eden had met Penelope Madison when they both worked at CamDames. Penny's screen name had been Penny Candi, going by Candi for short. A few months before Eden went solo, Candi reduced her hours to one shift a week and got a job at Vivace Coffee. When Penny heard Eden was quitting, she mentioned that Vivace was hiring and offered health insurance to part-time workers.

Health insurance had been one of Eden's biggest concerns about striking out on her own, and when her car died right after she'd invested all her savings in buying the townhouse and tech for the site, she knew she needed a part-time job to see her through until she built up her clientele to CamDames level again. It seemed like destiny that there was a Vivace Coffee within walking distance of the townhouse she'd just moved into. The only drawback was that there was one person working for Vivace Coffee who knew about her online work as Desiree, so Eden and Penny made a pact to keep each other's secrets.

"Wow. That's a crazy story, but I'm glad nothing worse happened."

"It was fine. Just weird."

"Anyway, I just wanted to say thanks. Sorry things got weird. If you ever need me to pick up a shift, I owe you. In fact, I'd love to grab a coffee sometime and catch up."

Eden gave a vague response to that before they hung up. Should she try to be friends with Penny in real life, or was that too risky?

Penny was younger than her by at least six years—which meant she'd begun working as a camgirl from pretty much the moment she turned eighteen. Eden worried Penny might have worked illegally before that, but there was an unwritten rule at CamDames that no one asked questions along those lines. If someone offered their background and personal history, no problem. But prying was out of bounds.

Much as Eden wanted to reach out to the younger woman to let her know she had a friend if she ever needed to talk about that experience and how it shaped her, she refrained. She didn't think it would be a welcome topic, plus no one at CamDames had known Eden was a grad student studying psychotherapy. She didn't want any crossing of the streams of her school and cam work.

Her coworkers at Vivace knew she was a student, but she didn't talk about her studies in detail, and she'd been careful the previous night not to talk about school with Tony, just in case he said something to Penny, who still worked one shift a week at CamDames.

It was vital that she wall off the two parts of her life. Her work was legal, and she had a healthy sexuality. There was nothing wrong with what she was doing, but that didn't mean she wouldn't be judged harshly by her fellow students. Dr. Dearborn might look for an excuse to eject her from the program.

So now she lived in a black hole where she couldn't tell her fellow psychology grad students about her side career and how it shaped her thoughts on human sexuality, she didn't discuss her schooling and life goals with her Vivace Coffee coworkers, and the only person in her world who knew about her secret life was Penny, who was more acquaintance than friend.

She didn't date at all, because it wouldn't feel right not to reveal her secret life to a lover, and she couldn't imagine finding a guy who would be okay with her line of work. She was a person who spent much of her days in social situations at school and work—both online and in the shop—and yet there was a part of her that felt deeply isolated.

Alone.

Last night's session with Falcon had been the first time in a while that she'd felt like the session was truly intimate in both directions. An emotional need of hers had been met in an unexpected way.

Perhaps she should look more in that direction for friendship rather than to Penny, but at the same time, she didn't want to leave the girl floundering if she needed someone to talk to.

Girl. No. Penny was a woman who'd been an online sex worker longer than Eden. But that was why Eden was worried about her. In the same years her sexuality was developing, she was putting it all on display.

Eden had been nearly twenty-five when she made the same choice, and she knew her eighteen—or younger—year-old self would never have been able to grasp the emotional and developmental implications.

A customer walked in the front door, distracting her from her thoughts. Once again, she was disappointed the customer wasn't Chase, but they were regulars, a gay couple who were always chatty and entertaining, and she spent the last thirty minutes of her short shift discussing the impact of Dave Filoni on the *Star Wars* universe.

Who needed to go out on dates when she could have her favorite kind of nerdy conversations with customers?

Maybe tonight she'd do a Princess-Leia-in-the-metal-bikini role play. Did Chase like *Star Wars*? Did he know deeply irrelevant details about the timeline of the Clone Wars that only other obsessive fans cared about?

She reminded herself it didn't matter if Chase liked *Star Wars* because she probably wouldn't see him again. She should focus instead on Falcon. Perhaps he'd taken his screen name from *Millennium Falcon,* in which case he'd definitely enjoy the Princess Leia role play.

Chase clicked the link Mothman sent and scanned the still images from the hospital security camera. They had a specific time frame—there was a ninety-minute window in which the goon had gotten medical attention before going back to Vivace Coffee—and Mothman was doing his best to grab images from every emergency room security camera within striking distance. It was a surprise he'd managed to snag these images at all, let alone less than twenty-four hours later, but still, Chase couldn't help but feel they weren't moving fast enough.

That the goons were comfortable going back to the coffee shop to spray-paint the rear door wasn't good. Plus there was the fact that a former CamDames camgirl had been behind the counter. Much as he wanted her presence to be a coincidence, that was highly unlikely. Was Eden somehow connected to the trafficking?

Should he out Eden to Mothman and Tricia? Tell them who she was? But that didn't feel right. If Eden knowingly had anything to do with the trafficking, she wouldn't have called Raptor.

He trusted her, right?

His stomach churned. The idea that he couldn't trust her didn't sit well.

He closed his eyes and ran through the shadowy memories from the time at his cabin when Parks brought the girl. He searched his broken memories for Eden's face. Was it possible he'd responded to Desiree immediately because he'd seen her before?

How long had Eden been a camgirl? His mental timeline was hopelessly skewed. He had no way of knowing when he'd seen the young girl's face. It could be any time after Parks first implanted the chip three years ago up until she'd been arrested eleven months ago.

He couldn't find Eden in any of his fuzzy memories. One thing he'd learned about infrasound and muddled memories was that most of the time, if he had a reliable event or image to jog his brain, the memory would sort itself out.

Both Isabel and Rav had experienced this in Alaska. Memories that were gone returned when the right stimulus was applied.

Eden was the right stimulus, but she triggered no memories. That had to mean she wasn't involved. She couldn't be.

But if one of the goons had recognized her from her CamDames days, it was entirely possible she was in danger now, and the spray-painted message had been intended for her.

Chapter Seven

It took a week, but Mothman finally got a hit on a private clinic security camera that showed the goon with the broken arm heading inside twenty minutes after the fight.

The sling made sense given the fast timing—doctors usually waited a day or two to make sure there was no swelling with that kind of break—but he'd probably gotten a splint and some strong painkillers to be able to show up at the shop and harass Eden, and Chase should have guessed the guy went to a private clinic given how fast he made it back to the shop. A DC hospital emergency room probably wouldn't have had a chance to examine him in the ninety-minute time frame they had.

But a private clinic, one in which the goon's employers probably paid for fast, discreet service, made a lot of sense. Hell, even Raptor had their own on-compound clinic with medics, but then, they recruited a lot of employees from the military, and medics were good to have around.

The shadow organization that operated through

CamDames' back door didn't appear to have their own medics on staff, but they clearly had an arrangement with someone.

With this lead, Chase wondered if the girls were treated by the same physicians. They were bound to have lots of health issues given the abuse they suffered.

Chase closed his eyes and remembered the flash of the face. The vague memory that cut to his core every time it surfaced.

The face that had set him on this path.

Parks had been a licensed psychiatrist and could write prescriptions. Chase was fairly certain she'd played the role of doctor for the backside of the organization, that she'd associated with them because she was looking for subjects to test the infrasound chips on after her success with Chase. Her previous test subjects had all been killed in a cover-up, and until Chase came along, it was possible she'd given up the research.

But then Chase and Isabel found themselves on her therapist couch. She couldn't touch Isabel—as the girlfriend and later wife of Alec Ravissant, any tampering with her mind and the surgery required to implant the chip would have been noticed.

Chase had been a different story. He'd bought a remote cabin within a few months of returning to work for Raptor and spent much of his time there, processing what he'd gone through alone.

His coworkers didn't know him well. He'd transferred from the Alaska compound and was the guy whose brain had been scrambled. They didn't know his habits or behavior.

Even the guys he'd worked with in Alaska didn't know who he'd been as a person before Godfrey got his claws into him, because Godfrey began "mentoring" him within weeks of his hire.

Chase had been alone and vulnerable, and Parks saw an opportunity to experiment on him. After she'd been successful—and he gathered he was her *most* successful test subject, because she'd combined her work with the groundwork done in Alaska—she'd wanted more subjects to experiment on.

Chase believed CamDames then became her new supplier for test subjects, but he didn't know how Parks became associated with the website, and he didn't have proof of any of this for the prosecuting attorney. Just vague memories with snippets of conversation that would never hold up in court.

None of what Chase was doing would hold up in court, which made his work all the more vital. Police couldn't do what he did. They needed warrants and probable cause. Chase required nothing of the sort, and because of that, he'd managed to intercept five girls in the last five months.

Now he sat in his Raptor SUV studying the illegally acquired photo of a guy whose arm he'd broken. Was the photo a valid reason to walk into the coffee shop where Eden was working? Maybe she wasn't in danger after all. A full week had passed.

He didn't *need* her confirmation that this was the guy. What were the odds that it was someone else in a sling outside that coffee shop a week ago?

But this was a perfect excuse to see her. Talk to her. Let her know he was following up—in ways the police weren't, but then, they didn't know who Jasmine was or why the men were after her to begin with.

Was it a mistake to involve Eden further?

He had her name and home address. He could run a full background check on her, but he'd chosen not to. He hadn't told Mothman she was a camgirl and used to work for CamDames. If he had, the tech wizard would've investigated her, finding out every private detail of her life up to and including her favorite brand of toothpaste.

Chase didn't want that for her. As someone who'd had his very essence stripped away, who hadn't even been granted privacy in his own mind, he didn't want to delve into this woman's life. Her job put her at risk for predators, giving her plenty of reason to hide.

He wanted to enjoy her as Desiree. He would not be a creepy predator.

But he also wanted to get to know Eden as Chase.

So he sat in the SUV, eyes on the coffee shop, where she was visible behind the counter. Her dark hair was swept up in a high ponytail that made her look younger than her nearly twenty-seven years. No wig. No makeup. Just pure, unembellished Eden. She was so freaking beautiful, even the glimpse through the window took his breath away.

He hadn't been online to see her since the night they met in person. He wasn't entirely sure why. The private session had been worth every penny. He wanted to do it again.

He *would* do it again.

Deep down, he figured he hadn't gone back to her site because he'd wanted the next time he saw her to be in person. Like this.

Except he was the only one who knew they'd been intimate, in a way.

As intimate as he could be, anyway.

That probably did make him a creepy stalker.

Shit.

Would he have been attracted to Eden if she wasn't Desiree?

He wasn't sure if he would ever know the truth there. He hadn't felt sexual desire for anyone else—online or in person—since the chip had been removed.

And he'd tried. When going out to bars failed, he'd

looked up the woman he'd been in love with in high school—the crush that had never gone away—on Facebook. She was pretty and single and appeared to be just as great as she'd always been and…nothing.

He didn't know if it was Eden or Desiree he was attracted to more, but she was the first woman who'd made him feel *anything* in so long. And she'd been attracted to him too. So much so, she'd wanted to proposition him, but instead had gone online and had used that desire to get them both off.

Yeah. It wasn't a great mystery as to why he was sitting in this parking spot mustering the courage to walk inside the coffee shop with his excuse of following up on what happened a week ago.

Would the same attraction zing between them? Had it been triggered by his recognizing her and she'd picked up on his arousal, responding instinctively? Or had the heat been natural chemistry on her part?

Could a woman as beautiful and sexy and confident as Eden actually want *him*?

He had zero doubt she met men every day at the coffee shop who wanted to date her. It was difficult to imagine she could want him over any of them. He'd never been much of a chick magnet—the stutter held him back, and he'd always been more shy than not.

With his high school crush, he'd been firmly in the friend zone, and that was true with a lot of women he'd been interested in when he was in his teens and early twenties. In the Before Times.

He opened the driver's door and stepped out. The longer he stared, the creepier and more stalkerish it would be, so it was time to face her.

He grabbed the envelope with the photo and approached the shop. It was quiet—afternoon lull—with only two customers sitting at tables and no one in line. Her back was to the door as she cleaned something behind the counter.

The bell above the door jingled. She turned to greet him, and surprise registered first, then her face broke into a beautiful smile.

A smile for him. His heart picked up rhythm. He felt his face flush.

His body's response to being near her was a foreign landscape. New. Different. Emotions he hadn't been able to access in years. It was exhilarating to experience this wild rush. It was as if she embodied magic that had woken him from a sorcerer's spell.

But even so, his reaction was also old, forgotten territory. He'd always been prone to blushing. That and the stutter had been the bane of his adolescence. If he hadn't been a black belt in karate by the age of thirteen, he'd have been brutalized. It helped having a father who was a martial arts instructor who'd started training him when he was in preschool.

His peers had respected him for that and didn't bother with the teasing. And for Chase's part, when he saw them picking on other awkward kids, he let it be known they were under his protection, and the bullying stopped. For an awkward teen, his adolescence had been strangely harmonious after that.

It was one of the things that had drawn him to police work. Protecting others. It had felt like it could be his calling when he found college wasn't a good fit for him.

He would never be an officer now, and he wasn't sure how he felt about that. On the one hand, there was no way he could do the kind of work he was doing now. He and Mothman were breaking a dozen laws to obtain their intel. And he had zero qualms about it.

Tricia stayed out of that part of it, because there were still a few cases she'd worked as a vice cop that could mean she'd be called in to testify, and she didn't want anything that could impugn her as a witness in a trial. She worked the legal end with Isabel, meeting the girls and getting them to the shelter.

This was particularly important right now, as she was recovering from a traumatic injury she'd suffered while in Indonesia nearly eight weeks ago. She was one of only four survivors of a massacre at a security conference and had been in a medically induced coma for several days, buying time for Raptor to fly her home for treatment.

She was back on her feet now, but would remain on medical leave through the end of the year, if not longer, while she rebuilt strength and underwent counseling. She'd insisted on being in the coffee shop last week—it had been her first time resuming the role she'd played in their little club since her injury.

Now she was eager to do more—she was bored in her recovery—and maybe, if Eden recognized the guy, they'd get another lead into the operation.

Yeah. That was totally not why he was approaching her at the counter, but he'd pretend it was.

He was braced for her to be put off by seeing him. After all, this wasn't the same coffee shop where the incident had happened, and she was protective of her information. But she'd also given this as her address, so she knew he had the information legitimately, and it was a damn sight better than showing up at her townhouse.

She was smiling, though, and it was genuine, so his presence wasn't unwelcome.

He opened his mouth to say hello, and the word wouldn't come. It wasn't his speech impediment that stopped him, it was the sudden thought that he stood just across the counter from the woman who'd licked an image of his cock.

Why did that memory have to jump into his head *now*?

He wasn't sexually savvy. He wasn't familiar with navigating the day—or week—after. Especially when only one of them knew what they'd shared.

This was a messed-up situation, but also wildly titillating.

She doesn't know.

Would she go online tonight and be hot for him again?

"Hey, stranger," she said, when he didn't speak. "You here for coffee, tea…or me?"

He laughed. "Y-you, ac-actually." He cleared his throat and dropped his voice so she wouldn't recognize it. Plus it helped with the stutter. "But I'll take a coffee too."

"Want anything fancy? Steamed almond milk, Irish cream shot, marshmallow sprinkles?"

He snickered. "There is no such thing as marshmallow sprinkles."

"It was worth a try. If you'd said yes, I'd have tossed in some Lucky Charms." She waved a hand toward the rack of individual-sized tubs of cereal for customers in need of a quick breakfast.

She leaned forward and spoke in a conspiratorial whisper. "I had a customer who poured coffee in their cereal once. It did not look appealing. I mean…if it had been iced with lots of cream, maybe. But it was straight java."

"That sounds revolting."

"Put me off cereal for weeks, to be honest." She grabbed a ceramic mug—not a to-go cup, he noticed—and held it up. "So just straight drip?"

He nodded. "Hold the cereal."

She filled the mug from the ready-made pot and set it on the counter before him. He pulled out his wallet.

"Your money's no good here. You helped us out last week. Least the owner can do is comp your coffee."

"It might have been Raptor's fault there was a problem to begin with."

"The girl did nothing wrong in having coffee in a coffee shop." She poured a second mug of coffee and leaned on the counter after taking a sip. "So what's up? I mean, much as I'd like to believe you're here for *me*, I have a feeling there's more."

Eden, you have no idea.

He stuffed a five dollar bill in her tip jar, then remembered the tip he'd given her last week, and he flushed with heat all over again. This blushing thing had to stop.

He attempted to muster a suave demeanor but remembered he'd never had one and this wasn't likely to be the time he figured it out. He took a sip of his coffee, then said, "This is a follow-up after last week. I've a photo I want you to look at."

He slid the envelope across the counter to let her retrieve the photo and study it. He wanted to watch her face as she saw the image for the first time and didn't want the distraction of being the one handling it.

She gave him a curious look, then pulled out the glossy eight-by-ten. Her eyes widened upon first glance, but then she tamped the reaction down, her face going carefully blank.

She'd recognized the guy. From when she worked at CamDames? If so, this confirmed there was crossover between the front and back ends of the business.

"You're wondering if this is the guy who was at the door? Sling Man?" she asked.

He nodded. "Is it him?"

Her brow furrowed, and he guessed she really wasn't certain, even though she'd recognized the face in the photo.

"Hard to say. I mean, it could be. This guy looks like he's in a crap ton of pain, between his face and the way he's cradling his arm. He doesn't have the sling yet." She shifted her focus from the photo to Chase. "Where did you get this?"

Her eyes were so damn pretty. She didn't have the heavy

smoky eye she sometimes wore on camera or the false eyelashes and colored contacts, and he liked her both ways. Girl-next-door Eden and sexy-siren Desiree.

His look must've given away his attraction, because her pupils dilated and she cleared her throat. "Chase?"

Nothing to do but give her an apologetic smile.

I find you so irresistibly hot, I can barely carry on a conversation.

"Sorry," he murmured. "Um. I can't tell you how we acquired the photo."

Her smile was knowing—attraction flared both ways and there was no pretending otherwise.

The bell above the door jangled, and a look of disappointment flashed across her features. She signaled with her thumb to the bar-height seats at the end of the counter. "Park yourself over there. You're not leaving while I handle these customers."

He couldn't help but grin. "Yes, ma'am." He settled on the far-end stool and watched her work. This was a good angle, as he could see behind the counter and had her in profile view. He already knew she had a spectacular ass, but this was a view of it he'd never gotten to appreciate—how she moved in her normal life, when every gesture wasn't intended to be arousing.

There was a small burst of activity as the first customer was followed by a second and third, and a full ten minutes elapsed before she could join him again. She pulled up a stool on her side and sat facing him. She let out a soft sigh. "It's good to get off my feet for a few minutes."

"You nearing the end of your shift?"

She hesitated before answering, and he realized his question wasn't a safe one for a woman to answer. She'd probably learned that lesson the hard way.

"Never mind. I shouldn't have asked." He let out a self-deprecating laugh. "Hard to believe I work in private security, isn't it?"

She smiled and leaned toward him. Like she wanted to be in his space. Smell him.

He felt the same way, so she was just making his efforts easier.

"From what I know about Raptor, you don't handle simple personal security like self-defense and women's safety."

"No. But I am aware of the issues. And I actually do teach self-defense."

She raised a brow. "Like the kind of classes you can take at a community center?"

"I haven't done that, but I have been considering it." *If thinking of it right now counts as considering it.* "I was referring to work I did last month in Portland, Oregon, when I volunteered to teach counterprotesters how to stand up to—and fight back against—white supremacists at the White Patriot rallies."

Her eyes widened. "Oh my God. You were there when the bridge bomb went off?"

He nodded.

"And then…there was the thing that happened in the office tower. When the rich guy was arrested. There were two Raptor operatives who were part of that. Were you one of them?"

He nodded again.

"Jesus. I need to do more than give you a lousy cup of free coffee—for which you tipped me almost double the cost."

Oh sweetheart, you have done more for me than anyone else. More than you can ever know.

But what he said was "First, this coffee is far from lousy, and really, I'm just in it for the coffee. Well, that and I can't stand bullies."

Oh hell. Now he sounded like he was parroting Captain America, but he wasn't. It was all true.

Another jingle sounded, and she slid off the stool. "You still aren't allowed to leave," she said as she headed for the order station.

He smiled as he watched her walk away, liking how she bossed him around.

That was new. A crack in his need-to-control-everything shell.

He could take orders from her any time.

Maybe he'd try that the next time he was Falcon.

Which would be tonight. No way would he be able to stay away after this exchange.

*C*hase Johnston wasn't just incredibly hot and disarmingly sweet, he was a bona fide *hero*. When she got home tonight, she was going to google the Portland racist rallies and see what she could find. There had been a lot of videos posted on YouTube. Maybe she'd see him in action.

Was that wrong? It wasn't like she was stalking him. She was looking up public information, right? It wasn't like she was trying to figure out where he lived…

But then, she knew where he lived because he'd mentioned living in the Virginia compound when he drove her home. Her townhouse had been on the way. She'd even taken a photograph of his driver's license.

It really sucked that she couldn't date as long as she had her online business.

At least she could fantasize. Chase revved her engines, which was something she needed to keep her online persona engaging. She could muster interest and enjoy the flirting and dirty talk, but having the fantasy of Chase in her head…well, last week had proven that was effective.

She'd made seven hundred dollars, which she'd desperately needed, plus she'd made Falcon happy. He'd come with her—a first for him. And they'd both had fun.

Win-win, and she had thoughts of the hot Raptor operative to thank for it.

He'd tipped her five dollars for a free mug of drip coffee, but really, she should be tipping *him*.

Before she googled Chase, however, she needed to call Penny and ask about the security guard from CamDames. It was strange that he might have been Sling Man, as she'd come to think of him. Was CamDames keeping an eye on Penny?

The name Jasmine flitted across her mind.

CamDames had a thing about animated princess movies. There were some women who used themed rooms built around the movies. Off-brand, of course, to avoid trademark lawsuits. But in the back rooms, management referred to them as the character names. They'd asked Eden to work the Snow White room once. She'd declined because not only was that not her thing—c'mon, if she was going to be a princess, she would be Princess Leia—but also, she never went on camera with dark hair. She knew the blonde, blue, red, and pink wigs weren't fooling anyone, but still, she didn't want to make it easy to recognize her.

The odds that one of her clients would come across her in real life were slim, especially now that she had the IP address blocker in place, but still, she couldn't be too careful.

Was Jasmine a reference to CamDames? Did Penny ever work the Jasmine room? Had it not been about the girl in the coffee shop that night at all?

She finished serving the new batch of customers, then picked up the drip pot and approached Chase. "Refill?"

"Better not. I have enough trouble sleeping as it is."

She wanted to explore that. Was it because of what happened last month in Portland? Or did other anxieties keep him up at night? Deep down, she wanted to understand people, and then she wanted to use that knowledge to help them know themselves.

"Can I get you something else, then?" She didn't want him to leave.

His gaze fixed on hers, and she figured he knew her motive. "I should go."

"But you haven't told me anything about Portland yet." That was brazen, considering he'd never promised to tell her anything. Perhaps Desiree's boldness was rubbing off on her.

His eyes flared with a sexy heat. "I suppose I could come back sometime. If that would be okay?"

She liked how this man was so conscious of her boundaries. She'd had customers who hit on her to the point of harassment who never once considered they were making her uncomfortable at work. Or rather, that she was uncomfortable was a feature, not a bug.

"I would like that. A lot."

He slid a business card across the counter. "My contact info if you should remember anything more about the guy in the photo."

She accepted the card and slid it in her back pocket, wishing there was a way she could tell him about the CamDames security guard without revealing herself.

*D*uring her short walk home, Eden pulled out her cell and dialed Penny. She had looked up her number in the store database because she'd never had reason to call

Penny personally before, but this was a call that she couldn't make from the shop, not without breaking their pact.

Not surprisingly, Eden's call went to voicemail. She never answered unknown numbers either. She left a message saying they needed to talk. One block closer to home, her phone rang.

"What's going on?" Penny asked.

"Is this a good time to talk?"

"Sure. I'm alone."

"Do you still work once a week at CamDames?"

She let out a sigh. "Yeah. It's hard to let it go. I make more in that one day than I do in a week at Vivace."

"Hey, you know you'll get no judgment from me. You were making bank. I'm surprised you dialed back in favor of being a barista."

"I had to… I…had a stalker. He found me in real life. I never should have put 'Penny' in my screen name, even if it wasn't used as much as Candi. Live and learn. So when I do my shift now, I look totally different. It takes two hours to do the baby-doll makeup, and honestly, it's a little freaky. I look like a comic book drawing, not a person. But it means I can do one shift a week and pay the bills, and stalker guy is blocked. I have a set list of clients and only accept new ones who've behaved themselves on the site with at least a thirty-day history."

Eden had asked for that kind of protection from CamDames, but she hadn't been the star Penny was, so they'd refused. It was another reason she'd decided to go solo. She'd wanted absolute control over managing the men she engaged with online.

"Why do you ask?"

"I was wondering if one of the security guards there is currently in a cast or a sling," Eden said. She wouldn't tell Penny about the security camera photo, not when she couldn't verify where it came from or how she'd seen it, but this was a reasonable question.

"Gosh. Wow. You think it might have been one of the CamDames guards who came to the shop last week?"

"Maybe? It was just so weird. And I got to thinking about the spray-painting on the door and the name Jasmine."

"And that made you think of the princess rooms."

"Yeah. You ever play Jasmine on camera?"

Penny made a sound that might have been a snort. "Good Lord. Who knows? I think I did them all before I had a following of my own."

"Be careful the next time you pull a shift. If you see a guard with a cast or a sling, let me know. And watch out for him. He might have been there for you."

"Thanks for the heads-up, but I'm sure it's fine. All the guards are super sweet to me."

"Yeah. That could be the problem. Promise you'll be careful. Get someone else to escort you to your car if you need it."

"'Kay. I promise, Mom."

Eden smiled. She'd been teased in the past by coming across as a mother hen to all the Dames. But damn, she worried about all of them. They were so young. Eden wasn't *that* much older, but she felt like she was.

"Penny?"

"Yeah?"

"Did you ever find out who your stalker was?"

"Not in real life, but his screen name was a bird. Eagle, I think? No, wait. It was Falcon."

Eden stopped in her tracks, a chill running up her spine.

No. There were plenty of guys who used animals as their screen name, and there had been an uptick in Falcons with the Marvel superhero's popularity. Just like she had a Thor and another regular who went by Loki.

But still, as she hit the End button, she felt a tingling at the back of her neck. Like she was being watched. She glanced around the busy street just two blocks from her townhouse.

She was imagining things. Even so, better safe than sorry. Instead of walking straight home, she cut through a park and went to a convenience store. Screw watching her weight every damn minute. This called for ice cream.

Chapter Eight

FALCON

Desiree usually starts her evening shift at eight p.m. and stays online until midnight—either in the open room or in private sessions. I now know this is because she has a day job and probably works afternoons with only the occasional evening. I can't imagine she does the morning store opening because the shop opens at six a.m. and four or five days a week she's working until midnight. But then, I don't really know her situation, and a lot of people who work two jobs burn the candle at both ends.

Many camgirls put in eight-hour days—I've researched the profession enough to know that the most successful ones keep consistent hours and treat it like the business it is. It's surprising that Desiree doesn't work full eights considering she has invested in quality cameras and props and a secure website with all the bells and whistles. She's not splitting her income with CamDames anymore, and her investment needs to earn out. The best way to do that is to up her hours. I'm certain she makes far more online than she does at the coffee shop, but then, she probably has to maintain a certain number of hours at the shop to get benefits like health insurance.

It's a screwy system, and I have no clue why she's made the choices she has. Hell, maybe she has zero interest in spending forty hours a week in front of a camera talking men through masturbation.

I can't really blame her there. It must get tiresome.

I wait until she's been online for at least thirty minutes before logging in. It's a risk that she's already entered a private room with another guy, but I'm hoping she's waiting for Falcon. Our last session was spectacular after she met the real me. Maybe she's looking for that again.

I will have to make a point of *not* logging in after the next time I see her in person, or she might notice a pattern. I will also log in between coffee shop visits. I need to be methodical if I'm going to keep this secret.

There are three others in the chat, including Thor, who'd been silent last time, and Hank, who is always chatty. The other name is unfamiliar, likely a new client she acquired while I was in Portland.

Desiree's eyes light up when she spots my name in the chat. "Falcon! Welcome. I've missed you."

I type a quick reply.

Falcon: Missed you too.

Then I drop a fifty into her account. Unnecessary to tip at this point, but if I'm going to get her into a private room, better to show some appreciation early.

"You're feeling generous tonight," she says as she positions herself in front of the camera so the unbuttoned top of her blouse reveals a nipple in side view. She's dressed in her sexy librarian outfit, no bra, but with a tight blouse that hugs her perfect breasts.

Falcon: I'm feeling hungry tonight.

Heat flares in her eyes. Yeah, she enjoyed our last session as much as I did.

I know it's her job to make me feel like I'm the only guy who gets her off when we're alone, but right now, we aren't alone. She runs the risk of alienating the others, so she doesn't say anything, but I know that look is for me.

Sure enough, one of the others chimes in.

Thor: You look hot tonight.

"Thank you. I'm in a bookish mood. And by bookish, I mean I want to get fucked in the stacks."

When she plays sexy librarian, she always spins fantasies of screwing in a library, with details that make me think she's referring to a specific library. She knows which areas are most private. All the hidden alcoves. Where she would go if she wanted to get caught by a group of coeds who could then enjoy the show. This fantasy works well for a group audience, because we can all decide if we're the voyeurs or the guy she's fucking.

It's one of my favorite games of hers. I think it's because it's something I would never want in real life. There is no control. No privacy. But it's hot as a forbidden fantasy, to have a woman that sexy and beautiful unable to resist me even for the amount of time it takes to go somewhere private.

Tonight, I won't be the voyeur. I'll be the guy she goes down on in front of the others.

Hank: What has you so horny tonight, Des?

I've never liked the word *horny*, but I've gotten used to it over the last months. If it were me asking the question, I'd say *hot* or *aroused*. Desiree deserves sexier language. But I know she doesn't care. She uses all the words and is really good at picking up the personal language preferences of her regulars because she always responds in their preferred vernacular. With some guys, she'll use the word *pussy* but with others, she'll say *kitty*. There's a vast array of words she uses in lieu of vagina.

I wonder if this is conscious on her part or if she's just that good at customer service. The next time I'm in the coffee shop I'll pay attention to how she talks to the customers. Does she apply the same skill there?

"Remember last week, when I told you all about the hot guy I met? The one I was desperate to fuck? I saw him again today. It was a public place, so I couldn't pull him aside and go down on him like I wanted to." She unzips the side of her pencil skirt and slides her hand under the tight fabric.

She's touching her pussy and thinking of me.

I go hard as a rock.

"I wanted to take him into the stacks. Have him fuck me from behind while I hold on to the shelf of literary journals."

She's pretending she works at the library. This is standard, but also the first time she's said it when I know it's a lie.

Even so, the scant words paint a picture, and I'm there with her, not bending her over a coffee shop counter, but instead spreading her legs and sliding deep, with the smell of old journals in my nose.

I want to touch myself, but I wait. I'll get my turn when we're alone. I'll enjoy this as foreplay.

She keeps her clothes on as she plays with herself. She rarely strips in the open room, especially if it's only regulars. She's already hooked us and knows we'll pay for more.

She knows I'm good for a few hundred at least tonight if we go private. It doesn't bother me in the least that this is a transaction for her. She's worth every penny.

I live rent-free in the compound, and meals are included. Raptor provides me with a vehicle—I had my own car a year ago because Parks couldn't have me driving a tracked company car when I did her dirty work—but after it blew up, I decided not to replace it. I've learned that being tracked twenty-four seven is a good thing for me.

I have everything I need. I also draw a good salary even though I was a shit employee for a few years—but they know that wasn't my fault, and Raptor was the reason I had my brain scrambled, so I have no problem collecting my check.

Basically, I have wads of money in the bank and little need to spend it. I can indulge in dropping money on Desiree. I can't think of a more deserving person. She's my therapy. At least the only therapy I will allow. I'm never going near an actual shrink again.

One game Desiree never plays is therapist or sex therapist, which is good because I'd have to exit fast. I don't want that in my head when I think of her.

I'd never get hard again.

She plays with herself and teases us with ideas for things she wants to do in private. I don't waste time and hit the five-hundred-dollar-tip button. I don't know how much the other guys tip, so I'm not taking chances. It's unusual for me to drop so much at the start, but why not? She's worth it.

She tells the others that she and I are going to go private. She usually gives a time to come back if they'd like a private session, but it appears my upfront payment has bought her time until midnight. It's gonna be embarrassing when I get off in just a few minutes, but I've been at half-mast since leaving the coffee shop so I can't imagine I'll last long. Not with the sexy librarian thing she has going on.

The first thing she says once we're alone is "I was really hoping to see you tonight."

"Because you want me to fuck you in the stacks."

"Yes, but not until after I go down on you."

She taps at her tablet and holds it up to the camera so I can see my dick pic. "I've been looking at this all week, thinking about taking you into my mouth. Running my tongue down the length. Sucking with the head touching the back of my throat."

Does she say this kind of thing about all the dick pics? Probably. But I don't care, because I believe her. She didn't have to search for the image.

When I sat at the coffee counter today, did she think about my dick? Are Falcon and Chase linked in her mind because I sent her a picture of my cock when I was Falcon, but she was already fantasizing about me as Chase?

It's a brain twister when I think about it. My cock is her mental stand-in for Chase's cock. It makes me want to tell her the truth, but I know if I do, I'll lose both Desiree and Eden. And I need Desiree.

She's helping me find my way to accepting the man I am now, because I'm coming to realize there is no returning to the man I was.

I know she doesn't like faking fellatio with a dildo. She's told us all she's tried different flavors so it doesn't taste like silicone, but nothing works and it's a libido killer for her. It's not just the taste, she's explained, it's the static nature of the toy. For her, the fun of blow jobs is the reaction. The feel of the cock getting thicker and harder in her mouth. The tightening of the balls in her hand as she cups them. The hard thrusts as she sucks and strokes. All that is missing with a manless cock.

Fake dicks, according to her, are great for vaginal penetration, but that's because she uses them with a vibrator for maximum self-pleasure.

On the screen, she does a slow striptease and plays with

herself as she describes what she'd be doing to my cock if we weren't separated by an entire continent.

This reminds me that I should say something about Alaska. I read daily news briefings from Anchorage because I'm committed to this role.

"Talk to me, Falcon. How am I making you feel?"

I stand from my bed and slowly strip. "I was fully clothed, but now that my cock is deep in your throat, I need to get naked. It's too fucking hot in this library."

She laughs. "You're stripping in public?"

"Why not? I've got a ripped body. People should see it."

I am ripped, but that's because there isn't much for me to do during my off-hours in the compound except work out and visit Desiree's private room. Well, that and search out runaways, but my brain isn't allowed to go there right now.

I'm naked in a library with Desiree, and she's on her knees before me with my dick in her mouth.

I risk touching myself and let out a groan.

On the computer screen, I see her smile. "Yes. See what I can do for you. Fuck my mouth, Falcon. Don't hold back."

"I will absolutely hold back. I'm not coming until I'm deep inside your wet pussy." Pussy is another word I had to get used to, but unlike horny, I like the word now.

It's one of the words that turns her on, so it's been positively reinforced enough that it makes me hot now too.

She scoots back and tilts her head up. She's shifted the camera so she's looking up at it with her mouth open. With my laptop on my bed as I stand beside it, it looks just like she's on her knees in front of me and just had my dick in her hot mouth. Her lips are slick with wetness. She's been licking them and might be wearing gloss.

She's fucking beautiful kneeling there. I can see down her unbuttoned top to the nipples that would be hidden by fabric at a different angle.

I'm struck by a deep longing for this to be real. In person.

I've never wanted that before. It's not safe. But maybe with Eden, it would be.

But this isn't Eden, and I'm not Chase right now. I'm Falcon and I'm about to fuck this woman in a library. Her moans will carry down the stacks, and people will watch us, and I'll get off on that too.

As this is something I *definitely* don't want in real life, it's a perfect fantasy to squelch the longing of a moment ago.

"Get up on your feet," I say, taking command of the fantasy.

She complies, tapping a button to change cameras. She's got an amazing setup that couldn't be cheap. I need to tip her more.

Her skirt is unzipped and disheveled. Her wig is up in a messy bun.

"Unclip your hair."

She does.

"Take the skirt off, but leave the shirt on. I want to fuck you with your tits tantalizingly peeking out."

Her eyes light up, and I realize she's been waiting for me to take charge. Does she imagine Chase is a take-charge-in-bed sort of guy? I know I would be if we were doing this for real, but it's not how I used to be. Do I project that air as Chase? Even with the stutter and blushing?

I'm not sure I understand why she's so hot for Chase, but I'll take it, whatever it is.

She wears a thong beneath her skinny skirt. She leaves the thin panties on because I haven't told her she can take them off. She is very good at relinquishing control.

"Spread your legs so I can drop down between them and look up at your wet pussy."

It takes her a moment to switch cameras—the new angle

comes from a handheld that she places on the bed, then she kneels over it, her legs slightly parted.

My screen shows her glistening wet pussy at a whole new angle. She's spread her legs for me plenty, but never like this, with a dedicated pussy cam.

It's fucking amazing, and I wish I could smell her.

"Spread your lips with your fingers and touch yourself."

She does, moving aside the small strip of fabric, then her fingers explore, but she doesn't touch her clit or slide inside her body. So I tell her to do just that.

The camera shows me everything, and I'm desperate to lick her for real.

I remind myself we're in a library. This is pure fantasy and not meant to ever be considered in reality.

"Get the tongue vibrator and make me lick you."

It doesn't take long before she's whimpering and moaning, having a very good time while I watch.

"What are you thinking about as I lick you, Desiree?"

"Nothing but your hot tongue."

I didn't expect her to say *Chase*, but we both know he's the man in her head right now. Is she imagining we're doing this in the coffee shop, or in her mind did she drag me to a library to fuck my brains out?

"C'mon. You aren't thinking about the library patrons who're watching me lick your pussy? Or that guy you saw today who made you hot?"

She lets out a groan and pulls the tongue vibrator from her clit. "Yes. To both."

"He got you hot. But I'm the one who's going to get you off."

She changes cameras again, I'm no longer getting the pussy close-up, but this is better because I can see her face again, and she's flushed and beautiful. On the edge and a bit desperate. Because of me.

Well, and her toys, but I'm playing a part here, and just like last time, this isn't fake. She wants this bad. She is on *edge*.

"You are so beautiful." My compliments are unoriginal but heartfelt. No one has captured my attention more than her. Her brazen sexuality adds to her allure. But she's also sweet and kind, and I want to lick her all over. I want to feel her hands on my body. Does she like wiry muscles, or is she more into the beefy bodybuilder type?

But maybe I know the answer to that already considering she wants to fuck the man from the coffee shop.

"You want me to fuck you from behind, or do you want to face me while I make you come?" I ask.

"From behind first to fulfill my fantasy of getting fucked as I lean over a bookshelf, but before I come, I'm going to turn over so I can see your body and watch you as you thrust into me."

We talk through her scenario, and she's up on her knees at an angle to the camera so I can see her side and back. She reaches between her legs and slips a dildo inside at the same time that I take myself in hand and thrust.

As before, it's intense to do this with her. The pleasure stronger than if I were alone and working from pictures or memory. We thrust and rock in unison, and she gets ramped up really fast.

She rolls over and resumes facing me now. She grabs a vibrator and looks at me expectantly. I haven't given her permission for that.

"Tongue first," I say. "Before I'm back inside you, I go down on you again."

She slides the dildo from her body, then switches vibrators and nearly goes off at the first touch. She turns down the speed and only lightly touches herself with it. She doesn't want to come yet.

She could. I haven't told her not to. But I like the fact that she wants to wait for me. I don't mind her going first at all. After all, until last week, that's all we ever did. But that's not what she wants, and even though I'm paying, this is all for her.

I love making her come, because it's my choice to do so.

"I'm going to fuck you again now."

I climb on the bed. I'm on my knees, facing the computer, and she spreads her thighs. I'm right there. She takes the dildo and slides it inside, and I stroke myself with the same rhythm once again.

She works the cock and vibrator in unison as she did before, her hands doing separate jobs that have her writhing on the bed as the pleasure builds.

I'm making sounds I couldn't hold back if I wanted to as I stroke my cock and watch her.

"Are you close?" she asks.

"Yes." The word comes out with a pant.

She turns up the dial on the vibrator, and leaving the dildo inside her, she releases it and places a hand flat on the bed, her fingers curling in the bedspread as her other hand works the vibrator.

It's that hand on the bedspread that does me in. It's not practiced or for show. She probably doesn't even know her hand is on camera. But it is and her pleasure is so intense, she needs to grip the blanket.

I orgasm, turning so I don't get cum on the laptop. I should have realized that could be an issue, but I'm new to this part.

On the screen, she comes too, letting out a deep moan as her body quakes with pleasure.

She lies on the bed, spent, splayed, and gorgeous.

I reach for my laptop to close it before I go clean up, but she must somehow sense what I'm doing because she says, "Don't you dare leave so fast again."

I hesitate. I'm paying her. One of the perks is no need for hanging around to wait for the sweat to dry. She won't deny my entrance to her room if I ignore her. I pay too well for that, and she likes me. I'm a good time and good money.

But I don't want to disappoint her because I like her too and want her to be happy. If this were a real date that culminated in sex, I'd stay as long or as little as she wants me. I might even want to stay the night.

I try to remember what morning afters are like, but Parks has messed with my brain too much. It's entirely possible I've never had a morning after.

Not by choice, anyway.

"Falcon?"

I've hesitated too long. It would be a dick move to disappear now. And I don't want her to think Falcon is a dick. I want to be her favorite client. I'm pretty sure I'm in the top three.

"Fuck, that was intense," I say by way of explanation.

"For me too. It's why I didn't want you to leave. I need time to process." She clears her throat. "Given this job…I don't get to date. Not for real. The orgasms are great, and I have the best clients. But sometimes I miss the other stuff."

"You want the postsex cuddle?"

"Sometimes. Yeah."

"I don't think I know how to do that."

"But do you want to…try? For me? This job can get… lonely for all that I'm interacting with men twenty hours per week. It's one-sided. And you've always been the guy who cared about my pleasure…so I'm hoping maybe you can be the guy who also cares about my other needs?"

There's so much sweetness in her words. This is Eden. The careful barista who protects herself with men as much as possible.

It makes sense that she doesn't date. I doubt many men

would be cool with her line of work, unless they also work in the industry somehow.

"What does that mean?" I ask. "We can't physically cuddle. What's the equivalent for you?"

"I don't know. Maybe we both get under the covers and…talk?"

I realize she might feel awkward. After all, she's still on camera, half-naked and spent, while I have the privacy of being nothing more than a voice.

"Okay. We can start there. But I'm not sure I'm excited by this talking idea of yours."

She laughs. On the screen, I see from her expression that she's relieved I'm sticking around. For a little bit, at least. I've made no promises.

I'm afraid of talking. I might slip and give her a detail about my life I shouldn't. Or start to stutter.

And now I have a new fear. What if I accidently whisper and she recognizes my voice?

This is a minefield.

But still, I want it. I want the same intimacy she's looking for. But I doubt I'm capable of it. Emotions are the hardest thing for me to process, let alone express. "Give me a minute to clean up."

She beams and says, "Same."

I go to my attached bathroom and do a quick rinse in the shower, then return to the bed with a damp towel to clean up the mess I made because, like a dipshit, I wasn't prepared for getting off.

I then grab a beer from my fridge, dim the lights, and slide under the covers. A minute after I'm settled, Desiree appears on camera wearing a skimpy satin pajama set. I have a feeling Eden might have something less sexy and more comfortable to sleep in, but I get that she needs to stay in character.

In moments, she's under the covers too. I sip my beer and set it on the nightstand.

"What's that?"

"I'm having a beer."

"Oh. That sounds lovely. When I first started this job, I would have a little wine to get my nerve up. But then one time, I had too much. After that, I made a promise to myself never to drink on camera again. But I'm not going back to the chat tonight. So it should be safe for me to have a glass."

"You're always safe with me, Desiree."

She smiles and blows me a kiss. "Be right back."

She returns a minute later with a glass of red wine, then crawls under the covers and lets out a happy sigh. "I know it sounds silly, but this is…perfect."

"Not at all." I feel it too.

"How old are you, Falcon?"

I consider the question and decide it's safe to go with the truth. "Twenty-seven."

"Oh! We're the same age. Well, almost. I'll be twenty-seven in a few weeks."

I'm surprised she told the truth, but then, I have a feeling that's what this whole cuddling thing is about. She wants to be herself. Or as much as she can be while wearing a wig and heavy makeup in bed.

I feel a rush of guilt that I won't do the same for her. I won't even turn on my damn camera.

I wonder why she chose me of all her regulars for this, but it might have something to do with how long I waited to get off while she was live on camera. She knows I was holding back for a reason, and something changed for me. Maybe she's curious, or maybe the fact that I waited for months makes her feel safe with me.

One thing she and I have in common is our need for safety.

I pull a big pillow to my side and hold it tight as a stand-in for her body and tell her so.

She grabs a pillow too and asks, "Are you on my left or right?"

"Your right."

She turns and holds the pillow as if we're facing each other. "I miss this. So much."

The longing in her voice cuts to my core. My guilt.

"I've never had this," I say. I almost whisper the words—a shamed admission—but I remember just in time that whispering is not allowed.

Because she's Desiree, I know she won't judge me, but I know my honesty will make her curious.

I also know that she won't ask why. But I want to give her the intimacy she craves, and at the same time, I know I need to tell someone about all the messed-up crap going on in my head.

Desiree is safe.

I close my eyes and hug the pillow and say the hardest sentence I've ever had to say. "I've been hurt, Desiree. And not just a little bit. I was tortured. Brainwashed. And sexually abused."

Chapter Nine

DESIREE

Falcon's words hang in the air. I'm stunned by what he told me, but also deeply touched that he trusts me with this.

Most of my regulars have shared at one point or another why they spend time with me, but Falcon has never said why he enjoys online entertainment, and I've wondered. I've even written down my theories on his motives in the notes I keep on all my clients. We've spent enough time together that I had a rough estimate of his age, from his voice and other cues. Our knowledge of popular culture has always been strongly aligned. I'd figured we'd graduated high school around the same time.

There has been a shyness about him that made me wonder if he was online because he found it difficult to talk to women in real life. And that may also be the case, but now I know the bigger reason, and while I had been correct about part of it, there was no way I could have guessed the full extent of what he just shared.

"Tortured?" I ask. "Are you in the military? Was this a deployment?"

"Kind of. It was work related."

I want to ask what kind of work, but I don't dare. He'll tell me what he's comfortable with me knowing. All I can do is be here for him. Listen. Validate.

Care.

"I'm so sorry that happened to you."

"Thank you."

"Have…have you told others about this?"

"Yes. Police. Doctors. Prosecutors. She's in prison now."

I feel a rush of relief. He's gotten some help, and even a small measure of justice.

"Good," I say.

"I got a letter from her two weeks ago. I don't know how she got it out, but she did. She had the nerve to tell me she was *proud* of me."

I want to ask why his abuser would take credit for him in such a way, but I can't push. "Did you report the letter to the prison or other authorities? She can be punished for that."

His voice is soft. "No."

I realize then that the letter probably included details his abuser knew he would never want shared, which is why he didn't report it.

I hate this woman with the fire of a thousand suns. I ache for Falcon that not only did he have to endure her abuse, but also because she found a way to attack him from prison. He is still being abused.

He's a survivor and ongoing victim at the same time.

All I can do is try to make him feel safe in sharing his confidence with me. "I'm always available if you want to talk. I never ever share anything about my clients, and the only thing I want is for you to leave our sessions satisfied and happy."

"Thank you," he says softly.

"I mean it. I love this job because my whole purpose is to make others happy. It's a great way to spend my time."

"You're very good at it," he says. "Spending time with you has helped me a lot these past months."

"I'm glad."

"I trust you, Desiree. And being with you—well, it's the only sexual desire I've felt in years."

Years? How long had the abuse gone on?

My heart aches for this man, whose face I will probably never see.

I run my hands over the pillow, remembering that he's watching me. It's weird that I forgot about the camera. I never forget. But I did. So now I say, "If we were really in bed together, I'd be running my hands along your jawline. I might kiss you, but only if you indicate you want to be kissed."

"I want to be kissed by you. I always want to be kissed by you."

And I wish I could kiss him. I miss kissing a lot too. There is no decent stand-in for kissing.

I think of Chase Johnston and imagine taking out my kissing frustrations on him. I bet he's a good kisser. He's got nice lips to go with those dreamy cheekbones. I bet he's all intense when he kisses and would cup both sides of my face in his big hands, giving my mouth one hundred percent of his focus.

Maybe I can find out.

I mean, kissing a guy isn't dating. It wouldn't technically violate the rules I've established for myself.

"Then I would be kissing you now. Softly. Letting you take the lead if you want it to go deeper."

I hear his soft chuckle. "After that last orgasm, I'd probably be done for the night, but then, it's been years since I willingly had sex with a partner. So, I think, maybe, if you were here with me, I'd be ready and able to fuck you all night long."

His words stir both heat and concern. Again, I'm wondering at the length of the sexual abuse he suffered. But I focus on the titillating part, because I'm pretty sure that's what he wants now. I let out a soft purr. "I would *love* to be fucked all night long. To have your beautiful cock at my beck and call for hours on end. It would be glorious."

"Damn, you're making me hard again."

I smile softly. I think he needs the redirect after sharing his trauma with me. I'll talk him through another orgasm if he wants, but I don't think he does. I think he wants to end our snuggle session on a sexy note. And I want him to leave happy—not just because it means a job well done for me, but because I want this with him again.

I *need* it.

Feeling lust for Chase has reminded me of all the things I can't have anymore, and I was feeling melancholy when I logged in tonight. I mean, I was also hot and ready, which was why I went for the sexy librarian role play, but beneath it all was the loneliness I'd felt since he left the shop.

When Falcon logged in, I suddenly remembered how he'd abruptly ended our session last time, and everything clicked into place. Of all the guys I get off online, he's the one I wouldn't have expected to bolt so fast after a more intimate session like we'd had. Which had triggered a tinge of disappointment.

It was an unconscious decision on my part to change that tonight. Instinct.

And here we are.

This has been by far the most intimate—as in the flow of intimacy being felt both ways—session I've ever had. I've had a lot of guys talk about stuff they'd never share with anyone else, and more than a few have cried over past or present issues. The women at CamDames and I would talk about how we all were therapists eighty percent of the time and sexy twenty percent. And even of the twenty percent, less than half of that went as far as sex toys and masturbation. Often, it was just taking off my clothes and…listening.

Falcon was different in every way.

And I want this with him again, so I will do what it takes to please him. It's always my goal anyway. "Do you want to play again?" I ask.

"No, but it's fun to imagine. Fucking you all night, then having regrets when I have to get up early for work, but knowing it was worth it."

"What time do you get up?" I ask. He's in Alaska, where it's four hours earlier. I look at the clock. It's nearing eleven, so it's not even seven there. I sit up. "Damn. I forgot about the time difference. It's not even close to time for you to go to sleep, and here I am making you crawl into bed with me."

He laughs. "I don't mind. The sun will be setting soon, and I'm more than used to going to bed when it's light out."

"How long have you lived in Alaska?"

"Since I was twenty-two."

Five years. That means the abuse happened there.

"Do you plan to live there forever?"

"No."

He doesn't elaborate, and I don't press.

I have no idea what he does for a living or if there are jobs elsewhere that would fit his skills should he decide to move. I'm not sure if he confirmed having been in the military earlier or not. But I suspect he's not in the service now, if he ever was, because as far as I know, it's rare to stay in the same place for five years.

I hope he'll give me another hint about his life, but I can't ask. It only invites questions from him, and I can't share.

A yawn overtakes me, and he notices. "You should sleep, Des. I'll be back again in a few days. I promise."

"You don't have to pay so much. To get me alone, I mean. Like you did tonight. You can go with my standard rate. I can't choose you over the others every time or I'll lose some of my best clients, but I'll take you as often as I can. No need to pay extra."

"I like paying you more."

"But you don't have to." While Falcon's five hundred up-front tonight means I don't have to go back online after this, it can't become a habit. Keeping regular hours makes all the difference in the long run, and random bonuses can't be counted upon as much as the faithfulness of Hank, Thor, and Wolfe. After all, even Falcon disappeared for six weeks. If I relied on him for everything, I'd be screwed.

"It makes me happy," he says.

He means it. I can tell from the warmth in his voice.

Regardless, I want Falcon to know I don't expect him to maintain that level of tipping. I'd rather earn less and have more of this than have him disappear because of the cost. "Okay. But really. You don't have to go overboard. I will choose you when I can."

The tip bar on the screen registers another five-hundred-dollar transfer from Falcon. My stomach drops with the shock of his generosity.

"Consider that an advance on our next session, then. Or better yet, a retainer. I want to keep fucking you, and now…I think I like this after part too."

Wow. I might be able to get a car sooner rather than later if he keeps this up.

I blow a kiss at the screen. "You're a sweetheart. Thank you for cuddling with me tonight."

"You're welcome. Good night, Desiree."

A message appears telling me he exited the room.
"Good night, Falcon," I whisper.

Chapter Ten

It required a great deal of self-control to stay away from the coffee shop for five days, but Chase didn't know if she worked on the weekends, and on Monday, a training inside the compound began, which kept him busy.

It was an easy three-day training with police officers from around the country. Raptor was attempting to incorporate sensitivity training for first responders integrated into the system, but the program needed some retooling, and Chase had his own doubts about retraining being the answer to stemming police violence against people of color. Best to fire the racist cops and start over.

But Raptor had always focused on training soldiers and officers for high-stress situations to prevent panic from escalating a bad situation into a nightmare, so there were some scenarios they ran that could be effective and save an unquantifiable number of lives.

Chase's role in the program was teaching unarmed combat skills, as that was his specialty. Parks might have scrambled his brain, but muscle memory was different, and Chase's muscles had begun training at the age of three.

His dad, who still ran a dojo in Arizona, was disappointed that Chase had no interest in taking over the family business, especially when at his core, he was teaching martial arts, but his father knew nothing of what Chase had gone through. He didn't know Raptor was Chase's only avenue for doing the kind of work that called to him.

Chase wasn't a cop, but on days like today, he was training them to be better at their jobs.

And maybe this was his true calling after all?

Day two of the training had been long and exhausting. He had two one-hour group lessons each followed by four thirty-minute individual lessons with varying degrees of skill level, for a total of six hours of highly physical work. Days like this, he didn't need to put in his regular hour in the gym, but often he did anyway because it was in his private work-outs that he could unleash fury on a bag if it had built up during the day.

But today had felt strangely harmonious. Five days later, he was still on a high after that last session with Desiree. All of it—the talking and the titillating—had somehow managed to drive away the darkness that tended to encroach upon his mind.

It was a long overdue mental break, the respite from anger and confusion. It would return, of that he had no doubt, but for a few days at least, his mind had remained blessedly silent.

He showered at the end of the long physical day, then headed to the employee dining room for dinner. The group lessons he'd taught earlier reminded him of Eden's question about teaching self-defense at community centers. He made a mental note to ask Keith Hatcher—Raptor's CEO—if they could run once-a-month safety classes for the community out of the gym.

It might not be possible given the complex security of the

compound, but it never hurt to ask. And then he could invite Eden here for some self-defense training.

She was helping him with his issues—even if she didn't know it—so the least he could do was help her by teaching some skills that could save her if the goons ever returned.

When he arrived in the large employee dining room, he spotted Tricia at her usual table. He quickly filled a tray from the buffet with an enormous amount of food. He'd burned a ton of calories today and needed to replenish. His body was lean to the point of having little to burn, so days like today required extra protein.

He set his tray in front of the empty seat next to Tricia and sat down.

She glanced at his plate and said, "Show-off."

She always joked about how unfair it was that he could eat as much as he did and remain as lean as he was.

"Sorry! I was running drills for a solid six hours today."

"I *suppose* that's fair."

After her injury eight and a half weeks ago, Tricia had changed her hairstyle. Her hair was still blue, but it was no longer braided. It was now free, vibrant blue curly locks that framed her features and hid the area that had been shaved with the careful placement of a clip at her left temple.

She wore glasses now as well, and it wasn't known if her vision had been permanently changed or if the need for glasses was temporary. They looked good on her, and she'd shrugged off concerns about blurred vision, saying it was better than being dead. She wasn't wrong, but he also suspected there was some bravado there.

It could be true that she was grateful to be one of very few survivors of a massacre, and also be upset that she might have long-term physical issues.

Much like he was thankful to be alive after all that was

done to him, but still carried barely banked rage over what Parks had done to his body and his mind.

He left to get a soda loaded with caffeine from the fountain and returned to the table as Tariq and another operative, Scott Howard, also took seats.

The four of them made up half of the Virginia compound's Falcon team. The other four were Sean Logan, Nate Sifuentes, Ian Boyd, and Jillian Archer, who'd been promoted when Josh Warner moved to Portland.

Of the four, only Jillian lived in the compound, and Sean and Ian worked more out of the DC office but pitched in on trainings when they weren't working private protection details.

Falcon team in Virginia was different from Alaska, because here the team was more likely to be scrambled in a pinch and sent on an op. It almost happened in August, when Tricia was injured, but by the time Keith was notified, the danger was past and the FBI investigating. Instead, Sean was sent to retrieve Tricia on the company jet. When the plane took off, everyone thought he would be collecting her remains. It wasn't until the plane was in the air that Keith was informed there had been a few survivors, including a Black woman with blue braids, as that was the only identification the Indonesian police had for her at the time.

Sitting next to Tricia now, no one would guess how close she'd come to dying two months ago. She looked good. The new hairstyle was flattering. But everyone on the team was watching out for her, and Chase was fairly certain their hovering had passed the point of pissing her off. But it was warranted.

Nobody else at the table knew about their sideline work with Mothman, and they were due for a meeting to discuss the search for Sling Man and the other guy, Terry, plus there was another runaway Mothman might have identified. They'd need to meet in one of their quarters tonight.

Dinner was enjoyable, and Chase was thankful to be in a position where he liked all the members of Falcon team. That hadn't always been the case—which was an understatement given what had happened in Alaska. But here, he knew he could trust everyone to have his back.

The people at this table and the other members of Falcon could even be trusted with the runaway rescue, but they were left in the dark for plausible deniability. No reason to take all of Falcon down if they were caught.

"What was the deal with you and Isabel Dawson at that coffee shop, Trish?" Tariq asked.

Chase was startled by the belated question. Twelve days had passed since then.

Tricia shrugged. "I'm helping Isabel with a personal project. One she's passionate about but doesn't want on the news, so it's hush-hush. Why are you asking now?"

Tariq frowned. "You didn't see the news?"

"No. I had physical therapy this afternoon. When I got back, I collapsed on my bed and wished I knew dark magic that would consign my therapist to hell. He's cute, but brutal. Why? What happened?"

She turned to Chase. He shrugged. He'd gone straight from the last training session to the shower to dinner.

"The coffee shop. It was hit with a pipe bomb a little over an hour ago."

*E*den stared at the TV screen, transfixed. The Vivace Coffee store she'd worked one shift at nearly two weeks ago was on the screen. Shattered glass littered the sidewalk. Fire trucks and ambulances were parked out front.

There was no word yet if there were fatalities, but the current report said at least five people had been injured.

It was the same small local chain she worked at four days a week, so even if she hadn't pulled the single shift, this would feel personal and scary.

But she'd been there, and there'd been an incident that night too. Was this bombing connected to that?

Chase had showed her that photo of the guy who might be a security guard from CamDames. She'd wondered if the guard was keeping tabs on Penny. She needed to talk to Penny again. God. What if Penny had been injured? And was Tony okay?

She still couldn't quite wrap her brain around it. Someone had *bombed* the coffee shop.

Given the way the guy cradled his arm in the photo, it had probably been Sling Man, but she hadn't seen Sling Man's face. What if it wasn't him and she identified the wrong guy? And she couldn't be certain the photo was of the guard from CamDames either. He was just a vague memory. She'd steered clear of the guards after one assaulted one of the Dames, claiming he'd paid her for sex and she hadn't delivered.

It was well known among the talent that they could earn extra money turning tricks with the guards and even some of the executives, so Eden avoided both as much as possible. It was especially unsettling with the guards. They were supposed to protect the Dames, but they'd proven to be their own threat.

She hadn't been certain it was the security guard and used that to justify not saying anything to Chase or the police.

But with this bombing, maybe she should tell someone? It might all be related.

She grabbed her purse and pulled out her wallet, where she'd tucked Chase's business card.

In spite of the excuse he gave at the time, she knew he'd given it to her because he was attracted to her, but wouldn't go so far as to ask her out. He'd hoped she'd call him. Now she was calling, but not for anything good.

Not because she was wanted to drag him into the back of the shop and get fucked against the wall, which was the fantasy she'd harbored for the last five days since seeing him and which had led to her selecting the sexy librarian fantasy that night.

She didn't have sexy barista in her repertoire because as far as she knew, except for the scantily clad baristas in drive-throughs near military bases, she didn't think there was any universal barista fantasy.

She pulled out her phone and noticed her hands were shaking. Her thoughts were all over the place as she processed the shock of seeing the burning coffee shop on TV.

She punched in Chase's number before she could over-think it. By calling him, she was giving him her number, but there was no helping that. She wasn't about to run to work to use their phone. Everyone there was probably in equal shock and horror. And the phone was probably tied up as family and friends tried to check in. Reporters were probably calling the seven other stores for a sound bite.

Chase answered on the first ring, his voice deep and serious as he said, "Chase Johnston."

"Chase. Hi. It's, uh, Eden." Oh Lord, she'd almost said Desiree. What the hell had triggered that? She never mixed up her worlds.

"Oh. Hey." His voice dropped to the almost whisper. "You've seen the news? I wanted to call you, but…"

He didn't have her number. Well, he did now.

"Yes. Listen, I want to know about that photo you showed me. How did you get it?"

There was a long pause, then he finally said, "Can we meet somewhere? To talk?"

She looked at her watch. She was supposed to go online in an hour, but this was important. And frankly, she didn't think she was up for being sexy tonight. Not after the bombing.

"Sure."

"Where do you want to meet?" he asked.

Her workplace was out. Her townhouse was also out—no one was ever allowed inside. She couldn't take the chance of anyone seeing her workroom. The Raptor compound wasn't all that far from her place, so it didn't make sense to go into the city. "I don't have a car, but my place is out."

"Tell you what. I'll pick you up and take you to a restaurant in Old Town Alexandria. The owner is a client and will give us a quiet booth or one of the private rooms if they aren't booked."

Was he trying to impress her? It was kind of working.

"Okay. I'll be ready and out front in fifteen."

She'd been halfway through getting ready for the camera when she saw the news, and now she scrubbed the makeup from her face and removed the fake eyelashes. She wanted to apply subtle makeup—after all, she was going out with a super-hot guy on the closest thing she'd had to a date in two years—but she didn't have time to do it right. And she shouldn't treat this as more than it was.

She wanted to know about that photo, and he probably had reasons why he didn't want to discuss it over the phone.

But still, she did put on her favorite pair of jeans that hugged her ass just so, and a cute top that highlighted her small cleavage. She couldn't dress this way at work—not without risking creepy customer attention—but she missed getting to dress for herself in public. She'd learned a lot about sex appeal in the last two years and never got to use what she'd learned in a public setting. She wanted to feel Chase's interested gaze. Wanted to be in a man's real-world orbit and feel the zing of his attraction.

Chase Johnston was interested in her, and she wanted to enjoy it.

The closest she'd come to that feeling online was with Falcon. Not that the others didn't think she was hot—they wouldn't give her such lovely tips if they didn't—but with Falcon, she felt the attraction could genuinely go both ways. There was a sweetness to him. Plus, he'd laid himself bare during their last session. And all of it mixed with the guy who was super commanding when it came to their simulated sex. It was a hot combo.

Sweet but dominant when he wanted to be. And he always wanted to make sure she was enjoying their time together. Like she mattered to him. She wasn't some bimbo in front of a camera to serve his whims.

She'd managed to cull out most of the regulars from CamDames who viewed her as nothing but meat. She preferred the interaction and consideration of men like Hank. They worried about her if she was late or absent.

The last session had done a lot to dispel any idea that Penny's stalker could be Falcon. No way. Besides, Falcon lived in Alaska. She was well aware that kind of thing could be faked, but why would he? He'd followed her from CamDames, where Desiree's room was open to all without geographical restrictions, and he'd mentioned Alaska even then. It was one of the reasons she'd allowed him to follow her to her private site.

She reminded herself to post a message on the site that she would be late and might not be online at all, but to check back around eleven. After all, if Chase got her hot, she could use it.

She was two minutes late in descending the stairs to meet Chase and wasn't the least surprised that he was in the front parking spot, waiting politely. He hadn't tried to rush her by climbing the outer stairs and knocking on the front door.

The minute she stepped outside, he was out his door and circling the vehicle to open the passenger door for her.

She reached the bottom of the stairwell, thanked him for picking her up, then climbed inside the large SUV. He closed the door, then circled around to the driver's side again. He moved with quick grace, his T-shirt hugging his lean muscles.

She wondered if he'd put on the tight shirt for her benefit, but given that he'd arrived so quickly, she couldn't be certain he'd even had time to make that small a change. But still, she wanted to believe he was as eager for her to admire his form as she wanted him to see her in her casual but sexy clothes.

This whole not-dating thing had really screwed with her mind. She got an abundance of male attention on a daily basis, but it wasn't the right kind.

"Where are we going?" she asked.

He named a restaurant she'd never heard of. She asked him to spell it as she texted Kelly once again with the restaurant name. He didn't comment on her caution, which was yet another point in his favor.

He seemed to take everything in stride. And she really liked that about him. But then, everything about his bearing made her feel safe, and she didn't usually feel safe around men—especially muscular ones—as she did with him.

She knew she was attractive—hell, she made very good money on her looks, so she'd better know what her assets were—and starting when she was thirteen or fourteen, her looks had made her a target for certain types of men. It only got worse when she ran away from her so-called husband at the age of fifteen.

So the idea that this tall, strong man who sometimes looked at her like he wanted to eat her for dinner could somehow make her feel safe was totally new.

And how was it that just being near him brought her most dirty fantasies to mind?

She was worried and scared, but still, as he drove to the restaurant, her brain was rapidly supplying scenarios of what they could do in a private room in the restaurant if they should get one.

She wasn't an exhibitionist. Desiree fulfilled any exhibitionist fantasies she might have harbored, and she was comfortable in that role, but she'd never wanted to make Desiree real. Never wanted to risk being caught.

But there was something about Chase that triggered a wildness in her. Like she wouldn't be able to resist him if they were alone in a room together.

She wasn't sure she understood it and should probably journal about it tonight. She was documenting all her emotions and reactions as much as she kept notes on the men she interacted with. She wanted to understand all of it, even though none of it would ever be published in a psychology journal or documented in any kind of study. Every day she was learning about the human brain and sexuality, and it utterly fascinated her. The changes the work had triggered in her own sexuality and overall comfort in her skin had been transformative.

Sometimes it made her sad that she had no one to share the data with.

They arrived at the restaurant, and Chase surprised her by parking in an employee spot in the back.

"Is this okay?" she asked.

He nodded. "The owner is the daughter of a superior

court judge who was targeted by Voight Forum." His voice was whispery with no hint of the stutter. Did she make him nervous, or was this the voice he used with everyone? She had a feeling it was the former, given that the two previous times they'd met, he'd tried to speak in his normal voice at first. "Both the judge and her daughter were doxed last year, and we're basically on permanent retainer after several incidents, and even had to put the restaurant owner and her children in a safe house for a month while we tracked down the people who threw bricks through her windows and threatened her kids. She told us we can always park here. I don't usually take advantage, but the street parking looked bad." He shrugged. "Warm October evening, and I think the ghost tours are ramping up before Halloween."

They circled from the private lot to the front street, which was full of locals and tourists on the mild early-fall evening.

She loved Old Town. Alexandria was so different from where she grew up in Idaho. The architecture of the city dated back over three hundred years and was charming with brick everywhere and narrow roads that had never considered automobiles in their design. Couples with small children strolled down the cobblestone street, and sure enough, there was a large group that looked like they were on a ghost tour.

Someday, she wanted to do the tourist stuff like that. She'd moved to the DC area just days before her first semester of grad school, and between school and two jobs, she'd never had time for sightseeing.

As it was, her hand itched to take Chase's and stroll like other couples. But they weren't a couple, and this wasn't a date.

They climbed the steps in front of the restaurant, which was in a building that had been built before the American Revolution, and Chase held the door open for her to pass through into a dark vestibule.

A tall white woman in her early fifties stood behind the host desk, and her face lit up when she spotted the man by Eden's side. "Chase! So glad you're back from Portland. Oh my, what you went through there." The woman circled the desk and hugged him, then kissed his cheek, and Eden was surprised by the warm familiarity, and suddenly realized he might have provided twenty-four seven security in the safe house for a month. That was the sort of thing that could definitely form a lasting bond.

What would it be like to spend a month with Chase as *her* bodyguard?

It was a delicious thought, and now bodyguard fantasies ran rampant through her mind. Would that be a role play she could try online?

Probably not, because it was *her* fantasy, not a client's. They wanted to fuck the librarian in the stacks and enjoy other fantasies that centered them in their world. But still, she could run it by Falcon and see if it interested him. He was always interested in her pleasure first. He might be game.

Chase introduced Eden to the restaurant owner in the quiet voice he'd used when they were alone in the car. The woman cocked her head. "You okay?"

His face reddened, and he said, "Stutter is acting up."

The woman looked at Eden, her gaze taking her in from head to toe, and she gave him a knowing smile. "I can see why."

Now it was Eden's turn to flush red, but it might be from heat rather than embarrassment.

"We have a nice table for you in the back. Sorry none of the private dining rooms are available. We're busy tonight with the good weather."

"I appreciate you holding a table for me."

"You always have a table here," the owner said. She met Eden's gaze. "Did he tell you he saved my daughter's life?"

She startled and turned to Chase as she said, "No."

He shrugged. "Well, it was sort of my job."

"Doesn't matter." There was a crashing sound somewhere in the back. "Gotta go." She turned to the hostess and said, "Table thirty-six."

The hostess led them through the packed dining room to a private booth in the back corner. Eden slid onto the bench seat opposite Chase as she took in the delicious scents of the dimly lit dining room. The hostess laid two menus on the table and asked if she could take their drink order.

Eden glanced at the menu and tried to stifle a sigh. She hadn't been to a restaurant this nice in ages. The food looked delicious, and there was something that smelled amazing, but this wasn't a date. It was a meeting she'd initiated, and she couldn't afford this place. "I'm afraid I've already had dinner," she said. It was actually true, if one counted low-fat cottage cheese mixed with grape tomatoes, cucumbers, and Italian dressing at three in the afternoon as dinner.

"Me too," Chase said. "Can we see the dessert menu?"

The hostess smiled. "Of course. Be right back."

After she left, Eden said, "I feel guilty taking prime real estate in the restaurant for just dessert."

"It's fine." He lifted the wine menu. "We'll order a bottle of expensive wine, and I always tip well."

She guessed that he didn't expect her to split the bill—after all, he was the one who asked to meet in person and had selected the restaurant—but still, she'd been caught off guard in this area before and had learned to be direct. She cleared her throat. "I'm afraid this place is a bit out of my range." Her face reddened as she said it. She wasn't even certain why. After all, wasn't she an advocate for open communication on all things in the early dating process?

But this wasn't a date.

He smiled and leaned forward so she could hear his whispery voice that never failed to turn her on. "Since I neglected to make it clear, this is my treat. You can order a seven-course meal if you want. If it means I get extra time with you after our business conversation is over, it will be worth every penny."

"This…this isn't a date." She wasn't allowed to date. It couldn't be a date. She didn't want to have to tell him the truth about herself. If one date led to another, they'd reach the point where either she'd have to end it or tell him the truth. And she couldn't see a scenario where she'd want to make either of those choices.

"What if I said I want it to be?"

She bit her lip. "I'd have to tell you that I cannot date you."

"Cannot? Are you seeing someone? Married?"

Seeing about twenty someones, actually. Or rather, they're seeing me. All of me. For money.

Instead, she said, "I'm not dating anyone, no. And not married. You?"

"No. No girlfriend. No wife." He opened the wine list. "Okay, this isn't a date, but I'd still like to treat you and enjoy your company for as long as you'll let me. Can I buy you wine and dessert? As a thank-you for meeting with me tonight?"

She liked that he didn't ask why she couldn't date him. His lack of questions there surprised her, actually, but then, he'd accepted her caution from the start.

"I would enjoy that," she said.

The hostess returned with the dessert menu and an appetizer sampler platter, which she explained was a gift from the owner.

Eden left the wine ordering up to Chase—there were few wines she purchased that didn't come in a box, and she guessed that none of those were on the menu—and they decided to hold off on ordering dessert until after they'd enjoyed the appetizers and had dispensed with the business side of their conversation.

She was still limited in what she could tell him. She'd made a promise to Penny, and she knew how upset she'd be if Penny broke the vow on her end, so she couldn't mention CamDames at all, let alone that Penny Candi had a stalker at one point and the guy in the sling could have been one of their security guards.

She'd tried to reach Penny immediately after seeing the news to follow up on whether or not she'd seen anyone in a cast when she did her shift this week, but her call had gone to voicemail.

For all she knew, Penny was online right now. Eden wished she'd asked which shift Penny pulled.

At the same time, she wondered if she could come up with some excuse to visit her old job site. She could claim she was interested in doing one shift a week like Penny or something.

But she'd never actually do it. Penny's decision to cut her hours so drastically and work for little more than minimum wage as a barista said everything there was to know about how unsafe working there could be.

At least baristas got tips. But then, Eden's whole life was tips these days.

Someday, she'd have her own practice, and she wouldn't work for tips. She'd help people heal and find their true selves. And when that happened, she'd be able to go out on dates with men like the one sitting across from her at this table.

She studied his face with those perfect cheekbones and masculine jawline. He really was a beautiful man.

He smiled as he took in her perusal. "What does that look mean?" he asked in that low, almost raspy tone.

"Does talking to me bring out your stutter?"

He smiled even as those cheekbones turned pink. "Yes. Absolutely."

"Why?"

"Because you're beautiful."

The unequivocal, direct statement sent heat straight to her core. "There are lots of beautiful people in the world. Do they all trigger your stutter?"

"No."

"Why?"

"Am I allowed to be frank? I don't want to scare you off."

"You might be surprised by what it would take to scare me. I'm not as inhibited as you might think."

He leaned forward, and she followed his lead so only inches separated their faces across the table. "There's something about you that turns me on. I think you feel it too. Felt it that night we first met."

The restaurant was definitely getting warm. Or maybe it was just their booth. It felt like they were all alone as the buzz of chatter from other tables became nothing more than a low hum. Her voice dropped to a husky whisper to match his. "Did you have dirty fantasies about me that night?"

"That night and every night since."

"Me too."

One corner of his mouth kicked up. It was a sexy, knowing smile. He knew what he did to her. He'd probably known when she was in his SUV and having fantasies of taking him to a hotel.

"I almost propositioned you that first night," she whispered.

"Why didn't you?"

"I was afraid you'd say no."

"I don't think I'd ever be able to say no to you, Eden." He leaned back, breaking the spell, and took a sip of his wine. "But it's better this way."

"How so?" she asked, following his lead and sipping her own drink. It was a nicely chilled, crisp white wine of some sort. She'd ask what it was for future reference, but would never be able to afford it. Not unless she took up cam work full-time, and she didn't want that.

"If we'd hooked up that night, there'd be no mystery left for us to discover. No time to get to know each other. And admit it, this intensity we're both feeling right now is kind of like a drug. I am positively high right now on two sips of wine because I'm alone in public with a beautiful woman I want to seduce."

Lord. He was right. She did feel it. It was this magical hot feeling that suffused her. It felt wonderful.

"But I told you I can't date you."

"So we won't date, but I don't see how that takes seduction off the table. Not when you're looking at me like that."

It was a fair point. She was the one who initiated this conversation after all, and who kept it going. She'd admitted to wanting him.

But still, she trusted that if she gave him a firm no, he'd respect it.

Right now, the last thing she wanted to do was tell him no.

Chapter Eleven

FALCON

I dropped Eden off at her place thirty minutes ago, and now I'm wondering if I should go online. I shouldn't risk it. Falcon can't keep showing up right after she spends time with Chase, or someone will notice a pattern. Hell, Hank or Thor might pick up on it even if Eden doesn't.

But damn, I want to see Desiree after my date with Eden.

And it was, without a doubt, a date, even if it didn't start out as one. It was wild being so straightforward with her about what I wanted and watching her reaction. She was turned on by my directness. But then, so was I.

I've spent a lot of time trying to figure out who I was, but maybe instead I should be focusing on who I am now, because in some areas, Chase 3.0 is an improvement, and tonight was a prime example.

At the end of the date, I drove her home and walked her to her door. I didn't try to kiss her, but we both wanted the goodnight kiss.

Given that she'd explicitly said she couldn't date me, I left it to her to initiate, and I think she would have if her cell phone didn't choose that moment to buzz.

She took one look at the caller ID and her happy mood was gone. She rose on her toes and kissed my cheek, then slipped inside as she answered the call.

I don't know if I was disappointed or relieved.

I can't date her either. Not without telling her I know her secret.

And I can't tell her I know her secret without losing both of them.

I shake my head at the thought. Without losing *her*.

I need Desiree for my mental health. And now I think I might need Eden too. She reminds me I'm alive. That I can feel, and even that I'm a man.

The last part makes me cringe, but it's true.

With her, I feel all the desire I thought I'd lost, and she looks at me—*me*—with those beautiful, sultry eyes that devour me like I'm the chocolate lava cake we shared at the restaurant. She sees me as a man and wants what she sees.

She's a drug. The best kind, because there are no side effects.

Well, except for losing her if I come clean about what I know and who I am.

So now I'm pacing my quarters wondering if I can risk going online to finish my date with Eden as our online alter egos.

I decide not to risk it. She probably took the night off anyway. I dropped her off at eleven, and she never works past midnight as far as I know.

My computer is open on my bed as I pace, and I hear the chime of an incoming message. My heart races as I see it's for the account I only use as Falcon. It's the one I load up with five-hundred-dollar cash gift cards so I can tip her generously and anonymously.

She has never sent a message to this account before.

I smile at the subject line. It's the universal code for a booty call: *You up?*

Yes. Yes, I am.

I open the email and see she's sent a link to a private room. No payment required.

I make sure the camera is blocked and off before clicking the link.

She's in full makeup and a sheer purple teddy. Her wig tonight is a short blue bob, and she looks hot in it. She looks nothing like the woman I just spent time with, but I see her beneath the disguise.

I'm infatuated with both, really, but I'll probably always fantasize about the real Eden in my mind now that I've seen her.

I want to whisper, but remind myself I can use my real voice. For some reason, I never stutter when I'm online with her. Maybe because she can't see me.

"You look hot."

"Thank you."

"Any particular reason you summoned me?" I say this as if I'm a genie. This thought makes me smile.

She slides a hand between her legs. "I want to play with you tonight."

"I didn't tell you to touch yourself."

She puts on a pretty pout, but I see the smile underneath. She wants me to take charge. To be the one who makes her come. That's why she summoned her favorite genie. She removes her hand from the valley of her thighs and says, "Well, technically, you didn't pay me for tonight, so I'm under no obligation to wait for orders."

I could remind her of the retainer I paid last time, but I know she's not doing this for the money. Not tonight. Plus, I like giving Eden my money.

Desiree. Not Eden. I'm paying *Desiree*.

I hit the button that drops five hundred into her account. It's becoming my default amount with her, and I have no regrets.

She gives the camera a stern look. "You didn't have to do that. I was obeying."

"I know. I like tipping you. Now spread your legs and tell me what brought this on."

She grins and spreads her thighs ever so slightly. Not enough. She's being feisty, and I really like it. "I went on a date tonight with that guy I mentioned before."

"Must not have been a good date if he's not deep inside you right now."

"That's the problem. It was a great date. I wanted to take him home and fuck his brains out. But I don't date. It's too risky."

"So you want me to fuck you instead."

"Yes, please."

"Okay, but this is going to be different."

Her eyes light up. "How so?"

"I'm going to fuck you up against the wall."

Her eyes go wide. This isn't a fantasy she's performed before, I think. Good.

"How do we do that?"

I point to the headboard on her bed. It's padded and about two inches thick. Just wide enough for her to position herself on top with her legs spread so I can imagine I'm holding her up with her legs wrapped around my hips. I've had a lot of fantasies about this.

I realize she can't see my gesture and say, "Your headboard. Sit on the top edge. Spread your legs."

She's eager for this scenario and tests out the top of the headboard as a support. "Oh, yes," she says. "This is hot."

"I've been eyeing that headboard for months," I say. Pretty much every time I see it, really.

She adjusts the camera until she's centered on my screen. She's a little farther back than usual, but it means I can see all of her. And she's so beautiful.

I tell her what toys she can use. How high she can turn up the vibrator. I draw out her pleasure for a long time. My own pleasure too as I stroke my cock slowly, not allowing myself to get too close to orgasm for the longest time.

Fucking Desiree against a wall is a fantasy I've had from the very beginning. I like it because I'm in total control. Holding her up, giving her my cock hard and deep. She's totally given over to me as I thrust into her. It's a surrender for her, I'm completely in charge.

Technically, it's still just a fantasy, but now that I see her like this, closer to real.

Desiree is on the edge now. I can see how much she wants to come. I love this, the way she lets me decide. She could cheat and turn up the vibrator, but I know she gets off on the dynamic we've built up. She trusts me and knows I won't deny her pleasure.

"Thrust faster," I say, pumping my hips as I hold my hand steady, as if I'm inside a woman who is pushed against a wall and can do little more than rock her hips to meet my thrusts as I do the work she wants. Needs.

"You feel me, Desiree?" I whisper.

"Oh God, yes. Please. Please. More."

"Turn up the vibrator to the highest setting." I remember not to whisper this time. It's good that she's so into the moment she didn't seem to notice.

She obeys and strokes her clit with it as she works the dildo, and all at once, she comes apart. Because she's upright, she doesn't curl in on herself like before. I see her whole beautiful body and her face with her closed eyes as she comes hard and holds the vibrator just so to keep the sensation going. Her body is open and her skin flushed. She is utterly beautiful as I spill my cum on the bed.

This is definitely the best first date I've ever had, which is a little strange considering it's the third time we've had sex like this.

Chapter Twelve

DESIREE

One would think that after two years at this job, I couldn't be surprised like that. *Feel* like that. But Falcon always makes me feel. And I don't mean pleasure. I mean like this is real. Like he's Chase and we went inside my townhouse and he fucks me against the wall in my living room because we were too eager to make it to the bedroom.

I've never been fucked against a wall, even though it's one of my favorite fantasies. But I've never been with a guy where we were hot enough for each other to pull it off. I work hard to keep my weight down, but I'm still not quite skinny, and it's a lot of work, I would think, to hold a woman up while thrusting like that. But I think Chase, with his muscular arms, could do it, and now I have Falcon, who helped complete the fantasy in a new way.

Sometimes I wonder why I've gone all in on this intense job, but nights like tonight—clients like Falcon—remind me how much sexual connection happens in the brain. And that's what this is about. I can connect with people both emotionally and physically using my brain.

I'm making it my life's work to study the human brain,

so the fact that this fascinates me makes perfect sense. Tonight, I'm going to journal about this after I log off with Falcon.

There is much to explore. Like, should I feel guilty about being intimate with Falcon after my date with Chase? I don't. This is my job, and I told Chase I can't date him for this very reason. But still, the thought remains.

I want to understand this sexual progression, how one kind of simulated sex can feel more intimate than another. Can even feel more intimate than actual sex.

I experimented a fair amount with sex in my late teens and early twenties. I'm no stranger to the physical, but crave the emotional.

My years of therapy have led me to conclude this all relates to my parents seeing me as nothing more than an instrument to uphold their religion. I was never a beloved daughter, I was a future baby maker for a man in their church. I was meant to be a pure vessel for an elder's sperm to propagate another man to keep the community going. My son would have been my master as much as my husband was supposed to be.

I know my mother's greatest disappointment was having only one child and a daughter at that. She failed the church that was her only reason for being.

My parents never loved me and sought to marry me off at fifteen to a forty-three-year-old man. And the state let it happen.

In most states, a married minor still has no rights—cannot enter legal contracts. Can't hire a lawyer to initiate divorce.

But I sneaked into our local library and found the loophole in my state. A married minor was considered emancipated. No one could force me to return to my parents if I ran away.

So at fifteen, I married. That night, before my husband could rape me, I escaped.

I found an attorney online who was willing to work pro bono and evaded child protective services, who sought to return me to the parents who'd married me off to a man nearly three times my age.

I'm one of the lucky few. I got the help I needed, and in my emancipated teen years, I found a therapist through an organization formed to help child brides—the same group that helped me find an attorney—and got the mental health care I needed. The woman was a social worker and remains the closest thing I ever had to a caring mother. She helped me work through my issues of never being truly loved by my parents.

It's been nearly a dozen years since my marriage and nine since I was able to obtain a divorce, and I'm thankful to the women who helped me—the attorney, the therapist, the advocates—for where I am today. I want to give back as much as they gave me.

And I never, ever want to be dependent on another soul for financial survival.

I began supporting myself at fifteen because as an emancipated—and married—minor, I didn't qualify for foster care. If I entered the system, I would have been sent back to my husband or parents.

So I got a job at a fast food joint and worked every hour that I wasn't sleeping or in school.

I lived in squalor and feared my husband showing up in the night to steal me back. Something the local police would have supported.

I haven't spoken to my parents since my wedding day and am happier for it. They never deserved me as a daughter. I'm sure they say the same thing, but with a different meaning.

Now here I am, an online sex worker who isn't ashamed

of my work or sexuality. I'm proud of the woman I've become and of the people I've already helped, and I'm still years away from being a practicing psychotherapist with patients.

What is online sex work if not a kind of therapy? And the man I'm online with now is someone I know I'm helping after our previous session, but he's also helping me, and that's new.

I've never been in love before, and now I long for that kind of emotional connection.

Is it Falcon or Chase who is waking that part of me?

Chase makes me want to be able to date and explore the chemistry that happens every time we see each other. He makes me want the physical.

Falcon gives me the physical and makes me want the emotional.

I want to confess my job that allowed me to afford this small townhouse. I want to share the ups and downs of my day with someone. I want to wake in a bed with someone who truly knows me and still loves me.

I want someone who can love me and accept what I do for a living. Not just a living, for security.

I need security more than anything, and money is security.

But I can't imagine ever finding such a man. Would Chase be repulsed? Horrified? Would he reject me?

It's impossible to guess. And I would feel devastated at seeing the heat in his eyes fade, or worse, turn to revulsion.

So for now, I can only get my emotional needs met by Falcon. He can't possibly judge, given our relationship. Yet I know many of my clients would judge me in real life.

People are strange.

And judgmental.

But I'm not ashamed and never will be. I'm a survivor,

and I help others. It's a good life, even if it is lonely in the day-to-day.

"What's going on, Desiree?" Falcon's voice is deep and warm. Maybe a little sleepy. I look at the clock, and it's only eight p.m. his time.

"Sounds like I wore you out," I say with a chuckle. "Going to sleep already?"

"Not at all. In fact, I was thinking I could do that again with a little encouragement. You turn me on endlessly, Des."

From what he shared last time, I know this is a big deal for him. "I'm glad. You make me hot too. No one has ever fucked me against a wall before."

"Never?"

"Nope."

"It was a first for me too. I think."

"You don't really know?" I pause, then add, "Were you drugged?"

"Sort of. My memories are all muddled. I don't remember much from before…the abuse. But I wasn't super sexually experienced, that I do know. And anything that happened under the influence of…well, it doesn't count. I didn't want or consent to it, even if I did orgasm."

There is a load of guilt and shame that comes with receiving unwanted sexual pleasure. I could write a dissertation on that topic alone. My heart aches for him. "I'm glad you want this pleasure with me and that you can take the pleasure you need. You make me feel amazing too."

"I didn't think I would ever want sex again until I found you."

I don't want him to see the heartache on my face—not when I can't hold him. I don't want him to think what I'm feeling is pity. It's not. It is a combination of rage on his behalf, empathy, respect for the work he's doing, and simple affection. "I care about you, Falcon. I'm always here to listen if you want to talk."

"Will you tell me something about you?"

In therapy, it's never about the therapist. The focus must remain on the client. But this isn't therapy, not really, and we've already established that a relationship requires some back and forth. My job, in its very nature, is me giving and my faceless client receiving. But he, more than anyone, always gives back to me, and he's made himself vulnerable in telling me of the abuse he suffered. I want to give him something in return.

I clear my throat and make my confession. "I was a child bride, forced by my parents to marry a forty-three-year-old man when I was fifteen."

My words hang in the air, and I find myself holding my breath. How will he react?

I haven't told anyone this story since I turned eighteen and didn't have to anymore.

Finally, Falcon says, "I'm so sorry."

I know he wants to ask questions. He wants to know the hows and whys and probably even if I'm still married.

But I don't want to talk about me. This isn't about what I went through to bring me to this place with him. This is about him and what he needs to heal.

"Do you want to date?" I ask. "I mean in real life, a real person and not someone four time zones away?"

"I didn't for a long time. Didn't think I was capable. Not only that I couldn't perform, but that I wouldn't feel. But I met someone recently, and…this time with you is making me think maybe I'm not a lost cause. Not too broken for love."

The jab of jealousy that stirs at hearing he's met someone —a ridiculous thought, given that he's my stand-in for Chase —is eclipsed by the last thing he said. "No one is a lost cause, and you're not too broken to love. You're worthy of love. You're lovable."

"You wouldn't say that if you knew what goes on in my head. The rage overwhelms me sometimes."

"It's normal to have rage against those who hurt you. I'm enraged on your behalf."

"This goes deeper. There's a violence inside me, and I don't know if it's me or what they put there. You said your parents forced you to marry when you were fifteen. Just hearing those words stirs all the rage. I want to find your parents and punish them. I want to go after the man who would force a child to marry him and break both his arms."

"Sometimes I want that too," I whisper. I clear my throat. "I've spent a lot of years claiming my autonomy. And I want you to know the woman you see before you"—I look down, waving my hand in front of my naked torso—"and I do mean *everything* you see, is being presented to you with full autonomy. I even started my own website so no one else would share in the profits of selling my sexuality. I can give as much as I want and take as much as I want. I am happy and not ashamed, and I want to share that with others who can benefit. Like you."

"So you don't feel the violence anymore?"

I cock my head, thinking. I want to be honest. Finally, I say, "I suppose sometimes, late at night, I'll dream of my parents and wake up with the unsettled part of my anger. But there can be no justice there. No one believes they did anything wrong or illegal, so I try not to think about them at all."

As I say the words, I can feel the rage building inside me, telling me that I have work to do in this area. This is a revelation to me. A reminder that I have some emotions that are still buried, waiting for me to deal with them when I'm in the right place.

I smile at the camera and say, "My best revenge is I didn't birth more monsters to run their church."

"Are they in a cult?"

"Not by the strictest definition—but yeah. Christian extremists who see women only as vessels for creating men. My mother was barely fifteen when I was born. I know she was a victim as much as I was, but she was so deeply brainwashed, she had no care for me. She thought I should be grateful they'd found me a husband who didn't already have sons, so I could be the lucky girl to give him one." I think of the mad light in my mother's eyes as she said this. She always resented my older half brother, especially when she was unable to carry another child to term. Unable to have a son.

"That's fucked up," Falcon says simply.

I laugh because it is. I touch my breasts for him and smile. "But this body is mine to do what I want with it now, and nobody tells me otherwise. I like role playing where you boss me around because it feels empowering. I'm choosing to submit. And I can choose not to. My choice. And I will only obey the commands that feel good to me. You always make me feel good, Falcon."

"I only want to make you feel good. I love watching you come. You're so open. Giving. You're what I've needed so much as I try to figure out what's happening in my brain."

"As much as I want to keep you as a client, if you've met someone in real life who feels safe and who turns you on, you should go for it. I understand it means you would probably have to stop seeing me. There aren't a lot of partners who would be comfortable with this. It's why I don't date."

"I don't think I'm there yet," he says. "I still have this rage I need to figure out. What if…what if I lose control of it?"

I wish I could see his face as he says, "They were trying to make me into a monster. I did bad things—most of which I don't even remember. I'm afraid the monster inside me is just sleeping."

Chapter Thirteen

FALCON

There. I've said the thing. My biggest fear. I wait for Desiree to sever the connection. I mean, this is crazy shit, and I can't even explain it. I can't tell her about infrasound and Parks. But this is the first time I've talked to anyone about this except Isabel since I left the hospital, because I've refused every shrink on the grounds that it was a shrink who did this to me.

Technically, Raptor requires annual mental health checks for all active operatives and trainers. I'm just past a year since my last evaluation, and Keith is letting me slide for the time being because he knows what happened to me, and I've performed better as an operative in the last ten months than ever before. But the day will come when I'll need to talk to a shrink, and I know I can't do it.

But that's a problem for another day. I want to know how much I've scared Eden with my confession that I might be some sort of rage monster.

No one thinks the Hulk is the hottest Avenger.

"Are you worried you'll hurt someone you care about?" she asks softly.

I close my eyes as I think about snapping that picture of Sean and Hazel in the forest last year. I hate myself for that almost more than the other stuff I did. "I already have."

"In the last year? After your abuser was arrested?"

"No," I say, glad for that truth. "But I have sent a few guys to the hospital. But they had it coming."

"Seriously?"

"Yeah."

"Did you get in trouble for that?"

"No. Like I said, they had it coming." It's true. I was lauded as a hero for what happened in Portland. And for saving the restaurant owner's daughter. Only Mothman knows about Sling Man.

"Do you feel bad for hurting them?"

"Not even a little bit. I'd do it again given the chance."

"You realize I'm dying to know what you do for a living now, right?"

"Sorry. That's top secret."

"Yeah. CIA is at the top of my list."

I smile. Better to let her think that than connect me to the guy she had dessert with tonight.

I hate lying to her, but I don't have a choice. "This isn't the snuggle session you were hoping for tonight, is it?"

"You're wrong there. This is exactly what I want. I don't get to share my life with anyone these days. And you've made me realize I still have some anger at my parents to process. Is this the kind of stuff other people talk about after sex?"

I laugh softly. "You're asking *me*? I have no idea. I've never had a girlfriend."

"I bet you'd make an awesome boyfriend."

I like to think I would, someday. Right now, my own brain scares me, so I don't say anything.

It's strange that I don't feel vulnerable with all the things I've confessed, and it's not because Eden doesn't know who I am. It's just…I feel safe with both Eden and Desiree. There's a kind, warm heart beating inside her perfect chest.

I imagine telling her who I am. Coming clean. Telling her about the trafficking happening through CamDames. She'd help me. I know she would.

But I keep circling back to the same truth. If I tell Eden who I am, I run the risk of losing the only person who makes me feel alive.

The only person who makes me think life is worth living.

Chapter Fourteen

Eden frowned at her checking account balance on the computer screen. She'd blown all her savings in buying the small townhouse, but it had been the only way to start her own business. She'd needed a private two-bedroom apartment and no roommate. It had been vital to be in control of her clients and be able to block local IP addresses, because she had practicum rounds next semester and couldn't walk into a situation and find herself face-to-face with someone who knew her as Desiree.

Worse, she could find herself in a position where they recognized her, but she didn't recognize them. This wasn't a recipe for establishing herself in the mental health business and could cause problems given the power dynamics of mental health work.

She'd done what she needed to do, but the fact remained, her savings were dwindling. Falcon's generosity these last two weeks had saved her butt, but she still wasn't close to being able to do more than pay the mortgage and put a little away for next semester's tuition. Fewer of the big spenders she'd cultivated at CamDames had followed her to her own platform.

There was no help for it. She was going to have to up her hours. Six a night instead of only four, and no more letting Falcon have her undivided attention for three hours. She needed to return to the group chat and convince other men to go private every single shift if she was ever going to pay off the townhouse and tuition.

All she wanted was security. To know she couldn't be sold again to a man because she wasn't earning her keep.

That had been what her mother had said that last day. A girl's job in this world was to make babies, and if she didn't get started, she wasn't worth the upkeep. And Cooper had paid a thousand dollars as if Eden was some sort of broodmare.

She would pity her mother if the rage didn't inhibit that feeling.

She rubbed her temples, thinking of Falcon and his rage. Did his rage come with the same feeling of helplessness? The same lack of outlet? Or did he find ways to let it out like steam from a boiling kettle?

He said he hurt people who deserved it. Was he a cop?

The idea that he took his rage out on suspects didn't sit well. Just because he said they deserved it didn't mean it was true.

There were plenty of innocent people in custody. Like when she'd been arrested for being a runaway two weeks before her parents married her off.

How was running away from parents—who had sold her, no less—a crime?

But even if Falcon was a cop, he wouldn't take out his aggression on a teen runaway. That much she knew about him.

She paused. But did she really? He could be anyone. He could be playing a role as much as she was.

No. She didn't buy it. His stark honesty when he shared what had happened to him had been real. He was a strong man who had suffered at the hands of someone, and he was trying to figure himself out.

She respected that. And it horrified her to know that his abuser had reached out to him from prison.

Cooper had never come near her again, but he had written to her. She'd never read the letters. She'd burned them and mailed back the ashes.

After the third time, the letters finally stopped coming.

She logged out of the bank website and pulled out her calendar. Her coffee shop hours were the usual this week. She worked eleven to four, Monday through Thursday, so she wouldn't have a problem starting the night shift two hours earlier. She even had an hour for makeup. She really should have made this change as soon as she decided not to take classes this semester, but she'd resisted because she'd hoped to use those hours to study ahead—get a jump on her course-work for next semester so the hours spent doing practicum work wouldn't cut into study time.

She worked twenty hours a week at the coffee shop, twenty hours in front of the camera, four hours at the lab, and next semester would have a full class load and ten hours of practicum per week. It would feel like she had two-and-a-half full-time jobs. But she'd do it.

She had to.

Her cam job paid the bills, the coffee shop provided health insurance and more money for bills, and the other one and a half jobs—school, lab, practicums—were the path to her dreams.

She would get her degree. She would help girls like her find a new life and healthy outlook. She would help trans teens become the person they were meant to be—the one they'd been all along.

There was so much she wanted to do, but not enough hours in the day or money in the bank.

Should she consider picking up shifts again at CamDames? Her mind instantly rebelled at that idea. No.

She'd invested so much in going solo, she needed to do the work so it would pay off.

She glanced at the clock. It was 5:00. She had just enough time to eat a quick dinner before she needed to apply the makeup.

If she was going to up her hours, no time like the present to get started. If she pulled in a thousand dollars a night for the next few weeks, she'd be back on track.

Her shift started slow—no surprise because her regulars knew she didn't usually log on this early—but she sent out some invitations to a few men who'd visited the room once but weren't subscribers, sending them a coupon for an "early bird snack," and two men took her up on it. While she was at it, she posted her updated hours and shared it with subscribers along with a photo she'd taken last week in the metal bikini with a survey question about which fantasies they'd like to see her perform.

She was deep in her regular shift when a new subscriber replied to the survey: *"Jasmine. Because she is ours and you owe us."*

*C*hase had logged into Desiree's room under a new ID. He shouldn't have done it, he knew, but he couldn't be Falcon with her again so soon, not after last night, but he'd had the need to check on her.

The coffee shop had been bombed yesterday, and they had no answers as to who or why. If it had to do with her or CamDames, whoever was behind it could know who she was and be watching her site.

So there he was, monitoring her chat room, writing down the login names of her clients. Searching for others who were new while remaining fully aware that one of the others could be doing the same to search for him.

Because she would be on longer tonight, she was putting more effort into the chat room, earning small tips from each of them as no one appeared to be ready to engage in a private session. He didn't know how much the others were tipping, but his guess was nothing big. Much as he wanted to give her more, he kept his tips to twenty-five each, for a total of one hundred. He wouldn't do a private chat with her as anyone other than Falcon.

He was about to log out when Thor indicated he wanted to go private, but at the same time, her expression changed from sweet and bubbly siren to confused to scared.

She'd been reading aloud answers to a survey question she'd asked earlier, and now she was upset.

What's wrong, Desiree? he asked in the chat.

He couldn't tell if she wanted to answer or not. Did she look…scared?

"Thor, it sounded like you were up for some fun? Guys, Thor and I are going to chat for a bit, but I'll be back later if anyone else is looking for company tonight."

A moment later, she and Thor were gone. Chase clicked the button to leave the chat, having no idea if he would log on later. Maybe Falcon should log in?

What did the message say? Was there any chance she would call him?

Everything about this situation sucked.

What if she was in danger because of him?

Eden called Penny as soon as she was done with Thor. She would make this call, then get back in the room. She'd only made half of what she needed for the night, but she still had three hours in her scheduled shift.

Who knew that in working for herself, she'd have to keep even more rigorous hours than before?

But then, with CamDames, she hadn't had any overhead. They'd even paid into her Social Security and Medicare. Now it was all on her.

Penny answered in a groggy voice. "Why don't you ever text?"

"Because I don't like written records of our conversations."

"Why? You doing something illegal?"

"No. I just don't want messages about CamDames on my phone. I figured you were the same."

"Oh. Yeah. I suppose. Why are you calling about them? You don't work there anymore. Aren't you living the high life as a free agent? Making all the money?"

"I wish. Listen, did you see a guard with a sling? I really need to know."

"You're still fixated on that?"

"Uh. Yeah. So did you?"

"I don't know. Maybe?"

"What do you mean maybe? Either someone is in a cast or sling or not."

"I don't really pay attention to the guards. Not unless I'm looking to score a bonus by turning a trick. But even then, it's more lucrative to screw an executive than a loser in security."

Eden stifled her sigh. Penny was a willing sex worker, but

still, there was a power dynamic in engaging with the men whose job it was to protect them and right up the hierarchy of the men who made them look good on the screen to the men who ran the company.

Everyone at CamDames knew that if a woman wanted a shift in a prime room where the high rollers frequented, a fast fuck with the boss could go a long way. It was hardly shocking given that they were all sex workers. But still, power dynamics were power dynamics, and that was one reason she'd opted to strike out on her own.

Penny couldn't be more than twenty years old. The CEO was fifty and raking in millions. Eden would have started a union if she thought she could get away with it.

"Listen, I got a message on my site tonight. It was the guy with the sling. He's after someone named Jasmine. I don't like anything about this. Your shop was *bombed*. I'm becoming more and more convinced this is about you."

"If it's about me, then why are they messaging you?"

Well, fuck. That was a good point.

"Because they know I would call you?"

But damn. Penny was right. They'd found her online, which meant he was from CamDames and he'd seen her that night. She'd taken more than half her regulars with her when she moved, and the company hadn't been thrilled by that. Company executives almost certainly knew her domain name and they could get around IP blockers with ease.

If they revealed who she was, they could ruin everything. She'd sunk her whole life into this. She needed the money for school. To live. To reach for her dreams.

They could destroy all her dreams by exposing her.

She wrapped up the call with Penny and hung up.

What should she do?

Had the response to her silly survey been a threat? Did they expect her to stand in for this Jasmine person?

Who was she, and why did they want her?

Should she call Chase and tell him everything?

Her heart squeezed at that. She didn't want to hear judgment in his whispery voice or see it in his eyes if she told him what she really did for a living.

But he might know who this Jasmine person was. She had no doubt he was keeping secrets about the reason the Raptor operative and Isabel Dawson had been in the shop that night.

She pulled up his contact info and debated calling, but in the end, she set down the phone and logged in to her website. She needed five hundred more dollars tonight before she called it quits. She'd slacked a lot the last two weeks and was paying the price with her low bank balance.

It was time to focus on the job that would pay for the schooling she needed to achieve her dreams.

othman had a line on another runaway. The grab would happen tonight—a damn short lead time that was probably the result of the interceptions Chase had made over the last five months.

From her photo, he guessed Ariel was fifteen.

The same age Eden had been when her parents had married her off.

Jesus. Every time he thought of that, he wanted to punch someone. How the hell had she become the confident, alluring, dynamic woman she was after that?

They didn't have time to do a detailed search for the girl based on her photo, but he could be in place to intercept her and get her to safety before Sling Man and Terry showed up.

The location was new, but that wasn't a surprise. But it was close to the CamDames office in the city, which did surprise him. But then, maybe they didn't have time to scope out a new pickup spot, and at least there, they controlled most of the street cameras.

Chase studied the map, then called Mothman. "Something about this isn't right. The timing, the location. It's too risky for them to pick up an unknown so close to head-quarters."

"I'm thinking the same thing." Mothman paused, and Chase figured his fingers were flying over his keyboard. He was the best hacker Chase knew, and that included Lee Scott, who did consulting work for Raptor on occasion. But Lee's government contracts meant he had to stay on the legal side of things, where Mothman was able to fly under the radar with steady employment by Raptor. As long as he kept Raptor's computers clean, no one looked too deeply into what he did on his own time and machines.

"I think it's a trap," Mothman said.

"Ariel is bait, and I'm the bird of prey."

"You think they know Raptor is involved?"

"If word got out that Isabel and Tricia were at the coffee shop, then yes. And the barista, Eden, told me she recognized Isabel. Who knows who else she told?"

"What did she say when you questioned her the other night, after the explosion?"

Truth was, they'd barely talked about the explosion over wine and dessert. Instead, they'd flirted shamelessly and then he'd gone home and fucked her alter ego virtually. But Mothman didn't know about Desiree. "She didn't talk about it with anyone at her usual store. But she said the guy she worked with that night, Tony, probably spoke to his cowork-ers. She gave me a list of names she could remember from the shift calendar in the back." He pulled out his notes. "A woman named Penelope, another named Zoe. The managers —Brian and Heather. The last names of the managers should be in the news articles."

"Yeah. I've already run down everything I can on them. I'll see if I can find last names for Penelope and Zoe. You should follow up with Tony."

Shit. Yeah. He should have right after the blast. What did

it say about him that he didn't even think of following up with the other witness? The one who actually worked at the store?

His brain was clouded by his attraction to Eden, and that was a big-ass problem.

Sure, it was more likely that Eden, having worked for CamDames, was connected in a way she didn't realize, but he needed to follow all leads, just like a detective would.

And shit. This meant he needed to tell Mothman about Eden being Desiree. It wasn't fair to have the guy working blind when Chase had a key piece of intel.

But this would mean Mothman would dive into Eden's life. Give him background information no one else knew, and that felt like an invasion.

She'd told him about her horrific marriage freely. He didn't want to know more unless she offered it of her own accord, just like he didn't want her to know more about what happened to him without him being the one to tell her.

This was messed up.

But he needed to focus on the current lead right now. A girl's life was more important than his messed-up brain. "Even if it's a trap, I have to go. We can't take chances when a girl's life could be at stake."

"I'm looking at the map right now. We need better intel on the location."

"Let's use a drone. One of Leah's new prototypes."

Raptor operative Nate "Hawk" Sifuentes's fiancée, Leah, was a coder for drones, and she'd been working on a prototype for Raptor for the last few months that was tiny and quiet with a powerful camera. Coming in around the size of a hummingbird, with motion that matched bird flight patterns, it was perfect for up-close surveillance.

"I'll ask if she'll let me run a test with it today," Mothman said.

"Good. I'll park nearby and be ready to move if there really is a girl. No Isabel or Tricia for this one. No way can we put them at risk when this is probably a trap."

"We need to send an email changing the meet time," Mothman said. "How early do we go?"

Last time, Chase had cut it close because he'd been spoiling for a fight. It had been risky for the girl and could well be what had endangered Eden, because they'd seen Jessica run into the coffee shop.

But if he made the meet time too early, there were other logistical problems especially if this was truly a trap. No need to let them know he was taking their bait at all.

"We won't change the time. Let them believe we never saw this exchange. Make them wonder if I'm going to be there."

It was an hour after her shift was supposed to end when Eden finally clocked out at the coffee shop. The evening shift replacement had a dead battery and had called and begged Eden to stay until she got there.

Being a team player who understood car troubles, she'd agreed, but it meant she'd have barely enough time to apply makeup before her online shift started at six.

She'd exceeded her goal of a thousand dollars last night and hoped to do the same tonight. She should have upped her hours months ago. If she had, she wouldn't be in the bind she was in now.

She hurried as she walked the mile between Vivace Coffee and her townhouse. She would have about ten minutes to stuff her face before the makeup ritual began.

One of these nights she'd just put on a masquerade mask and be done with it, but knowing her, she'd mess that up.

At least she didn't have to do full baby-doll makeup like Penny. That would suck. And, frankly, be a little freaky. Guys really liked that kind of thing?

She'd made a promise to herself when she started this job that she'd never do anything she didn't enjoy on camera. She'd indulge kinks as long as they worked for her. And baby-doll makeup had the double whammy of both not looking human and looking like a child.

Both were a hard no.

She was a living, breathing human woman and wouldn't turn herself into a caricature or animation for someone else's pleasure and definitely wouldn't look like a hypersexualized pubescent girl.

Her phone buzzed, and speak of the devil, the caller was Penny.

She slowed her hurried stride and answered. "Hey, Penny, what's up?"

Penny spoke in a hushed whisper. "He's here."

"What?"

"The guy in the cast you asked about. He's here. The security guard. And…I think…I think he might be my stalker."

"You think your stalker—Falcon?—is a security guard at CamDames—and he might be the guy who came to the shop that night?"

"Yeah. And maybe he bombed the shop too."

"Why do you think it's him?"

"Falcon always used voice when we were private. I know what he sounds like. His voice is very deep."

Eden thought of her own Falcon, who also had a deep voice she was certain she'd recognize if she heard it.

"I was outside the break room, and I heard two guys talking. One of them had that voice. I was stunned when he stepped out and it was a guy with a big cast on his right arm."

"Where are you now?"

"In the bathroom. I couldn't call from my workroom."

Yeah, everything that happened in that room was monitored.

"Eden, do you remember what he sounded like? That night at the shop? Can you come here and talk to him?"

"Sure but…your stalker happened months ago. Why are you just noticing his voice now?"

"He never spoke in front of me before. I think he knew I would recognize him if he did."

"How would I get him to talk? And if he recognized me through the window, he'll get suspicious."

"Shit. You're right. How about you meet me at my car? Like we had plans or something? Then we'll go inside and say I'm having car trouble and ask security for help."

"And what are you going to do when the car starts right up?"

"I'm a dumb bimbo to them. So are you. But if I have to, I'll pop my tire and ask one of them to change it."

It was reasonable. Lots of the women at CamDames socialized after their shifts. And no one would be surprised that she and Penny were hanging out considering they both worked for Vivace too.

"What time does your shift end?"

"Nine."

That would give Eden two hours before she'd have to catch the Metro and a bus to get to CamDames headquarters. Times like this, she really wished she had a car. But she needed to do this. If she could identify the guy from the shop that night—and he had a connection to Penny—this was information that could be taken to the police for the bombing investigation. It would mean revealing herself to the cops as a former employee of CamDames, but this guy had injured five people. People could have died.

It had to be done. Maybe the police would keep her identity secret.

"I'll be there by nine fifteen."

"Thank you!" Penny said. "I really appreciate this. "If he's my stalker *and* he bombed the shop, well, he needs to be caught."

As Eden hurried home, she realized there was another reason she was doing this. What if Penny's Falcon was also *her* Falcon?

She might not recognize the voice of the man who'd been outside the coffee shop two weeks ago, but she knew Falcon's voice. She heard it every night in her dreams.

Chapter Sixteen

$\mathcal{E}$den walked with purpose down the dark block. The bus stop was a few blocks away, and this time of night, walking alone was always questionable. But she used to work here and knew the street and how to walk. Plus, she had pepper spray.

She'd considered using a rideshare app once again, but rejected it for the same reason as before: she didn't like being alone in strange men's cars, and given that the drop-off point was a shop for online sex workers, it felt extra risky. There was no sign outside indicating what kind of business was inside, but it also wasn't the best-kept secret in town.

Her pace was brisk as she hurried along the cracked sidewalk. She hadn't missed this commute.

She glanced at her watch. Her timing was right on the money. Penny had texted her with the meet point by her car parked in the garage across the street. Then they'd go through the motions of noticing the flat tire—Penny said she'd jammed a knife into it during her break at seven—and go inside and bat their eyelashes at the security team and ask for a tire change.

If Sling Man didn't open his mouth in the exchange, Eden would ask him what happened to his arm.

She felt a prickling along the back of her neck as she entered the garage. It smelled of exhaust and oil and naturally had too many areas that were poorly lit. Parking garages must be designed by misogynistic men because they always felt like they were configured to terrorize.

And it worked. She avoided the even creepier staircase and walked up the ramp to the third floor, where Penny's car would be.

A bird flitted by. She was always amazed to see them in this most urban of landscapes. The garage didn't even have potted plants or anything close to resembling a natural landscape, but still, birds would find a way to nest even here.

Cars dotted the first and second floors, including a few luxury ones that indicated the executives were working late tonight. The garage had good security thanks to the CEO wanting to make sure his Tesla went unmolested. Unfortunately, said security might be Sling Man, aka Penny's stalker.

She rounded the bend of the ramp to the third floor and was shocked to see no cars at all. That was unusual. CamDames was live twenty-four seven, and while this wasn't the only office with rooms for the Dames to perform, it was the largest. There should be at least a dozen women on camera right now, and this was the Dame floor of the garage.

She felt a prickling of fear. Had they changed the floor designations? She pulled her phone from her pocket. No, Penny specifically said third floor.

So had she left already? But why would she do that? And how? She'd spiked her own tire.

There was a sound behind her. Footsteps.

Penny?

No. It wasn't the soft click of a woman's shoes. It was a man's heavy tread.

Eden darted forward, toward a thick concrete column to tuck herself behind while she figured out what to do.

Nothing about this felt right.

Her heart pounded as she clutched her phone. Should she call 911?

But a glance at the screen told her she wasn't calling anyone. "No Service" was in the top right corner.

Chase's heart drummed when the drone camera caught a familiar female shape entering the garage. What the hell was Eden doing here?

Fuck. This was more than a trap.

It was his worst nightmare.

Unless…Eden was one of them? Was she a honey trap?

Worse, was she a lure for the young runaways? A person they would instinctively trust?

For all he knew, she'd made up the story of being a runaway and forced child bride herself. He hadn't let Mothman dig into her past.

He'd failed the most basic test of an undercover op: everyone is a suspect.

Even the woman he might be falling for.

The drone followed her from high above. She glanced in its direction once, but then turned her focus to the interior of the garage.

She looked nervous.

What the hell was she doing there?

She walked deeper into the structure, heading up the ramp. The drone followed, keeping a safe distance and flying in a birdlike pattern. Leah had really outdone herself. If one wasn't paying close attention, it could pass as a real bird.

Chase was parked in the lowest level of the garage in an electric vehicle that Tariq had managed to plant earlier in the day when the garage was busy. Chase had slipped in at six p.m. with a group of employees from the adjacent business and settled into the vehicle with darkly tinted windows, sweeping the garage with the bird drone as he waited for Ariel or Sling Man to show up.

But what he got was Eden.

The minute she entered the garage, he turned on the engine, which remained silent even though he was ready to roll.

His gut twisted as he watched her ascend the ramp. Much as he knew he couldn't cross her off as a suspect, he didn't believe it.

She was a target. Bait. Not a complicit lure.

Not his Eden. She wouldn't work with child traffickers.

The bird camera showed her rounding the bend to the third floor and coming to an abrupt stop. He pressed the zoom button on the drone controls and took in her expression. She was terrified.

All at once, she bolted forward, running for the nearest concrete pillar. She stared at her phone, but after swiping across the screen several times, she shoved it back in her pocket.

The lights snapped off, plunging her into darkness. The drone caught the sound of footsteps and a low singsong male voice saying, "Desiree, come out, come out, wherever you are."

Chase hit the gas pedal and charged up the ramp. He should have done it the minute she was on camera, but like a dumb fuck, he'd hesitated. He rounded the final turn to the third floor and slammed on the brakes.

The floor was drenched in inky darkness. He turned on a strobe light to blind and disorient whoever was singing.

There, in the flashing light of the strobe, he saw a man wearing a hood over his head and a black cast on one arm grab for Eden as she ran for the stairwell.

The strobing light messed with Sling Man's night vision goggles and he missed the grab, buying Eden an extra step.

Chase launched himself from the driver's seat and raced after the guy. The strobing stopped just as he caught him and slammed him to the ground.

A knife appeared, and he swatted it away. Did this guy learn nothing last time?

They rolled on the ground, and then Chase felt a blow to his back.

Maybe he had learned something, because this time, Sling Man wasn't fighting alone.

*E*den made it to the stairway exit and yanked on the door, well aware that it might be a trap but having no other choice.

But the door was locked.

She waited for hands to grab her, but then heard the sound of fists on skin behind her.

The strobing had stopped. She ducked into the darkest corner near the stairs and turned to see what was happening.

Her heart had been pounding so hard in her ears—or maybe her breathing was too ragged—that she hadn't heard the vehicle that was now parked in the center of the parking row. The driver's door was wide open, but no lights were on. Only dim light from the street below gave any illumination to the scene before her as a man in a ski mask fought three men, two of which wore costume hockey masks and the last wore a hood.

As she watched, three became two. The guy in the hood and black cast—that had to be Sling Man—hit a concrete pillar and went lights out.

Then it was two men with knives on one unarmed man. She would wonder who to root for if she hadn't seen the unarmed guy in the ski mask launch Sling Man into the pillar.

Sling Man had been the one singing. She'd heard his voice and was certain he wasn't *her* Falcon. Thank goodness.

But she was confused as to why Penny wasn't here but Sling Man was.

And then there was Ski Mask. Who was he and why had he appeared in this parking garage right at this time—*with a ski mask?*

He moved like a blur. She felt like she was watching some sort of Jackie Chan movie as he somehow managed to choreograph his opponents' movements. Or maybe he anticipated them, but it looked like his every action triggered the desired reaction from his remaining opponents, who were quickly disarmed of knives, and then, even more alarming, of at least one gun.

Ski Mask's foot kicked out, and one of the guys let out a loud howl as his knee bent in the wrong direction. Ski Mask caught the third man in a headlock as Jacked Knee writhed on the concrete.

Eden's flicker of relief was short-lived when she felt something hard and cold press against her head. Someone pushed her forward at the same moment the garage was flooded with light.

Ski Mask turned to face her, still holding the last man in a headlock. Eden had no doubt he could snap the guy's neck if he wanted, given what she'd just seen.

"Let him go," the person behind her said. The voice was distorted. Computerized.

For a moment, she wondered if it was Penny, but the person was tall, whereas Penny was petite.

Ski Mask met Eden's gaze, and she caught her breath. *Chase?*

She contained her reaction. If it was him, she didn't want to give him away. He likely had a good reason for wearing a mask to a knife fight.

"I said, let him go," the distorted voice repeated.

"Remove the gun from her head, and I will." His voice was a low, menacing whisper.

The gun shifted, no longer pressing against her scalp, but peripheral vision told her it was still pointed at her head.

Orders were shouted at Jacked Knee to drag Sling Man to a van parked at the curve to the third floor.

Jacked Knee growled that he couldn't even walk, but he managed to hobble over to the unconscious man and grabbed his arm, pulling him as best he could toward the vehicle.

"Let the other one help," the distorted voice said.

"Give me the woman first."

Eden was shoved forward.

Chase released the third man at the same moment she was shoved in his direction.

He caught her, but instead of wrapping his arms around her, he pushed her behind him, and a moment later, a gun appeared in his hands. He pointed it at a figure cloaked in black—the person who'd held a gun to her head, who she was seeing for the first time. The person's body was disguised, the cloak draping over some kind of frame—like a Halloween costume designed to make a person look taller—distorting the person's height and shape.

It could be anyone.

"Leave," Chase said, pointing his gun at the figure. "And I won't shoot."

The guy who'd been in the headlock took over dragging

Sling Man. Jacked Knee hobbled to the open side door of the van and stumbled inside.

The cloaked figure walked backward to the van, keeping their gun on Chase. The unconscious man was dumped in the back. The lone uninjured fighter took the driver's seat as the cloaked figure climbed in the passenger side.

Chase kept the gun on the vehicle until it disappeared down the ramp.

The moment they were out of sight, he tugged her arm, pulling her toward the other vehicle.

"We need to get out of here now. There might be more."

Eden didn't hesitate and ran for the passenger door.

In moments, they were racing toward the exit. Right before they left the garage, Chase cursed and slammed on the brakes. He hit a button on the built-in computer console, and seconds later, something flew in the rear open window.

He closed the window and hit the accelerator, and they shot out into the dark streets. The van was nowhere to be seen.

Chapter Seventeen

$\mathcal{C}$hase guessed that Eden had a gazillion questions, but she was quiet, and she was probably also reeling.

She'd had a gun pressed to her head.

The image was burned into Chase's brain, and it triggered rage and horror.

It had taken everything in him to maintain control in that moment and not go after the cloaked monster and rip their head off.

Somehow, he'd managed to hold it together, letting them escape to save Eden.

It only worked because the cloaked person wanted to escape more than they wanted to keep Eden, which told him Eden had never been the target.

No. They'd been after him.

Once it was clear they wouldn't be able to take him, they'd used the only remaining weapon in their arsenal to cut their losses: Eden.

He'd brought danger to her door. They were using her to get to him.

Had they been watching the coffee shop? Watching her townhouse?

They likely knew he'd taken her to dinner.

Like a dumb fuck, he hadn't taken a surveillance detection route that night. It hadn't crossed his mind that it would matter.

He was taking an SDR now. But then, right at this moment, he didn't even know where he was really going.

His emotions were out of control. He was pumped with adrenaline and battling rage and arousal, riding the edge of that post-fight feeling that he didn't know how to process because it was more emotions than he knew how to deal with.

They hit a yellow light, and he slammed the brakes, first car in line at the stop.

He turned to Eden and suddenly realized he still wore the thin mask that covered everything but his eyes.

He whipped off the mask.

She didn't show any surprise, but he'd guessed the exact moment when she'd identified him in the garage.

Now her eyes flared with heat, and she said, "Kiss me."

He didn't hesitate and cupped the back of her head, pulling her toward the center console and meeting her halfway. His mouth covered hers, his tongue sliding between her lips, no foreplay as he tasted her fully, giving her a deep, carnal kiss that was just the tip of the iceberg of the intensity that coursed through him.

Cars honked, and he stroked her tongue with his one last time before he broke the kiss and returned his focus to the nighttime city streets and the green light ahead of him.

He tightened his grip on the wheel and sped into traffic.

He needed to find a place to pull over so he could kiss her again. And so they could talk, but mostly so he could kiss her and ride the high of the endorphins that had been released by getting to take some of his rage out on motherfuckers who deserved a beating.

This feeling should terrify him.

But for the moment, he felt like a god.

*E*den pressed her fingers to her lips as they raced down the streets. That might have been the single greatest kiss of her life.

And she wanted another one.

She had a million questions, and that kiss had wiped every single one from her mind. It had reduced her to nothing but a sexual being who wanted him inside her, to give her pleasure that made her forget the terror of the last thirty minutes.

He didn't say a word, but she knew he felt it too. Sexual energy charged the air of the silent vehicle.

All at once, she looked around the vehicle interior. "Wait, is this…a Tesla?"

He nodded. "I needed a silent car in the garage."

"So this is a Raptor vehicle?"

"Yeah. Raptor pays me well, but not Tesla well."

She ran a hand over the dashboard. "Well, look at me. Little Eden O'Keeffe, the poorest kid from poor town, riding in an honest to goodness Tesla."

He laughed. "You really the poorest kid from poor town?"

"No. But there were times when it was close."

Her brain filled with fantasies of having sex in this car, and she was tempted to tell him to find a private parking spot fast. The only thing that stopped her was knowing that while she could kiss him, sex remained off the table.

Besides, they had a lot of talking to do. Someone had tried to abduct her. They'd held a gun to her head.

And he'd fought three men like a badass ninja.

She cleared her throat. "You know martial arts."

"Yes. My dad was my first sensei. He started teaching me when I was three."

"Your first sensei? Is he…gone?"

He shook his head. "No. He's still alive and teaching. But I had other senseis. I studied several kinds of martial arts. When I was nineteen, I dropped out of college and went to Japan for two years."

"So you're, like, really good."

"I am." He gave her a sideways glance that was incredibly hot. "I'm Raptor's most skilled operative at hand-to-hand combat. No one—not even our best operatives with the most military and operational experience—has ever been able to beat me."

"That's not wildly hot or anything."

He smiled. "Thank you."

She turned serious as she remembered the fight. The blur of his movements. She placed a hand on his thigh. "And I'm grateful for your skills. I think you saved my life tonight."

He frowned. "But it was my fault you were there."

"How can that be?"

"We need to talk. Someplace private. Can we go to your place?"

Every part of her wanted to say no. No one entered her townhouse. But they did need to talk. And he had saved her life.

She lifted her hand from his thigh. "Fine."

He nodded and turned at the next intersection.

"You're going the wrong way."

"I know. Surveillance detection route. Something I should have done the first time I took you home."

"That would have totally freaked me out. I'd have been sure you were abducting me."

"Still, I should have done it. It might be why someone is after you now."

They rode in silence for the next thirty minutes as her mind chewed on that fact. But he didn't know about Penny or CamDames. This wasn't his fault. It was hers.

He parked in her driveway and asked, "Is the garage full? Can I park in there? If anyone is watching your place, it might be good to get this vehicle out of sight."

"It's empty. My car currently resides in a retirement home for vehicles whose parts are the only thing they're good for."

"Ouch."

"Yeah."

She jumped out and punched in the code on the keypad and stepped back as he pulled into her extra-deep garage.

He shut off the engine, and she closed the garage door, then led him to the door to the interior stairs and utility room. She unlocked the inside door, and he said, "Good call on keeping that door locked. Automatic garage doors are only the first line of security, not the best."

She smiled over her shoulder at him. "I'm a big believer in security."

"Good."

Inside, she keyed off the alarm, then closed the door and locked it behind him and keyed it on again.

She turned to go up the stairs, but he stopped her, studying the alarm console. "Again, I approve. This is a good system. The best you can get for a private residence in this area."

She smiled, glad she'd impressed him in his field, no less. "I did a lot of research."

Something in his eyes went hot, and he pulled her to him,

his hands on her hips. He leaned into her, and his lips brushed hers.

She let out a soft sound in her throat and opened her mouth to let him in. All at once, he scooped her up and pressed her back to the wall next to the keypad. His tongue stroked hers and she wrapped her thighs around his hips.

He was between her legs and her back was to the wall as he kissed her. His hips thrust, stroking her center with his erection, and she rocked against him, lost in the heat of the moment as he fulfilled a long-held fantasy.

There was no longer any doubt that Chase Johnston could definitely fuck her against a wall.

Maybe this wall. Maybe even right now.

His tongue slid against hers, hot and sensuous. God. How she'd missed kissing. Missed the feel of a hard body against hers. Missed the rhythmic thrust of pelvis to pelvis as part of intense kissing.

The wild, hot buildup of foreplay.

She'd missed all of this so much, but also wasn't sure it had ever been this good. This urgent. This scorching.

His arm under her butt supported her weight as he pressed her to the wall. She locked her ankles together as she gripped his shoulders and rocked her hips forward, feeling his thick erection against her clit in spite of the layers of clothing that separated them.

She ran a hand over his chest, loving the feel of his muscles under her palm. She wanted to slide her hands between them and stroke his erection, but it was impossible in this position.

She released his mouth, and his lips moved to her neck, leaving hot, wet kisses in his wake as he explored.

"I want to touch you," she said. "I want you in my mouth. I want to feel your cock deep inside me." She was positively frantic for all those things.

His body stiffened against her, and his mouth left her skin. His eyes closed with something that looked like remorse.

His reaction to her desperate desire sent a jolt of regret coursing through her. It was like ice water on heated skin.

Shit.

She was too much now. After two years of saying exactly what she wanted to men, she couldn't go back to being demure and hoping he'd figure it out. And he didn't like it. She was too bold. Too demanding.

She'd thought he could accept the sexual being she was, but she'd been wrong. She wiggled against him. His arms tightened around her.

"Put me down," she said.

He opened his eyes and frowned. "What's wrong?" He gently lowered her to the ground as he asked the question. His expression went from pained to confused.

"I'm sorry. I just—I didn't mean to turn you off."

"What?"

"When I said—"

"Sweetheart, you turn me on by breathing." His whispery voice sent new jolts of desire through her. "And what you said was hot as fuck. I just—I got a cold dose of reality. We can't do this now. We need to talk."

Oh hell. She'd been so caught up in her wants—her need to escape the trauma of what happened tonight—she'd blocked out all the reasons she couldn't have him.

He was right. They couldn't do this. And not just because they needed to talk about what happened in the parking garage, but because he didn't know what she did for a living, and that she had no intention of quitting.

What man would be okay with dating an online sex worker?

Chase followed her up the inside stairs—two short flights with a switchback turn on a landing at the midpoint—and into her upper-floor apartment.

The interior stair entrance deposited them in a large closet/pantry that was neatly organized and spotless. Combined with the utility/laundry room behind the garage, her townhouse had a lot of storage. From the pantry, they stepped out into an open-floorplan kitchen-and-living-room combination, with a low wall that separated an alcove for an office space full of packed bookshelves that was the first room along a hallway that must lead to bathroom and bedrooms.

The living room had a big front window with a small balcony. During the day, the room probably got a lot of sunlight.

"Nice place." He glanced toward the hallway with closed doors, figuring the one at the end was the master bedroom, which meant the closest door across from the office alcove was probably her cam room. "You live here alone?"

She nodded.

"Wow. Rent can't be cheap for a place this size."

She shrugged. "I inherited it."

The way she said it, he knew it was a lie. One she might be used to saying to others, but she hadn't been prepared to lie to him. She'd probably bought it but couldn't explain how she could afford it on a barista's wages.

Given what had just happened between them at the bottom of the stairway, he had to tell her what he knew, but he wouldn't do it here. Not now. For multiple reasons. Not the least of which was that he needed to process his emotions before he could speak, and right now, his brain was in a tail-spin from the violence. The kiss. The danger she'd been in.

It would take everything to get through this interview and leave him with nothing left. There was no way he could process her reaction in this state.

And then there was the fact that she needed to feel safe when he made that revelation, and from everything he knew about her, she wouldn't feel safe with him in the first moments of knowing he was her biggest fear. She'd done everything she could to ensure she would never meet a client in her real life, but she'd failed.

His admission would be her nightmare come to fruition.

Her feeling safe was paramount if they were going to be able to talk through the situation.

Even more than her feeling safe, he needed her to *be* safe. To that end, he wanted to search her home to make sure there were no intruders, but he knew she'd never allow that. Instead, he went to the front door alcove accessible from the exterior stairs and scanned the alarm system. "You should enter your code and get the activity report. See if there was any activity at the doorbell camera."

"Good idea," she said.

He liked that she didn't question the suggestion. Someone had tried to kidnap her. It stood to reason her home might not be secure.

She typed the code into the alarm keypad and then pulled out her phone to review the report.

"No activity after I left at eight."

"Good." He paused and then said, "So. Why did you leave? Why were you in that parking garage?"

She frowned. "Can I get you anything to drink before we start in?"

"Water, please."

The kitchen was separated from the living room by a counter lined with barstools.

Chase wandered into the living room while she rounded the counter into the kitchen and filled two tall glasses with ice.

He faced the gas fireplace and flipped the switch to turn it on, giving the room a soft, warm glow. He then turned off the overhead light and turned on a side-table lamp. This was the kind of thing he did when interviewing protection clients in a safe house, not a woman in her own home, but he needed her to be comfortable, and this conversation would be more fruitful with more shadows than light.

She entered the room with two glasses of water and an expression that was somewhere between amused and annoyed. "By all means, make yourself at home."

He smiled and took the glass of water she offered. Unable to help himself, he brushed his lips over hers, then said, "Thanks, I will."

Amusement won out, and she shook her head even as she smiled.

He wanted to set both their glasses aside and kiss her deeply. To settle on the couch and enjoy an endless make-out session that culminated with him sliding deep inside her and giving her the best orgasm of her life.

But he couldn't do any of that. Not with the amount of deception that remained between them.

It didn't mean he didn't want to be near her, though, and he sat on one end of the couch and patted the seat next to him. She smirked and dropped down on the far end, letting him know there was only so much control she'd give him in this.

Fine.

"So why were you in the garage?"

"Penelope asked me to meet her there."

He had no clue what he'd expected her to say, but for

some reason, it wasn't that. "Penelope, the woman you filled in for at the shop the night we met?"

"Yes."

"Why did she ask you to meet her, and why did you agree?"

She cleared her throat, then took a sip of water.

His heart pounded in anticipation of her answer. Would she tell him the truth? If she did, he'd have to tell her he was Falcon. Here. Now.

He wasn't sure he could process it all.

"Penny has another job in an office near the garage. She called me and said one of the security guards at her other job had a cast, and she wondered if he was Sling Man. She asked me to meet her on the pretext of hearing his voice and seeing his face to determine if it was him."

This sounded true enough. And it was the kind of thing Eden would do if it meant finding the bomber.

"Why didn't you call me? Weren't you concerned you were meeting a potential bomber to identify him?"

"I guess I didn't think he'd know why I was there. I mean, I wasn't certain he saw my face that night, and Penny and I work for the same coffee chain. As for why I didn't call you, I —I honestly don't know why. I didn't think of it. Maybe I thought I was protecting Penny? She doesn't want anyone to know she's a camgirl for a website called CamDames." She paused, then added, "You know what camgirls are, I presume?"

Yes. Yes, he did. "She's an online sex worker." He hoped she heard the lack of judgment in his whispered words.

Eden nodded. "It's not recorded content. The work is interactive. Which can be dangerous because clients can get fixated, so she doesn't tell anyone about her sideline. I only found out by accident. Just telling you this now, I'm violating her trust."

The lie about how she knew Penny was a camgirl told him that she wouldn't reveal more to him tonight. In a way, he was relieved. He needed to come clean before she did, or she might never forgive him.

He wouldn't waste time by asking what she knew about CamDames. If she wanted to tell him the truth, she'd offer it, and he didn't want to listen to more lies, even if he understood the reason behind them.

She fixed her gaze on him. "Why were *you* there tonight?"

He took a deep breath. It was time for her to hear at least part of the truth. "For the last eight months, I've been working with a small group of people connected to Raptor to intervene when runaway teens try to get a job at CamDames. CamDames—or individuals within the organization—is heavily invested in the sexual trafficking of minors. I had reason to believe a girl was about to be abducted in the garage, but instead, I found you."

*E*den thought she might be sick. *CamDames is trafficking children?*

She thought of Penny and her suspicion that the girl had been online since before her eighteenth birthday. She'd known it was possible the work hadn't been online, and it made her heart ache. She dropped her head in her hands and whispered, "You're certain?"

"Yes. I've intercepted five girls in the last five months. I know there have been more taken, but those are the ones we found out about in time to act. Our methods aren't legal, so we can't go to the police."

"The night we met. Jasmine was the girl?"

He nodded.

"And Isabel Dawson and your coworker…?"

"They were there to take the girl to a shelter for runaways. It's confidentially located, and Isabel's involvement must remain a secret or the shelter can be exposed. They're minors, and it's not safe to return them to their parents. It's not entirely legal."

"I understand." Did she ever. She'd have given anything to have a safe place to hide from her parents before she was married off.

"So where were you when Jasmine ran into the shop?" Her gaze jerked up to meet his as it all clicked into place. She'd seen him in action tonight. "You were breaking Sling Man's arm."

He nodded again.

"And that's why you came back to escort me home. You felt at fault."

"I *was* at fault. You were in danger because of me. Because I was too eager to beat the crap out of him."

Regret coated his words.

He might have regrets, but so did she. Her work in the online sex industry had lined the pockets of child traffickers?

She couldn't even begin to process that, so instead, she scooted closer to him and placed a hand on his knee. "You couldn't have known they'd come back."

"I wore a mask when I fought Sling Man, just like tonight. They might've gone to the shop and harassed you to draw me out."

"I don't buy that. We could just as easily have called the police. They had no idea we got a card from your coworker."

"But still. I should have known they'd keep an eye on everyone involved after we showed up at the shop that night. Our license plates identified us as Raptor. They could have followed us as I drove you home the first time. I watched for a tail, but didn't take an SDR. I led them right to you."

She supposed it was possible they'd monitored her to find him, as he described, but they might have been watching her anyway. She now believed Sling Man had recognized her that first night. He'd called her Desiree in the garage. Someone had replied to her survey with a threat.

The guards at CamDames could easily have known her real name and tracked down her work and home addresses. If they hadn't gotten Chase's license plate, they might have been monitoring her at work to see if their masked vigilante showed up, unmasked.

"If we're going to distribute blame, there's another person to consider." She closed her eyes as she thought of Penny, and a fresh jolt of betrayal hit her. "When I first walked into the garage and Penny's car wasn't there, and then Sling Man came after me, I wondered if she'd set me up. She must have. She's working with them."

"She was the one who was supposed to be in the coffee shop the night we met."

"Yes." Eden let out a heavy sigh. "So what do we do? We need to tell the police what happened tonight. Tell them everything."

He ran a hand over his face. "You mean tell the police my friends and I have been hacking and working as vigilantes to rescue girls who, if intercepted by law enforcement, they'd have to return to abusive parents? That tonight they used you as bait to get to me? I happen to know some of those officers are on the take. One of my coworkers—he goes by Mothman —is trying to figure out how to get the meagre evidence we've managed to collect to prosecutors in a way that will be admissible in a court of law. But until then, our best course is to leave them out of it."

"But the bombing…"

"The lead detective is on my list of questionable officers." He frowned. "You've seen what's been going on in this country the last few years. We've got a serious problem in our police departments." He rested his hands on his knees. "Another time, I'll tell you a story of something that happened to me. It's too much for tonight. But I'll tell you now I was part of a case where a sheriff and his deputies were involved in a criminal conspiracy that went on for years. I used to want to be a cop, but now I don't trust them."

Eden had her own issues with cops after their repeated attempts to return her to her husband, but she sensed Chase's mistrust ran far deeper for good reason.

He rose to his feet. "Let's talk tomorrow, okay? I'm not saying we won't go to the police, but if we do, we need to be prepared to be looked at as the criminals here. They're going to grill you about Penelope. They're going to want to know everything you know about her and assume you're involved with whatever it is she's doing. They're going to rip apart your life. Ask yourself, Eden, are you ready for that kind of scrutiny?"

His words sent a chill up her spine.

She'd never broken the law. Her work for CamDames was completely legal. But would the police see it that way, knowing they were involved in a sex-trafficking ring?

And a cop on the take from CamDames would be extra eager to point the finger at Eden.

Plus, she had school to consider. Even though she was innocent, even a passing association with an organization that was involved in sex trafficking meant she could kiss her career plans goodbye.

Chase glanced around the room. "I don't like leaving you here alone after you've been targeted."

She needed to think and be alone, and there was no way he could stay the night. If he shared her bed, they'd have sex. It was inevitable. And if she asked him to sleep on the couch, he'd wonder about why he couldn't use her second bedroom.

Worse, what if he searched her place in the middle of the night? And if she didn't trust him not to do that, he had no business being in her townhouse while she was sleeping.

"I'll be fine. I have a great security system."

"That's the only reason I'm not trying to argue with you right now."

He picked up his water glass from the coffee table and set it on the counter on the way to the inside stairs to the garage.

She followed so she could close up and reset the alarm.

At the base of the switchback stairs, where they'd kissed earlier, he stopped and pulled her to his chest.

She was surprised to receive a hug and not a kiss, but she settled against him and recognized it was a hug that she needed right then.

She sank into the warmth of his chest and encompassing arms, clutching him tight. It felt so damn good to be held and to hold in return. He made her feel safe. Special. Wonderfully alive.

It broke her heart to know that the next time she saw him, she'd have to tell him everything. Then he'd run as fast as his legs would take him out the door.

She was being a coward in not telling him tonight, but she needed to prepare herself for his rejection. It would be too much on top of what she'd gone through in the last few hours.

This might be the only hug she'd ever get from Chase Johnston. She needed to take all the human comfort from it she possibly could and remember this sweet warmth. The memory would have to sustain her in the future when she was isolated and alone.

Chapter Eighteen

$\mathcal{C}$hase took a full surveillance detection route home on the off chance he hadn't been identified by the CamDames goons yet. It was highly unlikely given that they might have found him by watching Eden.

Still, better safe than dead, so he did his job right and the ten-minute drive took forty-five.

Throughout the long drive, he wondered if Eden had decided to go online tonight. Did she want an escape from the night's horrors that Falcon could provide? Did she need the distraction of work after the ordeal? Not to mention straight up just needing to make money while she could because with each passing day, her online business was looking more and more risky.

All were valid reasons. Hell. She didn't need a reason that was valid in his eyes. She was a survivor, and that was what she needed to do now.

And part of survival was working.

Tomorrow, he would reach out to her about initiating a search for Penelope. Penny. He needed to know her

CamDames name. He guessed Eden would tell him since she suspected the young woman now too.

But would she tell him the rest?

Probably.

Which meant he had to tell her tonight. Before that conversation could begin. There was no way he could let her confess her secret life before he told her his truth. He had to be the one who told her first, because he was the one who'd lied every time they were together, either as Falcon or Chase.

She'd never owed him the truth of her sideline. It was her business. But each time he'd logged in and fooled around with her after he met her in person, he'd been taking something from her she wasn't willingly giving.

She'd showed him her body, told him about her marriage, all believing he was a client in Anchorage and not the man she'd met in a coffee shop.

He could see now what a violation that had been, even though he'd told himself at the time it wasn't wrong because he hadn't sought her out. He was certain now that it was no coincidence she'd been at the coffee shop that night, but still, it hadn't been his intention to find her and woo her in real life. He'd relied on a technicality to justify taking what he wanted.

And that didn't even touch on the fact that he'd endangered her.

He had to tell her, and he had to do it tonight.

First, he had to sort out the emotions that overwhelmed him to find the right words. He doubted the right words existed, though. She would never forgive him, and he couldn't blame her.

He arrived at the compound and parked the Tesla in the main operations garage and returned the key to the safe.

He could get in serious trouble for using the expensive vehicle for a vigilante mission, but he'd been all in on this for a while now, and there was no question that saving a young girl was worth the risk.

Saving Eden? That had probably taken years off his life.

He made his way to his quarters and keyed his code into the door.

He went straight to his laptop and logged in to Desiree's site, not allowing himself to think or hesitate. He might get lost in a spiral if he did.

He'd taken the easy way out in not telling Eden when he was in her living room, but he also knew it was the right thing to do, for her sake as well as his. Her online relationships were safe due to the separation. That safety was something she valued more than almost anything else. He wouldn't take it from her by presenting himself as her worst nightmare while standing in her living room.

He didn't know if he should be relieved or terrified that she was online. She was in a private session with another client, but the waiting room indicated she'd be back in fifteen minutes and he was first in the queue.

Chapter Nineteen

DESIREE

Hank is sweet as usual, but I have no patience for him tonight. I honestly don't even know why I logged in after Chase left. But I was so wound up and needed a distraction, so I did the fastest makeup job of my life and planted myself in front of the camera.

Might as well make money.

Because tomorrow, this will probably all fall apart. I heard what Chase was saying, but I don't see how we can avoid the police.

CamDames is trafficking children?

My heart wants to break every time I think of it.

I remember Jasmine—or whatever her name was—running into the shop with fear in her eyes. What would have happened to her if Chase hadn't been there? If Isabel Dawson and the Raptor operative hadn't been ready to take her to safety?

All three of them risked a lot to save that girl, and my heart surges as I think of Chase. He's like Batman, saving people when the cops won't.

Saving me.

He literally saved me tonight. And then he kissed me like it was his mission in life. I've never been kissed like that. I want more.

Truth is, I want to be his, and not just for one wild night. But I need at least four hundred thousand dollars before I can quit this job, and I wish I were joking.

Four hundred thousand would pay off the townhouse and equipment, cover the rest of my tuition, and get me a decent used car. With enough saved, I could get through the postdoc years where I'm doing my hours required to become a licensed psychotherapist. Actually, six hundred thousand would be better given the postdoc years. It would be nice to not have to work two jobs in addition to the required patient hours.

But if the townhouse were paid off, my monthly expenses would drop drastically, so I could make it work if I had four hundred grand.

I think I want the security of a paid mortgage more than anything. A home that is truly mine. I imagine Chase sharing my home, and it's such a sweet fantasy I can't help but smile.

"What's that smile about?" Hank asks.

Hank likes to ask me about other men when we go private. I think one of his kinks might be cuckold, but his wife doesn't want sex with him, let alone anyone else, so I'm his substitute. I often make up stories for him about all the men I'm supposedly screwing, painting a picture for his mind, sometimes while masturbating, but usually not. He never turns on his camera and sometimes mutes when I'm spinning a tale like Scheherazade, so I have no idea if he takes sexual pleasure in the moment or saves it for later.

When he does talk, he pretends to get jealous and talks about punishing me for being unfaithful, but then he asks for more details. It really gets him going.

One thing that I appreciate about this arrangement is

there is no feeling of sexual intimacy with Hank. Not like I've felt with Falcon, because he's not the man I'm screwing in my mind. And I'll be honest, sixty-five-year-old men don't interest me, no matter how I play it online. I like men my age with wiry muscles who are perfectly capable of fucking me against a wall.

I smile for the camera. "I met someone," I say. "And I'm pretty sure he'll fuck like a god."

"You haven't slept with him yet?"

I realize I didn't tell the lie I usually do—of having had sex already—because I don't want to share the fantasy of Chase with anyone. It's my fantasy, and now that I've kissed him, it's his too. Ours.

It's not like playing with Falcon, when fantasies of Chase spurred my pleasure. I might have been thinking of Chase, but I was following Falcon's orders. He was the man fucking me in the moment.

With Hank, I'd be the one sharing my fantasy of the very real man I want to have sex with. A man I have kissed. A man who wants to have sex with me.

Hank doesn't get to have that. It's mine.

And this is why I've avoided dating for two years. I never figured out how to set up proper boundaries between Eden's sexuality and Desiree's.

"No," I say. "We haven't even kissed."

"Tell me about him."

I find myself incapable of spinning a story, and I won't tell him the truth. I'm not a very good camgirl tonight. He's not getting his money's worth.

"Enough about me, Hank. What's going on with you? How was the visit with the grandkids?"

He launches into a story about his ten-year-old grandson who's a Little League star in Missouri, and I make sure the relief I feel doesn't show on my face. I'm dressed demurely tonight, fully clothed, and glad Hank isn't in the mood to watch me touch myself.

We wrap up our session, and I debate logging off for the night. I'm not into it. This was a mistake. I'm mooning over Chase and already grieving our coming breakup. A relationship that never was.

I'm about to sign out when my eyes flick to the waiting room and see the only name that could keep me online.

Falcon.

And he's already dropped five hundred dollars into my account.

Guilt seizes me. I want Chase. I enjoy Falcon. I'm not even dating Chase, and yet it feels wrong to fantasize about him with Falcon moving forward. So is it cheating on Chase if I fantasize about Falcon while fucking him virtually?

But how is it cheating when Chase and I aren't in a relationship?

Falcon and I have an intimacy that definitely would be cheating if I were seeing another man. And it's that intimacy I crave from both men.

And sex. I really want sex from Chase. And more kissing. Lots more kissing.

I don't know what to do with this emotional tangle, but Falcon has paid me five hundred dollars for my company, so I owe him my time. I send him a link to a private room and position myself in front of the camera. I consider unbuttoning a few buttons, but decide against it.

We'll just let this late-night session take its natural course. If Falcon wants sex, I'll give it to him, I decide.

I don't *really* owe Chase anything, and Falcon paid up front. I literally owe him something.

Falcon's smooth, deep voice enters my bedroom through the speaker mounted above the camera. "You look beautiful as always, Desiree."

I smile. "Thank you. I'm surprised you're here so late."

"I could say the same to you."

Once again, I remember that it's much earlier for him. I'm the one keeping odd hours. "I had…an errand in the middle of my shift, so I decided to pull some late hours. A girl's gotta eat."

I never pretend I'm not doing this for the money. They know it, and they tip me to keep me here.

"I know. That's why I always tip up front. I want you to have everything you need. Always."

"Aren't you sweet?" I unbutton the top button of my blouse. He should get a peek.

"No!" he says sharply.

I rear back, surprised by his tone. "No?"

"I didn't pay you for sex. Not tonight."

There's an edge to his voice that feels like a jab. I can't help myself, and I say, "You don't want me anymore?"

But this isn't the pouty thing, the begging for compliments that some guys like. No. This pain is real. I've opened up to this man. I told him about my farce of a marriage. What if he's saying goodbye?

"I always want you, Desiree. From the first time I saw your face, I've wanted you. I will keep wanting you for the rest of my days."

"You sound so certain."

"I am."

"Then why don't you want me to undress for you?"

"I want something else from you tonight."

"You want to talk? To cuddle?"

"No. I want you to listen. And to see."

There's a pain in his voice and I don't even know why, but my heart begins to pound. This is important. Deep in my heart, I know everything is about to change, but for the life of me, I can't figure out why. "What's going on? What do you mean by *to see*?"

"I'm going to turn on my camera."

A jolt of pleasure hits me. I'm going to get to see Falcon.

I have literally stared at his dick pic for hours in the last week. Which is ridiculous. I mean, it might not even be his dick!

But I think the picture is real, and now I'm going to get to see the rest of him.

His camera is turned on, and my screen splits with equal-sized windows for each of us in the gallery. But his camera is covered so his rectangle is black.

He removes the cover, and it takes a half a second for the image to buffer and clear.

In that half second, my whole life does indeed change.

I feel shock at first. Then horror.

Chase's expression is unreadable. But his mouth says, "I'm sorry."

Rage grips me, and I lunge for the camera to cut the feed. Instead, I knock it over, and it tumbles onto the bed. I yank at the cord, pulling the plug from the wall. No power. No image.

But the computer is still running. I'm still logged in. I can hear him say, "Eden, please—" right before I snap my laptop closed.

Chapter Twenty

Chase stared at the blank screen for five full minutes. Maybe she would come back.

But he knew she wouldn't.

His heart still pounded in his chest. His lungs still took in oxygen and expelled carbon dioxide. But everything was numb. He figured some part of him wanted to cry, but he didn't know how to do that anymore. Didn't know if it was even possible to feel that deeply.

Or maybe it was the opposite. He was feeling too much. He was in overload, and his emotion sensors had shut down.

Ever since the chip was removed, that was how he thought of it. Like he was Data on *Star Trek: The Next Generation* and his emotion sensor was out of whack.

Funny thing was, as far as he knew, he'd only ever seen a handful of episodes of that show. He knew the main character names. Their rank. For some, even the planet they were from. But he couldn't remember a single plot.

Had he been a Trekkie in the Before Times?

Maybe.

All he knew was tonight, he'd been through the most

intense emotional spiral of his post-chip life and he was now literally shaking with the inability to process.

He studied his trembling legs.

Legs with muscle memory that meant even in his most disjointed moments, he could fight. Find release in the gym.

And right now they were trembling.

He pressed his hands on his thighs to try to stop the shaking and wondered if this was adrenaline overload. Usually after a fight, he was swamped with adrenaline and would go for the gym. But tonight, he'd been with Eden, so he'd kissed her, and that had been an entirely different kind of high.

But those ups and downs hadn't prepared him for revealing himself. For her reaction.

The utter shock in her beautiful eyes. The pain. The agony of the sounds she'd made as she attacked her camera as if it were a predator.

He'd done that to her.

The only person who he'd felt a connection to since the chip was removed. The only person who made him feel. And he'd done that to *her*.

He'd had moments in the last year—ever since he'd woken up in the hospital and Isabel had gently explained what had happened to him—when he'd wondered if his life was worth living.

Was his brain salvageable, or was he nothing more than a tool programmed to do a monster's bidding?

More than once, he'd gone into a spiral, and in his disassociated state, the idea of removing himself from this earthly plane had appealed. But his Raptor family had pulled him back from that edge each time.

And then, when he'd embarked on the mission to save teens from trafficking, it had helped to solidify his resolve not to let those sneaky, deceptive demons, who whispered his life was without merit, win.

And then he found Desiree, and his limited emotional repertoire opened up to include sexuality. Pleasure. Joy.

Had he now lost all that?

Had his deceit cost him the one person who made his existence better than rote?

After everything that had happened, Raptor was his family, but even so, there were only a handful of people he could truly trust with the darkest part of his soul.

A few days ago, Isabel had shared that she was pregnant. He couldn't reach out to her or do anything that put her in the crosshairs. Josh was in Oregon. Hawk didn't live in the compound anymore. Tricia was recovering from a traumatic brain injury.

There was only one person he could turn to when he was still pumped with adrenaline after a fight with three assailants and seeing a gun pressed to the temple of the only person who made him really feel, then being rejected by the same woman because of the lies he'd let her believe. Only one person who wouldn't ask questions, wouldn't press for details.

A person who felt equally awkward among humans and who was one of the few who'd known Chase in the Before Times, even before Godfrey stuck his claws in his brain.

Mothman had been at the Alaska compound when Chase was a new hire and something of a golden boy with his hand-to-hand combat skills. But the computer specialist had never fit in at the compound full of high-testosterone operatives and former special forces operators.

Mothman was gay and on the autism spectrum and had admitted to being quite lonely in the remote compound, where his dating prospects were even fewer than Chase's.

They'd formed a friendship in the early days when Chase's mind had still been intact. Later, when Mothman transferred to the Virginia compound, they'd resumed the friendship with another layer: Mothman wanted private hand-to-hand combat lessons so he didn't feel like such an outcast amongst the operatives.

Chase had agreed, and over the last year, Mothman's skills had grown.

Now Chase called in a long-standing agreement. His emotions were in turmoil, and he needed to do *something*. It didn't matter that it was after one a.m. He needed a friend, and he needed exertion.

His text was simple.

CHASE

Spar in the gym in ten minutes.

Chase could easily beat on a bag as he tried to figure out his emotions, but he knew Mothman would show up and be the friend he needed, just as Chase would do the same in the reverse situation.

Sure enough, when Chase stepped into the gym, Mothman was already there—hair sticking up because Chase had pulled him from sleep—but still present.

If there was anyone employed by Raptor who was more different from the members of Falcon team, it was Mothman, who preferred to go by the moniker of a mythical West Virginian monster to his own name, which might be the most telling thing about him.

In the last year, as Chase struggled to figure out emotions, he found himself looking to Mothman, who had similar struggles. They were more alike in that regard now than they had been when they first met.

They were also of similar age and height, but where Chase was wiry, Mothman was lanky. Where Chase used muscle, Mothman used brain.

Mothman could speak Klingon, while Chase wondered how he knew so much about Data and Captain Picard.

There was a lot Chase didn't know about himself. And he was afraid he never would find out.

He should be focusing on the whos and whys of the night, but for the moment, he was more focused on Eden's reaction and wondering if she'd ever speak to him again. And trying to figure out how to process it all.

The only thing he could be certain of when it came to his muddled mind was she was everything to him. Without her, he didn't know if he'd ever find a path to feeling again.

"I was thinking you need to work on your roundhouse," Chase said by way of introduction.

"Yeah. I'm sure it was my roundhouse that has you worried at two in the morning." But even so, Mothman ran through his warmup exercises to get his body loose, then positioned himself in front of a bag and offered up a few half-hearted kicks.

Friends really didn't get any better than that.

Chase figured this other feeling that was bubbling up inside was gratitude. He took a second standing bag, and they practiced in parallel. Twenty minutes later, they were both drenched in sweat and the workout was no longer halfhearted.

Coming here was a good call. He'd needed the physical exertion after the adrenaline from the fight and then the sexual windup that couldn't go anywhere. But working out alone would have been a bad idea. He could spiral into a frenzy and not be able to pull out. More than once in the last year, he'd ended up bloody and bruised when he couldn't manage the onslaught of emotions and turned to the gym for relief.

Mothman was here to protect him from himself, no questions asked.

Forty-five minutes after the workout began, Chase collapsed on the mat, breathing heavily. "Thanks, man. I needed that."

Mothman sat on the floor and leaned back against the padded wall, then took a long drink from his water bottle. "You wanna talk about it?"

Chase's mind swirled. He did and he didn't. But Mothman had a need to know and should have been told everything two weeks ago.

Finally, he said, "I fucked up. I've been holding back an important piece of information from you. I'm sorry."

"I assume you are referring to the fact that Eden O'Keeffe worked for CamDames."

Chase startled. "You knew?"

He nodded. "I ran a search on her the night of the coffee shop incident. I recognized Desiree from our research in the spring. She went off my radar when she started her own site, but I still have the data I'd gathered."

"Why didn't you tell me?"

"I knew you must have recognized her. That you chose not to tell me was your business. If I'd found anything alarming in her background, I'd have said something."

"I f-f-f screwed up. It f-ffelt wr-wrong." *Dammit.* He was stuttering with Mothman now? He took a deep breath and resumed speaking. "I wanted it to be a f-fluke she was there." He took a sip of water. *Relax.* This was Mothman. "I didn't want to violate her privacy."

"You would have asked me to do a full background on anyone else in that situation. That you didn't with Eden was all I needed to know." He paused, then added, "There's nothing wrong with you enjoying Desiree's site."

Chase absorbed that statement. Mothman knew and didn't judge. He didn't ask that Chase justify or explain. He just accepted.

Mothman had probably logged in to Eden's site both when they were first investigating CamDames and again in the last two weeks. Did it bother him that his friend had likely viewed the nude images she posted behind a paywall and might even have had a private session with her?

It didn't matter that Mothman was gay and likely wasn't the least bit attracted to her. That wasn't the issue. What he needed to figure out was moving forward, did he have an issue with men—some even men he knew—viewing the content of Desiree's site? Others within Raptor might have visited. Might have had private sessions with her. And they still could.

If he did have a problem with that, he'd have to let that shit go fast, because Desiree belonged to no one and Eden needed her income.

He considered it from all angles. It would only bother him, he realized, if Eden, the woman he knew in real life, offered herself to Mothman or another operative, but he couldn't imagine her doing that. She didn't even want to date Chase as long as she was working as Desiree, and their chemistry was through the roof.

Her whole reason for not dating was just this situation. It would be hard to find a guy who wouldn't care that she showed off her perfect body to men online for money.

Chase could deal with it. Things never would have gone to the next level between them if he hadn't met her in person. If he hadn't then gone online and initiated sessions that invited more intimacy, breaking down Desiree's carefully crafted distance.

If Eden would have him, he'd wouldn't have issues with her online job. He wouldn't continue to visit her site, however. It would test his mettle if he had to continue watching her flirt with other guys. But then, knowing she was his and his alone in the real world would take the sting from that.

If only he had even a modicum of faith she'd ever be his. He'd blown it when he didn't tell her who he was as soon as reasonably possible.

"I assume you don't want the intel I have on her," Mothman said.

"Definitely not. I won't take the last vestiges of privacy from her like that. If there's something she wants me to know, I want her to be the one to tell me, not hear it from you first."

"As I said, if there was anything alarming I'd have warned you."

"And that's all I need."

"You told her who you are tonight?"

"Yeah."

"I'm guessing we're here because it didn't go well."

"I suppose it went as well as could be expected under the circumstances."

"If she's gotten to know you at all in these last two weeks, I think she'll come around."

Chase had no such belief, but he thanked Mothman just the same.

"You good?" Mothman asked, rising to his feet.

"Yeah. Thanks. For babysitting me tonight. And for keeping Eden's secrets."

Mothman offered a hand and pulled Chase to his feet. "You know I've got your back."

*E*den cried for a solid hour before finally drifting off into a fitful sleep. She woke to a gray fall morning in a bleak mood.

She still hadn't figured out how to wrap her brain around the hurt of it all. Chase Johnston was the first man she'd been interested in in a long time. And Falcon was the first man she'd felt intimacy with. The fact that both men were one and the same shouldn't have surprised her, but it hadn't just surprised, it had devastated. The ongoing deception of being in Alaska. Had he stalked her? Had he known who she was eight months ago?

She jolted upright in her bed. Was Falcon Penny's stalker after all? But then, could she believe anything Penny had said? Had Penny really had a stalker?

Could she believe Chase?

Chase had been the one who saved her life last night, while Penny had set her up.

Hell. She *had* to face Chase today. They needed to track down Penny.

She wished she knew someone else at Raptor. Anyone other than Chase would do. Which brought to mind another question, who else at Raptor knew her secrets?

She forced herself to rise and shower and face the day. No answers waited for her beneath the blankets. She didn't have a shift at Vivace on Fridays because of her research assistant gig, and she'd scheduled to go to campus an hour early so she could take a long lunch break with Kelly.

Man, she'd give anything to be able to discuss this with Kelly. As a psychology student, Kelly would have great insight into the psychological aspects. It would be an interesting puzzle for Eden too if she weren't in the middle of it.

A long shower at least helped with the puffiness around her eyes from crying last night. She applied makeup to hide what remained and was out the door in forty-five minutes.

She scanned the streets on her short walk to the Metro, not entirely certain if she was looking for Chase or the guys from the garage last night. Did she need to fear for her safety? Or was last night really about Chase and she was mere bait?

As she looked for potential assailants or online liars, she realized she'd yet to begin to process her trauma over what had happened in the parking garage. Her reaction had been muted by the blow of Falcon's big reveal. Deep down inside, she was probably still trembling, but one trauma at a time appeared to be all she could handle.

When she arrived on campus, she collected the week's new candidates for the study from Dr. Dearborn's office, then dropped the files in the lab by the computer before going into the graduate student office to let Kelly know she'd arrived early as planned.

She found Kelly at her desk in her cubicle and dropped into the guest chair, then snitched a wrapped mini chocolate bar from the bowl that always sat next to Kelly's pen cup.

"You must be stressed if you're eating chocolate," Kelly observed.

It was well known among the students that Eden didn't indulge in treats very often. They just didn't have a clue that her motivation was keeping her body at an unnatural level of slenderness for her frame.

Today, Eden wouldn't worry about the extra calories. Stress hardly began to describe her state of mind. "Yup," she said, popping the candy in her mouth and reaching for a second one. This might be the only pleasure she ever had again. She'd take what she could get.

"What's going on?" Kelly asked.

Eden figured she had to give some kind of answer. "Guy trouble."

"Oh my God, you're finally dating again? Is it that hottie Raptor guy? Wait, it must be. You went to a restaurant with him three nights ago."

Given that Kelly was her fallback person to text and vice versa, there was no denying it. "Yeah."

"So what's wrong? His cheekbones too perfect? His eyes too broodingly handsome?"

Eden laughed. "Yes. That is precisely the problem."

"Man, I wish I had your problems." She leaned forward and said, "Please tell me he's way too good in bed too."

Eden rolled her eyes. She had no idea if he was good in bed…except, well, actually she did. Sort of. Falcon knew just what to say, just the right commands. And he always put her pleasure first.

Her face flushed at the memory.

"Oh my God. You're blushing! He's a sex god. I knew it."

"Who's a sex god?" Tobias asked from the cubicle opening. He smiled when his gaze met Eden's. "You're seeing someone? I thought you weren't in a good emotional place to get involved?"

Kelly crumpled up a piece of paper and tossed it at him. "C'mon. If you haven't figured it out by now, that was Eden's gentle way of saying she wasn't interested in you."

That was true enough. She just wished he'd get the hint and leave her alone. Sometimes she wondered if he hit on her just to make Evelyn hate her. Sometimes she thought Tobias enjoyed the mind games. Like they were all rats in his behavior laboratory.

She was really done with being subtle and participating in his unwelcome cheese maze. "It is true both that I wasn't interested and that I wasn't in a place to date." She gave Tobias a smirk because after all, he was the one who brought up the awkward subject.

Kelly held up a hand for a high five. She was probably even more tired of Tobias's cheese than she was, having been in the department two years longer than Eden.

Tobias slunk away as Kelly asked loud enough for

everyone in the open room of divided offices to hear, "So what's the problem with the new hottie?"

She made a face indicating she didn't want to talk in the far-from-private setting. She'd make something up when they were at lunch.

The double-life thing was damn tiring. Truth was it had been for some time, but it got a lot harder once she struck out on her own and no longer felt comfortable letting anyone into her home. She hadn't realized how isolating that would be on top of the lies.

Chase was the first person she'd had over since her workroom had been completed. She'd been so relieved he didn't ask for a tour or to check for intruders—which would have been reasonable given the situation—but now she knew why.

On one level, she realized that Chase could be the answer to her loneliness problem. He knew what she did for a living. He was attracted to her—the real her, not the siren on the computer screen. No, last night proved he was as attracted to her as she was to him.

She just had to figure out if she could trust him. At least *that* was a true enough kind of problem she could share with Kelly.

"I just wanted to let you know I got here early so I'll have time to catch lunch with you whenever you want to go," she said.

"Oh crap! I forgot we'd made plans. Dr. Dearborn, Dr. Howard, and I have a meeting at noon to go over the latest MRI scans for my study."

"Bummer," Eden said, meaning it. "Next week?"

"Yes. I promise I won't schedule any meetings."

She rose and headed to the door, and as she passed Tobias's cubicle, he called out, "Eden, wait."

She paused. "What's up?"

"There's a group of us going out for happy hour at five. Want to join us?"

"Sorry. Busy."

"Hot date with the sex god?"

She gave him a tight smile. They were all equals in this office, and they frequently talked about sex and dating—it was part of what they were studying, after all—but Tobias's obvious interest in her, and the fact that he continued trying to get her to go out with him after repeated nos, was irritating.

She fully expected that if she ever committed to a happy hour, she'd arrive to find that everyone mysteriously canceled and it was just the two of them. Or maybe Evelyn would arrive later just so she could have a jealous meltdown.

Eden swore to herself that next semester, when she was back full-time, she'd let him have it if the games continued. "It's really none of your business, Tobias. Have fun tonight." She left the office without a glance in his direction.

In the lab, she settled in front of the computer. For the next four hours, she immersed herself in work, going over the files of children who were candidates for the autism study. This study was intended to identify markers for depression in children on the spectrum and collect data on how best to work with children who were likely to be poor candidates for antidepressants as their brain chemistry was different from children not on the spectrum and there might not be any safe or effective drugs available.

The study would include functional neuroimaging. Eden didn't plan to pursue cognitive neuroscience, but it was one of her areas of interest, and work on this study was a great opportunity for her to learn more about brain imaging and its applications while making a little money as a research assistant during the semester she wasn't taking classes.

She was deep in her work, having managed to block out

the nightmare followed by the heartache of last night. She needed this reminder of her life goals. She doubted cognitive neuropsychology was where she'd end up, but she wanted to learn everything she could about it as she chose her precise path.

She was so engrossed in the job, she must not have heard the door open, because she startled when Tobias spoke from behind her. "You're still here."

Her heart thundered. Was it possible he'd tiptoed in, intending to scare her? It was too late to hide her reaction, and she hated that she might have given him just what he wanted in scaring her.

She turned to face him. Better to call him out than to let him pretend it was an accident. "Was that fun for you?"

He smirked. "Kind of. Yeah."

Tobias was a good-looking guy. He was wicked smart. He'd made it more than clear when they first met that he came from money. She guessed that when it came to women, he'd pretty much always gotten what he wanted, and it vexed him that Eden wasn't interested.

She guessed that Tobias, for all his study of the human brain, didn't understand why his own was so fixated on her. Even the smartest of men could be so damn simple.

"What do you want, Tobias?"

He stepped in front of her, invading her space. She wished she hadn't swiveled the chair around to face him, because now she was trapped. His smile was downright nasty. "I was online the other night when I came across the most interesting website."

She kept her face blank. She wouldn't let him get any satisfaction from this conversation, any hint that what he was about to accuse her of was true.

"Here's the deal, Eden. You give it out for money online. You can give it out for me. I'll even pay you, because I'm generous that way. You refuse, and I'll tell Dr. Dearborn and you'll lose your nice, cushy research assistant job. Probably be kicked out of the program."

She gave him a tight smile even as her heart pounded. She could not let him see any kind of reaction as her body flooded with adrenaline. "I have no clue what you're talking about, but it sounds like you're trying to blackmail me into sex and are soliciting prostitution at the same time. Not only are both of those a crime, but my sex god of a boyfriend, who happens to be a Raptor operative with superhuman fighting skills, will happily kick your ass."

"Right. You expect me to believe that bullshit? You don't have a boyfriend. You barely even have friends."

"Chase is real, all right. Go ahead and google him. His last name is Johnston with a T. You'll especially enjoy the story about the guy in Portland who needed a whole lot of stitches after coming at Chase with a knife. And I'll point out that at the time, Chase was unarmed. Now get the fuck out of this office, and don't you ever try to threaten me again."

"There's nothing to stop me from going to Dearborn."

She just stared at him, blank faced.

He wouldn't assault her in this room. Dearborn's office was three doors down.

She would scream and dig her fingernails into his cheek and make sure there was evidence of his assault all over the lab. But that didn't mean her heart wasn't pounding. Didn't mean she had nothing to fear in the moment.

She didn't think he'd go to Dearborn. After all, she could turn around and point out he was trying to coerce her into sex. That wasn't an admirable trait in a psychotherapy PhD candidate. He was as likely to lose as her.

Problem was, she'd lose more, even though her job wasn't illegal and what she did with her body on her own time was nobody's business.

Could Dearborn kick her out of the program? Not for that, but it was possible he'd work to find another reason.

Tobias gave her a last hard glare and backed out of the laboratory. She stared at the door and waited for her heart rate to slow down.

This was not what she needed right at this moment when her life was in upheaval. Last night, someone had tried to *abduct* her, for fuck's sake.

There was one thing she needed to do before anything else. Just in case Tobias went straight to Dearborn. She pulled out her cell phone and logged in to her site, then took the entire, beautiful, money-making endeavor offline.

Desiree was taking an unplanned vacation, and there was nothing she could do about it.

Chapter Twenty-One

What did it mean that Desiree's site was down? Was she quitting? Had something else happened? He'd planned to give her space, to wait for her to reach out to him. But now he couldn't. He had to check on her. They needed to talk about Penny.

He texted her.

CHASE

Your site's down. Everything okay?

She replied almost immediately.

EDEN

Fine. Technical difficulties is all.

He didn't believe that for a second, but he wouldn't get anywhere with her by pushing for answers she didn't want to give.

Anything I can help with?

EDEN

Not at the moment.

CHASE

We need to talk.

No. *You* need to talk. You need to tell me the truth. Did you stalk me? Run a background check on me?

No. Never. Not even after the explosion when I should have asked Mothman to do it. It felt wrong. I couldn't violate your privacy like that. I swear.

He doubted she believed him, but he had to try. Later, he'd tell her that Mothman had done the search, but he didn't know what he'd found. But that kind of conversation had to be in person. There was too much nuance that would be lost in texts.

When she didn't answer, he tried again.

Please meet with me? You pick the place. I need to ask you about Penny.

There was a long wait for her response, during which Chase tried and failed to identify the emotions he was feeling. He decided to name whatever it was *tornado* because it summed up what was happening in his brain quite well even if it didn't hit upon an actual feeling.

It occurred to him he could use a cloud system for everything moving forward because at least clouds made sense. For example, today had started out very stratus but had shifted to cumulus when she responded to his first text. But now things were very, very tornadoey.

At last, sunlight peeked through the funnel as he read her

reply.

EDEN

Fine. Since I am apparently taking the night
off, we can meet at my place. Better that we
have this conversation in private. You're
bringing dinner. I want Thai food. There's a
good restaurant a few blocks from my house.

He smiled at her demands as the cloud began to turn
fluffy and white.

CHASE

Anything in particular you want?

I'll submit an order online. Tell me now if you
don't like spice.

No more than two stars for me. When do you
want me to show up?

I'm on the Metro now. Let's say six, to give
me time to decompress.

He wondered where she'd gone that she needed to
decompress, but again, he wasn't about to press her on
anything except the identity and location of Penny.

Fine. See you then.

He tucked away his phone and looked at his watch. It was
only four. He was done with his one-on-one training sessions
for the day. The best thing for him to do to kill time was go to
the gym. Physical exertion was the only thing that kept his
brain from tying up in knots.

Spending too much time obsessing over how he was going

to convince Eden to trust him might just destroy what was left of his cumulonimbus mind.

$\mathcal{E}$den paced her apartment, wishing she'd told Chase to come over earlier.

Better to get it over with. Better not to have time to think.

She was still trying to sort Chase from Falcon in her head. The confession of torture and abuse. That had to be real.

It was the kind of thing he would feel safer revealing as anonymous Falcon.

As scared and angry and hurt as she'd been, she felt new emotions surging to the surface. Empathy for the pain he'd gone through, warmth that he'd trusted her with his story after he'd met her in person.

It struck her then. He'd trusted her with his deepest wound after they'd met. She hadn't been an anonymous camgirl to him in that moment. And he'd chosen to tell her.

She had to proceed with caution around that aspect. He'd shared something she'd bet he hadn't told anyone he didn't have to—prosecutors, psychologists for the prosecution—but he'd likely never volunteered the information to anyone else.

As angry and hurt as she was, she needed to make sure he felt safe with her knowledge.

She remembered him telling her he hadn't shared the letter he received from his abuser and her suspicion it contained information he didn't want anyone else to see. There was so much about his abuse he had yet to process.

She couldn't turn her back on him there. Because dammit, she *cared* about Falcon.

She cared about Chase.

Should she continue seeing Falcon online? Did that even make sense?

But if online was the only way he could truly talk to her, maybe she should. As Falcon, he didn't stutter. Would he be forced to talk to her in a whisper when they were face-to-face tonight?

The brain scientist in her found that piece fascinating, but he wasn't an object of study and she couldn't be thinking of him as such.

It was true that she'd kept notes on her clients from the start in addition to documenting the changes within herself as she embraced a freer sexuality than she'd ever imagined, but she'd always been careful to code the notes to protect the client's anonymity. She had the basics of what they'd shared for the why of them seeking a camgirl for companionship and what they gained from the voyeuristic relationship. She knew for certain she hadn't added to her notes on Falcon since before he returned from his business trip.

His business trip.

Oh. Wow. It all clicked together. He'd gone to Portland to help train counterprotesters at the white supremacist rallies. He'd been there for the takedown of the White Patriot group. Had, in fact, played a key role in the arrests that were made.

Part of her wanted to pull out her old notes on Falcon and look for signs about his work. Hints about the abuse he'd suffered, but that felt wrong. He was Chase now, and she didn't want to face him armed with the psychological profile she'd been building on him for the last several months.

Instead, she paced her living room, waiting for six o'clock. Bracing herself for seeing him again. With each step, she found her anger and hurt diminished.

Last night, he'd kissed her against the wall at the bottom of her stairs, and she'd wanted him more than she'd ever wanted anyone in her life.

There was raw heat whenever they neared each other. Was it because he'd responded to Desiree instinctively that first time they met in person? Or was it their undeniable chemistry? Did they have a natural combustion point?

If her brain was scanned using fMRI when he was nearby, how lit would the results be? Hook him up to the same scan and would his brain show matching fireworks?

If Chase wanted her—*Eden*, not Desiree—he could solve a lot of her problems. She wanted sex but wouldn't sleep with a guy who didn't know about Desiree. Check.

The guy couldn't have issues with her job. Check.

Of course, that was a guess, but if he did have a problem, he'd be a pretty big hypocrite, and she didn't sleep with hypocrites.

She'd been feeling so lonely these last few months, and then Falcon reappeared, and she'd gotten the fake cuddling she craved. But with Chase, she could have *real* cuddling.

Was she crazy to even consider this after what he'd withheld from her? Or would she be crazy not to go for it?

She glanced at her watch. He would be here in twenty-five minutes.

She sent him a text.

EDEN

Adding one more item to the shopping list. I want Häagen-Dazs ice cream. Pralines and Cream.

*C*hase stared at the text in bemusement. Was a demand for ice cream a good sign or bad? Would he show up at her door with dinner and dessert only to have her take the food, then kick him to the curb?

He couldn't exactly blame her if she did.

He faced the complex puzzle of priorities on the short drive to her place. If he bought the ice cream first, it would start to melt sooner, and if he ended up waiting for the takeout order, it could sit in the car too long on what had proven to be a warm early-fall day. He didn't know he was going ice cream shopping when he left the compound, or he'd have raided the supplies for an insulated bag and ice.

If he got the ice cream after the takeout, their hot meal would cool before he reached her townhouse.

It wasn't exactly the most difficult problem, but it was the kind of thing that he found he had to process carefully since having the chip removed. Basic logic came harder and was frustrating as hell.

Scary, even.

Each time he struggled to process a simple decision like this, he had to wonder if he could still be a functional adult. He could work for Raptor because his job was physical and he'd been building the muscle memory required since he was a toddler. His body wouldn't fail him.

His mind was a different matter. He'd briefly tried living on his own but ended up back at the compound where basic living decisions, including most meals, were handled for him.

Sometimes he felt like he was a fucking toddler again. Only now he wasn't training his brain to manage physical reflexes. No, he was learning the most basic adult functions.

He also realized in this moment how much his coworkers had been coddling him over the years. They'd probably figured out that he stressed too much over ice cream first vs. hot food first and never left decisions like that up to him.

He pulled into the grocery store parking lot, finding the decision made because the supermarket was on the way to the restaurant, not the other way around. This was a factor he probably should have considered in the first place.

Who knew there would be so many variables to picking up dinner and dessert?

Inside the store, he faced another dilemma. Eden's message said "Pralines and Cream," but the store didn't have that flavor. They had Bourbon Praline Pecan and two flavors with cream in the name. But he didn't think Rosé and Cream or Cookies and Cream were what she wanted.

He googled Häagen-Dazs flavors on his phone and discovered Pralines and Cream had been discontinued.

Now what? He could text her a photo and ask her what to buy. Was that a normal thing to do? Or did it show indecisiveness? Weakness?

He leaned his head against the clear glass freezer door. He could fight off three goons at once and send two of them to the hospital, but he didn't know how to buy ice cream for a…date?

No. Not a date. A meeting with food.

There was only one logical solution. He grabbed a pint of every flavor that included the word praline or cream. But not cream as in *ice cream*, or he'd have to buy the entire aisle. Which, for a moment, almost seemed logical. But maybe that was because he was hungry.

He paused on that thought. He should pick out a flavor for himself. After all, he was supplying the food part of their meeting with food. He could pick something he liked too.

What did he like?

He couldn't remember. When did he last have ice cream? He had no idea.

Better start simple. Find out what he liked. He grabbed a pint of strawberry. His gaze landed on a pint of Pineapple Coconut Häagen-Dazs, and his mind returned to the weeks he'd spent in Hawaii at Rav's private estate between working in Alaska and moving to the DC area to work for Raptor's home office.

He didn't know it at the time, but Parks already had her claws into him, but she hadn't yet put the chip in his head. Those weeks on Kauai, he'd been gloriously free of her. He'd loved every minute of the peaceful break. And he'd had pineapple ice cream on the beach, looking out at the vast blue ocean with the hot sun on his skin. He'd felt like the whole world was before him, his mind was clear—clearer even than it was now, he realized—and he'd been starting over, recovered from the nightmare of his months in Alaska.

Until he met Desiree, it might have been the last time he felt deeply happy. Full of hope. It was an emotion-infused memory that was all his own. Parks hadn't messed with it because there wasn't anything sexual about it.

He put the pineapple-flavored ice cream in the basket, wondering if taste could deliver memories with the same power as scent.

The Thai food pickup went smoothly, and he realized how ridiculous it was to have made it so complex in his mind.

Would he ever be normal?

He'd bet a shrink would say there was no such thing as normal, but he had no intention of ever seeing a shrink again, so he was on his own figuring it all out.

He pulled into Eden's driveway, and the garage door opened automatically. She was inviting him to park inside. There was a metaphor there, but he would do his best to face her tonight and have the conversation they needed without showing signs of how much he wanted her.

She could well hate him.

He needed to assume her feelings toward him were on the hate end of the spectrum and work from there. Any movement to bridge the emotional chasm that separated them would have to come from her. All he could do was offer his apology and tell her the truth about everything.

Even his messed-up mind.

He climbed from the vehicle and grabbed the two bags of Thai food—apparently, she too was hungry—and the grocery bag full of ice cream pints and entered the interior switchback stairwell. She wasn't there, so he locked the interior door and started up the stairs. She had an alarm keypad by the front door to reset the alarm.

He entered her apartment, but she wasn't in the living room or kitchen.

"Eden?" he called out.

"Put the ice cream in the freezer and leave the food on the counter."

He did as instructed, then paced the room, waiting for her next command. He paused by the front door to check the alarm system. Fully engaged. Good.

He liked that she was careful.

But then, he liked everything about her. He wished he knew what to say to convince her he was sorry. Or explain that his brain struggled with ice cream purchases, so the idea of him properly tackling how to tell his favorite camgirl that he was a pathetic guy who paid her money to do dirty things online for his pleasure was beyond him.

And that might be the crux of it. His biggest fear. That she found her clients pathetic. That she secretly looked down on them. Even despised them. Despised him for what he made her do. It didn't fit anything he knew about her. He knew damn well she'd enjoyed their sessions. She'd opened up to him. But the fear remained.

After all, he *was* pathetic. Broken.

Ice cream incompetent, even.

He'd bypassed all the basic cloud metaphors and gone

straight to cat four hurricane status. His brain was now buffeted by wind.

His deepest, darkest fear surfaced under the onslaught of the gale. He'd told her what to do, and she'd obeyed because he'd paid her. Was he any different from Parks? Was he, in fact, *her* Parks?

"Chase?" Her voice came from the end of the hall.

"Yeah?"

"I need your help. Come into my room."

He strode down the short hall, his heart pounding as he approached the eye of the storm. He paused before the door, then took a deep breath and pushed it open.

There before him was Eden, lying on top of the king-sized bed, wearing a sheer purple teddy—one he'd never seen before—with both of her hands bound to the headboard in padded, matching purple wrist cuffs.

"I seem to have found myself tied up. Can you help me?"

Chapter Twenty-Two

The look on Chase's face made the hurry and difficulty she'd had in cuffing herself after resetting the alarm worth it. Thankfully, the cuffs had clips she was able to lock in one-handed, but it hadn't been easy, and she'd had to take a moment to catch her breath and prepare herself before calling him into the room.

And now he stood in her doorway, eyes wide with surprise as his gaze traveled over her body. His gaze returned to her face, and the heat was unmistakable. Which was good, because if this didn't turn him on, she doubted anything would.

"B-but this is j-j-just a meeting with food."

She raised a brow. "A meeting with food?"

His eyes narrowed as if he were focusing inward. When he spoke, he didn't bother with the whisper, but his words were clear. "This was supposed to be a meeting. Not a date."

"What if I said I want it to be a date?"

Studying his face as she was, she caught the exact moment when he realized she was echoing his own words from the other night back to him. But still, the confusion remained in his eyes.

"But—you—I..." His nostrils flared as his gaze roamed her body. "I screwed up. And you were rightfully hurt. And angry."

"Those are both true. But the way I see it, there are more truths for us to explore. One is that there was no way for you to tell me the first night we met that you'd recognized me. Not without revealing me to Tony, which I didn't want. And definitely not when we were alone in the car together, because I probably would have panicked."

He nodded. "And then when I went online, you said you wanted to fuck me. *Me.* And there was no way I could bow out of that private session. Or ruin it by telling you who I was."

She licked her lips. She wore just light gloss and makeup. Tonight, she was Eden. "What did it do to you, to hear me talk about how I wanted to take you to a hotel room and have my way with you?"

He stepped into the room, stopping at the foot of the bed. "It was the most erotic moment of my life. Until this one."

"Do you like this? Me tied up?"

"Very much."

She'd suspected as much. He liked to be in control. It probably had to do with the abuse he'd suffered. With the cuffs, he was assured she wouldn't touch him unless he wanted to be touched.

The bondage set was for sexual play, and she could get out of it easily if she wanted to. But it gave her limits. A reminder to keep her hands to herself until he was ready.

Plus, it would be fun. She liked the way he played.

She nodded toward the padded cuffs at the foot of the bed. They were two ends of a long strap that went between the box spring and mattress because the bed didn't have a footboard to hook the straps to. "If you want to cuff my ankles, keeping my legs open for you, you can." She spread her legs as she spoke, so he'd see the position she'd be in.

She'd exposed herself like this—not with the bondage toys, but still offering her body to men she couldn't see— hundreds of times online. Even so, her heart pounded as she offered herself up for real for the first time.

She was both exhilarated and a little scared.

He'd seen her naked. He'd seen her come. He'd made her come as much as he could from…not thousands of miles away, as she'd thought, but a dozen. Still, a dozen miles or a thousand, it was a long-distance orgasm they'd shared.

"We've had sex online. I want the real thing now. I want to feel you inside me. I want your kisses. I want to go down on you. And afterward, I want the cuddling. Some things are negotiable—if there's anything you don't want to do, just say the word. The one exception is the cuddling. If we fool around, you aren't walking out on me afterward."

"I'm fine with cuddling."

"And the rest?"

His brow furrowed in gorgeous confusion. "I feel like I should warn you that dinner is getting cold." He shook his head, like he felt ridiculous. "Never mind. That's probably not important."

He was adorably flustered.

"That's what microwaves are for. We can eat in bed after I've had my way with you. And then I'll lick my favorite ice cream from your chest."

His face fell. "Um, Pralines and Cream was discontinued. I got you a bunch of other flavors, though, including a praline pecan one."

That made her smile. "As long as I have ice cream and you, I'll be happy." She nudged the cuff with her foot. "Do you want this?"

He lifted it, running his thumb over the plush padded band. She wanted his thumb to do that to her. He dropped it on the bed and wrapped his fingers around her ankle. His big hand circled it completely. The touch was sensuous, his thumb brushing over her skin just like she wanted.

"No ankle cuffs," he said. "You need to be free to move. To react." He met her gaze. "Why the cuffs at all?"

"I figured…you'd like to be in control a hundred percent."

His face flushed with emotion. He murmured something that sounded like "Sirocco," then nodded and took a deep breath. "You trust me? This much?"

"I do. I'll tell you if I don't like something. I don't mess around with safe words. 'No' means *no*. Role-playing that I don't want something and doing it anyway is not my kink."

He nodded. "It's not mine either."

"No spanking or choking. Any hint of that and we're done. For good."

He nodded again. "Also not my kink."

She pointed with her chin to the bedside table. "Condoms are there. Along with water. Hydration is important."

He laughed. "You've thought of everything." He bent her leg, planting her foot on the bed and stroked upward to the back of her knee. His touch was light. Gentle, even. And it lit her right up.

"One last rule," she said in a breathier voice than she'd planned. "No blindfolds. I've been waiting for a long time to see your body. If I can't touch you, I at least get to look."

"Deal." He yanked his shirt over his head, revealing his ripped body, every bit as lean and muscled as she'd imagined.

"One more stipulation—"

"I thought the blindfold thing was the last rule."

"Not a rule. Stipulation. At some point in the next forty-eight hours, you are going to fuck me against a wall."

"Sweetheart, I can do that in the next ten minutes if you want."

"Not yet. Now get naked."

He sat on the edge of the bed and removed his boots followed by his socks, then rose and undid his belt buckle and dropped his jeans and underwear unceremoniously to the floor.

Instinctively she tried to reach out and touch him but came up against the bond at her wrist. Damn. What had she been thinking limiting herself this way? Her first time with a real male body in her bedroom in over two years, and she couldn't touch him.

But still, he was a feast for her eyes, and the moment was magnificent.

His smile was knowing and sexy as he stroked his cock. "You want this?"

She nodded and opened her mouth, hoping he'd take the hint and let her lick him. Taste him. If she weren't tied down, he'd be in her hands already. Maybe in her mouth.

He stroked his hard length again. He stood so beautifully before her, sinewy muscles, narrow waist. Dark chest hair trailing down in a line to his perfect erect penis.

Yes, the photo he'd sent her had been real.

She licked her lips again.

He chuckled. "Never fear, Eden, you'll get to touch me. Taste me. Eventually." His eyes narrowed, wicked and hot. "But first, I get to do all the dirty things I've been fantasizing about with you for months."

His voice was confident, firm. Just like Falcon. No hint of a stutter.

She was going to have both Chase and Falcon. Hot operative and dark lover. This was going to be utterly glorious.

He circled to the foot of the bed and climbed on, spreading her legs. He stroked her inner thighs with his fingers, his tongue following along on her left thigh until he reached her center, which was covered by a sheer panel of fabric held together with two small snaps.

He flicked the closure, and the taut fabric separated, revealing her pussy. His gaze left the place between her legs and met hers. "I've dreamed of smelling you. Of tasting you, for so long." His tongue spread her lips and dipped inside before moving up to find her clit, where the hot, wet strokes caused her to buck with pleasure. He then sucked her clit into his mouth, and she let out a whimpering groan.

He'd taken her from zero to a hundred with just a few flicks of his tongue. She was mesmerized, watching his head between her legs. He looked up, his gaze meeting hers as his mouth teased her. She wanted to close her eyes and sink into the pleasure, but she also wanted to see him. See her own body as he did the thing she so desperately wanted. And looking into his eyes as he toyed with her clit was intense beyond words.

She'd had months of fantasies that included Falcon licking her pussy, and two weeks of imagining Chase going down on her. The reality of having him at last had her straining against the cuffs. She wanted to stroke his head. She wanted to pull his mouth up to hers and kiss him. She wanted his hands on her breasts. She wanted everything all at once. She needed his hard length in her mouth.

"Chase," she finally rasped. "Let me taste you."

He raised his head. "You're sure? While your hands are bound?"

"Yes. I need to touch you. I need to feel what I do to you on my tongue, if not in my hand." She was absolutely desperate for him. She wanted to lay claim to that heavy erection. Hers. She did that to him.

He wanted her and only her. Even knowing what she did for a living.

He moved to her left side and scooted up the bed. Her head was propped on a pillow at a slight angle. She turned toward him and opened her mouth. He teased her lips with the tip of his penis. She licked at him until finally he slid the head inside, and she sucked, tasting his precum as he filled her.

He was slick, thick, and hot against her tongue, and the sound he made as she took him deep into the back of her throat was as thrilling as the look on his face when he'd stepped into her bedroom to see her splayed out for him.

"Eden." His voice was a ragged whisper. Her name reverent, like he was giving thanks.

She said *you're welcome* by stroking his length with her tongue as she slid her mouth as far along the shaft as she could take him. She sucked and licked and slid, and the feel of his hard cock against her tongue was a pleasure she'd been longing for.

He pulled back, leaving her mouth, his breathing heavy. This from a man who hadn't been winded after taking on three brutes in a parking lot.

He met her gaze. "Seeing my cock in your mouth… It's the hottest thing I've ever seen in real life."

"And what's the hottest thing you've ever seen that wasn't in real life?"

"You coming as I talked to you."

"Wait until you see me come as you fuck me."

He laughed. "I don't think I'm going to have to wait long for that."

"Better not. I'm going insane here." She wiggled on the bed. "I want this teddy off. I want your mouth on my breasts. I want you inside me."

"I thought I was in charge here."

"I promise I'll make freeing me from the teddy worthwhile."

"Darling, you make everything worthwhile. You've been my reason for breathing." He paused and held her gaze, his hazel eyes intense. "Desiree brought me back to life. Showed me I could feel."

His words made her belly drop. She could see from the look on his face that it wasn't hyperbole. He meant it.

"Kiss me," she whispered.

His mouth found hers, and his tongue slipped inside. His kiss was deep and intense. As intimate as the other sexual acts they'd just shared. As he kissed her, she felt his arm trail up along hers. He grasped her wrist and felt around, and a moment later, the plastic clip that attached the padded cuff to the headboard popped free.

He'd given her the use of one hand.

He raised his head and said, "Touch me. However you want. I trust you."

Her eyes misted at that. This was meant to be raw, intense sex, fulfilling needs they both had. Nothing more.

But it was so much more.

With her arm freed, she was able to roll to one side, facing him. He shifted so her bound arm rested beneath the crook of his neck and none of his weight pressed on the limb.

Their bodies were aligned lengthwise. She ran her hand down his bare back as his mouth covered hers again. She slid her tongue between his lips and stroked and explored as her hand caressed his smooth skin, moving down his back to his narrow waist and lower, to cup his perfect ass.

From there, she moved to explore his hip, abs, chest, and shoulder, only to move down again to take his thick erection in her palm. He groaned as she stroked him.

She released his mouth and shifted back to watch his face as her hand slid along his shaft. He'd closed his eyes, and his face was utterly beautiful as he gave himself over to the pleasure of her touch.

She was so utterly grateful she could give him this.

His eyes opened, and her belly fluttered at the hot intensity in his gaze. She brushed her lips over his and whispered, "I think you're the most beautiful man I've ever seen."

He stroked her cheek, tucking her hair behind her ear. "You will always be the most beautiful woman in any room. And I'm talking about Eden. Desiree is beautiful too. But Eden? You're breathtaking."

The reverence in his voice combined with the heat in his eyes triggered an intense rush of emotion. She slid her free hand up his chest as she kissed him and whispered, "Make love to me."

For a moment, she worried he'd react negatively to the phrase. The words had slipped out. It was Eden talking, not Desiree. Desiree didn't know heads or tails of making love.

Eden wasn't entirely sure she understood it either, but with Chase…those were the words that came to her lips.

He didn't react badly. In fact, he reacted *bestly*, his eyes burning with heat as he smiled and then kissed her tenderly as he nudged her onto her back again. His hips settled between her thighs, then he reached for a condom from the nightstand. He rose to his knees, freeing both hands to tear open the packet, but before he did so, he frowned at the purple teddy she still wore.

"How am I supposed to get that off you while you're tied up?"

"Velcro along the sides."

He smiled. "Brilliant."

The fastener was high quality, a thin discreet strip from armpit to hip on each side that separated easily when he tugged them apart, and she was freed from the tight garment she'd never worn before the camera because it was her favorite and she'd wanted to save something for Eden.

He'd seen her breasts dozens of times in the last eight

months, but this was the first time he could touch her, and the feel of his mouth on her nipples was yet another pleasure she realized she'd missed.

She reached between them and stroked his cock again as he played with her breasts. He raised his head and picked up the condom again. He ripped open the wrapper and placed the circle over the tip of his penis. Her free hand took over and rolled it down his length.

Then he was between her thighs, his hard, sheathed cock next to her opening. He slid a finger, then two inside her. His thumb stroked her clit, and she closed her eyes and let out a low groan as pleasure rocked her.

She opened her eyes to see the hungry look on Chase's face. Their gazes locked as he removed his fingers from her body and took his erection in hand to probe her opening. The tip penetrated, then he planted his fist beside her head and thrust. His thick cock slid deep, filling her as she'd so desperately needed.

He took her slow at first, his gaze never leaving hers. She didn't dare close her eyes. After months of longing to see him, the pleasure was more intense with the heady eye contact.

She made breathy sounds as he thrust inside her, the nails of her free hand lightly raking across his back as she rocked her hips in time with his.

He increased the pace of his thrusts, his body seeming to anticipate her needs as she wanted more, faster. Harder. It was their first time together, but also not, so it didn't surprise her that he seemed to know instinctively what she liked. He understood her rhythm. Her sounds. He probably knew her breathing patterns.

His thumb returned to her clit, again anticipating exactly what she needed. The feel of him inside her combined with the stroke of his thumb forced her to close her eyes, lost in the buildup to climax. She let out a low groan.

His breathing shifted, and she knew he was close. Probably as close as she was. He stroked her in and out with just the right amount of friction and speed. The buildup was intense as he played her body like a virtuoso. Then he held her at the precipice for a mind-blowing amount of time, all while sliding within her, building his own pleasure.

She whimpered with need, and he increased the pressure, sending her over. She came hard. Like a dam breaking. Like the earth moving. There was no metaphor that quite explained the intensity as pleasure washed over her. As she came, she felt and heard him plummet over the same edge.

She opened her eyes to see his beautiful face contorted with ecstasy as he thrust one last time while letting out a loud pleasured groan.

Spent, he paused and caught his breath, both arms still fisted on either side of her head as he held his body above hers. His eyes remained closed as he breathed deeply.

She stroked her free hand down his back, letting out a blissful sigh. After a moment, he reached up and unclipped her other arm, then rolled to his side, taking her with him, still inside her. He kissed her neck, then buried his face there. His body shuddered again, and she realized he was containing a sob.

Chase shifted so he slid from her body, then he pulled her close again. His emotions were overflowing. Out of control. He kept his face buried in her neck, breathing in her warm scent as his body quaked and his tears dampened her skin.

She knew he was crying. She had to. She slid her fingers through his hair. Stroked his back.

He raised his head, allowing her to see the tears in his eyes. His heart twisted when he saw the tears in hers.

This had been so much more than sex, for both of them.

But he had a feeling her tears stemmed from concern for him. He needed to explain.

"Ever since I've been…*free* of the brainwashing, emotions have been hard for me to manage. To even understand. Because for two years, I didn't get to feel. And suddenly, the restraint comes off, and it's like riding a bike without training wheels, when you never learned how to balance. But I *did* know how to balance once. It's just that the memories of how to ride were taken away. Or scrambled. So, in my memories, I still don't know which emotions were mine and which were hers."

She stroked his cheek, not saying anything. She was giving him time to organize his thoughts, which he was thankful for. She knew hardly anything about what had happened to him, but she always gave him space to think when they talked, like his coworkers at Raptor did. But they knew why he needed time. Her patience was one of the many things that made her amazing and just right for him.

"What happened between us just now, it's the first time I've felt the full range of sexual desire and everything else wrapped up in it that's all my own. My feelings. My thoughts. She destroyed all my memories of sex from before. But being with you… This is mine. Ours. She wasn't part of this."

Eden smiled as another tear spilled down her cheek. "I'm glad I could give you that. That we could share this." She kissed the tears from his cheeks, then brushed her lips over his.

"There's something else," he said. He stroked a thumb over her tear. A tear she shed for him. "I haven't been able to feel the highs and lows of emotions at all. It's felt like there's been some kind of barrier. Without the highs or lows, I haven't been able to cry. I've been *numb*. Totally and completely." He pressed his mouth to hers, kissing her deeply. The kiss was meant to show her how he really felt. The intensity he was feeling right that moment.

He raised his head to look into her beautiful eyes, which were now clouded with passion again as his kiss did the job of dispelling sadness. "I want you to know these are the first tears I've cried since I woke up in the hospital and found out what had been done to me. And Eden, these are tears of pure fucking joy."

Chapter Twenty-Three

$\mathcal{E}$den's face lit up like a star and Chase's heart swelled as she pulled his head down for another deep kiss. Freed of her restraints, she pushed him to his back and lay on top of him, kissing him like he was oxygen to starved lungs, and he loved every damn moment.

He was skin to skin with a beautiful woman who made him feel alive. He'd never imagined he could have this. Not even in his wildest fantasies did he think he was capable of it physically, let alone worthy.

That Eden could forgive him after what he'd done, that she could still want him and offer herself like she had. It was mind-blowing.

She raised her head, releasing his mouth. Her hair hung down, brushing his cheek. He gazed up into her face and tucked the soft dark strands behind her ear.

There was so much he wanted to say, including words that would probably terrify her. His brain might not be good at processing emotions or figuring out what to do, but he knew better than to say *that* now.

He wasn't foolish enough to believe he'd get more than a

few days with her. She'd invited him into her bed to fulfill a temporary need. Fine with him. He'd take anything and everything she was willing to give.

"What do you say we have dessert first?" Her voice was throaty. Sultry. But not Desiree's sexy tones he'd heard many times. No. This was pure Eden.

"I thought we just did?"

She laughed. "Oh no. I've got plans for my ice cream."

"I need to clean up and get rid of this condom first."

She nodded toward the attached bathroom as she removed the padded cuffs from her wrists. "You take that one. You'll find washcloths and towels in the cupboard." She grinned. "FYI, I do not like the taste of spermicide, and I intend to go down on you as part of my dessert."

"Duly noted."

She kissed him softly. "I'll clean up in the hall bathroom and get the ice cream."

She left him on the bed, and he lay there, watching the swing of her perfect ass as she slipped from the room.

The moment almost didn't seem real. As if it was one of his fevered fantasies from the before. When his mind wasn't his.

He did all the mental exercises he'd learned last fall, to check his own reality. He mentally reviewed the hours that had led up to now and found no gaps. There was a logical progression to getting here.

He rose from the bed to perform the final test, but first he needed to lose the condom that was making him itch— another sign this was real—so he stepped into the bathroom, tossed the condom, then jumped in the shower for a quick rinse.

Clean, he pulled a thick towel from the cupboard and dried off. The feel of soft terry cloth on his skin was another reality check.

This was real. Eden had made love with him. And she wanted to again.

He assumed this was nothing more than a convenient arrangement for her. She wanted sex, and he could provide it. He was okay with that. But still, he wanted more. He wanted everything he'd never dreamed he could have. With her.

In the bedroom, he plucked his cell phone from his pants pocket and performed the final test. He dialed a phone number from memory—something he'd always been incapable of in the fevered dreams. Any attempt to get help was impossible. His brain had been wired to fail.

Those wires had been cut nearly a year ago, but he still didn't trust it.

Mothman answered immediately. "Do you have intel on Penelope?"

"No. I'm having an *Inception* moment."

"Got it. You dialed from memory?"

"Yes. Went through on the first try."

"Running the scan on your Raptor phone. You're in Fairfax. Looks like Eden's address, if memory serves. You drove there straight from the compound, making two stops on the way. You arrived just after six."

Eden entered the bedroom, completely nude, carrying a pint of ice cream and one spoon. She cocked her head in question at finding him on the phone.

He had a moment of panic. Did he want her to know he was so messed up, he needed to call a friend to act as the spinning top in *Inception* to figure out if he was caught in one of Parks's mind fucks?

Did he have a choice?

"Last test," Mothman said. "Tell me the last thing you ate."

Eden. Chase flushed red. Mothman was referring to the lunch they had together earlier.

"Pizza."

"What did Tricia eat?"

This was a trick question. "She wasn't there. She was at PT."

"You're good to go. No gaps, no confusion. Vehicle and phone are at the same coordinates. Enjoy your evening with Eden."

"Wait. One more thing." His gaze met Eden's. Maybe he could pass this off as a work call. He lowered the phone and addressed her. "Can you tell Mothman everything you know about Penny? We don't even know her CamDames name."

"Mothman? You mentioned him before."

"He's the tech wizard for Raptor. He's trying to track her down. Her cell number isn't pinging. She's probably gone off the grid."

Eden nodded. She set the ice cream on the side table, then stepped into the bathroom. "Let me get a robe on first."

He nodded. It was an awkward conversation to have while nude, even if she was talking on the phone.

To Mothman, he said, "Just a sec." He handed Eden the phone when she returned in a silk robe that draped over her perfect body in the most enticing way.

She took the phone and sat on the bed while Chase pulled on his jeans.

"What do you need from me?" She hit the speaker button so Chase could hear both sides.

"Anything you can tell me. How long she's worked for CamDames, her aliases, where she lives. The address I found through Vivace Coffee was fake."

"Fake? Shit." She looked at Chase, and he saw the sadness in her eyes. "I was sort of hoping there was some sort of mix-up and she didn't set me up."

"It's not looking that way." Mothman's voice held the brisk tone of someone who didn't catch the social cue that called for a sympathetic response. He still missed that one, especially at times like this when he was listening for data that would set him on a technical hunt.

It made Chase feel less alone to know he wasn't the only one who had problems with communication.

"She's worked for CamDames for…I don't know…eighteen months? Maybe a little longer. She started a few months after me, but I gathered she had experience from elsewhere. I was concerned because I think she was only eighteen at the time."

"I've found conflicting ages for her. It's possible she was only sixteen eighteen months ago."

Eden let out a soft gasp. "Sixteen? You mean she's only *now* eighteen?"

"It's possible. I haven't been able to find a birth certificate and believe the name Penelope Madison is an invention."

Chase plucked the pint of ice cream from the nightstand to return it to the freezer. They wouldn't be picking up where they'd left off when Eden got off the phone.

It was selfish of him to regret it. This was why he'd come over, after all, and it appeared Penny was as much a victim as an accomplice.

Eden followed him to the kitchen and sat on a barstool with the phone on the counter. Chase began unpacking Thai food and sorting it for microwaving to reheat.

"The only screen name I know of is Penny Candi. She has a new name now that I don't know, but she said she uses full baby-doll makeup and looks more like a cartoon than a person. She told me the makeup is because she had a stalker who found her real-life identity." She met Chase's gaze. "Her stalker used the alias Falcon."

A rush of emotion—he guessed this one was shock, because it felt a lot like what he'd earlier dubbed *tornado*—

washed through him. Yeah. He definitely wasn't dreaming this.

"She said that after we met?" he asked.

"Yes."

"She was trying to make you suspicious of me."

Eden glanced at the phone, clearly uncomfortable with what Mothman was overhearing.

Chase said, "One second, Moth," and hit the Mute button. To Eden, he said, "He knows about Falcon. Or at least, he knows I found you online. He did a search on you that first night and discovered you were Desiree, who was on our list of people to investigate at CamDames eight months ago. You dropped off the list when you left."

Eden's face blanched. "You said you didn't run a check on me."

"*I* didn't. And I didn't know Mothman had. He didn't tell me the results. He figured I'd recognized you and had my reasons for keeping mum." He ran his fingers through his hair, praying she would believe him and would understand. "I didn't say a word to him until last night. After."

He rounded the counter and stood before her. "He doesn't know any details about Falcon. He doesn't know we just made love. All he knows is I told him not to share anything he learned in your background check because everything I know about you, I want *you* to have a say in me knowing it."

He studied her face, her delicate features expressing more emotions in this moment than he would be able to process. This was where the numbness had protected him. He ached with fear, his heart surged with hope, and anxiety threatened to put him in a cyclone.

He wanted to touch her, to assure himself he hadn't lost her already with this revelation.

She studied his face, then slipped from the stool, stood before him, and wrapped her arms around his neck.

He pulled her flush to his chest, his arms sliding over the silk robe as he took her in his arms. He buried his head in her hair, breathed in the flowery scent of her shampoo combined with the scent of sex on her skin.

Her words were muffled against his chest. "Okay. And thank you for giving me some choices here."

"I'm sorry Mothman invaded your privacy to begin with, but the work we're doing made it necessary."

"Has he…seen Desiree?"

"I don't know. Probably."

"Is he the judgmental type?"

"No. He doesn't give a damn. What you do with your body is your business."

She nodded, and he knew there would be more to this conversation. A lot more if they were going to continue seeing each other, which he wanted more than anything.

"Okay. Let's finish this conversation so we can get back to the fun part of our *meeting with food*."

He smiled. It sounded funny when she said it.

He released her and unmuted the call. "Sorry about that. Okay, where were we?"

"Penny told Eden that she had a stalker named Falcon, which was also conveniently the name you used as a login on Desiree's site. Which means it's likely that someone at CamDames had figured out that you are Falcon."

Mothman delivered it as straight facts, and his cold delivery was probably a lot easier for Eden to take than if he'd shown any kind of concern.

"How would they know any of that?" she asked.

Chase shrugged. "That's why we need to dig into Penny. As far as we know, the first connection anyone would have made between us was when I drove you home the first night.

Or if not then, then when I visited you at the coffee shop a week later."

"When did Penny tell you about Falcon?" Mothman asked.

Eden pulled out her phone and checked the call log. "I'm not sure. Either two weeks ago or just one. Probably just one?" She sighed. "The day after I filled in for Penny, she called me at work, and I told her about what happened and mentioned that Raptor had responded."

"So they could have started connecting dots then. And Falcon could have been suggested because they knew you had a regular named Falcon. They could have been trying to throw you off."

They wrapped up the call with Mothman and loaded plates with the various Thai dishes Eden had ordered, then took turns heating them in the microwave.

Eden poured them each a glass of wine, and they ate dinner on the couch in front of the gas fireplace.

"As much as I was disappointed by the change in direction from my plans to seduce you with ice cream, I'm glad we got that conversation over with and Mothman has what he needs to keep searching."

Chase took a sip of his wine. "Me too." He set the glass on the coffee table as she did the same.

He had so many questions about how to navigate this after-sex and possibly before-sex moment in time. He didn't know the process. What was normal.

Would she expect him to go home tonight? Or would she let him hold her all night long? She'd said she wanted cuddling, and he hadn't delivered on that promise yet.

She ate a bite of Pad Thai and then looked at him in confusion. She set down her fork and finished chewing. After she swallowed, she said, "You look...concerned." She glanced at his plate, which showed he'd barely taken a bite. "Is the food too spicy?"

He shook his head. If she could see it on his face, he might as well come clean. "I don't know how to do this."

"Do what?" Her face suddenly blanched. "Oh no. You're going to start the 'it's not you, it's that you're a camgirl' conversation already."

He jolted. "What? No! Not at all."

"Then why are you breaking up with me an hour after we got started?"

"Who said I was b-b-breaking up w-with you?" Shit. Now he was stuttering again.

"What don't you know how to do?"

He ran a hand over his face. "You are m-m-..." He paused, took a deep breath, and tried again. "Making my point. *This*—navigating the transition from bed, to talking, to, hopefully, bed again—I don't know how to do it. I want you, Eden. I want to make love to you in front of the fire. Against the wall. In the shower. And I'm not sure how to navigate because I've never really done this. At least, not that I know of. How do normal guys behave? Are there rules? I want to pull you on my lap and kiss you, but what if you're just trying to figure out how to send me packing?"

She gave him a soft smile. "It sounds like you should trust your instincts on this one."

"But that's the problem. I have no instincts."

She shook her head. "What was the last thing you said you wanted to do?"

He searched his brain. Sex in the shower? No. "Pull you on my lap and kiss you?"

"Spot-on instincts."

He reached for her and dragged her the short distance until her ass settled on his rapidly growing erection.

She let out a soft, happy sound as she wiggled her butt, then draped her arms around his neck, settling into place.

Her robe had come open revealing her perfect right breast with its pert, pink nipple. Instead of kissing her, he took that nipple into his mouth as his hand cupped her other breast still covered in silk.

"You have *very* good instincts." She let out a soft groan.

He raised his head. "You aren't bothered that I'm interrupting your dinner?"

"Not at all."

"Well, in that case…" He tugged on the sash of her robe, opening it wide, then lifted her, setting her in the corner of the couch with her back against the armrest. He spread her legs and scooted down so his face was level with her pussy.

Her eyes were lit with heat and humor as she held his gaze. "I'm afraid your dinner is getting cold again."

"That's what microwaves are for."

She laughed, and he licked her, turning that laugh into a gasp of pleasure.

He spent the next ten minutes devoting the entirety of his attention to ensuring he made her feel so damn good, she would insist he spend the night so he could do this to her again and again.

He wasn't great at communicating, but he was starting to think she was right, and he did have good instincts when it came to Eden.

Chapter Twenty-Four

For all that Chase was a badass warrior with a dangerous hobby and emotional scars, he was proving to be the sweetest, most attentive lover she'd ever had.

And yet he did it with the same take-charge manner he'd had as Falcon. He really did have good instincts—he always knew what she wanted, just as Falcon had known the commands to give to make her come.

It took them an hour to get through dinner, and during that time, she had two orgasms to his one.

His was her favorite, though, because she'd gone down on him in front of the fire, and the glow of his skin in the firelight as she pleasured him, the intensity of his eyes as he watched his cock disappear in her mouth, the way the flickering flames highlighted the hollows beneath his perfect cheekbones, had all blended together in a hot, intimate moment that was an entirely different kind of pleasure.

Giving him pleasure had instantly become her favorite thing in the world. It was better than ice cream *and* pizza.

And then later, she got to have him with ice cream, and damn, she was in joy overload.

They drifted off to sleep around midnight with promises of fulfilling her wall fantasies in the morning.

She woke early on Saturday and watched him sleep, his muscled chest bare as only a sheet was tangled around his hips. He must run hot, as the blankets were all on her side of the bed and askew.

She could fall in love with him. It was possible she already had. It felt like a daunting thing, loving someone, but at least with him, she could believe he cared about her too. Could maybe love her back.

It did make the prospect of returning to her night job a bit harder. It wasn't cheating. He knew about her work. She wasn't emotionally involved with her clients. Well, except Falcon.

She would snicker aloud except she didn't want to wake him. She'd given him quite a workout yesterday and had plans for him today. He needed sleep to build his strength.

She closed her eyes and relived some of her favorite moments from last evening.

She had her time as Desiree to thank for her easy, positive sexuality with him, something she knew he needed after what had happened to him. She also had Desiree to thank for finding him at all.

She would never regret her work as a camgirl. It had taught her a lot about sex positivity, and that might be the type of therapy she would practice someday, working with survivors of sexual abuse to develop a healthy sexuality. It would be meaningful.

A warm hand wrapped around her ankle, causing her to gasp as he pulled her down the bed toward him and his tangle of sheets.

She smiled and kept her eyes closed, and her belly fluttered when soft lips touched her ear as he whispered, "Tell me if I'm doing the morning thing right. All I've got to go on is instinct."

His mouth trailed across her chin and down her neck. He kissed her breasts, and within minutes, he was rolling on a condom and sliding deep inside her. The sex was languorous, perfect for fresh-from-sleep lovemaking.

After last night, she'd have been content to just feel him inside her, but he had other plans and slid from her, then nudged her to her stomach, lifting her hips so she was on her knees, before he filled her again.

He wrapped an arm around her and stroked her clit as he slid within her. He was no longer slow and gentle; now his thrusts were fast and feverish, bringing her to a rapid edge.

Thankfully, he was right there with her as she tumbled over the precipice. She let out a loud, impossible-to-contain shriek. The kind of yell that usually only the vibrator triggered when conditions were just right.

She collapsed on the bed, and he was on top of her, his hard muscled body slick with sweat.

"Damn," she panted. "You are good at mornings."

"Am I?" She could hear the laughter in his voice.

He rolled from her back, sliding from inside her as he did so, and she turned to face him. She smiled. "You're fishing for compliments now."

"But haven't I earned them?"

She chuckled. "Yes. Yes, you have." She faced the ceiling. "Whew. Talk about rise and shine."

He let out a bark of laughter.

She rolled to face him again. "I really like you, Chase Johnston."

His face turned serious as he stared into her eyes. He cleared his throat and said, "I'm a mess, Eden. And I know this is probably just a fling for you, but I'm going to just say it now. I want more than just today."

She kissed him as a dizzying heat spread through her. Now it was her turn to feel the prickle of happy tears. "This isn't just a fling for me."

"Really? I mean it when I say I'm a mess. Did you see how many pints of ice cream I bought? My logic skills are for shit."

"Chase, no man should ever be rejected for buying too much ice cream when commanded to buy ice cream." She stroked the stubble on his jaw. God. She'd missed morning stubble.

No. She'd never thought about morning stubble before. But on Chase, it was so damn hot, it made her regret all the previous days she didn't wake up to *his* morning stubble.

"Damn. You look like you made a deal with an evil genie to be this hot in the morning, all rumpled and sated."

"Evil genie?" he asked.

"Yeah. Or some other supernatural being. Your handsomeness breaks the laws of physics."

He laughed, his face relaxed and happy and her heart melted. He kissed her nose. "You're adorable. And wildly hot yourself. And I think I'm the luckiest man alive. Except this condom is driving me to insanity. I need to clean up."

She grabbed his hand before he left the bed. "Wait. We just agreed this was more than a fling, right?"

He nodded.

"I've got the five-year implant. Aside from being excellent birth control, it made my periods nonexistent, which, for a camgirl…"

He nodded. "After…what happened to me, I got tested for everything. All negative. And it's been more than a year."

She smiled. "It's been more than two years for me, and my last tests were negative too. So. If you want, we can skip the condom next time. But only if you're comfortable with that."

He leaned down and kissed her, then whispered, "My one regret is we just fucked, so I'm going to need a few minutes' recovery time."

She laughed. "Only a few?"

"I'm only twenty-seven. And I've got lots to make up for. Ten minutes tops."

She grinned. "I'll set a timer."

He impressed her by beating her timer by two minutes.

Chapter Twenty-Five

In the early afternoon, they found themselves lying on her couch, Eden tucked in one corner and Chase in the other, her feet on his lap as he massaged them simply because he couldn't stop touching her. They were both sated in a way he'd never imagined. He was pretty sure he'd broken some records for number of times they'd had sex since he'd entered her apartment last night.

Done for the time being, they were lounging and watching nature shows on her big flat-screen TV with the sound off. He liked that they didn't need to talk. They could just be. But at the same time, the talking was good too. He wasn't stuttering. He was fully himself, and that was who she wanted.

"I've never had this," he said softly. "This kind of intimacy."

She smiled and shifted her foot to caress his cock with the arch. Not to stimulate, just a pleasuring stroke.

He never imagined he'd be able to let someone freely touch his body again, but he trusted her.

He closed his eyes and remembered the weekends with

Parks in his remote cabin. When she'd used infrasound to trigger pleasure in his body that forced him to be erect. Eden knew he'd been abused, but not the extent of it. And this feeling inside him today was the antithesis of what Parks had done.

He cleared his throat, surprised that he wanted to share these thoughts with her. But he wanted her to know exactly what this meant to him. "One weekend a month for…two years, I think? I was forced to perform sexually. She—my abuser—used my body's response to certain infrasound frequencies to stimulate me and make me compliant. She liked to pretend we were lovers like this, sharing a romantic weekend getaway." He met Eden's gaze, seeing the compassion in her eyes. There was something else there too, and it warmed his heart.

What he didn't see was pity, thank goodness.

She crawled across the sofa and straddled him. She placed her hands on either side of his neck and cupped the back of his head, running her fingers through his hair as she held his gaze.

That she didn't flinch or look away—when she could use an embrace to hide from him—meant everything.

He smiled. He was totally falling in love with this woman. There was no other word for it. "I never gave her what she wanted. I never played her game. I wasn't able to resist the sex—she was in complete control of my mind and body—but I didn't give her the affection she craved. So when I say I've never had this before, it has a different meaning."

He touched her cheek, once again confirming this moment was real. "I never had the freedom to do this. To give and take as I pleased. To enjoy another person's body and allow them to enjoy mine. Everything about last night and today feels like a miracle. Like my long nightmare is over. And it's all you. Because you're amazing."

A tear spilled down her cheek, and she leaned forward, pressing her forehead to his. "I'm so happy to be sharing this with you. That you trust me with your body and your pain."

He cupped her face and brought his mouth to hers. His kiss was deep. She tasted like ice cream and smelled like sex. Like him.

He couldn't get enough of this. Of her.

The long kiss ended, and she stretched out on the couch next to him. She pressed her head to his chest, and he held her. There was nothing else that needed to be said.

He drifted off to sleep at some point. Or maybe it wasn't quite sleep as he found himself in a lucid dream.

His brain worked the problem of Penny's disappearance. But then, had she really disappeared? They'd never known where she lived to begin with, and the coffee shop she worked at was closed for repairs. He doubted she'd been at CamDames on Thursday at all. She could have called Eden from anywhere. Had Mothman been able to get the ping locations for her phone on Thursday? That question might be better suited to Lee Scott, who specialized in cellular security.

But Lee didn't know about what Chase was doing. They didn't know each other well, as Chase had avoided the inner circle of friends that included his boss, Keith, a few other senior Raptor operatives, and extended to Lee.

Chase had never felt comfortable around that group, and it was only made worse after what he'd done at Ian and Cressida's wedding.

He'd been doing Parks's bidding, but still, he'd been the one to take the photo. The one who'd set the bomb under the car.

The one who was ultimately behind the destruction of a structure on Rav's estate.

It was why he remained terrified of losing time again. He

wasn't sure what he was capable of. If he could hurt his friends, he could hurt anyone.

Even Eden.

He jolted awake.

Eden stirred against him. She'd drifted off to sleep too.

"You okay?" she asked.

He cleared his throat, which had gone dry at the thought of him hurting her.

He wouldn't. He couldn't. He'd resisted hurting Isabel—twice.

If he could resist hurting a friend, surely he could resist harming the woman he was in love with?

The woman who made him feel like maybe someday he could be whole again.

"I'm fine," he lied.

"It's okay if you aren't fine. I'm not going anywhere."

"I think I'm falling in love with you." The words were out of his mouth before he had a chance to stop them. Dammit. It was too soon for such a declaration.

But instead of pushing away from him and bolting for an exit, she leaned into him. Her lips brushed over his, and she said, "I'm pretty sure I'm in love with you too."

Tears sprang from his eyes. It was instant. Like a spigot. One second, his eyes were dry, and the next, overflowing.

He could feel this moment in all its glory. It was a cloudless warm breeze on a tropical beach. Endless blue sky and warm wind.

He kissed her tenderly. Slowly. Eventually, they found themselves on the rug before the fireplace, and he made love to her in the firelight, watching her face as he made her come.

He rolled over so she was on top of him, and she sat up, straddling him. He cupped her breasts, and she let out a groan, followed by the words, "I love you."

"I love you too," he said as he pitched over the precipice, his body pulsing with orgasm.

She collapsed on top of him and let out a soft laugh. "Okay, I was sure there was no way you'd have another orgasm today."

He laughed too. "Frankly, I'm also shocked." He stroked her hair. So soft. Another sensual pleasure against his skin. "Apparently, there's no limit to how much you turn me on."

She ran her hand over his chest. "Same."

Her phone, which sat on the coffee table, vibrated, making soft noise as it clattered on the wood surface.

She rolled away from his body and picked up the phone. Her face darkened with anger, and she set the phone down. Was her hand trembling?

"What's going on?" he asked.

She let out a heavy sigh and nodded toward her phone. "The guy who's the reason my site is down just texted me to be at his place in an hour."

"What? Why? I thought you said the site was down due to technical difficulties?"

She wrinkled her nose. "When we talked on the phone, I didn't want to get into it because, well, I wasn't sure how I felt about you. Plus, I was on the Metro."

He couldn't help but smile. She'd just told him how she felt as he made her come, so he was feeling pretty solid with her now.

"Will you tell me now?"

"Of course. Tobias is a fellow grad student—"

"Grad student?"

"Yeah. In my department—"

"I didn't know you were in grad school."

"Really? I…goodness, we've never talked about school? I guess it's because I'm taking the semester off. I didn't have money for tuition after buying this place and getting my own site up and running. I'm working as a research assistant this semester, which brings in a little money and keeps me connected to the department."

"So, you have three jobs." No wonder she always worked nights online and midday at the coffee shop. She must be exhausted.

She nodded. "Yesterday I was at the lab, and Tobias came in. He's always hit on me and I've always been firm in my no, but yesterday, he made sure I was alone and snuck up on me. He found my site a few days ago, apparently. He told me that if I didn't have sex with him, he'd tell my advisor about Desiree."

Chase reared back. "What the fuck?" Black rage filled him. He sprang to his feet and began pacing. "I want his full name."

Her eyes widened. "I'll deal with him."

He took a deep breath. He needed to get control of himself. He could tell he was scaring her.

He took another slow breath. In and out. The rage receded enough for coherent thought. "Mothman will need his name. It might be no coincidence he found your site now, when you're a target."

Because of me. She's a target because of me.

"Oh. Right."

Chase picked up his phone and started a text to Mothman. "Full name?"

"Tobias Redford."

"Do you have a phone number or address for him?"

She went to the office nook and woke her computer, then rattled off the number, which he typed into the text to Mothman.

Text sent, he approached her from behind and wrapped his arms around her. "I'm sorry I frightened you."

She turned in his arms and hugged him. "It's okay, but

this is something I'm going to have to figure out how to handle myself." She let out a nervous laugh. "Although I did tell him about you when he threatened me."

He smiled at that. Even when she'd been upset with him, she'd invoked him for protection. "I'm glad." He released her and stepped back. "So how big a threat is this to your schooling? What you do on your own time is your business."

"That's true, except in my field, it could make it hard for me to do my practicums. They could deny me the work because of the possibility I might find myself faced with an online client." She cleared her throat. "Like you, when you walked into the coffee shop. There's a power dynamic that would mess with the study in that situation. It's one of the reasons why I went solo. To block all IP addresses in the area."

Chase's brain was reeling. How did he not know any of this? Labs and practicums? He'd known she was smart; it shouldn't surprise him she was a scientist.

"What are you studying?"

"Oh!" She laughed. "I'm telling this all backwards. I'm working on a master's degree now, but my eventual goal is a psychology doctorate. It's a P-S-Y-D, or rather, PsyD, not a PhD, because I want to do clinical work, not research."

Chase felt the bottom drop out of his world. He released her and stepped back. His gaze scanned the packed bookshelves in her small office. Psychology book after psychology book. Textbooks. Case studies. Theory. Anatomy of the human brain. Books on neuropsychology. More on cognitive neuropsychology.

Cognitive neuropsychology. Parks's specialty.

His vision tunneled. "Y-you are s-s-studying c-c-c-ognitive neuropsy-sy-chology?"

"I've taken classes. I might specialize there. I don't know. Chase—what's going on? What's wrong?"

"I need to go."

He was in the pantry, heading to the interior stairs, when he realized he was naked.

Shit.

He returned to the living room, picked up his jeans from the floor, and tugged them on. Where was his shirt?

Bedroom. He hadn't donned it since last night.

He vaguely heard Eden asking him why he was leaving, her voice getting higher and higher pitched.

He didn't look at her. Couldn't.

Had she been studying him? Did she have a profile of him in her files? Was she studying all her clients?

Was that why she did it? To brain fuck people two ways instead of just one with therapy?

He found his shirt and boots and socks. The underwear he'd doffed last night and hadn't bothered with again. Phone. Wallet. Keys.

He had everything.

She followed him down the stairs. She was crying now.

He took comfort in the numbness that used to plague him. Nimbostratus clouds sheeted his mind, blocking the sun.

He yanked open the door to the garage, passing the wall he hadn't fucked her against and never would.

He vaguely heard the alarm beep, and she keyed it off. He hit the button to raise the garage door.

"Chase, what did I do? Why are you leaving?"

He paused by the door to his SUV. He probably owed her some sort of explanation. He wasn't sure, his brain too fogged for logic. She should have told him. He kept coming back to that.

She hadn't told him. On purpose.

She kept it from him. Who didn't tell the man they were sleeping with the major fact that they were in graduate school?

Was she working for Parks? Had she been the one to deliver Parks's letter to him?

"Please, Chase. I-I love you."

It sounded hokey now. Who said *I love you* after less than twenty-four hours of fucking?

He closed his eyes. *He did.* He had. He'd even said it first. Fuck. Was he screwing this up?

Was he the one in the wrong here?

He had no idea. No way to process or think because his brain was hopelessly broken. He met Eden's gaze. "My abuser, the woman who fucked me repeatedly against my will and pretended we were on romantic weekends like I thought this was, the person who brainwashed and controlled me, who made me do terrible things to my friends, the woman who tried to get me to kill for her…that woman was my shrink, Dr. Elizabeth Parks."

Her eyes widened. If she'd known that already, she was a good actress.

Was it possible she hadn't known?

Did it even matter? No one, *no one* would ever dig in his brain again. And there was no way a woman who was studying to be a psychotherapist or cognitive neuroscientist wasn't digging in his mind with every conversation they'd had.

She'd been studying him from the start. Like he was some sort of fucking lab rat.

"Goodbye, Eden." He climbed in his Raptor SUV and backed out of the garage.

Chapter Twenty-Six

*E*den watched the SUV disappear as it turned the corner at the end of her block. She was stunned. Completely flattened by the last…*five minutes?*

In a mere five minutes, the most perfect day of her life had been distorted by funhouse mirrors. Everything looked different now. Grotesque.

Dr. Elizabeth Parks. She knew about her, of course. They'd had long conversations about her in the grad student offices when the story made headlines last year, and again during sentencing this summer after the woman pled guilty to avoid the death penalty.

A psychotherapist who'd been experimenting on her patients had been big news in the department, especially when dozens of her "test subjects"—people who'd been abducted so she could experiment on them—had been murdered to cover it up.

Dr. Parks was Chase's abuser?

Eden wanted to vomit.

Much as it devastated her that Chase had run out without talking to her, she understood. If there was one thing she'd learned in her studies so far, it was that he wasn't in a rational place. He couldn't stay and talk in that state. He probably didn't even understand everything he was feeling. He'd said over and over he had trouble processing emotions.

She closed the garage door and reset the alarm. She needed to tell someone about Chase. A friend he might turn to.

He was in a dangerous mental state. Harmful to himself or others.

No.

She didn't want to believe that, but she remembered her session with Falcon when he admitted to beating up men who deserved it.

She'd seen him fight and knew he'd broken Sling Man's arm the first night they met. She'd seen him two hours later, and he hadn't had a scratch on him.

She grabbed her phone but was disappointed to remember that her conversations with Mothman had all happened on Chase's phone.

She googled Raptor and called the main number. A person answered, which surprised her, but then high-end security probably required exceptional customer service in a hurry when there was a crisis.

She remembered the bridge bombing in Portland and how quickly events could turn.

She asked for Mothman and was informed that there was no employee on file with that name. That was probably true, and who knew if the woman on the phone was just being difficult or if she didn't know all the employees' nicknames.

She hung up the phone and paced some more. She texted Chase and got no response. His phone didn't send read receipts, at least not to her, so she had no way of knowing if he saw her messages.

Her calls went to voicemail.

Should she just leave him alone? Wait for him to reach out?

Would he ever be able to forgive her for being the one thing he hated most?

The first call Chase made once he was away from Eden's was to Mothman. "Why didn't you tell me?" he demanded without preamble.

"Tell you what?"

"That Eden is in grad school."

"You didn't know?"

"No. Why didn't you say something?"

"You told me not to tell you anything."

"But you said she checked out."

"She did. Nothing tripped up or crossed wires with Penny except CamDames and Vivace Coffee."

"She's studying for a doctorate in psychology."

"So?"

"Just like Parks."

"Oh," Mothman said. But then he added, "It doesn't have to mean anything."

Chase pulled over. He couldn't talk and drive in this state, even with his Raptor headset.

Was he overreacting?

He had no clue. His brain was on overload.

He was having trouble connecting dots.

"But what if it does? I texted you the name of the grad student who threatened her. What are the odds he'd randomly find out about Desiree this week?"

"You're sounding like a conspiracy theorist."

"Are you trying to say you think I'm fucking crazy?"

"No! Of course not!"

Rage and pain simmered in the background of Chase's numbed brain. "Well then, you'd be wrong. My brain is fucked up beyond all recognition. I am a living, breathing FUBAR. And I'm going to get some answers."

Chase disconnected and ran the name Tobias Redford though the computer linked to Raptor's servers built into the dashboard console. He didn't need Mothman to find Redford's address, not when he had all Raptor's data at his fingertips.

*H*ours had passed since Chase left, and a sinking dread had settled in. Something was wrong.

She sent him a private link to chat with Desiree. The site was offline, but she could still do private chats because they were run through an app that was separate from the public site. She sat on the bed in the middle of her workroom, ready to go on camera if he responded.

She texted both Chase and the link she had for Falcon, using her Desiree account.

DESIREE

Please reply. We need to talk. I'm sorry you didn't know. I love you.

Would he believe her? Was he even capable of it? Or did he only see ulterior motives and suspicion when it came to her in the state of mind he was in?

She knew he believed he was broken…but she would never apply such a term to him or anyone. There was healing to be done for Chase, but it wasn't about fixing. It was about working with the tools he had available to process emotions and events in a way that made sense for him.

He was a hundred percent capable of feeling, processing, and handling what the world threw at him. Hell, look at what he'd managed in the last year?

Holy hell. She still couldn't believe he was one of Dr. Parks's victims.

No. Not victim. Survivor. He'd survived everything she'd done to him, and he was building a new life. Learning how to love.

Her eyes teared.

Learning how to be loved too.

All she wanted to do right now was love him. Let him know he wasn't alone. He could count on her. She would support him in his feelings of distrust and hurt even though they were directed at her. He'd been blindsided at discovering what she studied.

She swiped at her tears. He wasn't going to respond to her.

Who would he talk to?

Her attempt to reach out to Mothman had failed quickly. Who else was there? She couldn't remember the Black operative's name, but she did know the name of the white woman who'd been with her that night.

She dialed Raptor again and identified herself to the woman who picked up. "I need to get a message to Isabel Dawson. Tell her that the woman from the coffee shop needs to talk to her about Chase Johnston." She paused then added, "And Jasmine. And CamDames." One of those had to do the trick.

"Ms. Dawson doesn't work for Raptor," the woman said.

"I know, but she'll want this message." Eden gave her number and added, "Tell her it's urgent."

She hung up and paced her workroom, fighting more

tears. She couldn't help the feeling that it might already be too late to find Chase.

Isabel Dawson shocked the hell out of Eden by knocking on her door thirty minutes after she'd left the message with Raptor's twenty-four-hour call line. Equally surprising, Isabel's husband, Senator Alec Ravissant, stood by her side.

"Ms. Dawson—I—I—"

"Is Chase here?"

"No. That's why I was trying to reach you. He left a few hours ago. He was very upset. I'm worried." Eden stepped back and waved her arm toward the living room. "Come in."

"Alec would like to do a quick inspection to make sure the apartment is empty if you don't mind, then he'll wait in the car."

Eden was taken aback. "I do mind. Very much. Please have Mothman call me." She started to close the door. She wanted Isabel's help, but that was a massive violation of privacy to show up uninvited and then demand to search her home. By a US senator who owned a private army, no less.

Maybe she was wrong and Raptor wasn't the good guys?

"I told you it was a ridiculous demand," the woman said to her husband as the door clicked closed. She pitched her voice higher so Eden could hear. "Go wait in the car, Alec. I'll be fine."

A deep male voice responded, "I don't like the secrets you're keeping from me."

"Well, consider us even from last year, then."

"Iz—"

"Go, Alec."

She heard the sound of footsteps descending the stairs. "He's leaving," Isabel said. "Can I come in?"

Eden opened the door and met the gaze of the pretty freckle-faced redhead with abundant curls. "I'm sorry about that," she said. "It was the only way I could get him to agree to the detour. We were on our way to the compound when I got your message."

"Why didn't you just call?"

"Because we were in the car, and he can always hear my cell phone conversations. I swear he has superhuman hearing."

"And you don't want him to know about Chase?"

"He knows all about Chase. What I don't want him to know about is Jasmine."

Eden led her to the couch where she and Chase had cuddled just hours ago. She set her phone on the coffee table, faceup, so she wouldn't miss a text from Chase should it come in, and took a seat in the same spot she'd occupied earlier when Chase was here and wondered if Isabel could smell sex in the room.

Oh well, drop in uninvited and you might not be greeted with the fresh scent of Febreze.

"I'm worried about Chase," she said, launching into the extreme CliffsNotes version of the story. "We've gotten involved since we met at the coffee shop that night, and last night, he spent the night here. I didn't realize until a few hours ago that he didn't know I was in grad school." She paused and said the hard part. "Because I also work as a camgirl, I'm pretty careful about sharing details of my life. Habit. And school never came up."

She studied Isabel's face, looking for signs of revulsion or judgment and seeing none.

"And?" Isabel said, prompting her to continue.

"So, anyway, when I told him what I'm studying, he lost

it. He said goodbye and left. Like, *left*, left. As in 'we're done for good' and jumped in his car. This was just…I don't know…thirty minutes after telling me he loved me?" She swiped at a tear. "I'm so worried about him. He was irrational. I'm worried he's a danger to himself. Or others."

"I feel like you're leaving out an important piece, Eden. What are you studying?"

And here she was, doing it again! She'd berate herself later. Right now, she needed to know Chase was safe. "I'm working on my psychology doctorate."

Isabel bolted to her feet and took two steps toward the door, then stopped. She faced Eden, and the look on her face was abject horror.

Okay, so the woman had zero reaction to Eden being a camgirl, but psychology horrified her? "What? Why are you doing the same thing he did?"

"Did he tell you *why* it upset him?"

"Right before he left, he said Dr. Elizabeth Parks was his abuser. I know who she is. From the news, but also at school, we talked about her in a seminar last spring."

"Parks was my psychotherapist too." The woman took another step toward the door. "I—I don't know if I can help you."

Tears streamed down Eden's cheeks. "Please, Isabel. I just want to find Chase. Make sure he's okay. I'm not asking you to bring him back to me. If he can't deal with who I am— what I do for a living—so be it."

Wasn't that ironic? The one man who could accept her being a camgirl couldn't accept that she wanted to be a psychotherapist. Wait until he found out his tips had paid for several of her classes.

She suppressed a bitter laugh. There was nothing funny about this situation. It was all just one kind of pain layered over another.

She followed Isabel to the door. "I'm sorry for the pain you and he both suffered. I'm not the person who harmed either of you, but I am the woman who's falling in love with Chase. He had a breakdown and left, and I'm scared for him. Scared for others. He's mentioned his rage and that he's taken it out on deserving parties. But what will he do if there isn't a deserving party at hand?

"He might be going to CamDames to beat up the guys who tried to abduct me to get to him on Thursday night. We need to find him before he gets hurt. Or before he hurts someone so bad, there's no way to protect him. And that's what you've been doing for the last year, isn't it? Protecting him?"

Isabel's hand dropped from the doorknob, and she turned to face Eden. "Someone tried to abduct you?"

"Four someones. Chase fought three of them off. The fourth held a gun to my head."

Isabel closed her eyes. "I'm sorry that happened to you."

It wasn't until that moment that Eden realized she hadn't even begun to process that horror. Her entire brain had been filled with Chase from the moment he kissed her in the car, to the moment he broke her heart as Falcon, to the moment he broke her heart again by walking out on her.

"Yeah. I didn't like that part at all."

"I didn't either," Isabel muttered. She pulled out her phone. "We need Mothman. He can track him through his phone and vehicle. He messaged me earlier and asked me to come to the compound to meet with him and Tricia. That's why we were on our way there when I got your message."

Isabel sent a text and a minute later said, "Mothman spoke to him right after he left here." She frowned as she read. "He says Chase was upset. About you. Mad at Mothman for not telling him about you being a student."

A minute later, her phone buzzed again. "He monitored

him for the first hour. He reached out to me when Chase disappeared from the tracking systems. I didn't get the message until an hour after he sent it."

"What does he mean, disappeared from the tracking systems?"

Isabel was typing on her phone. "I'm asking exactly that."

A moment later, she raised her gaze and met Eden's. Her eyes were bleak. "Both his phone and vehicle went offline. Mothman can't track either." She glanced at the screen again and murmured, "That's not even supposed to be possible for a Raptor vehicle."

Dark despair filtered through Eden.

No. NO. No. *No.*

"What does that mean?"

"It means that wherever Chase is, he doesn't want to be found. "

*C*hase woke with a jolt, disoriented. He must have fallen asleep at the computer again.

Except he wasn't at the computer. He didn't know where he was. The room was pitch-dark.

Room? No. Not a room. A vehicle.

But it wasn't his work vehicle. No. It was a nice car. A Lexus, if he wasn't mistaken. Raptor had a few they used when escorting wealthy clients to events where they didn't want to show up in a beefy SUV.

Was this a Raptor vehicle? He hit the dome light. It flared bright, practically blinding him.

And then he saw the blood.

His hands were covered with it. Dry, but still damp in patches.

Revulsion spread through him. He searched for his phone but didn't find it, his bloody hands leaving streaks on the car's center console. Or had those already been there?

He reached for the ignition and turned the car on. It wasn't a Raptor vehicle, or it would have a computer.

The digital clock glowed in the dash. *3:42.*

He didn't need to call Mothman to perform memory tests and check his tracking. There was zero doubt he'd lost over ten hours.

Chapter Twenty-Seven

CHASE

I turn on the headlights to figure out where I am. The beams cut through the darkness and show me hills and trees. Given the amount of time I've lost, I could be anywhere, but this feels like western Virginia to me.

I've got three-quarters of a tank of gas, so I'm not in danger of running out if I explore to figure out where I am. The car doesn't have built-in GPS, and I don't have a phone. But this is good because I don't want anyone to locate me or this car before I know what's going on.

Before I know what I've done.

I pull out onto the road, and after a mile, I see my first crossroad sign. Not far after that, I come upon a corner with a gas station and convenience store. Covered in blood as I am, I won't be going inside to ask for directions. Thankfully, I see a sign for a highway entrance up ahead, and I know where I am.

The compound is a half hour away. I could go home. But I'm not ready to do that. I need a cell phone with internet so I can check the news. Find out if I'm a wanted man. But I can't get a cell phone until I've cleaned up.

It hits me then. I have the perfect place. I promised myself I would never return there, but now it's my only option, and it's not far.

Twenty minutes later, I'm turning onto the long driveway. Not just any driveway.

My driveway.

I round a bend, and there it is. A house I've never seen before, but it's my house. My property.

I bought this place three years ago with money I received from Raptor as compensation for what I'd gone through in Alaska. It was a "bonus," but everyone knows it was reparation. Not that what had happened to me could have a dollar value, but I'm no fool. I took the money and bought my dream cabin.

It became my nightmare.

I'm still not sure if Parks planted the idea of purchasing the place in my mind, or if she saw an opportunity when I told her about it.

Chicken and egg. Does it matter? Once she used it to control and rape me, nothing else mattered.

Yesterday was probably the best day of my life, and now, less than twelve hours after I bolted from Eden's place, I'm back in my nightmare, at the one place I hate more than any other.

The cabin was burned to the ground a year ago. Parks had one of her accomplices set the fire in an attempt to kill my coworker Sean and his fiancée, Hazel, but the fire was also meant to destroy the physical evidence of Parks's presence in my cabin. After two years of using it as a place to torment me and exploit my body, her DNA was all over the place. Not even the fire was able to destroy it all.

It was one of the reasons she'd pled guilty. They had so much evidence against her.

I might have just let the place stay a burned heap of charred nightmares, except I figured I should sell the place and Raptor's insurance stepped up to pay for the rebuild. It was complicated, but what happened was related to Raptor, so while my normal homeowner's policy balked at the arson, Raptor stepped up. I suspect Isabel's husband, the owner, paid out of pocket. Technically, I saved their lives by not murdering them on Parks's orders.

It's a bit twisted, but they get it. Isabel especially. She and I bonded after Alaska, but even more so in the last year. She's one of the few people I know I can trust no matter what. She's the big sister I never had.

I never met her brother, Vin, but he was murdered by the same people who hurt me, and that right there created an unshakable bond.

If there's anyone in this world who is a hundred percent rooting for me, it's Isabel.

So I didn't question it when the money came in for the rebuild. One way or another, Rav was making sure I got my cabin back. I could keep it or sell it. I approved the plans for the new structure and signed the necessary papers, but that's it. The work was completed while I was in Portland, but I haven't been here to see it. Nor did I visit at any point during construction.

I never planned to come here again.

But now it's my only refuge. The house is fully outfitted for me or to rent out as an Airbnb, which is one of the ideas I had during construction. I hired a company to furnish the place and set up Wi-Fi. I even purchased a desktop computer for the office.

I think subconsciously, I wanted this place ready to go should I decide I needed it.

And now here I am, needing it.

I need to wash off the blood. I need computer access to run searches to figure out what I might have done.

Did I hurt someone?

The blood on my hands is like a Magic 8 Ball that says, *"Signs point to yes."* It's hard to argue with the signs, but at the same time, I suspect the source. I mean, half the possible responses are positive and only a quarter are negative. I'm *supposed* to believe this.

And that right there is what doesn't feel right.

This blood on me, it's not how I defend myself. Not how I attack. I'm not a killer. I'm a defensive fighter. I hurt—break bones—to end the fight. Because broken bones are better than slit throats or gunshot wounds.

This blood is something else entirely.

But ten hours are gone. Really, anything could have happened.

I cannot underestimate Parks.

How did she get to me? She's in prison. But then, how did her letter find its way into my mailbox?

I think I've been bracing for this since receiving that letter. I knew she was gearing up for something. But how did she know about Eden? How did this all come about?

I feel like that's the missing piece, how Eden is connected.

My panic at learning her major was triggered by a deep-seated fear that she's working with Parks. That the woman I'm falling in love with is one of her disciples, doing her bidding.

It's irrational, but also not, because no one knows Parks like I do.

It might even be my most rational thought ever. Parks had followers—people who were eager for her brain experiments, like the guys at CamDames. They hoped to use her research to make the girls they abducted more pliable.

And what I mean by pliable is pliable in the way I was. It

took drugs and infrasound, but she could make me hard against my will and unable to resist.

It's why I'm desperate to find the girls and intercept them before what happened to me becomes their nightmare too.

I—an absolute expert at self-defensive hand-to-hand combat—was unable to use my skills to save myself. Parks took away my one superpower.

It's my greatest nightmare and shame that the techniques Parks "perfected"—using her terminology—on me have been used on teenage trafficking victims. Because I was *compliant* for Parks, numerous girls may have undergone the same "treatment," resulting in having their bodies' sexual stimulation used against them like mine was on me.

This is perhaps the greatest source of my rage. This is where the violence inside me threatens to break free.

I know it's not my fault, but still, I feel the responsibility for it. The crushing weight of my inability to overcome the sexual stimulators she used against me. Every orgasm my body experienced was a betrayal.

It meant so much to be able to reclaim that with Eden, to feel arousal without shame, to come without horror. But now I'm wondering if even that was Parks's doing, and the darkness inside me grows.

During my missing hours, did I go on some sort of berserker frenzy?

Is that what the blood on my skin and clothes means?

It's not my blood. It's not my car.

But then, not even my *mind* is mine.

The last thing I remember clearly is getting Tobias Redford's address. Is this his car? His blood?

If it is, do I regret doing whatever it was I did to him? He threatened Eden. Demanded she fuck him in payment for his silence. As if the fact that she's a sex worker meant she has no right to consent to whom she shares her body with.

The rage that clouds my broken brain at this is debilitating.

He has payback coming.

Did I deliver it?

There's a big difference between a broken limb and death. And a continuum for meting out punishment. He didn't actually assault her. He threatened her. If I broke his nose, no problem. I wouldn't lose sleep over that. I'm just a guy defending a woman's right to bodily autonomy.

I'm a huge advocate for bodily autonomy, as it turns out. I don't have a college degree, but I still might know a thing or two on the subject. I've had the kind of schooling no one ever wants to go through.

Broken nose, hell, broken limb, and I wouldn't feel the slightest twinge of guilt.

But if I killed him… Well, that's straight-up murder.

Is it possible I killed a man during my lost hours? To the best of my knowledge, I never have before.

The assholes in Alaska tried, but they couldn't make me do it. Parks tried, and I resisted.

But what if this blackout, what if these lost hours, came from *me*? No orders, just rage?

I really am the Hulk, unable to control myself and far too powerful for my own good.

I'm sitting in my driveway, staring at my house—one I've never seen before because I was too much of a chickenshit to come here—and my heart pounds with the anxiety of unanswered questions.

I focus on my surroundings to get my breathing under control. The new structure is in a different location, an improvement over the old one. Better sunlight, the builders promised. I can't tell because it's just after four a.m. in early October. It's dark but for my headlights on the house that is too big now to be called a cabin anymore.

The new location for the main structure means I can walk the ground where the old cabin was. I decide to do that before I enter my fancy new house for the first time so I can wash off the blood of a man I may or may not have killed.

Not the homecoming I'd planned, but then, I'd never planned a homecoming.

Before I get out of the Lexus, I check the glove box for vehicle registration. As expected, this car belongs to Tobias Redford.

That strikes me as bad. But then, would any name on the registration have been good news?

I want to call Mothman, but I need more information before I reach out. One call to Raptor and they'll send a team to take me in. For my own protection, ostensibly, but if I killed—or even simply hurt—Redford, I need to recover my memories of last night. ASAP. Before I find myself in a jail cell. Raptor can't hide me like some kind of fugitive. That would put too many people at risk.

I will not be the reason Mothman faces prison time.

Worse, if I'm locked up, given my history, I'd be sent straight to the mental health unit. Shrinks would be the only people they'd let me talk to.

I have precious little time to figure this nightmare out.

My gut says I've hurt no one. It doesn't feel like the lost time when I was under Parks's control. But my gut feeling can't protect anyone from jail.

All I know is in the past, regaining my sense of self after lost time had been similar to waking up with cottonmouth after drinking too much. There were certain hangover symptoms to coming off Parks's mind games. I always had a stabbing pain in my head, behind my right eye, and there was vertigo that was likely triggered by the infrasound. The fluids in my body had responded to the super-low frequencies in ways that meant unbalancing the pressure in my ears.

But I don't have a headache now and no vertigo.

I climb from the Lexus and cross to where the cabin used to be. The charred remains are gone. Cleaned up and destroyed by professionals. Good riddance.

Now it's just a flat rectangle of grass. If I keep this property, I could put a hot tub here. Or better yet, a swimming pool. I used to love to swim, and if I had a pool installed here it would mean the place I hate most in the world was nothing more or less than a hole in the ground.

My mind wanders, and I find myself imagining a lake.

Eden and I can swim in fresh water stocked with native wildlife, then make love on the shore of my private lake paradise.

My heart aches at that. For the first time since I left her apartment, I feel pain. Real pain. Debilitating pain.

This is one of the lows I haven't been able to feel. Yesterday, with Eden, I felt my first high since Parks got her claws in me, but now I feel the low, and it's so bad, I drop to my knees as tears spill.

I'm crying. Really crying, experiencing all the pain I haven't been able to feel since I woke up in the hospital a year ago.

Is it because of the way I left Eden, or is it because I'm standing here, in the place where Parks fucked me and begged me to treat her like a cherished lover?

I pause on that memory, which hits me with unexpected force, probably brought back thanks to sensory details like the smell of the woods. I remind myself that no matter what she called it, and no matter how I responded, she didn't fuck me. Rape is the only appropriate verb. I wasn't a willing participant, and as a verb, "to fuck" can be quite excellent.

I spent nearly twenty-four hours alternating between fucking Eden and making love to her. And it was the best day of my life. Fucking her was hot and intense. Wild and carnal.

As the word implies. I like the word *fuck* in that context. Parks can't have it.

I apply the word *rape* to my memory. Just because I had an erection and came doesn't mean it wasn't rape. I never consented. I was never given the chance to say yes or no. But if I had been, my answer would have been a firm *no*.

I have spent many hours in the last year trying to remember everything Parks did to me, not because I wanted to remember but because I wanted clues as to who the girl was, the one who led me to believe CamDames is involved with child trafficking. But one thing I refused to do—even though I knew it might open up the memory floodgates—was return here. To the place where I first saw the girl. To the place where Parks raped me.

But now here I am, and there is no hiding from those memories. I need to know. Not just for myself, but for Eden.

For the girl. Whoever she is.

I close my eyes and I remember the skylight. The one I lay beneath as Parks did her thing. I remember staring at the patch of sky and waiting for my nightmare to end.

Now I look around and try to figure out where the living room was. Where the skylight would be.

A large tree was scorched in the fire. The branches that overhung the house were trimmed back in an effort to save it. I remember those branches. One had sometimes crossed the plane of the skylight when the wind was high. I now go to the corner of the property closest to the tree. This must be the living room.

I lie on the cold ground and shift my position until I think I'm beneath the ghost of the skylight. I look up at the starry sky as my body shakes with sobs.

Real sobs. *My* sobs. Pain in all its glorious awfulness.

As I cry, I slide back in time and sink into the memory that has remained elusive for a year. I stare at the predawn sky, and the memory plays out as if it's happening now. I'm back in my nightmare as if I never left and have no idea of what is yet to come.

I refuse to kiss Parks, and she slaps me, but I don't care. I stare up at the skylight and wait for her to finish. She pumps her body up and down on my unwillingly erect penis.

I feel the fade of the sting on my cheek and take pride in it. I am not a hundred percent compliant. She doesn't control all of me.

It thrills me that I made her angry. That I don't satisfy her.

In moments, I will have my orgasm and be done. It's up to her to get herself off before I come and go flaccid.

A male voice says, "That's quite enough, Elizabeth!"

Parks ignores the man and keeps raping me. I'm flat on my back, doing nothing, and she's riding me as she massages her clit. She picks up my hand and tries to force me to do it. My knuckles bump against her but don't give her anything she'd enjoy.

"I said that's enough!"

"No. No. I'm so…" Her voice is breathy. I'm dead inside. I'm about to come, but there's no pleasure in it. It's an automatic response. Like a sneeze. And not even a good sneeze.

My body pulses with orgasm, and she stops pumping up and down and focuses on massaging her clit until she comes.

She then climbs off me and says to the man who is out of my line of sight, "If he were younger, the refractory period would be much shorter. I've found that it generally takes an hour or two to get him hard again."

"I accept your data. I didn't need a demonstration."

"Are you jealous? You know I'm doing this for science."

"You fucked him in front of me because you knew it would piss me off watching you with your toy."

Parks's voice takes on a lilting edge. "Think of that the next time you watch your precious Desiree. Or fuck your wife."

"I don't fuck my wife, and you know it. And Desiree is also a scientific study. That she happens to be young and beautiful is only a bonus."

"I just fucked a beautiful young man in front of you. His cum is still inside me. Do you want to fuck me now? To erase him by spraying your cum over his?"

All I can think is *Fuck her, whoever the hell you are, so she'll leave me alone.*

And he does. They screw on the couch so I can watch. Parks says she wants to see if I'll get erect at seeing them.

I don't. Nothing about Parks turns me on, but I'm trapped on this floor like I'm under a spell. It feels like my whole body is being pressed on like a weighted blanket, but the weights are attached to invisible manacles. I can't escape. Not until the evil witch releases me from her magic.

After they screw, they speculate on my refractory time because I failed to respond to their exhibition.

They debate whether or not there's something wrong with me, because I'm only twenty-five. It doesn't seem to cross their minds that Parks repulses me.

I think she believes I'm sexually attracted to her. I have a vague sense that she's messed with all my memories of sex before now, either to put herself in my partner's place or to steal from me memories of women who aren't her.

"Let's see if he responds to other stimuli," the man says.

He boots a computer, and the first images he shows me are even more repulsive than Parks.

I'm seeing children. Girls who can't be more than fifteen. Their bodies aren't even fully developed.

I close my eyes. It's the only rebellion I can manage. They can't make me look.

But it turns out they can. Parks has something in her toolbox. My eyes pop open. I don't know what it is, but I think I can just hear the high-pitched squeal it emits.

In front of me is a girl with wide brown eyes. She looks terrified. This appears to be a test subject for one of Parks's experiments, because the girl doesn't want to be there even more than I don't want to watch. Someone off camera says, "Starting test," and the look on the girl's face goes from terror to unwelcome pleasure.

The truth is spelled out for me on my large computer monitor. Parks is testing infrasound on her. To make her compliant. Like me. To trigger pleasure sensors so she has no say in her body's response. So people can lie to her and say she enjoyed it so what's the big deal?

I want to vomit.

Lying on my back as I am, I might drown if I vomit. I can't move thanks to the paralyzing spell. Would my body fight it? Would I be able to roll over? Or would I die?

Would Parks guess it was suicide? Would she know I'd welcome death rather than be her victim any longer?

The girl on the screen is asked her name. She says, "Penny," in a meek voice.

The man off-screen says, "No, give your screen name."

"Oh. I think it's….Candi? With an I," she says in a dull voice. Her face flushes. The infrasound is getting to her.

I heave.

But there's nothing in my stomach, so I don't get the escape of drowning.

"This isn't going to work for him. He likes older women. Like me," Parks says.

"Forget the test subjects. Go to CamDames," the man says.

They browse through the options, showing me women of various ages. All these women are of legal age, and I think, unlike the girl—Candi—these videos aren't recordings. This is live. Women in the outside world. Not recorded in a place of pain like Candi, nor are they stuck in a nightmare like the one I'm trapped in, as far as I can tell.

If I could touch the keyboard, I could type a cry for help. But I know that come Monday, when I'm back in the real world, I won't have any memory of my latest weekend with Parks. I'll have hundreds of opportunities to cry for help, but will ignore every single one.

My brain has been partitioned off like a computer hard drive. The data doesn't all work together, and it's not made to. Or maybe it's more accurate to say that right now, I'm on both the C drive and an external F drive. When F is plugged in, I can remember all my weekends with Parks. Plus, I can access my C drive, including some of the partitioned data. But come Monday, the F drive will be ejected and I'll only have access to what C knows.

C doesn't know F even exists when it's not plugged into the USB port. C doesn't know what happens to me when I visit my cabin.

Parks is a world-class brain fucker, and someday I'll kill her with my bare hands.

The man takes control of the computer, and a new face fills the screen.

The woman is young, but not like Candi young. She's probably around my age, and she's breathtakingly sexy. She has long blonde hair but dark eyebrows, telling me her hair is either bleached or a wig. Probably a wig or her brows would be bleached too. Her eyes are wide and beautiful. She's vivacious. Full of light and energy. Warm and inviting.

If I could type a message to this woman to beg for help, she'd help me. I know it.

She's fully clothed, but as we watch, she receives a tip with a request to show her tits.

"You're paying for everyone to get a peep?" she says with a laugh. "That's generous of you."

The man's fingers fly over the keyboard, and I realize he must be Mr. Generous. He's paying so I can see the woman's breasts. I think he wants to make Parks jealous.

The woman cocks her head, her eyes focused to the side. She must be reading the chat. Then she smiles. "Oh. That's sweet of you. Give me his email, and I'll be sure to send him a card with a picture. In the meantime, everyone gets to enjoy his present." She unbuttons her top, revealing her breasts, which are the most perfect I've ever seen. Probably a C cup. They're round and fit her petite frame. I want to lick her pert nipples.

She blows a kiss at the camera then says, "Happy birthday, Chase," and cradles her breasts with both hands.

Is it my birthday?

No. It can't be. My birthday is in July. I look up at the skylight. The branch that sways over the window is bare. I think it must be late fall. Maybe winter.

I turn back to the screen. I will enjoy my present even though it's a lie.

"He's getting hard again," Parks says. She doesn't sound pleased. This is another gift.

"Desiree could get an erection out of stone."

"Are you fucking her?"

His voice has an edge as he says, "If I were, it would be for science."

Instead of making Parks jealous, as I think he wanted, she lets out a deep laugh. "A twenty-five-year-old rocking that body would never look twice at you."

"Maybe so, but you have to use infrasound on your boy toy for him to get it up for you, my dear." The words are said with bittersweetness. I don't know if these people think they love each other but there's a whole lot of jealousy and anger muddling their relationship.

Maybe I'll get lucky and they'll murder each other before the weekend is over.

Wouldn't that be sweet?

I focus on the siren on the monitor. She squeezes her perfect breasts for the men watching—and I can see the list of people enjoying this peep show. Eight or ten men. She responds to comments that pop up on the screen and someone asks her to take off her short skirt.

She smiles and says, "You know I only do that in private sessions. First guy to drop two hundred gets a pussy peek."

Mr. Generous reaches for the computer, but Parks slaps his hand away. "No."

"But it's for science, my dear. Look at him. He's getting harder by the second."

"Then you will watch me fuck him so we can test his refractory period again."

The man turns off the computer. I would sigh in relief if I could.

Desiree is beautiful, but there's no way I want Parks to abuse the erection I got from looking at her.

It's the first erection I've attained in months that wasn't forced on me. And the fact that the bitch is up in knots because Desiree made me hard and Mr. Generous prefers her over Parks gives me another small dose of satisfaction. Happy not-my-birthday to me.

I would smile if I could.

Parks reaches for my penis, and I deflate instantly. Refractory period reset.

She'll force another erection on me soon, but for the moment, I'm safe.

And now, thanks to the woman on the computer screen, I know my body is still mine. I can still feel. And maybe someday, when I'm out of this nightmare, I'll find Desiree and learn to feel again.

Chapter Twenty-Eight

Warm, wet tears streamed down Chase's face as he left the memory that had spent the last year in hiding in his mind.

So much made sense now. His immediate reaction to Desiree. The face of the girl he'd been searching for since last fall.

Penny Candi was the terrified teen. The memory had probably taken place about twenty months ago, after Eden was established at CamDames but before Penny showed up. Since then, Penny had been thoroughly brainwashed. Abused. Used. Manipulated. Was she working for Parks now?

It was possible—even likely—but there was no doubting she was a victim, just as Chase had been when he committed crimes for Parks.

He'd never been quite certain why he fixated on CamDames as the source of the trafficking, but he'd trusted his subconscious, and now he knew why.

He played through the memories in his mind. Unlocked now, they didn't fade or shift like the teasing hints he'd only been able to get fleeting glimpses of in the previous months.

It was like they'd been replanted with roots, and the memories now branched from a solid trunk.

He wondered if he hadn't come back here in the months since the fire because Parks planted a trigger to keep him away. This was also possible. Even likely.

One thing he, Isabel, and Rav had discovered in the early months of their recovery from Alaska was that no memories were truly lost. They could be scrambled and buried, but once the memory was triggered by a stimulus—be it scent, image, or other sense—and the barriers were breached, the memory would return.

Chase lay on the cold grass as dawn inched upward across the sky and felt the tears cool on his cheeks.

Eden.

Was the entire foundation of his attraction to her due to Parks's influence? The thought sickened him.

Could he have nothing for himself? Not even the beautiful woman who made him feel?

Was it all a fantasy because she gave him a hard-on once? Did it have nothing to do with who she was? Who *he* was?

If he'd glimpsed a different camgirl that day, would she have become his fever-dream woman?

No. His brain's rejection was instantaneous.

No.

No.

Eden was special. There was something about her that had spoken to him then, spoke to him now. He'd needed to see her open, healthy sexuality in that moment, when he'd just seen Penny's torment and he'd been deep in his own nightmare.

She'd been a bright joyful spot. Offering him a reason to get an erection that didn't come with guilt or shame.

And that was what she'd been for him at first. But now

that he knew her, had, in fact, made love to her repeatedly, she was so much more.

She was everything.

He bolted to his feet.

Oh fuck.

He'd abandoned her, believing she might be in on it with Parks, but the memory had shown him that she was a bystander in Parks's twisted game with her lover.

And the man he'd seen in the memory had been a fan of Desiree. Did he know who she was in real life? Parks had asked if he was fucking Desiree, which sounded like he did know her.

If so, that meant that not only was Eden innocent, but also she was in danger.

Chapter Twenty-Nine

EDEN

My phone vibrates, and I check the screen. Chase has called at last. I've been sitting on the bed in my workroom since Isabel left sometime before midnight. She promised to keep me in the loop, and I think I believe her, but no one has reached out to me in the intervening hours.

I've been sitting here waiting for Chase's call, holding my phone, not sleeping, but not awake either.

And now I see his words on the screen. He's responded from his Falcon account.

FALCON

I'm sorry.

I need you.

I think I did something.

The messages arrive in a row, before I have a chance to respond.

I'm coming over. Open the garage. I need to
hide.

I finally have a chance to respond. I'm replying from my online account too.

EDEN

Where are you?

A few miles away.

What happened?

I'm not sure. I'll explain when I get there.
Please, open the garage for me. I can't let
anyone see me.

Of course. Everyone at Raptor is looking
for you.

You can't tell them I'm going to your place.
They will be forced to turn me in. I need to
figure out what I've done before that
happens.

My heart aches. Do I listen to him? I promised Isabel I'd let her know immediately if I heard from Chase.

But Chase already doesn't trust me because of my intended profession. If I violate his trust now, I'm certain it's all over. He'll never trust me again.

I can't live with that outcome. I know it happened ridiculously fast—but also it didn't, as I've known him online for months. I really have fallen in love with him. Both hims. Chase and Falcon.

If I believed in soul mates, he would be mine. But it's actually not something I believe, so instead I just know that mentally, we're right for each other. There is a connection there we've always been able to tap in to even when I couldn't see his face and our relationship was nothing more than transactional titillation.

So now I make a choice and I don't call Isabel. Instead, I go to the keypad next to my front door and key in the code to turn off the alarm and open the garage door. I key off the interior door lock so he can enter the stairwell.

I then go to the front window and watch the street in front of my building. A car turns the corner. In the streetlight, I can see it's not Chase's Raptor SUV, but that makes sense. If he were driving that, Raptor would know exactly where he was.

Hours ago, Mothman said it was like his vehicle had been swallowed by a black hole. It simply blipped out of existence.

Where did he get this vehicle? Does he even know?

The sedan pulls into my driveway and disappears into my garage. I return to the keypad and close the garage door and reset the alarm.

He can enter through the interior door because that alarm is turned off. I love this system because I can control every detail.

I didn't skimp on anything when I bought this place and set up my business, and I don't regret it even if I did blow my savings and made it impossible to afford classes this semester. I'll get caught up.

At least now I know I'm safe and Chase is home safe too.

Chase is home. I hope he wants that. *This* with me.

I don't see how I can continue working as a camgirl if Chase lives here, but it's something I'm willing to try to figure out if it means I can be with him.

I wait for him to come up the stairs, but there's no sound of footsteps.

My phone vibrates.

FALCON

Promise me you are alone. That I haven't walked into a trap.

Is he still in the garage? I want to run down to see him, but I respond to his text instead.

EDEN

Of course I'm alone.

No one from Raptor is there?

My heart aches that he doesn't believe me. But have I given him reason to trust me?

Use the link I sent you for a private session. I'll turn on my camera and show you no one is here.

I tap the app on my phone that allows me to do remote privates. I don't use it often because I prefer being hands-free when I'm Desiree and watching the feed on my big-screen desktop in the workroom. But the system, like everything else I bought when I set up my business, is seamless.

I'm live, and I see that Falcon is watching. Before I pan the room, I center my face in front of the camera. "I meant it when I told you I love you. I want you to trust me more than anything. No one is here."

He doesn't respond, and I see that his microphone is off.

I wait for a text and when none comes I show him the living room and kitchen, followed by the pantry with the door to the stairwell, then the hall bathroom, my office nook, master bedroom and attached bath.

A message appears in the chat.

FALCON

What about the other bedroom?

I know he means my workroom.

He damn well knows I'd never let anyone from Raptor in there. Hell, I didn't even let *him* see it, and he knows better than anyone what I do in that room. It's important to me to keep the space separate from the rest of my life.

But I also want him to trust me, so I pull out my key and unlock the knob. It's not a dead bolt, but it is meant to be an exterior door lock, so it's solid. I step inside my workroom and pan the camera over the bed, the dresser that holds my supply of sex toys, the array of cameras that point to the bed. This room connects to the hall bathroom, and I unlock that doorknob with the same key to show him it's a room he's already seen.

I then turn the camera to my face again. "See? No one here. Now please, come up and talk to me."

A familiar voice behind me sends chills up my spine. "You've got a sweet setup here, Desiree."

I turn and face Penny in my workroom as the open hall door to the bathroom slams closed.

Through the phone speaker, I hear the distorted voice that I heard on Thursday night as someone held a gun to my head. "It's time for your final performance as Desiree."

In that moment, I realize I have a Trojan Horse parked in my garage. The person on the other end of the text messages hadn't been Chase at all. And I foolishly unlocked the gates and welcomed them in.

Sling Man and Jacked Knee both point guns at me and watch me change into one of my Desiree outfits. Without the masks they wore the other night, I recognize both men. They were definitely security guards at CamDames. I don't remember their names. It would have been so much easier if I did. I wish I'd told Chase the truth when he showed me Sling Man's photo a lifetime ago.

But then, if their names could be found through the legal side of the corporation, I'm sure Mothman would have done it by now. So they probably were never officially on the payroll.

They're working for the computerized voice that emits from my phone, and I wonder who it could be that he—I'm assuming the person is a he—is being so careful to not let me hear his voice.

It makes me think of Chase and Falcon and why I didn't recognize his voice, and so I have to assume this person is one of Desiree's regulars. I have about twenty to choose from, which is too much for my brain right now.

The voice sounds like something from a science fiction horror movie, and that alone fries my brain and derails my thoughts.

But still I try to focus, fighting through the fear. Aside from being a regular, does the voice belong to someone I know in real life? Is it the CEO of CamDames? I met him a few times. I would recognize him. But it could just as likely be someone lower in the hierarchy. I've met all of them too.

The fact that I don't hear his voice gives me hope that they plan to let me live.

And that is why I cooperate. I want to live.

I will do whatever is necessary to survive.

Given the leers from Sling Man and Jacked Knee, I'm pretty sure I know what they have in mind.

I'll do it too. But make no mistake, even though I will appear to be willing, it will be rape. I do not consent to what is about to happen to me.

But I won't fight if it means I'll live. I will suffer, but I will live. Right now, that's the primary goal.

I'm naked in front of two men and Penny. Sling Man snaps photos like he's a gawking tourist in Times Square.

I tell myself not to care. I've been on camera naked hundreds of times. I post nude photos behind a paywall. I'm comfortable with my body and my sexuality, and it has earned me a lot of money.

But of course, this is different.

This man is probably going to rape me on camera sometime in the next hour.

I will survive.

I dress in a lacy teddy that's bright red and feathered. It's not my favorite because it's not really that pretty. It's meant to be over the top, more costume than actually sexually appealing. My personal style is less ostentatious.

But whatever. I will survive. I hardly care that they chose my ugliest teddy for whatever is about to happen.

I reach for a wig, but Jacked Knee stops me. "No wig. No makeup."

They're making certain either I'll never willingly work as a camgirl again or that I'll never become a psychotherapist. Possibly both.

Fine.

I will survive.

And then I'll figure out how to pick up the broken pieces of my life. Of my dreams.

Whatever happens, *I* will not break.

I will be messed up and angry and bleeding inside, but they can't break me. Breaking implies fixing, and there will be no fixing this. There will be healing. There will be hurting, and then there will be finding new tools to process and move forward.

Even as I tell myself these things, I imagine taking a knife and sliding it across Sling Man's throat.

I've never entertained a violent fantasy like this before, and I realize these men have already changed me.

They've shown me there's violence I would do if I could. I would strike right now, and they haven't even touched me yet.

All they've done is make me get naked and leered at me, and let's face it, getting naked in front of men so they can leer at me is literally in my job description.

But of course, none of that happens in person. I've wondered if I could work at a strip club. I have considered it.

My total and utter lack of ability to dance prevented me from ever trying it. I have no rhythm. It would be ridiculous, and my tits aren't good enough to not have talent. I'd starve from lack of tips.

But now I see how much I embraced the distance of the camera. The safety of not seeing the men's faces. Of smelling their breath.

Of being out of reach of their groping hands.

I never had it in me to be a stripper, and I was fooling myself in thinking I could handle it.

"Sit on the bed," the imperious robot commands over my phone's speaker.

I follow orders and position myself in front of the cameras.

Penny brings my laptop forward and tells me to enter my password to take my site online.

I meet her gaze, and for the first time since she arrived, she doesn't flinch or look away. I stare hard, and I think I see the lost girl who's screaming in agony even now.

Penny is a victim. She always has been. She's currently an accomplice but wasn't Chase an accomplice at one time too?

But this doesn't have to do with what happened to Chase a year ago, does it? This is about CamDames and sex trafficking. This is about stopping Chase from continuing to mess with their business by rescuing girls.

This can't be connected to the torture he underwent with Parks or what Isabel went through in Alaska. Isabel told me she doesn't think Parks experimented on her, but she also said she'll probably never know and the fear would sometimes wake her in the middle of the night. Now that she's pregnant with her and Alec's first child, she has a new fear that the nightmares and mental health issues will make her a terrible mom…but like Chase, she's afraid of seeking professional help.

I was stunned that she opened up to me like she did, but I'm also one of the few people who has an inkling of what happened, and it slipped out.

She's even afraid to tell Alec of her fears because she knows he'd wrap her in bubble wrap and not let her volunteer at the shelter that has given her life meaning the last six months.

She told me that Jasmine is doing well and seeking legal separation from the stepfather who was sexually abusing her.

I cried at that.

Now I remind myself this is why I'm in this situation now. Because Chase saved Jasmine, and no matter what, I'm so glad he did.

"Enter the password," Penny says with a hard edge to her voice.

It's only been about ten seconds, but my brain traveled quite a distance in that time. It's a coping mechanism I perfected when I was a runaway child bride.

I reach for the laptop to settle it on my lap, as the name suggests. "No," Penny says. "And don't get cute."

I nod and type my password while she holds the computer. She tilts the screen ever so slightly, and I see the minimized icon on the bottom right.

My fingers fly lightning fast, so neither Sling Man nor Jacked Knee can catch the extra strokes as I open the app and push the notification. I'm going live from my apartment, and all my subscribers will be notified. Maybe one of them will call the police.

Given what the world is about to see, this really is my last outing as Desiree.

I minimize the app, but it's running. This won't be a private session with—I presume—Chase. Nope, the whole world is going to see what happens here, and Penny is the one who wants that to happen.

Is she sabotaging me or helping me? I have no clue, but I'm better off with the coming events airing live than I am without it.

I will survive.

And maybe so will Penny.

"I'm logged in," I say.

"Give her the letter to read," Mr. Roboto says.

Penny hands me an envelope that isn't sealed. Before I can open it, she says, "Not yet." She hits the button for the video feed and says, "Now. Read it."

I slip the single piece of paper from the envelope, and my eyes tear when I read the first line.

I face the camera, clear my throat and say, "My dearest Chase, you have refused to talk to me or acknowledge my messages, so I'm forced to reach out to you in a way you cannot ignore. Your slutty replacement for me will read my words as I remind you of how much you enjoyed being my lover for the two years we were together…"

Chapter Thirty

CHASE

I watch in horror as beautiful, sexy, amazing Eden sits in a garish red teddy I've never seen before and reads words on a page meant to gut me.

I'd be lying if I said they didn't.

It doesn't matter that tears are streaming down Eden's cheeks as she says the words, I'm still hearing Parks in her voice. The woman who took everything from me is now taking Eden and tainting her with my nightmare. Making her part of it.

She was my one happiness. The one pleasure and joy I managed to find on my own.

At least I thought it was on my own. But that was Parks's partner's doing.

Eden reads the speech, and I block out the words. I can't listen. It could be a ransom demand and I'd have no clue. My brain can't process it. We've moved so far beyond the intricacies of buying ice cream.

But Parks knew this. She planned this. She knew my brain would shut down. That was her goal, to render me useless while Eden is in danger.

I'm inside my new cabin that is too big to be called a cabin. The place is actually quite nice. It's a one-eighty departure from the one where I was tortured.

The new place is sleek and modern, right down to the integrated Wi-Fi and computer. I'm spitting distance from the wilderness of the Appalachian trail, and I have my own satellite internet connection so I don't have to wait for the phone or cable company to finally lay cable or a cell tower to go up to give me my 5G or whatever the current level of G is now.

I didn't waste time exploring the house, I went straight to the computer and logged in. I was going to message Mothman and tell him some of my suspicions and let him know that I don't have my phone or vehicle—and whoever does has a backdoor into Raptor—when I read the direct message from Desiree that a session was about to begin. The first message was only to me, but then a second went out to all her followers, and I knew then that something bad was going down.

Much as I wanted to keep this on the down low with Mothman, if what I suspect is true, Eden is in critical danger. Before the session began, I blasted the message using the urgent Rap App, a company-wide alert that delivers to every on-duty but not covert operative's phone accompanied by a loud, screeching tone that defies all silencing.

It's after five a.m. Time to wake up and save my girl. Woman.

Soul mate.

Every one of my coworkers is now probably watching Eden read the nightmare message from Parks. A message the bitch had probably crafted down to the very last detail with the intention of destroying me.

Would it work?

Maybe. Probably.

It doesn't matter as long as it doesn't destroy Eden.

I open a chat with Mothman.

CHASE

My phone and vehicle were stolen sometime in the night.

MOTHMAN

I know. I think they used your phone to trick Eden into letting them in.

Not my SUV?

No. They were in a different car.

How do you know?

Because Alec used a device to grab the security code when Isabel left late last night. I've worked with her security company and have a portal. I'm in her system. Have access to her cameras. I control the locks. Falcon team is mobilized.

I rock back in my seat and read the words again, stunned. My team doesn't just have my back, they have Eden's too.

Are you saying the team is there? Inside?

They're in the interior stairwell now.

I feel a sharp burn of anger as Eden sobs on my computer screen.

Then why the fuck haven't they moved in?

MOTHMAN

> Two reasons. One, they wanted to know what the plan was with Eden. Don't worry, we've got Leah's nanodrones crawling all over. Isabel planted them last night. It's how we got the specs on the security system. If anyone touched Eden, they'd have moved. No one has laid a finger on her. Promise.

No. They just made her go live, destroying both her business and her dream of being a psychotherapist in one fell swoop.

CHASE

> And the other reason?

> They killed one of Eden's fellow grad students and set you up for it. Hoping something they do here will give us more evidence against them in the murder.

I stare at the words, amazed that I can achieve an uncharted level of stunned heretofore not recorded by trackers of human reactions. This is a cat ten hurricane.

> Tobias Redford?

> Yes.

> What makes you certain I didn't kill him?

It's Mothman's certainty that shook me to cat ten. I pause, then type the words that could shatter me.

> I lost time. The car I woke up in belongs to Tobias.

MOTHMAN
Aside from the fact that you aren't a killer
and never have been?

There is always a first time.

In all the years you worked for Raptor, you
have never once used your gun outside a
training session.

Wrong. I pulled my gun the other night.

They had a gun to Eden's head. Doesn't
count. Also, you didn't pull the trigger. You
insist on teaching unarmed fighting, even
though the majority of our trainees are armed
ninety percent of the time. Even when you've
gotten in fights protecting clients or saving
teens from CamDames, you've always
entered the battle unarmed. My dude, you
have a problem with guns.

All at once, I'm sent back in time. A memory from Alaska
that haunts me. I'm bound to a chair in one of the shoot houses.
We're about to rehearse a hostage scenario that will be incorpo-
rated into the next training session, and I'm the hostage. Godfrey
and I are alone. The cameras aren't running because the practice session hasn't begun yet. Godfrey decides to play with me.
He points his pistol at my head and dry fires repeatedly.

My terror that he's about to shoot me in the head is very
real. I nearly piss myself, but I don't call out for help. I can't.
I'm deep under Godfrey's control at this point, already
stalking Isabel and I don't even know it. Godfrey would have
done what he could to obscure this memory if he had the
opportunity, but Brad Fraser enters the room and nearly
comes to blows with Godfrey in my defense.

Godfrey ended up suspended for two weeks after Brad reported what he did, but he wasn't fired. Months later, I learned that Brad's report on the incident was buried by one of Godfrey's accomplices, saving his job so he could continue to torture me.

Mothman is right. I don't like guns. Not anymore.

CHASE

I take it Redford was shot?

MOTHMAN

Yes. Shot to the heart. But that's not the only reason we're a hundred percent behind you.

What else?

Hawk went to Redford's house to find you around midnight. Door was wide open, so he went inside. He found Tobias dead on the floor of his living room. He immediately called the FBI. Given the connection to you and the bombing, it's likely they'll have jurisdiction.

While he was waiting, he noticed Redford was wearing an Apple Watch. On a hunch, he put on gloves and unlocked the phone that was still on the coffee table using the face recognition—thank goodness Redford hadn't been shot in the face.

Hawk dumped all the data he could grab to Raptor's cloud, just like I taught him. He made sure to suggest the feds do the same while they can still unlock the phone with face ID. Apple still isn't playing nice with feds on that, even when the person is the victim.

MOTHMAN

> It'll probably take a bit for the feds to confirm, but the watch's fitness tracker is a pretty good gauge of time of death and marked when his heart stopped beating. According to his watch, you were still at Eden's when he was murdered.

CHASE

> His killer texted Eden with Redford's phone to bait me to go there?

> Looks like it.

And I walked right into their trap. They must have hit me with infrasound the moment I arrived.

Chapter Thirty-One

*E*den finished reading the ridiculously long, nightmarish letter. The only thing she learned from the experience was that this had *everything* to do with what happened to Chase last year. Somehow, Dr. Parks was still getting people to do her bidding.

How?

Her gaze fixed on Penny, and she remembered what Isabel had told her about infrasound and the implant in Chase's head.

Had Penny been chipped? Probably.

But who was continuing Parks's experiment from prison? And how had they gotten mixed up with CamDames?

She faced Sling Man. The camera was still rolling. They weren't done with this game of torturing Chase from afar.

She clenched her jaw. Maybe she should fight instead of being compliant. But would fighting get her killed?

She wished Chase had taught her some self-defense as they'd discussed during her shift at the coffee shop forever ago.

But they'd never had a chance for that, and it hardly

mattered now, because even if she could fight the man physically on her, there was another man with a gun, plus Penny remained a wild card.

Sling Man stepped to the foot of the bed. "After two years of watching you online, I'm ready to finally get a piece." He nodded to the camera. "And if you perform well, we can monetize it on a hard-core site." He wrapped his castless hand around her throat. "The dirty motherfuckers on the paywall sites love a good choke fuck."

Eden tried not to show fear. He would just get off on it, but it proved impossible as a shudder went through her.

Sling Man's thumb ran over her throat as if he were looking for the best place to press.

All at once, the room erupted in chaos as men in combat fatigues entered through the bathroom and hallway doors.

Sling Man jolted as he was hit with something—had someone shot him?—and he spun around with the impact.

Jacked Knee found himself in a headlock by a Black man, as the white guy who might have shot Sling Man pinned the prick to the floor and cuffed him.

Eden looked to Penny, whose face had gone white as a sheet. She probably expected these men would tackle and cuff her too. She faced Eden, and it looked like she was trying to say something. She managed to squeak out a single word: "Help—" Then her body jolted, going bolt upright, her face a mask of pain and terror. She dropped to the floor.

Eden knelt at the young woman's side and placed a finger on her throat to check her pulse, which she felt immediately. Her chest rose and fell. She was breathing.

"I—I don't get it. What happened?"

The Black operative who'd subdued Jacked Knee dropped to the opposite side of Penny's limp body. "Same thing happened to Chase when he tried to ask me for help when he was still under Parks's control."

"How is that possible?"

"We think there was a posthypnotic suggestion that activated the implant when he resisted orders or tried to ask for help."

The man gently turned the girl's head and touched her scalp behind her ear. "I think I feel a scar."

The other operative cursed. To Sling Man, he said, "Who chipped the girl?"

"Don't know what you're talking about. And I only talk if I can get a deal."

The man had been about to rape her and he was already trying to cut a deal while Penny lay unconscious. She hoped he rotted in prison for the rest of his life.

"Can I punch him?" the white operative asked the Black one.

"Better not. Leah's drones are recording everything, and we'll have to turn it all over to the FBI if we're going to clear Chase."

The dark-haired man grumbled something about maybe a gap in the data not being a big deal. He had a chiseled jaw coated with at least a day's growth. Dawn was just breaking, and she guessed these men had been pulled out of bed early if they'd ever had a chance to sleep at all.

"So, who are you, exactly?" she asked as her gaze bounced from man to man.

The one who'd checked Penny's scalp answered. "I'm Sean Logan." He nodded to the other operative. "That's Ian Boyd. We're on Falcon team with Chase."

y the time Chase arrived at Eden's, she was sitting on her couch wrapped in a thick robe, talking to an FBI agent who was frequently called in when Raptor was involved. She was a personal friend to Curt Dominick from back when he was a US attorney for the District of Columbia.

Curt, who'd then moved on to be the US attorney general for a few years, and Senator Alec Ravissant were good friends. Curt would never cross a line or show favoritism, but whenever Raptor was involved, he followed the investigation to make sure nothing was overlooked, and often Agent Sara Seong would be part of that review process.

Chase knew Agent Seong well after having been at the center of two such investigations. He liked the woman but was still braced for being hauled off and Mirandized with murder charges. Raptor had data that proved Chase was innocent, but the FBI had to confirm it first.

At least with Agent Seong involved, he knew he could speak frankly, and odds were she knew exactly what information Raptor had and how they'd obtained it.

He wasn't surprised the FBI was investigating. Last year, they'd been the go-to agency because they'd needed to bypass a local sheriff who'd been a suspect. Then the bombing had a US senator as a potential target, which made it a federal case. In the end, the crimes were classified as hate crimes—Parks had selected her victims based on race—and hate crimes also fell under federal jurisdiction.

He presumed it was the connection to last year's case, and the fact that Penny was now in the same hospital he'd been sent to when he collapsed with the chip in his head that had been the connection they needed to tie it all together and keep it federal. Otherwise, it was unclear if the feds would have jurisdiction in the Redford murder.

Mothman had been hopeful, but he hadn't been able to assure Chase he wouldn't be arrested if he showed his face to a federal agent. But he came anyway because he had to see Eden.

Her gaze met his, and she bolted to her feet. "Chase!"

The room went silent. Or maybe his hearing cut out, because all his brain could take in was Eden, dwarfed by her fuzzy blue robe. He crossed to her, wrapped his arms around her waist, and lifted her to his chest.

Her arms circled his neck as her body draped against his. He turned and marched down the hall. His hearing returned, and he heard Agent Seong say, "Five minutes, Johnston, then we need to talk."

That she was letting them have a few minutes alone was a good sign.

He kicked Eden's bedroom door closed behind him and settled on the bed with her in his arms, snuggled on his lap as he leaned against the headboard.

Her body shook as she quietly sobbed. Finally, she met his gaze, her cheeks damp with flowing tears. "I'm so sorry I read her letter."

He ran his thumbs over her cheeks, wiping away tears only to have more take their place. "Shhh. I know they forced you. It's not your fault. I didn't listen past the first line anyway."

"But it is my fault. I let them in. Jesus. I was so stupid."

"They had my phone. That was *my* fault. If I hadn't played right into their hands, none of this would have happened. I'm so sorry, Eden. My stupid meltdown caused you trauma and could have killed you." Now his own tears fell. "I'm so sorry I ran out on you."

She cupped his cheek, taking a swipe at his tear with a thumb. "Your reaction was perfectly understandable given what happened to you. I know you hate me for it, but I do have a degree in psychology and enough graduate classes to understand. You were doing the best you could in the moment. I accept that."

"I could never hate anything about you, Eden." He pressed his lips to her forehead. "I meant it when I said I was falling in love with you. That didn't change when I found out about your studies, I just couldn't cope in the moment. It stirred every irrational fear I have."

"I think given what happened to you, your fear is completely rational." She brushed her lips over his. "And I love you too."

A tiny bubble of joy filled his chest, but popped as he realized what he needed to tell her. "I remembered something this morning. Before you went live."

"What is it?"

"Mothman told me you met Isabel last night."

She nodded. "She was only slightly happier to hear about my studies than you were."

"Did she tell you what Parks did—about infrasound and the implant?"

"A little. She also said there was a lot she wouldn't say, that it was for you to decide if you wanted to tell me." She rubbed his chin, her fingers stroking the bristles along his jawline. "She cares about you a lot and is quite protective."

"She's the big sister I never had." He smiled thinking about how much he'd needed Isabel's support this last year. "Did she tell you how the memory shit Parks did works? Memories of infrasound events are never truly erased, but they can be buried?"

"She did."

"Well, this morning a memory came back to me, and I discovered why I reacted so strongly the first time I visited your room at CamDames. I saw you when I was under the influence of both infrasound and I think some hypnotic suggestion and possibly even a drug cocktail she cooked up to keep me compliant. The combination was how she managed to get away with raping me one weekend a month for two years. The hypnotic suggestions were how she kept control of me when she wasn't around."

"So you think…hypnosis, drugs, and infrasound frequencies…are the whole reason you're attracted to me? That she planted me in your brain?" Eden pulled back, wrapping her arms around herself. As if she was afraid to touch him now.

"Honestly, I don't know. It's entirely possible knowing her. And it horrified me at first, this idea that I can't even have this—you—without her vile touch being on it."

Eden's face crumpled, and the tears that had stopped flowing now overflowed again. "You think…this thing between us isn't real?"

She pulled her knees to her chest and wrapped her arms around them tight, completely cutting herself off from him.

He gently took her hand and brought it to his lips. "No. I love you, Eden, and even though it fucks with my head to know she's insinuated herself between us, it doesn't change the fact that you're the only person who's made me feel since my long nightmare began."

She unfurled from the ball she'd made herself into and reached for him, hugging him again. "Oh thank God. Because I need you, Chase."

"I need you too, sweetheart."

She tucked herself on his lap again. Her soft dark hair tickled his chin. He was in heaven with her in his arms, it was that simple. "When you appeared on the computer screen, my reaction to you was instantaneous. And by reaction, I mean erection. And it made Parks jealous. Which was satisfying in that I liked anything that pissed her off or upset her. She wanted to believe I was really her lover and not a guy she had to use stimulants with so she could use my body. Make no mistake, her raping me had the same power and control dynamic that occurs when the victim is not a cis male. Her desire to believe I wanted her was just another layer."

"Well, I'm glad I gave you a moment of satisfaction in what must have been a horrifying time."

"Honey, you gave me hope. It was the first natural reaction I had to anything when she controlled my body. My mind. My whole world. It was you, Eden. And it might have only been your body at first, but it was also your light and energy. I connected with that when I needed light. And later I found you on my own and it was the same feeling. You were the light I needed in my life. The light I still need."

"I need you so much, it's scary," she whispered. "Like, I don't even know where this feeling is coming from because I've never *needed* anyone. Not since I ran away from my so-called husband when I was fifteen."

His heart surged at the idea her feelings were as intense as his, that a woman as amazing as Eden O'Keeffe could love him back.

There was a knock on the door. "We need to talk, Johnston," Seong shouted through the door.

"Five more minutes," Chase responded, not even making it a request.

"I'm setting a timer," the FBI agent said.

"Fine." He hadn't been certain she'd agree, but that told him he was in a better position than he'd feared.

He turned his attention to the woman in his arms. "So my memory told me a few things we need to discuss. One, I think Penny Candi is the girl I saw—in a different memory— that set me on my quest to uncover CamDames' trafficking of young girls. I've never actually seen a photo of Penny. I think it's possible the reason Penny asked you to sub for her that first night we met was because Parks—or whoever is running the show now—suspected I was the guy who was intercepting girls, and if I saw Penny's face, my memory barriers might fail.

"I never go into the shop when we do an extraction, but they were probably being extra cautious. And then when you called us—that made their caution worth it, but also a mistake, because Penny probably would have convinced Tony not to call."

"Penny is a victim. Like you," Eden said.

He nodded. "Absolutely. She probably really would have been a clueless barista that night. But she would have recognized the goons outside the window as being from her legit job at CamDames, which might be why they returned to the shop that night. They didn't know Penny wasn't working. They might have figured she'd answer their questions. But then they saw you and had to go all in to figure out what you knew. I have a feeling they're in the dark about Parks and are working for someone else altogether."

"Who are they working for? I mean, I know it's the creepy cloaked guy with the robot voice, but who is he?"

"I was wondering if you'd put it together yet."

She shook her head. "I'm still reeling that all this is connected to what happened to you with Parks."

"It's connected to you too. The memory I recovered today was an important one. We've long suspected Parks had a lover, but couldn't find a trace of who it was. Now I know I met him. And he's one of the regulars at your site."

Chapter Thirty-Two

$\mathcal{E}$den reeled at that and then wondered why it even surprised her. *Of course he was a regular.*

Why it hadn't crossed her mind was the bigger question. "Who is it?"

"I think he knows you in real life. He's been watching you and putting you on the screen to make Parks's jealousy spike. She was jealous of his infatuation with you, and it turned to something darker when I got an erection just looking at you. I think her lover is—or was—married, which is why they kept the relationship a secret. He said something about never screwing his wife."

Married. Didn't screw his wife. It clicked into place. "Hank. Mr. Roboto is Hank."

"He's the old guy who drops in frequently?"

She nodded, thinking of the last two years and how many times Hank had shown up when she was online. Weekly, certainly. Sometimes more. Rarely less. "He was always so sweet. In the beginning, he wanted more of the kinky private sessions." She shook her head. "I think the first time I had to masturbate for a client was with him. I faked my orgasm to get it over with."

She closed her eyes. Had she actually had virtual finger banging with the monster who'd held a gun to her head?

She hadn't faked it every time with Hank, but it was close. Thankfully, since she went solo, he hadn't paid her premium fees for private sessions very often.

She bolted from the bed, leaving Chase's warm body, and ran to the toilet, where she lost the meager food she'd managed to eat this morning after Sling Man and Jacked Knee were arrested.

The man she'd shared her body with online multiple times was the same person who had enslaved Penny. Who worked with Parks to enslave Chase.

Done heaving, she rocked back on her heels and wiped her chin with toilet paper and dropped it in the bowl before flushing.

Chase was by her side, with her even in this. She leaned against him. "I hate everything about this. I was *good* at being a camgirl and had a healthy attitude about it. I am not ashamed. I will never be ashamed of enjoying full body autonomy. But now…I feel sick and dirty. He took my sense of autonomy from me. Made my job dirty. I've never looked at my performances as dirty—in a bad way—until just this minute. I figured I was helping people—like you, and I thought, like Hank. Giving them a safe and healthy way to explore sexuality when other avenues weren't available."

"I'm sorry, Eden."

She leaned back against the wall, not ready to leave the basin just in case nausea rose again. "So what is Parks's connection to CamDames?"

Chase leaned beside her, threading his fingers through hers. "So here's the part where my horror and shame kick in. I think she was working with CamDames to make the girls more compliant during sex." He shook his head as if he was erasing the last word he said from his mind. "Not sex. Rape. They wanted the girls compliant, like me." He took a deep breath and continued, "Maybe if I'd been able to resist, Penny wouldn't have gone through the same nightmare. I was Parks's greatest success, and she wanted to replicate it. She no longer had her supply of undocumented immigrants, so she turned to teenage girls to keep her experiments going after she perfected her technique on me."

Eden raised their joined hands to her lips and kissed the back of his hand. "You were a victim. You're a survivor now, but you were a victim then and she attacked you from a direction that was impossible to resist. You could be the best ninja fighter in the world—and I've seen nothing that indicates that's not a straight-up fact—but all the muscles and skills and reflexes and weapons in the world couldn't have stopped her. She had access to your brain's internal wiring, and nobody knew it. I'm so, so, so sorry for everything she did to you and the pain you suffered, and not a single thing was your fault. And it definitely isn't remotely your fault that she committed similar atrocities on others."

"I know all these things on one level, but I don't know if my soul will ever believe it."

"I want a future with you, Chase, and I promise right now that I don't want to be your therapist or muck around in your brain. Anything you declare is off-limits will be a hundred percent off-limits. But if there's one thing I wish I could help you with, it's that point—understanding that everything she did is on her and none of it is on you."

He squeezed the hand entwined with his. "We'll have to take that aspect one day at a time."

"That's a solid offer. I accept."

He let out a soft laugh, and her heart warmed. Together,

they could get through this. And it looked like together was possible.

Well, if he wasn't arrested. "We should probably go talk to Agent Seong."

They both rose from the floor, but before leaving the bathroom, she stepped up to the sink and dipped her head down to the faucet for a mouthful of water. She swished it around, then spit it out and followed up with a swish of mouthwash. She turned to face Chase, who leaned against the doorjamb with an unguarded smile on his lips.

She felt the same adrenaline rush—or whatever it was— she'd felt the first time she saw him. It had been wild, and she'd wanted to invite him to a hotel and explore every inch of him with her mouth.

Now she had explored him with mouth and hands, and she only wanted more. Even now, after the intensity of the morning.

Maybe especially now, to forget the intensity of the morning.

He seemed to be thinking the same thing, because he pulled her against him and kissed her slowly, nudging her mouth open with his tongue, and then he was inside and her entire body wanted to melt with the sweet, hot, tender burn of his kiss. When he released her, he whispered, "I'm counting the minutes until all this is behind us so I can take you to bed again and we can both forget everything except the feel of each other's bodies."

She smiled and ran her hands over his erection, sadly covered by thick denim. "I can't wait." She pushed back from his chest. "But first, FBI."

"Oh, for a dollar for every time I've heard that line."

She snickered.

Before leaving her room, she quickly changed into yoga pants and a tank top, pulling on a soft, light hoodie over the top. Now that Chase was here, she didn't need the comfort of her plush robe to fight the chill that had encased her heart after the assault.

After she'd changed, they left her room, walking down her short hallway hand in hand. Every pair of eyes in the room turned to them and conversation stopped. She saw the looks of concern on people's faces, and while she understood it all came from their care for Chase, she couldn't help but wonder if this was a look he received all the time from the members of Falcon team.

It was wonderful to know they all cared, but still, she guessed the concern probably weighed on him.

It was Nate—aka Hawk—who broke the heavy silence. "So when Agent Seong leaves, we all want to hear the real story of how you kicked three men's asses at once."

"We need to check the bird drone Leah made and see if it caught video," Sean suggested.

Chase rolled his eyes. "You don't need video to believe it. You know I'm the best."

That was met with grumbling laughter, in which all the grumbling was clearly fake. "They hate it that none of them can beat me when we spar," Chase said to Eden in a stage whisper.

She laughed. And it was a real laugh, tension cut.

"You should have seen them pumping me for details on the fight in the garage," she whispered loudly back. "It was like I was giving them a sneak peek at their favorite comic book and they wanted details about every panel."

"Did you tell them about how I jacked the guy's knee at the same time I got the other one in a headlock?"

"Wait," Ian said. "That happened simultaneously?" He looked accusingly at Eden. "You didn't say that. That's the best part."

Eden refrained from pointing out that was the moment

the gun was pointed at her head, because that wasn't the purpose of this conversation. They were telling Chase they respected him in a way he could hear it. They really were a lovely team. She hoped she could fit in with this part of Chase's world.

Would his friends judge her for being a sex worker? Did they deep down believe she deserved what almost happened to her this morning? She didn't think so, but it would take a while for her to believe it.

She didn't expect acceptance and could understand why it wouldn't be forthcoming. She would do her best not to judge even if people judged her. But this was one important reason why she'd never told anyone who wasn't associated with CamDames about her other job.

"Chase told me he suspects Mr. Roboto is one of my regular clients," she said, owning her job in a roomful of people who might not approve, but who were friends of Chase so she had to accept them even if they didn't accept her.

"One of your regulars?" Seong asked. "Do you have a name?"

She shook her head. "His screen name was Hank, but it's almost certainly an alias."

"But he was a subscriber, so you'll have financial records we can trace."

"Odds are he paid like I did," Chase said, owning the fact that he was a client and making her love him even more. "Untraceable prepaid Visa cards. I bought them with cash." He gave Eden an apologetic smile. "I was concerned about my employment with Raptor—there are always people looking for weaknesses to exploit. You were mine. Unfortunately, Parks already knew about you."

She wrapped an arm around his waist and squeezed, leaning her temple against his chest, stunned that he'd say this in front of his team. He wasn't shying away from how they met at all. "No need to explain."

She then straightened and nodded to Agent Seong, tilting her head toward the workroom door. She hadn't entered the room since she'd left it after Sling Man and Jacked Knee were subdued.

She'd learned their names at some point earlier, but she'd ignored the input, preferring the names she'd given them in her head. It was less personal that way.

She would reach out to her therapist—the woman who'd helped her so much when she was sixteen and who remained an important fixture in her life—and discuss what was healthy in that regard.

It crossed her mind she could probably talk to her fellow grad students—

Her mind killed the idea off mid-think. Tobias had been murdered, and Chase was, in theory, a suspect, even if Tobias's fitness data, combined with Eden's alarm system data—which had logged the time Chase had left here yesterday—and Chase's SUV and cell phone data, which had his GPS location at the same time, would exonerate him eventually.

It would take time for that information to be released by investigators. Until then, there would be no turning to her fellow grad students. She might not even return to grad school.

She didn't believe for a minute that Chase had murdered in cold blood, but until the FBI named a different suspect, no one in the department would believe anything else.

Personally, Eden's money was on Sling Man as the shooter.

Tobias had been a pawn in this whole little nightmare, and like many a pawn, he'd been the piece taken in a move aimed at checkmate.

With Chase being the king who was blocked in from all sides.

She shook off the miserable thoughts. They would just have to find Tobias's *real* killer. Now. Today. Not the guy who pulled the trigger, but the guy who pulled the strings. Hank.

She settled in front of the computer in the workroom and opened up the payment app. "I'll download the transactions and send everything to you."

"Will you let Mothman have access to your account?" Chase asked. "I can guarantee he'll be able to track things down faster if he's legally authorized. He'll leave the money alone, of course."

Eden gave him a sharp nod. "Also of course. Anything that gets us answers faster works for me."

"I need evidence that's valid in a court of law," Seong said in a clipped tone Eden had grown used to. The Asian American agent had a brisk, no-nonsense style that was comforting. She'd said she'd worked the Parks investigation last year, and Eden guessed no one else in the FBI knew more about Dr. Elizabeth Parks than she did. There had been enough evidence to put the death penalty on the table, and that had been what pushed the psychologist to plead guilty and accept life without parole.

"It'll be a hundred percent legal if Eden authorizes Mothman's access and a thousand times faster than the FBI could get a warrant and access."

Seong nodded. "Do it."

While Eden showed the agent her transaction register and pointed out the payments from Hank, Chase texted Mothman.

In a matter of minutes, she'd given a stranger whose real name she didn't even know access to her online bank account. She should be terrified by this, but strangely, it wasn't even a blip on her fear radar.

She trusted Chase, and that was enough.

"Tell me everything you know about Hank," Seong said.

"I kept a profile on each of my clients," Eden said. "It's in my file cabinet." She rose to grab it, then saw Chase's face.

It hit her then, what she'd just said and what it would mean to him.

"It wasn't psychological. It was to help my memory so I would know what to ask and talk about. Know their preferences. Even preferred language." She lowered her voice and said, "But yeah, I made notes on what I suspected would fit in their psychological profile too."

It had been an interesting exercise for her, and she'd developed a lot of theories about men and their relationships with camgirls in the process.

"You have one on me?"

She had no choice but to say the truth. "Yes."

His face was unreadable, but he said, "Get your files for Seong."

"If you're certain Mr. Roboto is Hank, that's the only one I need," Seong said. Eden would laugh that the woman had adopted her nickname for the monster, but the moment was too fraught with the strained look on Chase's face. He was struggling with this new information.

"No," Chase said. "Get Falcon's file too. There might be information there that can help us."

Eden ran to her office, passing by the Raptor operatives who showed no signs of leaving. Not that she minded. Protection was a good thing.

She unlocked the top drawer of her cabinet and pulled out her client files. Seong could have them all as far as she was concerned. She wouldn't be going online again. Desiree was history.

She returned to the workroom and dropped the stack on the bed. "This is everything. Do what you will with them. I'm

not a psychotherapist, and there's no confidentiality require-
ment or even expectation."

Seong nodded. "We'll start with Hank."

Eden grabbed his file, which was thicker than the others.
He'd been one of her first fans.

"Do you think he's one of the executives at CamDames?"
she asked Chase and Seong.

Seong shook her head. "I know squat about CamDames
because *somebody* didn't give me a hint about what he was up
to." Her irritated tone was clearly directed at Chase. "But
that doesn't feel quite right. Might be someone lower than an
executive. CamDames is extremely profitable. It's hard to
understand why the CEO or anyone making the bigger bucks
would risk screwing that up with trafficking when the legal
stuff was making bank."

"I wondered about that too," Eden said. "From the
minute Chase told me about the trafficking, I wondered why
the hell they'd do that when there were weeks I pulled in ten
K in twenty hours." She glanced around at her very nice
townhouse. "I wouldn't be broke except I only worked for
them for sixteen months part-time and used most of the
money to buy this place and set up my own site."

"So what are you thinking?" Chase asked Seong. "It has
to be someone connected to CamDames. The guys who tried
to abduct Eden were security guards there."

"Definitely connected. I think an investor. Someone who
made money from the site, but didn't work there," Seong
said. "I think there's another connection to Eden." She
paused and studied Eden. "It's no mistake that a grad student
found out about Desiree and threatened you at just the right
time that you would threaten him back with Chase."

Eden had confessed to that earlier, before Chase arrived,
and now she focused on the connections Seong was making.

The text from Tobias had been sent after the man was

dead. It was bait, obviously. But how had anyone known to clue Tobias in in the first place? There was only one answer. "You think it's someone in the psychology department."

Seong nodded.

"It makes sense," Chase said. "Parks was a psychologist. She could have known faculty there. Even students. And as I already told you, we've long suspected she was having an affair with a married man. Anyone who fits that bill?" Chase said.

Eden's gaze jerked to his. "You mean like my advisor, Dr. Elliot Dearborn?"

Chase's brow furrowed. "Maybe. I never heard his name. But I saw his face."

Eden crossed back into her office. Chase and Agent Seong followed. She reached for a hardcover book from her shelf and flipped it open to the back, where the author photo was printed in crisp color on the flap. "Is this the man you saw?"

Chase's face went pale, then he gave a slow nod. "That's him. That's Hank."

Chapter Thirty-Three

$\mathcal{E}$den's files were spread across the coffee table. After a private discussion between Eden and Chase about how much of his history with Desiree and how much of the abuse he suffered he was willing to share, he'd decided he trusted everyone in the townhouse: Seong, Rav, Isabel, Ian, Sean, Hawk, Tricia, and of course Eden. Nothing was off-limits, and everything would need to be discussed openly if they were going to figure out exactly how Dr. Elliot Dearborn was involved and find proof of who really murdered Tobias Redford.

Likewise, nothing was off-limits as far as asking Eden about her work with CamDames and her solo enterprise. None of her sessions were recorded, so all they had were her notes.

Each person in the room was given a file to examine. Chase took his own. Eden and Seong were going over Hank's file together, talking softly as they sat on the barstools at the kitchen counter.

Chase would read through his file before anyone—even

Eden—took a look at it, and he would have the final say on if it would be shared with the others.

He settled in a plush recliner with the file on his lap and braced himself for Eden's psychological observations based on their conversations over the last eight months.

The first notes were just the simple facts of a new follower: screen name along with any details offered as far as background, amount of time he was in the chat, and amount spent. He hadn't paid for a private session for several weeks. It had taken that long for him to build up the courage.

In those first weeks, she'd noted his language preferences —did he like to talk dirty or preferred to say nothing at all— and he marveled at her memory because she'd been on camera the whole time, but then he realized she'd had the transcript of the chat for reference when the shift was over.

"Eden, do you have access to the chat transcripts from CamDames?" he asked.

She looked up from where she'd been scrutinizing something on the page with Seong. "No. They would let me view them right after my shift, but that was it. The minute I left the building, it was their data, not mine."

"But you have the files from the last six months," he confirmed.

"Every word."

"Is there something you're thinking of?" Seong asked.

"Nothing in particular. Mostly I was wondering if there was a shift in Hank's behavior when Parks was arrested and again when she pled guilty."

"How so?"

"Given my memories of the night I told you about, there was a messed-up dynamic with him and Parks. A love-hate thing. But the events of the last twenty-four hours, right down to the letter that Eden read that was supposedly from Parks, feels like revenge against me for what happened to her."

"Why do you say supposedly?" Hawk asked.

He was the only person in this room aside from Isabel who had known him in Alaska, before he'd been changed forever. And even Isabel hadn't really known him, because he'd been too shy to talk to her. The few times he wanted to, he'd been afraid his stutter would embarrass him, and so by the time he did speak to her, he was no longer himself.

Given his history with Hawk, he probably trusted him more than anyone because he was one of the only people who knew who he'd been once. Or maybe it was because Hawk knew who he *could* have been.

"I don't think Parks wrote that letter." Chase hadn't listened when Eden read it online, but he'd scanned the text before settling in to read his file. The FBI had allowed Eden to make a copy before they claimed the original as evidence. "And now that I think of it, I don't think she wrote the one I received in my mail a few weeks ago either. It's not quite...her speech pattern. One thing I know is Parks's words. And Agent Seong has confirmed the FBI has no idea how she would have gotten the letter out. She hasn't had any visitors or any mail in or out since she was transferred to the max facility in July after sentencing."

"So you're saying someone who knew the intimate details of what Parks did to you wrote the letters, but they didn't get her language usage quite right," Seong said.

"Yes. And maybe the transcripts that Eden does have will bear out the language part."

"Good idea," Seong said. "We'll look at those after we go through Hank's file."

Chase nodded and turned his attention back to Eden's notes on Falcon.

He jolted when he read the summary after their first private session.

Falcon is probably white, midtwenties, and socially adept. Online, he knows how to talk to women and isn't the type to send an unsolicited dick pic, not even to a camgirl. I don't think he's visiting my room to get his engine revving for a date. He was hesitant and reserved during our private session. I think he wanted to take it sexual but was concerned about moving too fast, almost like it was a first date. He might simply be shy, but it's also possible he's recovering from sexual trauma. Either way, he'll need coaxing to attempt explicit sexual play, if that's what he wants.

She underlined the last sentences.

<u>If he indicates he wants explicit play but seems reluctant or hesitant, that is when he can be coaxed, not before. Do not push him. Every sexual step must stem from his wants and desires. He needs to feel in control at all times.</u>

Holy crap. She'd gotten all that from their first session alone, for which there had been no transcript because he'd been on voice for the first time.

He wanted to tell her she was very perceptive, but this wasn't the place or time, so he kept reading.

And then the weirdest thing happened. Over time, Eden went from describing Falcon's words and their interactions to her reaction to their deepening sexual relationship. The entries became more and more about Eden's thoughts and feelings as he dominated and bossed her around with words, and how much it turned her on because his style wasn't that of an overbearing dom. No, she'd been drawn to how he commanded her pleasure, and she grew frustrated that he didn't masturbate with her. That she was alone in her apartment with just a voice that was always in control.

Her notes were more about her physical and emotional reaction to their sessions than they were about him and his psychological makeup.

Had she been falling in love with him even then?

But how was that surprising when he'd been falling in love with her at the same time?

It was entirely possible to fall in love with someone you'd never met in person when you could communicate as deeply —even have sex as they had—online.

He looked at her, sitting at the counter, head close together with an FBI agent, and realized he'd probably been in love with her before he ever stepped foot inside that coffee shop, and now he knew that she'd already been falling for him.

Had they both tapped into that chemistry that night? She hadn't known who he was, of course, but he had, and maybe he'd emitted the right pheromones to tip her off or something?

Somehow, she'd picked up on Falcon's vibes.

He'd dreaded reading these notes. He'd feared she was looking at him like a lab rat, as Parks had done, but the gift he'd received was the opposite. He'd gotten to read the opinions she'd had about him and how they'd grown into deeper feelings. There was nothing objectifying or scientific about the words she wrote. It was all feeling and a gift.

How many men were lucky enough to know all the best parts about their partner's emotional journey to falling in love? To read the admiration and desire in her own neat script?

And all this was including, not in spite of, the fact that she'd guessed at some of the abuse he'd suffered and worked hard to make sure her words and actions always felt safe for him.

Was it any wonder he was in love with her?

He turned to the last page of the file and saw it ended before he went to Portland. She hadn't taken notes after their session the night he returned to her room. He smiled at that. She'd kept it intimate and personal by not adding him to her client notes.

Every person in this room except Tricia and possibly Seong—they'd never discussed her personal life—was in a happy, committed relationship. He'd spent the last year wondering if such a thing was even possible for him.

Now he knew he could have it all. As soon as they nailed Dearborn.

***

It was difficult to read the notes she'd kept on Hank now that she had Dr. Dearborn's face in her mind. But the more she read, the more she knew Hank and Dearborn were one and the same. And she hated herself for never guessing.

But then, she hadn't guessed Chase was Falcon. It had never crossed her mind that anyone in her real life would visit

Desiree. She'd felt stupidly safe due to the IP address blocking she'd learned how to do. It never occurred to her that everyone apparently utilized VPNs when accessing online sex sites. But still, she didn't think so many could employ the kind that bounced to a different location halfway around the world to work around her locational blocks. She should probably be banging her head on the counter at her failure to predict any of this. The majority of her clients probably didn't use virtual private networks, but clearly the important ones had.

Earlier, she'd wondered aloud why she hadn't recognized his voice. She'd started working for CamDames just weeks before starting in the master's program, and she'd listened to Dr. Dearborn give lectures at least twice a week at the same time Hank was visiting Desiree's CamDames room with the same frequency.

Seong suggested that Dearborn had used software that changed the pitch of his voice, which made sense. Unlike Chase, Dearborn had known from the start it would be necessary, as Eden had been his student. In her notes, she had the date of Hank's first private session with her, which was just six weeks after she began classes.

She read through the notes, pointing out phrases that connected to her advisor. The FBI agent needed a solid legal basis to connect them, and it might be possible to get a search warrant and seize Dearborn's computers. One was bound to have evidence of the many, many visits he'd made to her site as Hank. And maybe it would have information on his affair with Parks too.

It was a long shot. But long or not, it was still a shot.

She read through the notes she'd jotted after a particular private session and jolted. "Chase, when did you say you think the memory of Dearborn at the cabin happened?"

"It's hard to say, it's all so muddled, but my guess is around eighteen or twenty months ago? Parks had been abusing me for some time—I'm certain of that. But I think it was the first time he witnessed it. Parks mentioned that I was twenty-five at the time."

"I'm sorry," she said, "but it's important that we're clear on this point. You said he watched Parks rape you, then they screwed on the couch, hoping you would watch?" She hated saying this in a room filled with his friends, but reminded herself it was okay. They already knew. They'd agreed that everything was open to discussion.

"Yes."

"Did he orgasm?"

"I think so. Parks taunted him. Asking if he could cover my cum with his." He said the words with surprising ease. He'd accepted the need and was probably compartmentalizing.

"Why does this matter?" Isabel asked. Her question had a slight edge to it. Eden knew she was protective of Chase and was glad for it.

"I think I've figured out why Dearborn visited Desiree." She cleared her throat. "*Me.* I've been working on a few theories since I started in the sex trade. One conclusion I've come to is that everyone has a reason to visit a camgirl. And by that, I mean *deep-seated*. They might not even know it. Camgirl work isn't free. And there is plenty of free porn available to get a person in the mood. But camgirls are interactive, and we cost money. You don't keep going back if you aren't getting something more than an erection from it. Because you can get an erection for free at one of the other sites."

"Not always," Chase said pointedly.

God, she loved him and his brave honesty.

She nodded. "Exactly my point. It's sometimes men—not always men, but the majority of visitors to camgirl sites identify as male—who have difficulties in that area who turn to camgirls because they need the interactive element to achieve an erection."

"But I thought we figured Dearborn was following you because of his connection to CamDames and trafficking?" Tricia said.

"I'm sure that's why it started but you don't show up at least two nights a week for two years for that. He could have checked in every other week and been done with me. The ledger tells a story. We now know he paid me between one hundred and five hundred a week, occasionally having private sessions in which he tipped even more. I think I've figured out why." She glanced at the workroom door where she'd been so close to being assaulted this morning and let out a soft gasp.

"He even tried to get it today. This wasn't about Parks. She was never going to see that tape in lockup. This was about him and his kink. And today he was getting revenge on Chase by using me for the only thing that gets him off."

"And that is?" Seong asked.

"If I'm right, then around the time he was at Chase's cabin, Hank started asking me to tell him stories of me having sex with other men. He wanted me to describe it with him as a spectator usually in the role of cuckolded partner."

"So cuck fantasies were his kink," Chase said.

Eden nodded. "And it started after he watched the woman he was trying to have an affair with rape you. I think that was the first orgasm he'd had in a long time. In my notes, I speculated that he could achieve an erection, but they didn't last long and he was unable to satisfy his wife. He was unwilling to perform any other kind of clitoral stimulation, so his wife gave up on him. This is all speculation, of course, but you get to know a man in my business even if you only have their voice to go on."

"So watching Parks with me triggered something in him that turned him on."

"Yes. And then he tried to get me to recreate that fantasy. I was probably a stand-in for Parks or his wife, and he enjoyed the idea of watching. There might have been a punishment element in his mind in the sex that followed, whether he had it with a partner or masturbated."

She glanced around the room and finally met and held Chase's gaze. "This is about revenge and CamDames, sure, but there's more to it than that. If he just wanted revenge, he'd have ended the game when he set you up for Tobias's murder. Or he would have had me killed or abducted me from here. Those things would hurt you, and I'm sure he has issues with me too, so bonus revenge.

"But first he wanted me to read a letter as if I was his incarcerated lover, and then he wanted to have one or two men rape me while it was recorded so he could watch that video over and over. It was a violent cuckold fantasy played out against the woman who abandoned him. Not willingly, but still abandoned to the degree that he hasn't been able to speak to her in a year without fear of revealing himself as her accomplice." She paused. "This is all just my personal theory, by the way, I haven't studied this area enough to claim any sort of expertise. But it fits with the behavior and how Hank chose to present himself."

"How does Penny fit in all this?" Seong asked.

"I'm not sure. I think it's safe to assume that apart from Chase," she met his gaze and added, "I'm sorry, but—"

He nodded. "I was Parks's first true success. And Penny was her second."

Eden nodded. "You had a life to return to, so she had to bury your memories of your weekends in hell. But Penny had no one. Did she ever get to surface from the nightmare of being controlled? Was she internally screaming inside, even as she went through the motions of her days?"

"You said she started working at the coffee shop a few months before you did," Chase said. "Maybe that was a sign Parks's control slipped when she was arrested. Maybe Penny was breaking free?"

"And then Dearborn reeled her back in?" Isabel asked.

Eden cocked her head. "Actually, it might be the opposite. Once Parks was arrested, Dearborn had to fear your memories returning. He knew you might remember him. He wouldn't know if you'd heard his name or not. And he knew you'd seen Penny too. So she stopped performing as Penny Candi. They tucked her in a coffee shop to give her something to do. It was convenient that Sling Man and Jacked Knee did all their pickups of runaways nearby—"

"Someone disabled the coffee shop cameras," Tricia said. "I think Penny started working there and disabled the cameras, and then they started using the side street with the dark alley as the meet spot."

"And then Chase started intercepting girls they hoped to nab for trafficking and sending them into the coffee shop, where Tricia and I waited," Isabel added.

"When did you intercept the first girl?" Eden asked Chase.

"It was about six months ago."

"Right around the time Penny suggested I apply and after you were already a client. I wonder if Hank—or rather, Dearborn—figured out from the start that Chase was Falcon," Eden said.

"Possibly. If he didn't then, he did the night we met. You showed up in the group and said you'd met someone that night. I'm guessing they knew Raptor responded to the call. Then Falcon showed up." He stopped there, but Eden finished the connection in her mind.

Falcon dropped enough money for Desiree to forgo all pretense of entertaining the group and they went private. If Dearborn hadn't put two and two together before, then that sealed it.

"We'll probably never know if Penny suggesting I apply at Vivace Coffee was a coincidence or not. It was a very normal kind of thing to do, and we don't know how much of her life and actions are hers. We don't even know how old she really is, but my guess is she's not twenty if the first time you saw her in the video clip from your memory, she looked only fifteen or sixteen."

Eden paused, feeling her eyes burn with tears for the girl. "This morning, when I looked into her eyes, I saw pain. And she set up the blast message to let everyone know I was going live."

That was met with nods and understanding. Everyone here had accepted that Penny was a victim, no matter what she'd done, and Eden realized they'd already been through that with Chase.

They had less problem wrapping their minds around it than she did. Seong included. But then, a year ago, Seong's job had been to investigate everything about Chase to find if there were any holes in his claim of innocence. She'd already told Eden she'd found nothing. It was one reason she'd readily accepted his innocence in Tobias's murder. It reeked of a setup, she'd said.

"I'm guessing they started watching you, if they weren't already," Chase said, "after the coffee shop incident. When I walked in to show you Sling Man's photo, that just sealed it. Dearborn didn't even have to do research to figure out who I was. He'd met me. Probably more than once, but I only remember the one time so far."

"Do you really think they're trying to find Jasmine?" Isabel asked.

Chase shook his head. "No. The first night, sure, but not anymore."

"Good. It's important to keep the shelter a secret. We're on shaky legal ground as it is with the fact that we take in minors who are supposed to be returned to their parents. If Voigt Forum finds out about it, they'll dox us for sure."

Chase looked up. "What is Voigt saying about me?"

Alec looked up from his tablet. "Nothing yet. Keith assigned one of the office staff to monitor all right-wing social media for mentions of you, Eden, and Redford or anything associated with CamDames or the Vivace Coffee bombing."

"I'm confused about that," Eden said. "Why bomb the coffee shop?"

Chase jolted and Eden cocked her head, realizing no one else had noticed his reaction. But they were all deep in their own internal mapping of the situation, it seemed. "What is it, Chase?"

"It just occurred to me the bombing could have been a test for Penny. She could have been ordered to do it to show she was still in their control. They did that with me a few times prior to last fall. Small sabotages that no one would ever guess was me." He looked to Seong. "Was Penny investigated after the bombing?"

"All coffee shop employees are being investigated. I don't know how far they got with Penny." She rose and said, "Let me make a few calls." She slipped from the room and went to the interior staircase for privacy.

After she left the room, Eden said in a whisper, "I have a plan for how we can corner Dearborn. But it won't work if the FBI is involved."

Chapter Thirty-Four

Chase hated everything about Eden's plan, but he was outvoted by his so-called friends. They had to put off the actual plan discussion until after Seong left to share everything she'd learned with her associates at the FBI.

When she finally left, she impressed upon Chase the need to stay put, but it was unofficial in that there was no arrest warrant being served. He'd given her his statement and Redford's vehicle had been seized the moment Chase parked in Eden's driveway, as previously arranged.

Even so, it wasn't until early afternoon that Seong left.

"You aren't going into his office alone," Chase said for the dozenth time. His jaw was clenched so tight, he wasn't sure why he hadn't broken a tooth yet.

"There is no way he'll talk if anyone is in the room with us. And I'll have the nanodrones that Nate's girlfriend designed. We'll get his confession from sixteen different angles."

"He's not going to confess. He's going to bolt, and he might take you hostage."

"I won't let that happen," Nate said softly. He had been

assigned the role of Eden's bodyguard at the evening candle-light vigil on campus for students and faculty to honor slain student, Tobias Redford. Eden was determined to show up and corner Dearborn. Everyone agreed Chase was out as bodyguard, so Nate had stepped up.

"It should be me. I didn't kill Redford."

"But Dearborn will freak if he sees you," Isabel said. Probably repeated. Chase was having trouble letting this point go. He couldn't stand the idea of Eden facing Dearborn without him when he was the best unarmed fighter in Raptor and they all knew it.

"He doesn't have Sling Man or Jacked Knee," he said. They'd all adopted Eden's names for the goons. "And Penny is safe in the hospital."

"But there was another guy in the parking garage," Sean said. "Whoever he was, he won't hesitate to shoot first if he sees you."

"What if that was Tobias?" Chase asked. Anything to get his way.

"Wait, what?" Eden said. "You think Tobias was more than just a victim here? You think he was Dearborn's accomplice?"

He shrugged. "No clue. But maybe. Could it have been him?"

Eden closed her eyes, and he guessed she was trying to picture the shape of the man he'd had in a headlock in the garage. Finally she shook her head. "I have no idea. The mask completely covered his face. I didn't even see his eyes, like I did yours. But the build could be right."

"If it was him, then the third henchmen isn't a problem. Dearborn is on his own."

"Let me do this for you, Chase," Nate said softly.

His tone caught everyone's attention and Chase wasn't the only one who looked at him questioningly.

Nate let out a deep sigh. "I didn't have your back in Alaska." He glanced at Isabel and added, "I didn't have Vin's back either. If there's anything in my life I regret, it's that I missed my Falcon teammates' cries for help. If I'd seen what was really going on, Vin might still be alive. And you"—he held Chase's gaze without flinching—"might not have suffered all you did. We might not be *here* right now at all. Parks never would have gotten her hooks in you."

"It's not your fault, Nate," Isabel said, echoing Chase's thought.

"Maybe not, but I still have regrets, so give me this, Chase. Give me a chance to have your back. I'll protect Eden with my life."

Chase knew that. The operative was a former Green Beret, and he'd been with Raptor longer than anyone in this room—including the company owner. And there was no arguing with that plea. Bastard.

"You know one of the things that sucks about learning how to feel again? All the fucking emotions." Chase didn't spill a tear, but just barely.

Isabel covered her smile with a hand, while Eden leaned into him, wrapping her arm around his waist. Her eyes did spill over with tears as she said, "Emotions, man, they're the *worst*." Then she laughed, and everyone, including Chase, did too.

He brushed his lips over her forehead. She was doing this for him. To put his nightmare to rest once and for all. "You'll be careful?" he whispered for her ears alone.

"Always. Remember who I am. Caution is my number one rule. I didn't even give you my number that first night. Or proposition you, even though I wanted to."

He kissed her again and faced the group. "Fine. Nate accompanies her. But I'm on campus. Just in case."

Keith wasn't here, so the statement was directed to Sean,

who was the ranking operative on the team. But of course, this wasn't an official op. There was no client. This was his friends gathered to figure out how to clear his name and take down one of the people who'd nearly destroyed him.

But habits die hard, and Chase always respected the boss, who, in this instance was Sean.

Sean nodded. "I want a floor plan of the building."

"I could probably sneak one or two of you into the lab. I have keys," Eden said.

That idea perked him up. "How close is the lab to Dearborn's office?"

"Is three doors down close enough for you?"

He gave a slow nod, for the first time not entirely hating this.

"So you'll sneak us in, then you and Nate will go to the vigil, and you'll convince Dearborn to meet with you in his office—presuming he's at the vigil, of course."

"If he arranged for Tobias's murder, I'm pretty sure he'll be there."

"Why did he kill Tobias?" Tricia asked.

Eden shrugged. "Convenience? No clue except that it was easy to pin on Chase once I told Tobias about him. I'm starting to think that Dearborn is frustrated because he was Parks's partner and nobody gives him credit. He could be disassembling as we move closer to the first anniversary of her arrest—which is just a week away. He hasn't been able to talk to her at all from that moment. And now he's lost his one connection to her—Penny—and his two goons. He's on edge, and the idea of a private talk in his office with me will be too much to resist. Make no mistake, he's a brilliant man. He earned his PhD thirty years ago. He knows more about human psychology than I probably ever will…now." The last word said it all. Eden was accepting the loss of her dream.

"What makes you think you can outsmart him, then?" Isabel asked.

"One, he doesn't respect me as an equal, doesn't think I could ever possibly figure out the scam he's been pulling on me for two years, and two—"

She stood and pulled open the light hoodie she'd donned over a tight tank top when she'd dressed earlier. The tank hugged her curves and highlighted her narrow waist, while her yoga pants showed off her round ass. She swept a hand down her spectacular body. "He wants this. So much so that he's paid me over twenty-eight thousand dollars over the course of two years just to get a peek."

"It's kind of hard to argue with that," Tricia said with a grin. "I mean with both the body and the money."

Eden grinned. "I had to give up ice cream to get this body. At least it was worth it financially." She turned to Chase, "Sorry, babe, enjoy it while you can, because if I'm not paying the bills with it, I'm having ice cream and garlic bread. But not at the same time."

Chase burst into laughter. A full belly laugh that shouldn't be possible right then, but damn. She was the light he'd needed for so damn long and her strength and fearlessness was an absolute turn-on.

He pulled her onto his lap and tugged the hoodie closed at the front. "Okay, then. We've established that Dearborn doesn't stand a chance. What time does the vigil start?"

"Seven p.m.," Nate said.

"So Sean and I should be in place in the lab by six."

Heads bobbed around the table in agreement.

"We leave at five fifteen, then." He checked his watch. "That gives us four hours."

His meaning was clear, and the members of Falcon team plus Rav and Isabel all rose. Isabel said, "Alec and I will ride this out at the estate. Keep us posted."

Eden had risen, and Chase stood to receive the kiss Isabel bestowed on his cheek. "We'll be fine. And congrats again on the baby. I can't wait to be an honorary uncle."

Isabel beamed and patted his cheek. "Watch out. This kid is going to wrap Uncle Chase around their tiny little finger."

"Can't wait."

Isabel and Alec left, followed by the team. All but Tricia would be ready to roll by five. Tricia would be in the Virginia compound's version of God's Eye with Mothman, monitoring the video feeds from Leah's drones. Ian, Sean, and Nate would all go to the campus with him and Eden.

One way or another, Chase's nightmare would end tonight.

Chapter Thirty-Five

Chase made love to Eden in the sweetest, tenderest way possible. For a guy who claimed not to understand emotions, he was most excellent at expressing them physically.

Afterward, she curled against his side. "Cuddling for real is one of my new favorite things."

"Oh yeah? What else is a new favorite thing?"

"Your cock inside me."

He laughed. "Funny you should mention it, because that's one of my new favorite things too."

She grinned. "But not the cuddling?"

"Oh no. I love the cuddling too. Every moment with you. It's almost too much happy for my broken brain."

She cupped his cheeks to hold his gaze. "Enough of that. You aren't broken. You never were. Wounded, yes, but never broken. I wish you could see the man you are from my view. I see a beautiful, whole man who is the first to care about other people in all situations. You fight unarmed even when your opponent has a weapon. I mean, who does that? Someone who has more humanity than this world even deserves, that's who."

"It's worth noting that I still kick their asses and break their bones."

"As you should! They had knives! And so did the guy in Portland."

"I just don't want you thinking I'm some kind of saint, Eden. Because I would happily kill Dearborn with my bare hands."

"I know you're processing the violence that simmers after what has been done to you, but none of your *actions* bear that out. You've only fought in defense of yourself and others. And I want Dearborn dead too—but I also want him to live because I think he'll squeal like a pig and we'll finally get answers to everything Parks did to you and others."

He kissed her and said, "Fine, I'll try not to kill him if he can be taken alive."

She grinned. "See? You are positively civilized."

The gleam in his eyes turned wicked. "But not when it comes to you. With you, I have the dirtiest thoughts."

Heat coiled in her belly. No one had ever turned her on like this. Sweet, shy, fun, dark, daring, dirty. He was the full range, and she looked forward to exploring the entire spectrum that was Chase.

Maybe even especially the dirty parts.

The respite of the afternoon had been welcome, but when it was time to leave Eden's townhouse and go to the vigil, Chase was ready for that too. He was wired. Angry.

Ramped up to see Dearborn again.

If all went well, he wouldn't, though. Eden would secure Dearborn's confession and Hawk would take him down, and that would be that.

Was it wrong to want to take a swipe at him? Would Eden understand? Would she forgive him? Would she finally see that he really was a monster?

He would do his best not to kill anyone tonight, but he wasn't entirely certain his best was good enough.

Still, he didn't have a weapon. Didn't even want one. A minute alone with Dearborn, and he wouldn't need one. The guy was a brain fucker on the cusp of retirement. Physically, there was no way he could take on a Falcon team member in his prime. And as the youngest-ever—and still current youngest team member company-wide—Chase was most definitely in his prime.

An old prick like Dearborn didn't have a chance without his team of goons.

And Chase had beaten them too. Only one remained— what were the odds he'd be at the vigil? If the third man hadn't been Tobias, that is.

The more he thought about it, the more Chase was starting to believe Tobias wasn't just one of Dearborn's students. It was entirely possible the murdered man had been in the parking garage Thursday night.

But even so, if it wasn't Tobias, it was unlikely Elliot would want his last remaining henchman to taint the vigil, especially now that he had to have figured out the other two had been arrested this morning. It was also telling that Chase hadn't been arrested for murder. But then, Dearborn probably expected the guy who pulled the trigger to take the fall for that.

They took two vehicles to the campus, Sean and Ian in one, and Eden, Hawk, and Chase in the other. A surveillance detection route was required, so the drive took thirty minutes longer than necessary, but no one followed them.

Once on campus, they entered the building that housed the psychology department and they all skirted the cameras as much as possible—which was very possible as there were easy gaps in coverage, and once they were inside, there were no cameras at all.

First, they set loose Leah's drones, which were small enough to scuttle under doors and settle into nooks and crannies in Elliot's office, then Eden let them into the lab. "Don't look at any of the computer stuff. It's protected data and blind studies. All confidential."

"Promise," Chase said.

"I might not have a future in psychology, but I do still have ethics."

"We promise, Eden," Sean said.

Chase pointed behind him toward Sean and said, "He's the boss. We'll be good." He then kissed her nose. "Be careful out there."

"Will do."

I love you, he mouthed.

Her face lit up, and she rose on her toes and whispered, "I love you too, Falcon." Then she and Hawk left.

He watched her leave, realizing it was the first time she'd called him Falcon like that. It was kind of hot. She loved all of him. Even the wounded parts.

When they were alone in the quiet, dark lab, Sean said, "Eden's great. Not that it matters, but I approve."

Chase smiled, feeling another glow of warmth. He was glad a man he respected recognized the spark that made Eden special. Sean didn't appear to be hung up on the fact she was a sex worker. In fact, none of the members of Falcon team had shown signs of disrespect. It was nice to know his faith in his team was warranted. He was also glad he wouldn't have to quit his job because he worked with closed-minded assholes.

While the guys at Raptor might not have ventured into the paid end of internet porn, Chase had zero doubt that everyone there had visited the free online sites. Especially in Alaska where prospects were limited in remote Tamarack.

So if anyone *did* express disdain, he'd call them out for being hypocrites, but remained glad that didn't appear likely to happen.

"I could see her and Hazel talking for hours about the intersections between anthropology and psychology. In fact, I'm already bracing myself for that."

This was a reminder that as a student of brain science, Eden would fit right in with the women who were partnered with the men on Falcon team. Leah and her drones. Hazel and her bones. Cressida and her sunken boats. Eden and her brains.

He liked the idea that he could give her friends—family, really, as that's what they were to him at this point. Eden had said the last two years had been lonely. He could help change that, and not by himself.

Tricia's voice carried over the headset. "Drone cameras in Dearborn's office are in place. Everything checking out on your end, Johnston?"

He and Sean each pulled out their laptops so they could watch the dozen camera feeds on something larger than a phone. "Everything looks good here," Sean said.

As they watched, new cameras came online, these set loose in the area surrounding the fountain where the vigil would take place.

Eden smiled as one tiny drone faced her. She put her fingers to her lips and blew a kiss at the insect-like drone's camera.

"She's cute, Johnston, but if she starts getting mushy with

the camera, you'll need to put a stop to that," Tricia said. "I'm in the middle of a long dry spell, and I don't need to see this much cute happiness right now. I'm recovering from a head injury. Show me some mercy."

"Sorry, Trish—" Chase started.

"Kidding! Mostly. I'm happy for you. I mean it when I say she's adorable. And that body. Whew. But still, I don't think giving up ice cream is worth it."

There were more chuckles and more drones released as Ian positioned himself outside the vigil zone, but within quick sprinting distance.

With everything in place, Hawk and Eden retreated into the shadows and waited for the first students and faculty to arrive. They would wait until the event was in full swing before Eden showed her face.

Twilight came and went quickly, and on the computer screen, Chase could see the glow of candles as students gathered and touched wax sticks to spread the flame from one person to the next.

The vigil had begun.

Chapter Thirty-Six

$\mathcal{E}$den watched the people who'd been the closest thing she had to friends gather to grieve Tobias Redford.

For herself, she grieved for the victim of a heinous crime, but she didn't have much in the way of loss of a friend. He'd never been a friend. He'd been a man who wanted to sexually harass her either out of the program or into his bed—probably both, because if she'd slept with him, he definitely would have wanted her gone afterward.

In fact, it was worth looking into to see if there was a pattern of women leaving the program after a liaison with Tobias. He was the head honcho grad student, just inches from his PhD, and he'd found it maddening that she wasn't interested in or in awe of him.

He was used to new female grad students being impressed by his star power. Evelyn was a prime example. Even Kelly had admitted to being caught in his spell once upon a time, but she'd told Eden that one night of lousy sex had cured her.

Needless to say, Tobias had tried to run her out of the program after that. But Kelly was more tenacious than a burr. But now there was Kelly, crying with the others.

It was sad that Tobias had been murdered, and in a different situation, Eden would be grieving with the rest of them, but still, she had to wonder how much of Kelly's tears were shock at the violence and abrupt loss and how much was true grief.

She waited until Dearborn showed his face. He walked slowly, as if weighed down by sorrow. If she didn't know better, she would absolutely believe he was devastated by the loss of his most senior student. The one who'd clearly been his favorite.

The one he'd had killed twenty-four hours ago.

Early on, Eden had learned that people were sometimes put off by her interest in becoming a psychotherapist. They feared she might try to psychoanalyze them. And admittedly, it was hard to turn off that wiring once it was hooked up. But Dearborn and Parks were prime examples that psychologists were not the hallmark of sanity.

She had no clue what Parks's diagnosis would be, but from what Chase had described, she guessed borderline personality disorder. BPD was often hard to distinguish from narcissism, which, she guessed, was where Dearborn landed.

Eden looked to Nate and nodded.

Nate spoke into a hidden mic. "We're going in." He had an earpiece that was so tiny, it was only noticeable if one was looking for it.

"I am not going to repeat that, Johnston." Then he winked at Eden, and she realized he was joking. Setting her at ease.

She liked the people on Chase's team. It was fascinating to her that they went from casual first names and nicknames like Hawk when chatting to last names when an op began. She was always curious about the ways in which people used language to signal different things. Like code switching from AAVE when a Black person was talking to other people of color and using different words and syntax when talking to white people. It was a brilliant skill and a sophisticated, nuanced language.

Maybe she should look at a graduate degree in linguistics. Not to study code switching and AAVE—that work was best left to people of color whose culture and language were embedded in the study—but perhaps the intersection between language and psychology.

But first, she needed to confront her professor and advisor.

She approached the group, holding out her candle.

She made a beeline for Kelly, her closest friend in the department. Kelly jolted at seeing her and pulled back her candle, not letting Eden's wick touch her flame. "What the fuck are you doing here?"

"I'm here for Tobias, just like you."

Craig, who was probably Tobias's best friend among the grad students stepped forward. "You shouldn't be here. When Tobias told you he'd found out you were a whore, you had him killed to shut him up. But it was too late and he already told us all about you."

Eden reined in her reaction. She'd been expecting this. And really, it didn't matter if these people thought she was turning tricks in person or working online. Either way, it was her body, her choice. But as far as the department went, it mattered that the online work she did was legal.

She cocked her head. "Oh, if you know about my online job, then maybe you saw what happened this morning, when I was forced to read a letter at gunpoint and was threatened with rape? The sympathy you're showing is a fine sign of how awesome a therapist you'll be one day."

"Back off, Craig. I saw the video, and it was horrible."

Eden jolted, realizing her defender was Evelyn. She scanned the other faces in the crowd and figured it was split fifty-fifty. Being psychology students like herself, many were open-minded. But the other fifty percent had just lost a friend to a horrific murder, and Eden was under suspicion for her role in that.

Even so, it was the look on Kelly's face that cut the deepest. Kelly didn't even like Tobias.

Eden lowered her voice. "I didn't have anything to do with Tobias's murder, Kelly."

"Bullshit. You *told* him you were going to send your Raptor boyfriend after him. He turns up dead twenty-four hours later. You think we're stupid?"

She'd known all her fellow students were plenty smart. But that didn't mean they weren't gullible, as Kelly was proving.

"So Tobias told you how he threatened me? That if I didn't fuck him, he would tell Dr. Dearborn about my online job? And you're taking *his* side?"

Kelly looked like she wanted to cross her arms, but it was hard to do when holding a lit candle. So she just squeezed the wax stick and said, "Nice that you're making yourself the victim, when Tobias was the one who was murdered."

Eden tilted her head in acknowledgment of that statement. "There are multiple victims in this story."

"You're a sex worker and you want to play the victim card?" Kelly said. "Please. So Tobias hit on you after he found out you'll do it for money. Big fucking deal. It's not a capital crime." Kelly glared at Eden and raised her candle. "This vigil is for Tobias Redford. How dare you show up after you sent your boyfriend to kill him."

"He's not my boyfriend," Eden said, returning to the script they'd agreed to back in her townhouse. She couldn't let herself get derailed by their horrific, uninformed, grief-stricken accusations. She pointed at Nate and delivered the cover story they'd planned. "He is."

"You told Tobias on Friday that Chase Johnston is your boyfriend and that he was going to beat him up because he hit on you. And you can't deny you said Chase, because you sent me a photo of his ID. I *know* he's the guy. And the police said he killed Tobias."

"The *FBI* said he's a 'person of interest,' and they've spoken with him and me. That's all. I don't know if Chase killed him, but I didn't send him after Tobias."

She hated lying about Chase, but they needed Dearborn to believe the FBI was only looking at Chase right now, or she'd never get him alone in his office.

"You're lying," Craig said. "And you've tainted the entire department. At every job interview, I'm going to be asked why I didn't recognize you were a sociopathic slut who sent her boyfriend to murder a fellow student."

Wow. If he thought *she* was tainting his job prospects, wait until he found out about his *advisor*.

Craig was a lost cause. She didn't care about his opinion. It was the condemnation from Kelly that she didn't understand.

Was it because she'd never disclosed she was a sex worker? Or was it all just ugly grief?

In private, she and Kelly had discussed many times the need for safety for sex workers. Kelly talked a feminist game, but when she learned her friend was a sex worker, in front of the crowd, she went for blood.

Eden cleared her throat. This wasn't going as expected. She needed to get the conversation back on track. Not everyone here felt the same as Kelly and Craig. She could win the others over. "Listen, I had nothing to do with Tobias's death. I'm as horrified as you and wanted to honor him tonight. And I brought my *real* boyfriend because I figured you all would want to talk to him."

"Why would we want to talk to the ultimate cuck?" Craig

said. "You really don't care that she fucks other guys for money?"

She'd never liked Craig, and now she knew why.

"Shut up, Craig." Again, it was Evelyn who'd spoken on Eden's behalf.

She met the younger woman's gaze and saw the compassion that was missing from Kelly's eyes. That was also unexpected. Eden had underestimated the young woman. It was possible her eyes had been opened to Tobias's manipulations. Or she just was better at looking at the situation from the outside and seeing the truth. Whatever the reason, Eden was thankful for not just Evelyn's support, but for her willingness to speak up in such a charged situation.

She shook off her reaction. She was here for a reason, and it wasn't to suss out which of the grad students were true friends, it was to trap Dearborn. Craig's words gave her an opening, and she would use it. She smirked at Craig. "Why would you presume he doesn't like watching?"

Let Dearborn and his cuckold fantasies take that in.

Right on cue, the professor joined the discussion. "I think it's best you go, Ms. O'Keeffe."

"But you all haven't heard what Nate has to say."

"Why would we care?" Kelly asked.

"Because I'm the one who found Tobias's body," Nate said.

His words shut everyone up. There was an extended silence, and finally, Craig broke it. "When did you find him?"

"What happened? The news didn't even say how he died. Just 'suspected homicide,'" another student said.

"How do we know you didn't kill him?" said another.

Nate rolled his eyes. "I went to his house just after eleven p.m. to see if my coworker Chase Johnston was there."

This was part of his rehearsed speech. They'd discussed exactly what Nate would reveal. The students were bound to be curious given the lack of information online and Nate wasn't bound to any kind of secrecy except they wanted Dearborn to believe Chase was on the verge of being arrested. It was a win/win having Nate play her boyfriend in this moment and they would milk it for all it was worth.

"The front door was ajar, and I called out and got no response. It was unusual and I didn't have a good feeling about it, so I entered the residence."

"Holy shit," someone muttered. They were riveted, and he'd barely said anything yet.

"I searched the downstairs and found Mr. Redford lying flat on his back on the living room carpet. It was clear that he was dead, but I checked for a pulse as trained, then called the police."

She liked the way he left out cause of death. Let them pull it out of him.

"But how did you know he was dead? I mean, how did he die?"

"GSW to the heart."

"GSW—gunshot wound?" Dearborn asked.

"Yes."

"If he was shot, how come no one reported shots fired? He lives in a quiet neighborhood."

When Eden first heard the story, she'd wondered that too. She'd been to Tobias's house for study sessions more than once. It was a suburban neighborhood, but houses were still close together.

"It appears the shooter used a belt to tie a pillow completely around a handgun to muffle the sound. Near the body I spotted the belt wrapped around a folded-over pillow with a hole in the fold. I didn't touch it to see if the gun was inside, but I don't think it was."

"I thought that was bullshit? You can't silence a gun with a pillow."

"No, but it would muffle the shot enough that it might not be distinguishable as a gunshot and not a door banging closed. I doubt anyone inside the house would be fooled, but the neighbors might. For what it's worth, the police canvassed the neighborhood to determine if anyone heard anything late last night."

This was a fib in that the police were really asking about early evening, specifically the time of death provided by Tobias's Apple Watch.

"Wait," one student said. "That means…shooting him was premeditated."

Nate nodded.

Eden had spent the day wondering if Tobias had been murdered purely to set up Chase for the crime or if he'd been the victim for another reason.

"Are you allowed to tell us this?" a female undergrad asked.

"Shhh, Debbie. We want to hear this."

Nate shrugged. "I'm not in law enforcement. Nothing keeping me from saying what I saw."

"How do we know you didn't do it?"

"Airtight alibi for the time of death."

"What was the time of death?"

"As far as I know, there is a window of two hours before I found the body," Nate said. "Based on messages and social media posts by the victim."

This, of course, was a straight-up lie, given that they knew Tobias had died around five p.m., not after nine.

One student said, "Yeah. He posted on Facebook last night at eight. Never imagined that would be the last time he'd ever reach out to us." The speaker—a pretty undergrad Eden vaguely remembered seeing in the lab a few times—promptly burst into tears.

While chatter resumed among the group of approximately thirty students, and Nate was busy answering questions, Eden stepped to the side to get Dearborn's attention.

He was fully in his role of aloof professor. In the moment, she had a hard time reconciling him with Hank. But she didn't waver in her conviction. She was absolutely certain of who he was.

Chase had even seen his face.

Now she needed to get proof that would hold up in court.

"Dr. Dearborn," she said softly so no one but him would hear. "I'd like to talk to you about…my online work and what it means as far as me continuing in the program."

"This is hardly the place, Ms. O'Keeffe."

She glanced over her shoulder and saw the group was eating up every tidbit Nate could spill. "Then how about we go into your office?" She faced Dearborn and dropped her voice even lower, letting it take on the husky tone she used as Desiree. With her secret out, plenty of people would expect her to cut a deal with her body—just as Tobias had demanded on Friday—but she needed to be subtle in front of the others. Dearborn wouldn't take a chance if anyone was watching him.

She ever so slightly licked her bottom lip, then bit it. Only he could see her face; only he knew she was adding the tiniest bit of come on to her facial movement. "Please, Professor. I need to explain. Alone."

"What about your boyfriend?"

She gave him the answer that would turn him on the most. "Oh, Nate doesn't mind what I do."

Dearborn's eyes widened ever so slightly, then he gave a sharp nod. "I need to say something to the students, then I'll head to my office. Follow a few minutes later. Come alone, and we'll see if we can come to an arrangement."

Wow. He wasn't bothering to hide that this would be a negotiation either. It kind of made her wonder if he had a habit of sleeping with students. But given his potential issues with maintaining an erection, maybe he hadn't tried.

Of course, that issue could be new and merely a function of age. He'd been teaching for nearly thirty years.

Dearborn addressed the crowd, giving a short speech about how devastated he was at the news of Tobias's tragic murder and that everyone should wait for the police to do their job before casting judgment.

When Sling Man and Jacked Knee had been questioned in her apartment that morning, the only information they offered was that they didn't know who Mr. Roboto was. They'd only seen him the one time in the garage, and he'd kept the hood on in the vehicle.

It sounded implausible to Eden at first, but given Dearborn's relaxed manner tonight, she could believe that he really didn't think the two men could be connected to him. He was absolutely confident that no one would suspect him. And even if he left fingerprints or DNA at the crime scene, he could easily say he'd been at Tobias's house a few days before. Tobias always bragged that they hung out together.

After the speech, Kelly stopped him, and they had a moment of private conversation in which he held her hands in a gesture of sympathetic grief. Not hugging, it was a more appropriate handclasp between professor and student. Then Dearborn left, and Eden checked her watch. She would wait exactly five minutes.

Her presence was still not quite welcome with, she estimated, about twenty-five percent of the students. They studied her and stood back as if she had a sexually transmitted disease that might be airborne.

Worked for her. This was still Nate's moment. It would be best if she slipped away while everyone's attention was on him, so she texted him, saying she was going to talk to Dearborn and to follow when he could.

Mothman had dumped a fake text history thread in her phone that included texts with Nate dating back a week to support the boyfriend lie.

They were leaving nothing to chance.

She set off across the darkened campus the moment the five minutes were up.

Usually, she'd avoid the darkest route, but she had nanodrones following her and Ian was somewhere hidden nearby, tracking her. It was best no one realize immediately where she was headed. She needed to keep up the charade for Dearborn.

The building was locked this time of night, but she had a prox key like all the other grad students, and she waved it in front of the sensor, and the door made the familiar clicking sound as the light turned green.

Someone at Raptor had managed to make a copy of the RFID signal using equipment they had at the compound earlier today, so Nate had his own key to enter the building without her, as did Ian.

The halls were empty as she took the stairs to the second floor. When she reached Dearborn's office, she knocked.

"Dr. Dearborn?"

"Come in, Eden."

She entered his office to see the lighting was low—only the floor lamp next to the desk was lit. She had no clue if the nanodrones were able to amplify the light source, but hoped they could. Their cameras were very small, but from a distance of six or eight feet, they could get a decent-sized window view.

Eden stepped into the room, swinging her hips ever so slightly. More than she'd ever done in this building before, certainly.

She knew how to turn it off and how to turn it on in slow

degrees. She'd learned a lot during her stint as Desiree. Right now, she told herself she was in front of a camera—actually more like a dozen—but she was pretending Dearborn was the only lens. Hank. The difference tonight was she could see him too.

"Close the door," he said.

She grinned. "Of course."

She didn't lock it. She didn't want to make it hard for Nate to join the conversation on cue.

She turned and strode toward him. His eyes swept down her body as she gave her hips a slight sensual sway.

She'd donned a dark knee-length pencil skirt and fitted blazer over a pale button-down silk top. It was very sexy librarian, which she knew was one of Hank's favorite games because he could pretend he'd caught her fucking another man in the stacks.

This outfit wasn't one she ever wore as Desiree—she never wore Desiree's outfits in public—but it was close enough in style to trigger a reaction, plus it was dark and appropriate for a candlelight vigil.

"I'm so glad you agreed to talk to me, Elliot."

She saw heat flare in his eyes at her use of his first name. This was almost too easy. She stopped a few feet in front of his desk so he could still see the full length of her.

He rose from the seat behind his desk and circled it to sit on the front edge, bringing them even closer. "I'm not sure if I can help you. This department has a reputation to worry about."

"I feel certain we can come to an agreement. My work was perfectly legal, and I won't be doing it anymore."

"That may be true, but I'd be risking my professional reputation."

She dropped her voice. "I'm sure I can find a way to make it worth your while."

She fiddled with the button on her blazer, then popped it open.

He gave her the slightest nod, telling her to continue. So very careful not to verbally respond.

She slid the blazer off and draped it on the back of a chair. "Why don't we get more comfortable for this discussion?"

His eyes narrowed the tiniest amount. "How do I know you aren't recording this? Blackmail would be one way to get back in the department. Show me your phone."

He was more careful than she'd hoped, but thankfully, she was prepared and handed him her phone.

"Tell me your code."

"I'll unlock it."

"Your code or no deal."

She gave him the six-digit pin and wondered how good his memory was for things like that.

"Your boyfriend texted you. He said he's on his way. I told you to come alone."

"I did. I'm here alone, and Nate knows everything." She smiled at Dearborn and whispered, "He likes to watch."

"How long have you been together?"

She shrugged. "A few weeks. We met through Chase. I actually dated Chase first. Nate came into the room and, well, that's how I found out he likes to watch." She smiled. "He also likes threesomes."

The heat flaring in Dearborn's eyes was off the charts, and his slacks tented at the crotch.

He tapped a few buttons on her phone, and when he appeared satisfied she wasn't recording anything, he set it on the desk next to him.

"You could be wearing a wire."

She shrugged and started unbuttoning her top, slowly.

"What are you doing?"

"Stripping to show you I'm not wearing a wire." She dropped her voice. "You can do a body cavity search if you want."

"Proceed," he said.

She slipped the top from her shoulders, and instead of going for the skirt next, she unhooked her bra and dropped it to the floor. She was naked from the waist up.

Dearborn was nothing but a camera, and this was a means to an end. She was doing this for Chase.

And honestly, this didn't bother her. As Hank, he'd seen her naked more than anyone, if she thought about it. She felt bad for the operatives watching who were probably uncomfortable right now, but she was fine. She was used to performing naked.

She reached up a hand and lifted her breasts to show him the underside. "See. No wire here. Nothing but these perfect tits."

Hank preferred the word *tits* over all others when it came to breasts.

The door burst open, and Eden turned, expecting to see Nate ruining her trap before it was laid.

But no. It was Kelly.

Chapter Thirty-Seven

Chase was surprisingly calm for being in a position of watching the woman he loved strip for a sex-trafficking murderer.

"You okay, man?" Sean asked.

He nodded. "Yeah. She's okay with it. That's what matters. She's Desiree right now. She knows what she's doing."

He saw the minute she slipped into Desiree's skin. Her posture changed, her voice, her everything.

Right now, Dearborn was some poor sap on the other side of the camera she needed to win over to get paid.

It was that simple.

Until a voice on his headset said, "Oh shit. Incoming!"

"What's happening?" Sean asked.

"One of the grad students is heading for Dearborn's office," Ian said.

"Can Hawk stop them?"

"I don't think it would help the situation if I did," Hawk replied. "It's the woman who was the most suspicious at the vigil. I think she's just being nosy. Not dangerous."

Shit. The woman would ruin Eden's chance of getting a confession, though.

And a moment later, Dearborn's office door flew open and slammed against the wall.

A white woman about the same age as Eden stormed into the room. Her face turned bright red at the sight of a half-naked Eden standing in front of the professor.

Eden, who had her hands on her breasts for Dearborn, chose to drop her hands instead of covering her nipples. She straightened her shoulders and stood proud like a statue of a goddess.

She was glorious in her implacability. "Kelly, how nice to see you. But really, it's polite to knock."

"Dr. Dearborn told me to come here. And to not bother knocking."

Eden turned to the professor. If she was rattled by the wrench he'd thrown into her plans, she didn't show it. "Hoping for the threesome after all? I could have arranged that."

Dearborn's eyes narrowed. "I wanted Kelly to witness your attempt to use your body to get back into the department."

Eden shrugged. "I could claim you told me to strip before you'd consider my request. She didn't see anything."

"Who are people more likely to believe? The tenured head of the department or the sex worker?"

Eden cocked her head, her steady gaze moving from Dearborn to Kelly. She smiled and shrugged. "Fine. I was trying to use my body to get back in the department. It failed. I guess I'll just have to sue the department for allowing Tobias to sexually harass me. I'm sure the female students he ran off in the years he was here will stand with me."

She met Kelly's gaze. "Won't it be ironic when you're called as a witness to corroborate my story?"

Kelly's face reddened. Chase had to marvel at the resolution of the drone cameras. He could see the struggle on the woman's face. Eden had described Kelly to him, and he knew that until this morning, she'd been Eden's friend and unlikely to support Tobias in anything.

Dearborn picked up Eden's silk blouse from the floor while she grabbed her bra.

He handed her the shirt, and Chase caught a slight reaction when their hands touched. What was that? A ripple of revulsion?

She straightened, and then Chase saw her slip something into the small pocket of her skirt before she pulled on her bra.

What was it? A note?

Eden dressed quickly, then left the office without so much as a nod to her professor or former friend.

There was nowhere for a drone to hide in the hallway and they might be spotted if they followed Eden out, so she disappeared into the void of the corridor.

Chase waited for Nate to give an update. He was on the floor, around the corner and out of sight. But before Nate said a word, Eden barged into the lab. "Shit!" she said under her breath as she thrust out a piece of paper.

Sean took it, read it, cursed, and passed it to Chase. Into the radio, Sean said, "Dearborn passed Eden a note that says he needed Kelly as a witness so when he reinstated Eden later, no one could claim he'd done it in exchange for sex and to wait for him in the lab."

"All the drones are in the office. We can't move them without Dearborn seeing."

"What about the ones that were with me at the vigil?" Eden asked.

"Once you entered the building, Ian collected them," Chase said. A glance at his computer showed Dearborn and

Kelly in his office, but Chase figured the professor would get rid of the student and make his way here within minutes. "It would take too long to get them here, and Kelly might spot them on her way out."

"You need to get out of here," Eden said.

Chase shook his head. "Not going anywhere."

Eden's gaze darted around the room. "There's no closet. And you can see under all the tables. There's nowhere to hide."

"Not true. The cabinet under the counter at the end is empty."

Eden glanced toward the cupboard he indicated. "That's too small. You'll never fit."

"Sean and Nate won't fit—they're too bulky. My frame is smaller."

"You'll be contorted like a carnival exhibit."

"Twenty-four years of martial arts means I'm very flexible."

Chase was glad he'd spent the downtime looking through the unlocked cupboards and had noted one remained empty. Eden had said to stay out of the computers, but she never mentioned the cabinets, and as an operative on a stakeout, it was always important to scope out potential hiding places.

"Hurry," Eden said. She turned to Sean. "You need to leave. Now. Before Kelly steps into the hall. Take your computer."

He grabbed the slim device and went to the door without a word of argument. There was no time for a plan B, and there was no better moment to trap Dearborn than now, when he was clueless.

Chase grabbed his computer and brought it with him into the cupboard. It would be a tight fit, but there was no way in hell he was leaving this room.

Chapter Thirty-Eight

From the lack of voices in the hall, Eden guessed Sean was out of sight when Kelly left Dearborn's office. She listened with her ear to the door as Kelly's footsteps padded by. She turned to see that Chase had disappeared inside the cabinet. She couldn't believe he'd managed it.

She tried to quell the trembling of her hands. Stepping back from the door, she took a deep breath. She could do this. Chase was here.

Less than a minute after Kelly's footsteps had faded, Eden heard the doorknob rattle. She'd locked it to buy time, and now Dearborn was fiddling with his keys.

Her heart pounded, and her hands refused to stop shaking. This change in plans had thrown her for a loop.

She'd been certain she was in control of the situation and didn't like the realization that he'd outsmarted her.

She'd underestimated him.

How much had he figured out?

Only one thing was certain, he never would have sent her into the lab if he'd guessed Chase and Sean were here. So even if he'd figured out some of it, he didn't know everything.

The door swung wide and without preamble, he bent over and scanned the room, searching under the tables. He straightened and smiled as he stepped into the room then turned and locked the door. He placed a wedge between the door and the frame.

"What are you doing?" she asked. The tremor in her voice matched her quaking hands. She wasn't acting this time.

"Jamming the door. The bolt is now wedged against the plate. Even with a key, you can't unlock this door. It's convenient for when I want time alone with one of my favorite students."

And that was the moment her stomach dropped, when all her egotistical ideas that she'd figured him out—bested him at his own profession, no less—crashed and burned. He was a predator who'd been abusing his students for a long time.

Maybe it hadn't been Tobias who'd run them out of the department after all.

His cold gaze scanned her. He held up her phone. "You forgot this in my office."

Shit. Shit. Shit.

"Thankfully, you gave me your passcode. Now strip. I want to know you aren't wearing a wire. And yes, my dear, there will be a body search. And I recorded you consenting to it when you gave me your phone earlier."

He touched the screen and she heard herself say: *"You can do a body cavity search if you want."*

Holy fuck.

Play along. Chase is here. He won't let this go too far.

She doffed her clothes, skipping the slow striptease this time.

"What's going on, Elliot? I thought we were going to have mutual fun?"

"Oh, I'm going to have fun, all right. But I'm afraid it won't be mutual."

He paused to look at her naked body, exposed to his gaze once again. "Beautiful," he murmured. "You have a body that's worth a lot of money, Eden. And I've come to collect."

"Because you've spent over twenty-eight thousand on me in the last two years?" She might as well say it. Pretenses were gone.

"Figured out I was Hank, did you?" He cocked his head. "Tell me, Desiree, how did that make you *feel*?"

Hell. That was his therapist voice. Shit. The motherfucker was totally in her head. He knew. He fucking knew.

Smile and play along. Be Desiree. He likes Desiree. He wants to fuck Desiree. Or at least he wants to watch Desiree with another man. And then he wanted to make her screw him as punishment.

She wasn't wrong on that point. She knew it.

"How hot did it make you to hear me speak for Elizabeth this morning? I know you wanted to watch your goons rape me, and pretend it was her getting fucked by Chase. Just like that first time. When you watched your lover get off on raping another man and it gave you an erection that wouldn't quit for the first time in months...or maybe years?"

Dearborn's nostrils flared, his eyes turning steely. Bull's-eye.

"And then she abandoned you and you haven't been able to get off since. So what's the plan here? I mean, you and me? It's not going to happen, and we both know it because you need another cock to prime the pump, so to speak."

God. She would never talk this way to a man with erectile dysfunction if, well, he wasn't a nightmare incarnate.

He'd been running the psychology department for how long?

"You realize it's all your fault, don't you?" he said.

"What's my fault?"

"Me finding CamDames. Investing in the company. I'd never even visited a camgirl site until we discovered my new favorite student worked there."

"*We?*"

He shrugged, ignoring her question. She assumed *we* meant Parks and Dearborn.

"It's your fault we found CamDames, and it's Chase Johnston's fault my Elizabeth went away. You both have to pay."

She suppressed a shiver. She didn't want to show this man her fear. "You tried to punish me this morning and failed."

"Never fear. I have a backup plan. You see, Elizabeth left me her notes and equipment. I assisted her with Penny. I know what to do."

He took a step toward her. "Want to know why I shot Tobias?" His words were a whisper. Chase might not have heard him.

"*You* shot Tobias?" She projected her voice.

He nodded. "I shot him because when I told him we were going to turn you into a Penny, he balked."

"Turn me into a Penny? You mean chip me, like you did Chase?" Her brain was reeling. When he'd said *we*, he'd meant Tobias, not Parks. Or, more likely, all three of them.

"Yes. You see, I figured after twenty-eight thousand dollars, it was time to get my money's worth."

Dearborn turned and went to the cupboards.

Eden's heart beat double time. *Does he know Chase is there?*

But instead of going to a lower cabinet, he unlocked an upper one and pulled out a device that looked like a parabolic microphone or tiny satellite dish. He turned to face her.

"I'm afraid we never know how a person will react until after the first hit. We must calibrate from there. So brace yourself, this might hurt."

He pressed a button, and Eden felt a disturbing sensation in her ears that triggered an instant migraine-like headache.

She dropped to her knees, blinded by the agony.

A mewing sound emitted from her throat. Was she dying?

Somewhere in the pain, her brain managed to register that this must be infrasound.

Then the world went black.

Chapter Thirty-Nine

Chase erupted from the cabinet the moment Eden collapsed. He would have been out sooner, but he'd been unable to position himself to make a smooth exit and his legs got caught.

Startled, Dearborn twisted and saw Chase coming at him. He turned the infrasound device on him, and Chase felt the nightmarish jolt flow through him as he body-slammed into the psychologist, sending the device flying.

It was only momentum that saved him, because infrasound was the one weapon Chase's muscle memory was useless against.

Dearborn hit the floor. He surprised Chase by pulling out a gun.

In a flash, Chase saw that the bullet wasn't intended for him. Dearborn's fallback was a bullet through the brain.

Chase hesitated for just one moment, but then kicked the gun away as it fired. Blood sprayed over the floor. The change in trajectory meant the bullet had taken out Dearborn's ear, but he'd probably live.

The gun clattered to the floor a few feet away, and Chase

flipped the man over and cuffed him. He then turned to Eden and pulled her into his arms. "Sweetheart, speak to me."

"*Motherfucker*, that hurt like nothing I've ever felt before."

He nodded. "I know. I'm sorry I didn't stop him before he zapped you."

There was pounding on the door, but Chase ignored it. He needed to make sure Eden was okay.

"Did we get him? Did you hear what he said?"

"Better than that. When he unlocked your phone, I sent Mothman a message, and he turned on your camera and mic. We got everything. Even the words he whispered."

"Oh thank God." She wrapped her arms around his waist and held him tight. "I was going to be pissed if we went through all this for nothing."

"Chase!" Sean said as he pounded on the door. "Let us in. The FBI is on their way."

"Can you dress without help?"

She nodded. "Let them in now. No need for you to wait until I'm clothed."

He brushed his lips over hers. "You were brilliant. Thank you for everything you've done here. I think I might finally, truly be free now."

She smiled and kissed him back. Sweet. Tender. "Thank you for trusting me to do this. And for not freaking out about what I had to do."

"I trust you with everything, Eden, starting with my heart and my body, but most especially with my mind."

Epilogue

Virginia
Seven Months Later

They both had wanted a small wedding, intimate and personal, with only their closest friends and Chase's dad, as he was the only biological relative either of them had. Well, Eden's parents were still alive, but they weren't invited.

The social worker who'd helped her and become something of a foster mother to Eden flew across the country to attend, and she was given the honorary role of mother of the bride.

Chase's dad walked her down the aisle, which was really just a gap in the gathered standing guests. They didn't bother with more than a few rows of chairs for nursing moms and those in need of seating for the short ceremony.

The wedding ceremony was performed by a judge who was friends with Alec Ravissant and took place in the woods on Chase's property near the Appalachian trail.

Chase had planned to sell the place, but given that the old

structure had burned down and the new house had no memories to mar it, he'd asked Eden if she'd be willing to spend every other weekend with him there to see if he could love the place again.

The first thing he did was hire landscapers to create a pond where the old cabin used to be, so there would be no spot of earth to remind him. Instead, he'd see something beautiful.

Within two months of the experiment, they'd both agreed the property was worth keeping. For Eden, it was wild to have the security of two homes after the poverty of her childhood followed by the homelessness of her teens.

During the week, they lived in her townhouse. Her workroom was now a second bedroom and someday would hopefully be a baby's room.

She'd never even known she wanted to have children—it hadn't been on her radar as a possibility until she met Chase. And seeing him with friends' children, and now Isabel and Alec's newborn son—who had bright hair that looked like it would be carrot orange like his mom's—had sealed it for Eden. She wanted children, and she wanted them with Chase. He was going to be an amazing dad someday.

And now here she was, facing him in the forest behind their blissful cabin, saying words that bound them together forever.

He was breathtakingly handsome in his tux, and she'd laughed when he showed her his cuff links—small gold falcons.

His face was bright with love and warmth as he said his vows. The dark shadows were fading from his mind.

He still struggled with the violence that surged at times— usually triggered by an injustice that set off feelings of powerlessness. He'd developed mental exercises to work through the feeling, so he could dispel the powerless feeling and replace it with something positive or something he could control.

But he did all this work with a very good therapist Eden had helped him find. She was his partner—and in moments would be his wife—and not his therapist.

She said her vows, and finally, they got to the kissing part, where he proved he could still take her breath away even with a tame kiss.

The man was pure catnip.

It was a hot May day in Virginia, and they retreated from the forest to an area where they'd set up two large tents for shade. They would eat, and then a live band would perform and she would dance with her new husband.

They held hands as they wandered through the small gathering, hugging friends and accepting congratulations.

Isabel was gently bouncing six-week-old Vincent Ravissant on her shoulder. "Can I hold him?" Eden said.

"You sure? He's liable to erupt from either end at any moment."

"Don't care. I'm only wearing this dress once anyway." Her white wedding gown was simple and sweet, and she loved it to pieces, but really, if her dress stopped her from holding this beautiful baby, what was the point?

Isabel draped a clean cloth diaper on Eden's shoulder, then handed Vincent over. The baby settled against her and closed his eyes.

"Oh my God. You're hired," Isabel said.

Chase wrapped an arm around Eden's waist as he looked down on the baby. "How do you deal with how cute he is?"

"Told you my kid would wrap you around his tiny little fingers."

The photographer appeared in front of them and snapped photos of Eden holding the baby while Chase gazed down, and a little bubble of joy grew in Eden's belly.

This was really her life. After growing up with parents who didn't even try to love her, she was surrounded by a new extended family that overflowed with it.

They all cared deeply about Chase, and in the last seven months, she'd recognized that it wasn't pity or guilt inspired. They respected him and admired him as much as she did.

He remained the youngest operative on Falcon team, and he'd never served in the military or been a police officer—the only member of Falcon team to have achieved that rank without that background. He'd confessed to her months ago that he'd thought he'd achieved it when he was twenty-two because it was part of the mind games, but now, with his brain clearer, he could see, as could Eden, that none of his coworkers believed that. They respected him as the equal he was.

And it meant everything to him.

A couple with a teenage girl—guests Eden hadn't met yet—approached, and Eden passed the sweet baby back to his mama so she could give them her full attention.

Chase and the man hugged, then Chase moved to hug the woman. Eden smiled at the man. "You must be Josh."

He hugged her. "It's great to finally meet you, Eden."

There were more hugs as she met Maddie and Ava, and they all promised to sit down and chat later.

Next up came Agent Sara Seong, who had become a friend in the last seven months as the murder of Tobias Redford was sorted out.

Not long after his failed suicide attempt, Dearborn had confessed that it was Redford who initially tipped off Dearborn that Eden was working for CamDames. He'd stalked her when she first started classes and spotted her arriving at work and entering the building more than once. There was no name on the building, and the internet didn't readily provide the organization, so Tobias had bribed a guard to find out what Eden did there.

From there, it was a muddled slippery slope—they weren't sure how much they could trust Dearborn's account. But both Dearborn and Tobias had grown interested in the work of camgirls—from a psychological perspective, he said—and Eden didn't doubt it, but he also saw a money-making opportunity. He'd invested in the company, but it wasn't enough.

At some point—Dearborn claimed Tobias did the dirty work—they set up an online portal to lure girls into their trap. Before they were sold, Parks experimented on them to see if she could make them compliant. She was testing infrasound again, and Dearborn and Tobias were providing test subjects with the help of hired muscle—the same guard Tobias had bribed initially and one of his coworkers.

CamDames, the official website, had been a lure for the girls—a real, lucrative job with dormitory housing—but as far as Seong could tell, the actual business had nothing to do with the trafficking. As they'd speculated that early October day, the executives in the company were making too much money on the legal side to enter the illegal sex trade. Dearborn, Redford, and Parks had been selling the girls they abducted without any actual association to CamDames other than the guards they'd hired to abduct the girls.

After Parks was arrested, they had no more need for test subjects, but they'd become part of the supply chain for girls, so Tobias and Dearborn kept the business going.

Dearborn initially claimed it was Tobias in the cloak in the parking garage, but the men who were arrested in her apartment eventually caved and identified Tobias as the third goon and Dearborn as Mr. Roboto.

Sling Man and Jacked Knee had gone on to say Dearborn had shot Tobias and then called them, demanding they help frame Chase by driving his unconscious body to another location and leaving him covered in blood in the driver's seat of Redford's vehicle.

They did it, no questions asked. The two men didn't know—or particularly care—why one partner had killed the other.

Seong thought Dearborn's claim that Tobias had balked at putting a chip in Eden's head had the ring of truth. Dearborn needed Tobias's help because Parks had entrusted the younger man with information on the procedure. It seemed she played the two men off each other. When questioned about whether or not Parks was sleeping with Tobias Redford, Dearborn claimed he didn't know.

Eden suspected it was another reason he'd wanted to punish his lover.

Penny was another loose end Seong was taking care of. They'd learned the girl had, as Chase suspected, tossed the pipe bomb that injured five people. Seong was giving her the same care she'd given Chase and ensuring the young woman didn't face charges for crimes she committed when she was under Dearborn's control.

Today, Sara was full of smiles after months of heartbreaking investigation. "You both look radiant!"

She kissed Chase's cheeks and hugged Eden. She whispered in her ear, "You have no idea how thrilled I am to see you both so happy, and Chase…he just holds a special place in my heart. I'm so glad he found you."

Eden teared up at that and hugged the woman tightly.

During a lull in greeting guests, Eden slipped her arm around her husband's waist and squeezed. "I think this is the most perfect day of my life—so far."

He grinned down at her. "And we haven't even gotten to the best part yet."

A happy exhaustion filled Chase as he picked up his bride and carried her over the threshold of the cabin that was too big to be called a cabin. The wedding was over; their guests were departing down the long driveway. It was just him and his new wife at last.

The day after tomorrow, they would catch a flight to New Zealand for a two-week honeymoon. It was a bucket list destination for them both, and they figured it would be a good time to explore before Eden buckled down and resumed classes with the summer term. It had taken months to sort everything out, but the issue of Eden's very legal sex work was nothing compared to the fact that the head of the department had murdered a student, sex-trafficked young girls, and experimented on them. Then there were the students who had been sexually harassed by both Redford and Dearborn coming forward and demanding action from the university.

Basically, the school was bending over backward to give scholarships and reenroll everyone they could.

Eden was back in business.

Desiree, of course, was not. She'd retired. Her last airing had been the morning she'd been forced to read a fake letter at gunpoint.

All that was behind them, though. For the first time since Alaska, Chase believed the darkness and storm clouds would stay behind him. He no longer feared losing time.

No longer feared losing his mind to the rage.

Penny was on her own road to recovery.

And he had Eden. The light he'd found in one of his darkest moments. With her, he felt whole again.

He kissed her softly but deeply as he unzipped her wedding dress. They were both exhausted, but having her perfect body next to his energized him.

She peeled off the layers of his tux, and it wasn't long before they were both naked and eager.

He smiled down at her. "I've been planning this night ever since you said yes."

She grinned. "Have you now?"

"Yes. I figured we needed to make it special. Something we've never done before."

She cleared her throat. "Ahem. I don't think there's much unexplored territory in that area."

"I beg to differ."

Her eyes widened. "What is it? You know how I feel about spanking."

He laughed and kissed her nose. "No spanking. I promise. You've got to leave the room for just a minute."

She nibbled on his jaw. "Okay. I can't wait to find out what you have planned."

He grabbed her butt and squeezed. "Scoot."

It only took him a minute to get into position because he'd set up everything ahead of time, but he waited an extra moment to get his heart rate to relax. He'd be lying to himself if he didn't admit to being a bit scared. But he trusted Eden with everything.

Finally he called out. "You can come in."

She opened the door, and her jaw dropped when she saw him splayed out on the center of their bed with his wrists wrapped in padded cuffs and bound to the headboard.

"I was thinking it's time I let you have complete control."

"Oh, Chase."

"I was also thinking it's my turn to be blindfolded so I can't see you, but you can see me. A reversal. Falcon gets a taste of his own medicine."

"Oh, Chase," she said again. "You're amazing."

He grinned. "And that right there is why I didn't put the blindfold on yet. Seeing your smile, that's the best part of this perfect day."

Acknowledgments

This book wouldn't have been possible without the author friends who have kept me company online and off: Kate Davies, Serena Bell, and Kris Kennedy. I can't wait to resume monthly tapas night.

Thank you to the women who work as camgirls who have shared information on their profession in documentaries, news articles, and on personal blogs. I appreciate your openness and honesty in sharing your world.

Thank you to my #1k1hr team who held me accountable as I drafted this story: Darcy Burke, Toni Anderson, Julie Kenner, Annika Martin, Jenn Stark, and Elisabeth Naughton. Knowing you were there with me each day always makes the work more satisfying.

Thank you to my children just because they are amazing people. Extra thanks to my daughter for her on-going Photoshop lessons.

As always, thank you to my husband for being my anchor.

About the Author

USA Today bestselling author Rachel Grant also writes thrillers as R.S. Grant. She worked for over a decade as a professional archaeologist and mines her experiences for storylines and settings, which are as diverse as excavating a cemetery underneath an historic art museum in San Francisco, survey and excavation of many prehistoric Native American sites in the Pacific Northwest, researching an historic concrete house in Virginia (inspiration for her debut novel, CONCRETE EVIDENCE), and mapping a seventeenth century Spanish and Dutch fort on the island of Sint Maarten in the Caribbean (which provided inspiration for the island and fort described in CRASH SITE).

She lives in the Pacific Northwest with her husband and children.

For more information:
www.Rachel-Grant.net
contact@rachel-grant.net